Writing the Prizefight

Writing the Prizefight

Pierce Egan's *Boxiana* World

DAVID SNOWDON

PETER LANG

Oxford · Bern · Berlin · Bruxelles · Frankfurt am Main · New York · Wien

Bibliographic information published by Die Deutsche Nationalbibliothek
Die Deutsche Nationalbibliothek lists this publication in the Deutsche Nationalbibliografie;
detailed bibliographic data is available on the Internet at http://dnb.d-nb.de.

A catalogue record for this book is available from the British Library.

Library of Congress Cataloging-in-Publication Data:

Snowdon, David.
 Writing the Prizefight : Pierce Egan's Boxiana World / David Snowdon.
   pages cm
 Includes bibliographical references and index.
 ISBN 978-3-0343-0990-5 (alk. paper)
 1. Egan, Pierce, 1772-1849--Criticism and interpretation. 2. Boxing stories--History and
criticism. 3. Sports stories--History and criticism. I. Title.
 PR4649.E45Z88 2013
 824'.7--dc23

                        2013016671

Cover image: 'Thomas Belcher' (London: 1811), by Thomas Douglas Guest
© Trustees of the British Museum.

ISBN 978-3-0343-0990-5

Peter Lang AG, International Academic Publishers, Bern 2013
Hochfeldstrasse 32, CH-3012 Bern, Switzerland
info@peterlang.com, www.peterlang.com, www.peterlang.net

Contents

List of Short Titles   ix

CHAPTER 1

The Rise in Popularity of Pugilism and its Reporting   1

     In this Corner, Introducing Pierce Egan and the 'Boxiana Style'   15
     Pugilistic Interest Peaks and Declines   26
     Aspects of Egan to Consider   28

CHAPTER 2

Flash!: The Language of the Metropolis and the Prize Ring   35

     Linguistic Factors: Authenticity and Illicitness   38
     Fancy Connection: The Metropolitan Slang of Life in London   43
     Early Boxiana Volumes   48
     Sports Talk: Reported Speech   60
     Egan's Sporting Newspapers and New Series Boxiana   65
     Post-Boxiana Series   68

CHAPTER 3

Sporting Theatre: Spectacle and Social Dynamics   71

     Drama Boxiana: Accentuating Spectacle in Pugilistic Affairs   75
     Social Conflicts   85
     Different Perspectives on the Performance   94
     The Arts, and Further Classical Connections   103
     Racial Neutrality: Boxiana's Pugilistic Unity   110
     The Human Equivalent of the Cockpit   115
     Theatricality, and Re-packaging the Sport for Wider Appeal   118

CHAPTER 4

The Nation – Military and Moral   127

   Transferring Sporting Attributes into Martial Combat   132
   Native Enmities: Rivalry between Britons   153
   Conciliation and Integrity v Revenge and Dissipation   162

CHAPTER 5

Enlivening Reality: The Egan Touch   179

   The *Boxiana* Style in Political Satire and Parody   181
   Boxiana Traces in Selected Nineteenth-Century Literature   192
   A Watershed, and Eganesque Sports Reporting   208

CHAPTER 6

Post-Fight Observations   229

APPENDIX

Glossary of Nineteenth-Century Flash and Sporting Terms   237

Bibliography   249

Index   255

Pierce Egan (1821)
Artist: George Sharples. Engraving: Charles Turner.
© National Portrait Gallery, London

Egan alerted readers that prints of this portrait would be available for purchase: 'On Tuesday next will be published a LIKENESS of PIERCE EGAN, in his UPPER STORY, asking HIMSELF a FEW QUESTIONS' (*Egan's Life in London, and Sporting Guide*, 17, 23 May 1824).

List of Short Titles

Annals of Sporting – 'Jon Bee', *The Annals of Sporting and Fancy Gazette; A Magazine, Entirely appropriated to Sporting Subjects and Fancy Pursuits*, 13 vols. (London: Sherwood, Neely, & Jones, 1822–8)

Bee's Sportsman's Slang – 'Jon Bee', *Sportsman's Slang; A New Dictionary of Terms Used in the Affairs of the Turf, the Ring, the Chase, and the Cock-Pit; with those of Bon-Ton, and the Varieties of Life; Forming an Original and Authentic Lexicon Balatronicum et Macaronicum, Particularly Adapted to the Use of the Sporting World, For elucidating Words and Phrases that are Necessarily, or Purposely, Rendered Cramp, Mutative and Unintelligible, Outside their Respective Spheres. Interspersed with Anecdotes and Whimsies, With Tart Quotations and Rum-Ones; With Examples, Proofs and Monitory Precepts, Useful and Proper for Novices, Flats, and Yokels* (London: W Lewis, 1825)

Book of Sports – Pierce Egan, *Book of Sports, and Mirror of Life: Embracing The Turf, The Chase, The Ring, and the Stage, Interspersed with Original Memoirs of Sporting Men & c.* (London: Tegg, 1832)

Boxiana I – Pierce Egan, *Boxiana; or, Sketches of Antient and Modern Pugilism; From the Days of the Renowned Broughton and Slack to the Heroes of the Present Milling Era* (London: Smeeton, 1813)

Boxiana II – Pierce Egan, *Boxiana; or, Sketches of Modern Pugilism, From the Championship of Crib to the Present Time*, vol. II (London: Sherwood, Neely, & Jones, 1818)

Boxiana III – Pierce Egan, *Boxiana; Sketches of Modern Pugilism, During the Championship of Cribb to Spring's Challenge to All England*, vol. III (London: Sherwood, Neely, & Jones, 1821)

Boxiana IV – 'Jon Bee', *Boxiana; Or, Sketches of Modern Pugilism, Containing All the Transactions of Note, Connected With The Prize Ring, During the Years, 1821, 1822, 1823*, vol. IV (London: Sherwood, Neely, & Jones, 1824)

Boxing Reviewed – Thomas Fewtrell, *Boxing Reviewed; or, the Science of Manual Defence, Displayed on Rational Principles. Comprehending a Complete Description of the Principal Pugilists, from the Earliest Period of Broughton's Time, to the Present Day* (London: 1790)

B/P – Paul Beale (ed.), *A Dictionary of Slang and Unconventional English, Eric Partridge* (London: Routledge & Kegan Paul, 1984)

Bucks and Bruisers – John C Reid, *Bucks and Bruisers: Pierce Egan and Regency England* (London: Routledge & Kegan Paul, 1971)

CBP – Bernard Shaw, *Cashel Byron's Profession* (London: Constable, 1886)

DNB – *Oxford Dictionary of National Biography* <http://www.oxforddnb.com>

EB – *Encyclopaedia Britannica Online* <http://www.britannica.com/eb>

Egan's Grose – Pierce Egan, *Grose's Classical Dictionary of the Vulgar Tongue, Revised and Corrected, With the addition of numerous slang phrases, Collected from Tried Authorities* (London: Sherwood, Neely, & Jones, 1823)

Egan's Life in London, and Sporting Guide – *Pierce Egan's Life in London, and Sporting Guide Connected with the Events of the Turf, the Chase, and the Ring* (1824–7)

Egan's Weekly Courier – *Pierce Egan's Weekly Courier to the Sporting, Theatrical, Literary, and Fashionable World* (1829)

Fistiana – Vincent Dowling, *Fistiana; or, The Oracle of the Ring* (London: Clement, 1841)

Grose – Francis Grose, *Classical Dictionary of the Vulgar Tongue* (London: Hooper, 1785)

Lexicon – Anon., *Lexicon Balatronicum. A Dictionary of Buckish Slang, University Wit, and Pickpocket Eloquence. Compiled Originally by Captain Grose. And Now Considerably Altered and Enlarged, with the Modern Changes and Improvements, by a Member of the Whip Club* (London: Chappell, 1811)

Life in London – Pierce Egan, *Life in London, or, The Day and Night Scenes of Jerry Hawthorn, Esq. And his Elegant Friend Corinthian Tom, accompanied by Bob Logic, the Oxonian, in their Rambles and Sprees through the Metropolis* (London: Sherwood, Neely, & Jones, 1821)

New Series Boxiana – Pierce Egan, *New Series of Boxiana: being the only original and complete Lives of the Boxers*, 2 vols. (London: Virtue, 1828–9)

OED – *Oxford English Dictionary*, 2nd edn. (Oxford: Oxford University Press, 1989)

Pugilistica – Henry Downes Miles, *Pugilistica: Being One hundred and Forty-Four Years of the History of British Boxing*, 3 vols. (London: Weldon, 1880)

Real Life in London – 'An Amateur', *Real Life in London, or, The Rambles and Adventures of Bob Tallyho, Esq., and His Cousin, The Hon. Tom Dashall, Through the Metropolis; Exhibiting a Living Picture of Fashionable Characters, Manners, and Amusements in High and Low Life*, vol. I (London: Jones & Co., 1821)

RIPM – William Vasey, *Remarks on the Influence of Pugilism on Morals; Being the Substance of a Speech Delivered at the Newcastle Debating Society, on the Fourth of November, 1824* (Newcastle: Newcastle Debating Society, 1824)

Sporting Anecdotes – Pierce Egan, *Sporting Anecdotes, Original and Selected; of Persons in Every walk of life, Who have acquired Notoriety from their Achievements on the Turf, at the Table, and in the Diversions of the Field, With sketches of various Animals of the Chase: To which is added, an Account of noted Pedestrians, Trotting-Matches, Cricketers, & c. The whole forming a complete Delineation of the Sporting World* (London: Sherwood, Jones & Co., 1825)

Tom Crib's Memorial – Thomas Moore, *Tom Crib's Memorial to Congress* (1819)

Trial of Thurtell – Pierce Egan, *Account of the Trial of John Thurtell and Joseph Hunt. With an Appendix Disclosing Some Extraordinary Facts, Exclusively in the possession of the Editor* (London: Knight & Lacey, 1824)

Warreniana – William Frederick Deacon, *Warreniana; with Notes, Critical and Explanatory, by the Editor of a Quarterly Review* (London: Longman, Hurst, Rees, Orme, Brown and Green, 1824)

The Rise in Popularity of Pugilism and its Reporting

Any study of pugilistic writing in the early nineteenth century requires some elaboration on the ways in which sport, and particularly prizefighting, played a major role in society during the period. Sporting events provided diversion, or consolation, amidst more onerous issues at home and abroad or simply the toil of everyday metropolitan life. National anxiety at news of precarious military situations on foreign soil or radical unrest at home could be, for some, assuaged by reading reports of the latest prizefight, race-meeting, pedestrian wager, and so forth. Readers avidly sought the alternative, and perhaps illusory, climate of the sporting world. Even proceedings in the House of Commons, hectic amidst scandal in the first year of George IV's reign (1820), were downgraded when competing with sporting events: '[Thomas] Creevey reported the "rage" of the House of Lords at being compelled to attend in October: "It interferes with everything – pheasant shooting, Newmarket etc."'.[1]

Honourable, or chivalric, precepts were claimed as being commonplace in the pugilistic ring and, in the wake of conflicting emotions arising at news of the naval triumph off Cape Trafalgar (20 October 1805), and death of Horatio Nelson (1758–1805), reports of the honourable conduct evinced by Hen Pearce (the 'Game Chicken'), in his fight against Jem Belcher (1781–1811), provided welcome distraction as news emerged of Napoleon's victory over Russian and Austrian forces at Austerlitz (2 December 1805).

---

1   Exiled in Europe since 1814, the King's official wife Caroline of Brunswick returned in 1820 claiming her royal rank. The King instigated divorce proceedings, and a subsequent 'Queen's Trial'. Donald Thomas, *Cochrane: Britannia's Sea Wolf* (London: Cassell, 2001), p. 102.

[6 December 1805] PEARCE threw BELCHER upon the rope, and while his body was balancing in that unprotected, yet fair situation, the *Chicken* had an opportunity of ending the fight, by one of his tremendous blows, but his generous mind spurned the committal of a deed that would have grieved his soul. (Pierce Egan, *Boxiana I*, 1813, p. 149)

This sporting ethos was perceived as mirroring Britain's military prowess and magnanimity in victory. In the same year, a piece penned by William Cobbett (1763–1835) railed against state interference in sporting practices:

All athletic and rustic sports, every exercise requiring great bodily exertion, and tending, under the name and the feeling of pastime, to strengthen the frame, and to produce hardihood and valour, seem to be doomed to extirpation, and that too, by the instrumentality of those very laws, under the mild spirit of which they have so long flourished and so long contributed to the forming and the preserving of that at once resolute and amiable character, for which the people of England have ever been distinguished.

The tone is precursory of the rhetoric repeatedly produced by the foremost pugilistic writers as they promoted the national benefits to be derived from vigorous sporting exercise. This is underscored by Cobbett's recommendation, in this same piece, of pugilism as a preferred 'mode of terminating quarrels amongst the common people', perceiving it to be a non-fatal method (theoretically).[2]

Some of the earliest evidence of a rise in pugilism's popularity was 'the erection, in 1723, of a boxing-ring in Hyde Park, "by order of his Majesty", in which disputes among the lower orders, as well as professional fights, could be settled according to the rules of the sport'. The natural progression was that public interest in such contests could be partially satiated by publishing reports on the action. There appeared 'an increasing number of books, periodicals, broadsides and instruction manuals', such as Thomas Fewtrell's *Boxing Reviewed; or The Science of Manual Defence* (1790).[3] An

---

2   *Cobbett's Political Register*, VIII, 12 (21 September 1805), pp. 418–19.
3   Christopher Johnson, '"British Championism": Early Pugilism and the Works of Fielding', *The Review of English Studies*, 187 (1996), pp. 331–51 (337, 10).

extract from a profile of Tom Johnson (c. 1750–97), demonstrates the ponderous diction of this early pugilistic text:

> He has never yet engaged, without previously studying not only the powers and manner of fighting, but also the constitution and disposition of his adversary [...] If his opponent be cool, he himself is cooler; if warm, he makes him still more so by taking every justifiable measure to irritate him. (*Boxing Reviewed*, pp. 61–2)

References such as 'stage', 'enemy', and 'system' foreshadow recurring topics of performance, foreign foes, and aggressive martial tactics tempered by 'coolness':

> Unlike most fighters, who seldom attend to rules for their guidance in a combat, until they find themselves upon the stage, he regularly forms [...] a system of conduct most adapted to himself, and contrary to his enemy; and to effect this, he calmly balances the respective abilities and tempers of each. (pp. 62–3)

The explicatory tone is maintained throughout the near one-hundred-page text, and no fight reports or commentaries are featured. With the exception of some general profiles of the more renowned prizefighters, the text constitutes a defence of the sport.

Here is Dennis Brailsford's account of the subsequent increase in press coverage afforded to the sport, and the gaming motivation:

> More gambling nourished the appetite for more sport at a time when the two were considered inseparable, so much so that the *Sporting Magazine*, on its first appearance (October 1792), promised to set out the circumstance of every match, event, and wager as it was made. The publication of a monthly sporting journal was itself a remarkable development, its editor claimed to be 'astonished' that among all the magazines there was not a single one 'expressly calculated for the sportsman' [...] Whatever it might loftily say about 'bruising' in its editorials, the *Daily Register*, in the month before it became *The Times* (1788), was acknowledging that pugilism was now the fashion and deserved notice.[4]

---

4   Dennis Brailsford, *Bareknuckles: A Social History of Prize-Fighting* (Cambridge: Lutterworth Press, 1988), p. 31.

'Pugilism was also featured in Captain Topham's *The World* (from 1787) [...]
Bell's Weekly Messenger (from 1796), and the *Weekly Dispatch* (from 1801)'.[5]
But, unlike horseracing and cock-fighting, bare-knuckle prizefights often
depended upon the inconsistent leniency of local magistrates. Considered a
barbarous activity, cock-fighting also became illegal in 1849, but it too man-
aged to continue. Ironically, it had been a lost bet, in 1750, by the volatile
Duke of Cumberland that exacerbated pugilism's slump into illegality. He
ordered the closure of the principal amphitheatre and exerted influence on
the magistracy to adopt an unfavourable stance against the sport. Brailsford
states that prizefighting 'attracted the idle, the criminal and the cheat [...]
It became exposed to the laws on breaches of the peace, creating an affray,
and by the 1760s on duelling; while a death in the ring could bring a manslaughter charge'.[6] This general view is underscored by Lord Ellenborough's
remarks at the trial (May 1803) of four pugilists charged with 'conspiracy
to fight a duel, riotous assembly [...] and breach of the peace':

> It draws industrious people away from the subject of their industry; and when great
> multitudes are so collected, they are likely enough to be engaged in broils. It affords
> an opportunity for people of the most mischievous disposition to assemble [...] In
> short it is a practice that is extremely injurious in every respect and must be repressed.[7]

By its very nature a violent sport, the pugilistic world was inextricably associated with gambling, drinking, and the demi-monde. Consequently, there
was an opportunist element about the arrangement of fights, and 'the Fancy'
would often favour venues situated near county borders. Collectively, 'The
Fancy' comprised those who followed sporting events, but the term was
particularly applied to prizefighting votaries. One fight between Samuel
Evans (Young Dutch Sam) and Ned Neal (18 January 1831), originally
planned for Newmarket, was swiftly relocated to Bumpstead in Essex (over
twenty miles away):

---

5   Edward Topham, journalist and playwright (1751–1820). Dennis Brailsford, 'Morals
     and Maulers: the Ethics of Early Pugilism', *Journal of Sport History*, 12, 2 (1985),
     pp. 126–42 (129).
6   Brailsford, *Bareknuckles: A Social History of Prize-Fighting*, p. 13.
7   Edward Law, first Baron Ellenborough, judge (1750–1818). Ibid., p. 45.

Just as the combatants had arrived on the ground, and all was anxious expectation, to the great dismay and vexation of the amateurs, the Beak popped in his nose [...] He proved inexorable to all the gammon[8] that was pitched to him [...] and nothing less but a removal would satisfy his duty. (Egan, *Book of Sports*, 1832, p. 297)

In *The Pickwick Papers* (1837), Charles Dickens (1812–70) outlined a similar intervention boasted by one magistrate ('Beak'): 'I rushed into a prize-ring [...] attended by only sixty special constables; and, at the hazard of falling a sacrifice to the angry passions of an infuriated multitude, prohibited a pugilistic contest between the Middlesex Dumpling and the Suffolk Bantam.'[9] Pierce Egan's report focused attention on the unsuccessful attempts to persuade, or corrupt, the law-enforcer, including the appropriate slang expressions. Dickens preferred the humour of the pompous magistrate's sham courage, together with the droll sobriquets assumed by the two fighters.

Either way, the accounts reflect a harsh social reality for the sport – it was prone to judicial interference. Sparring sessions involved the performance of fighting motions, usually wearing gloves, and delivering more moderate blows. Such exhibitions were more leniently regarded as a form of entertainment, or instruction, but this acceptance was not universally applied: '[Jem] Belcher was prevented from appearing at an exhibition at the Sadler's Wells Theatre and the magistrates went so far as to close down the theatre for the whole of the rest of the season.'[10]

Despite obstacles, a groundswell of popularity enabled the sport to operate amidst its supposed prohibition. It had formerly received a welcome impetus (1786):

Royalty again condescended to throw its shield over the national game, and men of the highest rank and consequence [...] encouraged and were present at those 'prize-fights' which became the rage, and were attended by thousands [...] of all ranks. A guinea was the price of admission to the combat [Humphries v Martin, 3 May 1786], a sum which hundreds willingly paid, and it was calculated that from thirty to forty thousand pounds were hazarded on the event. (Vincent Dowling, *Fistiana*, 1841, p. 33)

---

8   'Gammon' was synonymous with 'nonsense or cant' (*B/P*), but in the *Boxiana* series it was most frequently applied in keeping with the sense 'to humbug or deceive'.

9   Charles Dickens, *The Pickwick Papers*, ed. by Robert L. Patten (London: Penguin, 1986), p. 412.

10   Brailsford, *Bareknuckles: A Social History of Prize-Fighting*, p. 48.

This improved status, together with upper-class endorsement, appears to have endured and Lord Byron (1788–1824) 'accompanied another pugilist to John Sebright's Park in Hertfordshire to see a bout (10 May 1808) between the champion John Gully [1783–1863] and Bob Gregson [1788–1824]'. He also attended lessons at the Bond Street rooms of former champion John 'Gentleman' Jackson (1769–1845), and communicated these sparring sessions with 'the Emperor of Pugilism' in letters written to Thomas Moore (1779–1852).[11]

Although the sport oscillated between notions of courageous dexterity allied to humanity, and unlicensed brutality, there was an increasing awareness that it offered a form of safeguard against a perceived national emasculation: 'Pugilism and the Prize Ring were, almost by definition, the antithesis of effeminacy [...] supporting those virtues that would save the country'.[12] Conflicting issues, associated with unpredictable law enforcement, were encapsulated in the main question debated at a meeting of the Society for Mutual Improvement (April 1820):[13]

> Ought the Magistracy of England to be considered worthy of censure for a negligent execution of the laws against PUGILISTIC COMBATS, or of approbation for their prudence in not too violently opposing public taste, and winking at what affords much amusement and keeps up the spirit and courage of the country? (Egan, *Boxiana III*, 1821, p. 577)

This echoes Cobbett's earlier complaint concerning the judicial stance against pugilism.

A common interest in sport encouraged the dissolving of social barriers, and a mixed assortment of characters were to be found attending the prize-ring or cockpit. Lords and MPs would mingle with coal merchants,

---

11   *Byron's Letters and Journals*, ed. by Leslie A Marchand, 12 vols. (London: John Murray, 1973–82), I, p. 162. See letter of 9 April 1814, *Byron's Letters and Journals*, ed. by Marchand, IV, p. 91.

12   Peter Radford, *The Celebrated Captain Barclay: Sport Money and Fame in Regency Britain* (London: Headline, 2001), p. 62.

13   Established under the patronage of Jeremy Bentham, philosopher, jurist, and reformer (1748–1832).

caulkers, and costermongers, membership of the Fancy not being confined to a specific class. Equality did not usually stretch to lower and upper-class combatants meeting in the ring, the wealthy amateurs and aristocracy predominantly occupying the roles of patrons and promoters. In theory, an egalitarian mandate existed for a low-bred navvy and a peer of the realm to settle a conflict with their fists, but the delicate balance between this classless philosophy and customary practice was rarely bridged. Various fight reports mention the many vocations of the pugilists, ranging from butchers and bakers to watermen and soldiers. Brailsford expands on the composition of their followers:

> Less remarked upon by historians [...] in bringing some stability to the prize-ring, was the backing of a solid body of middle-class citizens who had made their money in manufacture and trade [...] The view that the prize-ring was the preserve of the aristocracy and the roughest of the lowest classes alone is far from the truth.

Amongst the attractions for aristocratic onlookers was the 'opportunity for sporting participation [...] another outlet for the passion for gaming [...] and the excitement of the cockpit in human form, with the added spice of illegality but virtually no danger of prosecution'.[14]

Inside the ring, Pierce Egan's *Boxiana* series (1812–29) advocated a set of moral rules that would, had inter-class contests taken place, have transcended any conventional social hierarchy. Disappointingly, there were few examples of a meteoric ascendancy in fortunes such as that enjoyed by John Gully, who worked his way via pugilistic success from debtor's prison to become a proprietor of various collieries, and an MP. He also became a successful racehorse owner, winning the Two Thousand Guineas (twice), the Oaks, and the Derby (twice). Although it has been suggested that these achievements were 'sunk deep in many devious and dishonest practices',[15] Egan's description of Gully appears to encourage similar aspirations in others:

---

14 Brailsford, *Bareknuckles: A Social History of Prize-Fighting*, pp. 25–6.
15 Henry Blyth, *Hell and Hazard: or William Crockford versus the Gentlemen of England* (London: Weidenfeld & Nicolson, 1969), p. 133.

With a knowledge of the world, he unites the manners of a well-bred man, unassuming and intelligent upon all occasions, which has gained him respect and attention in the circles which he now moves [...] proving, in himself, a lively instance, that ALL *pugilists* are not deprived from entering into polished society. (*Boxiana I*, p. 186)

The importance attached to the attendance of 'Corinthians' (upper-class sportsmen) is apparent by the fact that it frequently warranted a mention in fight reports, the writers intimating that their presence augmented the credibility of proceedings. An added attraction was that, despite class interaction, the sport was considered unlikely to radically disturb the social equipoise: 'It was a traditional English sport which offered a space where different ranks could come into contact, but without threatening the social hierarchy'.[16] Nevertheless, pugilism's precarious social status was susceptible to extraneous political events, and there was concern over the government's introduction of the 'Six Acts', which included the prohibition of large public meetings and drilling.[17] This endangered the attendance of fights as well as the pugilists' training. Prizefighting continued to suffer the same erratic intervention as before, and ambivalent feelings towards the sport emerged following a major contest between Spring and Langan (champions of England and Ireland) at Worcester Race Course (7 January 1824):

The writer of an anonymous article[18] [...] describes how over the last generation the sport has 'spread like a mania among the coarse-minded and profligate as well as some of the *would-be* decorous' [...and] notes that the recent fight between Spring and Langan had been tolerated by Worcestershire magistrates, whereas 'a meeting of a few dozen radicals would have set all the Dogberries in the county in motion'. The 'exhibition of coarse, vulgar blackguardism' was allowed to take place, it is suggested, 'because the gain made by the neighbourhood from the motley assemblage, which swarmed from all points to the scene'.[19]

---

16   David Higgins, 'Englishness, Effeminacy, and the *New Monthly Magazine*; Hazlitt's "The Fight" in Context', *Romanticism* 10. 2 (2004), pp. 173–90 (175).

17   An attempt, in late 1819, to quell Reform agitation, the Metropolitan Police Force not being established until 1829.

18   'Tokens of the Times' in *New Monthly Magazine* (January 1825), p. 90.

19   Higgins, 'Englishness, Effeminacy, and the *New Monthly Magazine*', p. 180.

The writer's repulsion is evident, but the popularity suggested by 'mania' and 'swarmed' is clearly conveyed, as well as the attendant benefits for local traders.

As for overseeing its own activities, John Jackson helped to establish the Pugilistic Club in 1814. This was a period in which Jackson was sparring regularly with Byron, and the newly-founded society boasted some influential recruits along with its revisions to supervisory arrangements at fights: 'Its articles recorded the express determination of the members to see fair play [...] Indeed, the Fives Court itself became almost decorous, with a roped square for a ring to keep out over-enthusiastic or spoiling spectators, and official "bouncers".[20] The Fives Court in Little St Martin's Street, was the Fancy's top venue for benefits and sparring exhibitions. It featured a three-sided court for the game of 'fives', which involved striking a ball by hand. Also, this location was not subject to the same constraining magisterial controls that governed theatres. Members included the Royal Dukes of York and Clarence, the Duke of Queensbury, and wealthy Welsh landowner Sir Watkin Williams Wynn. The club's ornamental whips, perhaps, betrayed unease that their pugilistic crowds were not so 'decorous' as they wished.

Although only fighting on three occasions, Jackson built up such a reputation that he was often called upon as an arbiter in disputes. The club did not amend the sport's first set of organised rules, which had been introduced by former champion John Broughton (c. 1703–89). These rules, 'agreed to by the PUGILISTS' (August 1743), were not, primarily, concerned with defining illegal blows or behaviour within the ring. Instead, they concentrated on maintaining order, avoiding betting disputes, and the division of takings:

1. That a square of a yard be chalked in the middle of the stage; and every fresh set-to after a fall, or being parted from the rails, each second is to bring his man to the side of the square, and place him opposite to the other, and till they are fairly set to at the lines, it shall not be lawful for the one to strike the other.

20   Birley, *Sport and the Making of Britain*, p. 169.

2. That, in order to prevent any disputes as to the time a man lies after a fall, if the second does not bring his man to the side of the square within the space of half a minute, he shall be deemed a beaten man.

3. That, in every main battle, no person whatever shall be upon the stage, except the principals and the seconds [...]

4. That no champion be deemed beaten, unless he fails coming up to the line in the limited time, or, that his own second declares him beaten. No second is to be allowed to ask his man's adversary any questions, or advise him to give out.

5. That in by-battles the winning man to have two thirds of the money given which shall be publicly divided upon the stage, notwithstanding any private agreement to the contrary.

6. That to prevent disputes, in every main battle, the principals shall, on the coming on the stage, choose from among the gentlemen present, two umpires, who shall absolutely decide all disputes that may arise about the battle; and if the two umpires cannot agree, the said umpires to choose a third, who is to determine it.

7. That no person is to hit his adversary when he is down, or seize him by [...] any part below the waist; a man on his knees to be reckoned down.

(*Boxiana I*, pp. 51–2)

Perversely, the Fancy believed contests to be almost self-regulating, forming part of a pugilistic community that was governed by in-built codes of honour. This quixotic vision claimed a moral ascendancy for this socially diverse branch of the sporting world, as well as maintaining that such superior conduct was thoroughly English:

> The cult of sportsmanship is often located within a project to distance genteel lifestyles from vulgar [...] Making 'sportsmanship' a national rather than an aristocratic asset did much to define a distinctive English civility [...] English pugilism was a species of honour not known in any other parts of the world [...] The emphasis was on strict adherence to unspoken and unwritten rules, binding competitors and spectators in recognition of the necessity of fair play.[21]

Published fight reports reinforced the increased influence of pugilistic affairs, and the leading players entered into public consciousness. The Georgian fight scene appeared to revel in its physicality, the commentaries often reflecting this, which is one aspect that would come under the disapproving gaze of the Victorians. William Vasey, in a speech at the

21   Paul Langford, *Englishness Identified* (Oxford: Oxford University Press, 2001), p. 149.

Newcastle Debating Society (4 November 1824) couched his recognition of the boom in pugilism's popularity in terms that suggest an insidious element: 'so greedily do persons follow the study and exercise of this art, that there would seem to be a sort of fascination about it which proves fatal to all those who come within the circle of its allurement'.[22] This debating society was established in 1822, assembling in High Friar Street, before meetings discontinued in 1825. Vasey was one of the most distinguished members, being a clerk in an attorney's office and then a counsellor's chambers. Here, Vasey proceeded to elaborate on the possible desensitisation of society to witnessing general brutishness, claiming that, rather than being inclined to 'shudder at the inflicted severity', spectators would inevitably 'grow callous to human suffering and thirst for scenes of additional barbarity' (*RIPM*, p. 15). Vasey apparently equated the mushrooming of interest in pugilistic affairs to a miasmic craze, and the sport's followers as 'those infected with its spirit' (p. 5).

Another issue that pugilism had to confront was the position of London as the sport's capital. Bristol fighters renowned in their home city could only have their feats recorded with any regularity by fighting in the London area. To rouse interest in the sport, prizefighters embarked upon countrywide tours performing the role of pugilistic missionaries:

> Provincial tours had always been a useful source of income (and publicity) for successful fighters [...] Manchester, Liverpool, Bradford, Leeds, Newcastle – these were the staple venues in any sporting tour, but no town of any size was without at least an occasional visit from one of the country's greater or lesser pugilistic heroes.[23]

Notwithstanding his opposition to pugilism, Vasey confirms the impact of the 'mania' on society in 1820s Newcastle: '[Pugilism] produced two of the largest assemblages of people that the Newcastle Theatre has ever contained, on two successive nights [...and] called out, to the distance of about ten miles, five or six thousand people to witness a Prize Fight' (*RIPM*, p. 4).

---

22 William Vasey, *Remarks on the Influence of Pugilism on Morals* (Newcastle: 1824), p. 3. Vasey died of consumption in December 1826, aged twenty-four.

23 Brailsford, *Bareknuckles: A Social History of Prize-Fighting*, pp. 119–20.

This extension of the performance aspect, entreating the better-known pugilists to exhibit their skills on the stage, was well established. Black American fighter Bill Richmond (1763–1829), who turned to pugilism when he moved to London at the turn of the century (*DNB*),[24] was one such performer: 'BILL, in company with other pugilists, has exhibited his knowledge of the SCIENCE [...] at the *Olympic Pavilion* and *Regency* Theatres, with satisfaction and applause from numerous audiences' (*Boxiana I*, p. 449). There is evidence that this may have proved a lucrative sideline for some, and Daniel Mendoza (c. 1765–1836) records, in 1790, that he was 'continually receiving from the proprietors of various country theatres, letters containing very liberal offers of engagements.'[25] The additional publicity generated intensified public anticipation for prizefighting and, significantly, the ensuing published accounts. Thus, the 'gospel' of pugilism was spread:

> Have not our classic theatres [...] possessing all the advantages of authors the most exalted and refined; actors the most inimitable [...] scenes and decorations, in point of magnificence and splendour, unparalleled – invited PUGILISM to their boards, and the names of some of the first rate boxers enriched their play-bills; and the audiences (of whom no doubt can attach to their respectability) testified their approbation by loud plaudits, at the liberality of the managers in thus publicly displaying the principles of Pugilism! (*Boxiana I*, p. 8)

A demand to view well-known fighters evidently existed, and a capacity for the sport to be adapted in order to prove acceptable to female tastes is suggested:

> In 1791 Pugilism was in such high repute, and so strongly patronized, that *Dan Mendoza* was induced to open the small theatre, at the Lyceum, in the Strand, for the express purpose of public exhibitions of sparring; and, in his managerial capacity, assured the public [...] that the manly art of boxing would be displayed, divested of all

---

24 'Brought to England (in 1777) by General Earl Percy, later Duke of Northumberland'. Marke Zervudachi, 'Prize-fighting in England circa 1660–1860', in David Fuller, *Noble Art: Prize-fighting in England 1738–1860* (British Sporting Art Trust, catalogue of Newmarket exhibition, 2005), pp. 10–11.

25 *The Memoirs of the Life of Daniel Mendoza*, ed. by Paul Magriel (London: Batsford, 1951), p. 68.

ferocity [...] and the whole conducted with the utmost propriety and decorum, that the female part of the creation might attend, without their feelings being infringed upon, or experiencing any unpleasant sensations. (p. 9)

This is one example of the sporadic attempts to depict pugilism as palatable for a refined audience, but my discussion of concerns over declining masculinity, increasing 'effeminacy', national identity, and martial readiness considers that these idealistic calls to extend the sport's appeal lacked conviction. Possibly, such pieces expressed unrealistic, even insincere, pretensions to attract a diverse audience, and the degree of 'flash' jargon content further confuses the issue of audience accessibility.

Eventually, specialised volumes were dedicated to chronicling the most significant prizefights, one of the first being *Pancratia, or a History of Pugilism* (1812).[26] Although anonymous, the author was 'almost certainly' the book's printer, William Oxberry (1784–1824),[27] a typical fight report reading:

[14 July 1807] A battle was fought on Windsor-forest, between Flowers, the Berkshire coachman, and one Sweet, recently a waiter in the vicinity of Bath. At ten o'clock the parties met, and a ring was formed in the presence of about 200 spectators; the combatants set to; at the beginning Flowers seemed intending to make a short job [...but] having suffered severely on the left side by his adversary's hits, he found that plan would not do, and dropped it. Sweet was now untouched, and bets two to one in his favour; Sweet supported a superiority for half an hour, when Flowers put in a tremendous blow under his opponent's ear; still Sweet fought undismayed, but his strength soon failed him; he, however, shifted, stopped, and hit with great science, and had the advantage to the end of 40 minutes; but Flowers proved a complete GLUTTON,[28] and although severely beaten, never appeared shy. In the thirty-sixth round Sweet was quite exhausted, and unable to withstand the fury of his antagonist, who with great violence hit him down. (*Pancratia*, pp. 288–9)

---

26 The Pancratium was a sporting contest in ancient Greece, combining wrestling and boxing (*OED*).
27 Brailsford, 'Morals and Maulers: the Ethics of Early Pugilism', p. 129.
28 An expression denoting a pugilist who exhibits stamina, or 'fortitude in taking punishment' (*B/P*).

Here, there are traces of persistent aspects that would appear in subsequent reporting: a little slang terminology; typographical variation; update of betting odds; and information on the social background of the fighters.

Pancratia culminated with accounts of the two famous battles for 'the Championship of England' between national hero, Tom Cribb (1781–1848), and the black American challenger, Tom Molineaux (c. 1785–1818). These contests took place on 18 December 1810 (at Copthorn, Sussex) and 28 September 1811 (at Thistleton Gap, a few miles from Grantham). The clamour, and scrutiny, surrounding the build-up and outcome of these tussles engulfed not only the sporting world, but also supplanted concerns over campaigns being fought by the Duke of Wellington (1769–1852). For many, the pretensions of a foreign pugilistic invader constituted the more tangible national threat: 'In such uncertain times the nation's morale depended heavily on the outcome of the contest between Cribb and the American [...] as much a test of British character, many felt, as that which faced the nation in Spain'.[29] News of the major contests now piqued public curiosity, especially when heralded as involving greater issues than personal glory. There appears little doubt that English prestige was felt to be at stake in the above battle, but reports of such fights manipulated the situation, adopting a highly charged tone by promoting emotive national matters. There was little danger of understatement, and it may not be coincidental that *Pancratia* and the first *Boxiana* serialisation followed soon after these momentous clashes, seeking to exploit the interest generated and capture a wider audience.

---

29   Defending Portugal as a base in 1810, Wellington's situation was considered grave as he constructed the Torres Vedras lines across the Lisbon peninsular. Birley, *Sport and the Making of Britain*, p. 165.

In this Corner, Introducing Pierce Egan and the '*Boxiana* Style'

Although probably born in Ireland (see footnote), Pierce Egan (c. 1772–1849) was raised in London where his 'Irish migrant father worked as a road labourer'.[30] Experience gained in the printing trade (he became a 'skilled compositor', *DNB*) would be displayed in the linguistic and typographical brio of his *Boxiana* series, which was infused with quotations, allusions, literariness, as well as ornate footnotes. John Reid provides a useful overview of Egan's social sphere and mind-set, portraying him as a 'valued member of a considerable number of sporting and drinking clubs', who inhabited 'the underworld of literature and journalism', and someone fully conversant with 'the ephemera of his day'.[31] By 1812, he was working for the printer and publisher George Smeeton (fl. 1800–28) in St Martin's Lane.

Egan did not immediately acknowledge authorship of his first publication, *Boxiana I* (1813),[32] the reader being guided by 'ONE OF THE FANCY' through the predominantly London-based sphere of prizefighting.[33] This sporting set embodied much of pugilism's inherent controversies and contradictions, which was exacerbated by Egan's use of the flash language most closely associated with the Fancy. Egan developed its use in further volumes of the series – *Boxiana II* (1818), *Boxiana III* (1821), *New Series Boxiana I* (1828), and *New Series Boxiana II* (1829). If the Fancy was associated with the demi-monde, and Egan described as 'a man of the

---

30   *An Oxford Companion to the Romantic Age*, ed. by Iain McCalman (Oxford University Press, 2001), p. 492.

31   John C Reid, *Bucks and Bruisers: Pierce Egan and Regency England* (London: Routledge & Kegan Paul, 1971), pp. 10–11. Reid also discusses his failure to definitively establish Egan's precise date and place of birth (p. 4).

32   The completed volume, published in 1813, retained its 1812 serialisation title page. Ibid., p. 232.

33   This is how Egan signed the dedication to 'Captain Barclay' (Robert Barclay Allardice, 1779–1854, the renowned Scottish gentleman farmer, pedestrian, and pugilistic trainer).

underworld', then perhaps this author's chronicling of sporting men's movements has something in common with a 'disreputable radical underside', as McCalman explains:

> Part of the fascination of this circle lies in its fluid, ambivalent position within the popular political milieu and wider society. Tracing the lives and careers of individual members reveals a long and intricate overlap between the allegedly separate spheres of 'respectability' and 'roughness'.[34]

Ambivalence in issues of respectability, masculinity, and morality is a recurring theme in this book, but it is contested that any political undertones ascribed to Egan's writing are incidental or inadvertent, the writer's prime concern being to hone an entertaining style. Often commentating on the same basic details as other writers, it was the linguistic flourish and specific drama that Egan instilled which distinguished his pugilistic reports. This linguistic element is supported by references to *Egan's Grose* (1823), his updated version of Francis Grose's *Classical Dictionary of the Vulgar Tongue* (1785).[35]

The identity of the *Boxiana I* author had been suspected, and anonymity was dispensed with for its 1818 reprint. In the interim, Egan had played his part in establishing sport as a more prominent feature of newspaper journalism. The exact year that his writing duties commenced at London's *Weekly Dispatch* is uncertain, but there is sufficient evidence of his distinctive style for Reid to proffer the following outline regarding the development of sports reporting in that newspaper: 'up to 1810 the *Dispatch* printed little or nothing to do with sport […] It increases until by 1814 there is a substantial quantity […] Various turns of phrase in 1816 accounts leave little doubt that by that year he was well established'.[36] The *Boxiana* series pursued a relatively consistent format; an introductory disquisition on the

---

34 McCalman, *Radical Underworld* (Cambridge: Cambridge University Press, 1988), p. 3.

35 Egan devoted a piece to 'eminent antiquary' Francis Grose (c. 1731–91) in his volume of *Sporting Anecdotes* (1825, pp. 68–78). Further editions of *Grose* were published in 1788 and 1796.

36 Reid, *Bucks and Bruisers*, p. 27.

most pressing topics favoured by the author was followed with 'chapters' largely profiling one particular fighter, including commentaries on his most recent fights. In Egan's volumes, sections on the more renowned pugilists were often preceded by bust-style portraits of the fighters in fashionable dress.[37] The columns of Egan's two sporting newspapers (*Egan's Life in London, and Sporting Guide* (1 February 1824 to 28 October 1827) and *Egan's Weekly Courier* (4 January to 26 April 1829) printed fight accounts in the '*Boxiana* style', and some were reproduced almost verbatim in his *New Series Boxiana* and *Book of Sports* (1832).

It was Egan's very public disagreement with the *Boxiana* publishers (Sherwood, Jones, & Co.) that presented a great rival, Jon Bee, with the unexpected opportunity to supplant him as author of *Boxiana IV* (1824). 'Bee' was the pseudonym of John Badcock (fl. 1810–30). A court judge awarded Egan the right to continue his *Boxiana* writing on condition that any such text's title was prefixed with 'New Series'.[38] The *Boxiana* style remained undiminished, with Bee's approach allowing a seamless course for the series. Bee is an integral part of any study of pugilistic writing, which is further augmented by his editorship of *The Annals of Sporting and Fancy Gazette* (biannual, published 1822–8). His lexical publication, *Bee's Sportsman's Slang* (1825),[39] also informs the debate on the specialist jargon of the ring, as well as the flash language of the Fancy. Unfortunately, some of Bee's energy was channelled into a negative challenging of Egan's proficiency. Bee became so piqued by what he perceived as Egan's efforts to either anticipate or eclipse him with rival publications that he permitted resentment to impinge upon his treatment of certain reports and lexico-graphical definitions.

Bee was swift to highlight the favourable reports that Egan lavished on the fighter Jack Randall (1794–1828). Although Egan generally proved an unbiased observer, he almost invariably referred to Randall as '*the*

---

37 The images in *Boxiana II & III* were the work of George Sharples, who also produced the only known portrait of Egan (1821).

38 Court proceedings of 24 July 1823.

39 A revised edition of Bee's dictionary that was originally published in 1823.

Nonpareil'. Consideration of Randall's Irish parentage was a bonus for Egan who proudly refers to the 'prime Irish boy', 'Young Paddy', and so forth. The tone was set as Egan introduced his *Boxiana* readers to the prizefighting hero:

> JACK RANDALL, DENOMINATED (*THE Prime Irish Lad, otherwise the* NONPAREIL.)
>   The Prize-Ring (1818) does not boast of a more accomplished boxer than RANDALL; nor of any pugilist, who, in so short a period, has made greater progress towards arriving at the *top of the tree* than he has done (*Boxiana II*, p. 260).

A couple of pages later, the unstinting nature of Egan's praise is rendered quite evident; his opinions of Randall's abilities have veered away from the straight path of objectivity with any pretensions of journalistic impartiality seemingly abandoned:

> RANDALL is a complete *rara avis* in the ring; but does not appear to use any *finesse*. His position is erect, and natural fighting is his forte. His *look-out* in battle is equal to any admiral upon the station; and he turns the neglect of his adversary to account with the utmost promptness and judgement. He is a most excellent judge of his *distances*, and *floors* his opponent with tremendous severity. His ONE-*two* are put in with the sharpness of lightning [...] As a *fibber*, he has no superior [...] On his legs he is wonderful, and he gets over the ground with all the agility of a dancing master; but, notwithstanding these rare requisites towards victory, he does not trifle with any of them, but fights with the greatest caution. He leaves nothing to *chance*. In the heat of battle he is cool to a degree; but his most prominent feature as a fighting man is – in retiring from all his contests [...] scarcely exhibiting a *scratch!* (*Boxiana II*, pp. 262–3)

Egan the fan? Egan the social acquaintance and fellow tavern carouser? Egan the Irish patriot? Probably all of these. But, accusations of biased reporting can, to some degree, be fended off by the need to pique the reader's interest – to excite. And, in this area, plaudits and general exaggeration of qualities are excusable, possibly to be expected. Less easily ignored, or justified, are some of the gushing eulogistic traces amidst Egan's writings on Randall, the man and his fights. The profile that Egan created (partially fabricated?) is, overall, an entirely positive one almost devoid of either censure or exposure of any sporting or personal shortcomings.

In terms of being considered an all-round worthy human being, Randall was portrayed as the antithesis of Tom Hickman ('the Gas-man'), a controversial figure who provoked ambivalent emotions within Fancy circles and, by natural progression, amongst the writers recording confrontations in and out of the prize-ring. Hickman will be discussed at greater length later, and Bee would criticise Egan for failing to swiftly expose some of Hickman's particularly bad-tempered cruelty which Egan had witnessed. Bee's view of Egan's subtle (and some less subtle) promotion of carriage lamps, shooting guns, and hostelries, in *Book of Sports*, is not known. Possible vested interests, together with the championing of favourite pugilists, forms another dimension of the sports-writing debate, as it can be considered another factor that compromised Egan's claims for impartiality. One unanswered question remains: to what extent could the pugilistic genre have been advanced by the two writers working in tandem, or at least co-operating to avoid duplication of publishing projects?

Returning to the sport itself, on a practical point, it should be noted that Jack Randall was not a 'heavyweight' fighter, and therefore not to be directly compared to former champions and *Boxiana* cult heroes such as Tom Cribb and Tom Belcher (1783–1854). The bigger prizefighters usually weighed approximately thirteen to fifteen stone. Although official weight divisions were yet to be legislated, it was generally accepted that only a foolhardy man, not a brave one, would challenge a fighter more than about two stone heavier than himself. Randall weighed in at '10 stone 2 lb.' for an April 1817 fight (*Boxiana II*, p. 269), and slightly heavier, '10 st. 10 lb.' (*Boxiana III*, p. 198), in September 1821. His height was recorded to be '5 feet 6 inches' (*Boxiana III*, p. 175). Thus, anyone relishing the prospect of seeing Jack Randall fighting for what was definitively recognised as 'The CHAMPIONSHIP OF ENGLAND' (*Boxiana I*, p. 112) would have been harbouring an unrealistic hope.

The theatricality of a major prizefight was an element explored by Egan, Bee, and, perhaps most famously, William Hazlitt (1778–1830) in his essay 'The Fight'.[40] All attempt to capture the sense of drama and anticipation of

40   First published in the *New Monthly Magazine* (February 1822).

the hours preceding the contest, including the journey to the venue (often shrouded in secrecy until the day), the badinage and betting frenzy outside the ring, the tournament-like sporting of colours, and the almost gladiatorial entrance of the combatants. Egan's brand of pugilistic commentary offered a knockabout hybrid of accurate reportage and imaginative licence, but he consistently touched on themes of national significance such as patriotism, military defence, moral rectitude, and general humanity. Neither did he disregard the unsavoury side of ring affairs, featuring the drinking and gambling culture of the Fancy and its inherent criminal element. Egan was a leading figure in the ethical debate surrounding prizefighting.

Unsurprisingly, the *Boxiana I* dedication to the much-respected Captain Barclay does not dwell on profligacy but, rather, on qualities that could be harnessed for national benefit, albeit delivered with a playful undercurrent:

> To those, Sir, who prefer *effeminacy* to hardihood – assumed *refinement* to rough Nature [...] or would not mind pugilism, if BOXING was not so shockingly *vulgar* – the following work can create no interest whatever; but to those persons who feel that Englishmen are not automatons; and [...] would ultimately be of non-effect were it not animated by a native spirit, producing that love of country, which has been found principally to originate from, what the fastidious term – *vulgar Sports!* BOXIANA will convey amusement, if not information. (*Boxiana I*, pp. iii–iv)

When including some accounts of early-eighteenth-century fights, Egan acknowledged his primary source: 'To Captain GODFREY'S *Treatise upon the Useful Science of Defence*, (now extremely scarce) [...] we are, in some degree, indebted for an account of the characters of the *Fancy* within his time' (*Boxiana I*, p. 21). In the conclusion to his report of a 1733 contest between a 'Venetian Gondolier' (Tito Alberto di Carini, brought to England by Leader of the Opposition, William Pulteney) and Bob Whitaker,[41] Egan inserted some of Godfrey's commentary:

> He, ran boldly in beyond the heavy mallet, and, with one '*English peg*' in the stomach (quite a new thing to foreigners) brought him on his breech [...He] was compelled

---

41   '1300 spectators paid upwards of a guinea'. Zervudachi, in Fuller, *Noble Art: Prize-fighting in England*, p. 8.

> to GIVE IN – to the no small chagrin of the foreigners, who were properly *cleaned out* [...] Godfrey concludes, 'the blow in the stomach carried too much of the English *rudeness* for him to bear, and finding himself so unmannerly used, he scorned to have any more doings with his slovenly fist'. (*Boxiana I*, p. 25)

The phrasing of a fighter being 'unmannerly used' appears somewhat stilted, but the vitality of the scene is adequately conveyed. And, the notion of an antipathy towards foreigners, or at least a pro-English bias, is established at this early stage.

Egan demonstrated his inflated style, and sense of justice, in his pro-file of George Nicholls (1775–1832), who was the only fighter to defeat Tom Cribb (20 July 1805). Egan was aware that some 'friends of the CHAMPION' had encouraged the myth that Cribb enjoyed an unbeaten career by 'withholding the name' of his vanquisher (p. 389), but was determined that his publication would not perpetuate injustice: 'For want of a BOXIANA, to record their valorous deeds, Heroes and Tyros of the fist have [...] been suffered to "steal ingloriously to the grave", and their quali-fications buried with them' (*Boxiana I*, p. 19). Egan consistently asserted that he would record episodes of pugilistic excellence that might otherwise go uncelebrated:

> [He] might have reached the very summit of glory – but who can now only be remembered as a meteor in the pugilistic hemisphere, whose dazzling qualities caused a momentary blaze, then disappeared, and all its brilliancy has since been lost in oblivion. However, we were glad to find, that the Temple of Fame is not so com-pletely filled with heroes, but what a small niche has been preserved to do justice to the memory of NICHOLLS. (p. 196)

Egan faithfully recounts some of the crucial moments from this contest: 'the coolness and good temper of NICHOLLS appeared so predominant throughout [...] that not only his fortitude was preserved, but added vigour to his judgement [...] CRIBB became rather puzzled and perplexed from his tactics being thus foiled' (p. 197). Egan was eager to emphasise the martial aspects of contests, implying that most pugilists, regardless of previous edu-cation or profession, were capable of deploying military-style tactics in their efforts to outmanoeuvre their opponent. Egan rarely ignored opportunities to underscore the national benefits to be derived from pugilism.

Egan's view on the social levelling effect of the sport appears idealistic. In *Boxiana I*, he eloquently claimed:

> Distinction of rank is of little importance when an offence has been given, and in the impulse of the moment, a PRINCE has forgot his royalty, by turning out to box, to prevent the imputation of a coward – a DUKE, his consequence in life – and a BISHOP, the sanctity of his cloth; displaying those strong and *national* traits. (p. 3)

I find no evidence in the *Boxiana* writings of such illustrious persons entering the ring to thrash out a grievance. Indeed, in upper-class society, where serious affront had been sustained, honour was more likely to be satisfied by challenging the offending individual to a pistol duel. Egan and Bee regularly discredited this practice, implying that there was something un-English about resorting to weapons away from the battlefield. They firmly placed 'foreign methods' of settling altercations in a clandestine vendetta culture that nurtured the furtive, dishonourable code of an assassin. Resentment at a lack of judicial even-handedness was not new:

> The sword and pistol have their professors and patrons; but the mischiefs resulting from the use of them are never mentioned, while, on the contrary, if a melancholy accident takes place in pugilism, it is magnified into a tremendous evil, which requires the interference of the legislature. (*Boxing Reviewed*, p. 6)

Although Bee included news about the latest duels in his *Annals of Sporting* series, the reports are sometimes couched in a derisive tone that imparts a sense of slapstick to proceedings. Fewtrell's 1790 text anticipated a 'lesser of two evils' argument contested by factions supporting and opposing the sport; 'that pugilism, by the rules of morality and nature, is preferable to all other modes of violent decision' (*Boxing Reviewed*, p. 7).

Regardless of a pugilist's social background, there is little hint of prejudice in *Boxiana* volumes. Certainly, there is a liberating impartiality throughout Egan's exuberant commentaries, with any references to a fighter's vocation, colour, religion, or even physical impairment confined to a penchant for wordplay. When a pugilistic butcher challenged Johnson, Egan related that 'the *Knight of the Cleaver* was, in a few minutes [...] completely *cut up*' (*Boxiana I*, p. 92). Also, a fighter named Fry 'got so much *broiled* [...] TOM walked off the ground not even *pinked* (p. 93). The latter term acts both as a continuation of the 'cooking' theme, and as a play on the flash sense 'to pink', to strike an opponent with the visible effect of drawing blood (usually referred to as 'claret'). Ultimately, the reports maintained a neutral stance, and news of admirable or shameful conduct within the pugilistic environment was recorded with a candour that underscores Egan's aspiration to achieve accuracy and objectivity, and avoid succumbing to stereotyping.

The pugilistic reports of the period conflate to suggest that the Fancy, and general public, harboured the following mind-set: limited success enjoyed by black and Jewish fighters was acceptable, and could even be celebrated in a bonhomous spirit of sporting camaraderie, but if they evinced an ambitious hankering to dispute the 'natural' supremacy of the country's finest pugilists they were regarded as menacing interlopers. In short, they constituted a threat to the national citadel that was the pugilistic championship of England.

Pancratia registers the pervading blend of anticipation and discomfort over the first battle between Cribb and Molineaux: 'the NATIVES felt somewhat alarmed that a man of colour should dare to look forward to the championship of England, and threaten to decorate his sable brow with the hard-earned laurels' (*Pancratia*, p. 346). Never miserly in appreciation of a fighter's qualities, Egan had heaped praise on black and Jewish pugilists such as Richmond and Barney Aaron. Remarking upon the above fight, Egan congratulated Cribb on *'vanquishing* his BRAVE OPPONENT' (*Boxiana I*, p. 363). This epithet is consistent with the author's even-handed approach, but there exists some uncertainty whether he is striving to redress the balance for what he had perceived as unsportsmanlike bias, even hostility, directed against Molineaux: 'the applause and cheering was decidedly upon the part of the CHAMPION [...] the *man of colour* received, generally, a very different sort of reception' (p. 367).

Egan had previously supplied an indication of his justice-for-all philosophy when railing against the partisan demeanour of the crowd attending the fight between Humphries and Mendoza at Doncaster (29 September 1790):

Prejudice so frequently distorts the mind, that, unfortunately, good actions are passed over without even common respect; more especially, when they appear in any person, who may chance to be of a *different* COUNTRY, *persuasion*, or *colour*: MENDOZA, in being a Jew, did not stand in so favourable a point of view, respecting the wishes of the multitude towards his success. (*Boxiana I*, p. 265)

It should be noted that some resentment towards fighters from the home countries was also discernible. Irish pugilists were sometimes viewed with an animosity that also betrayed fear of their fighting qualities, whilst Scotland's contribution to the sporting 'science' was spoken of in disparaging terms.

Constantly aware of opportunities for publicity, Egan readily reproduced any complimentary remarks made about his work. In the aforementioned meeting of '*the Society for* MUTUAL IMPROVEMENT', the debate was ostensibly about the merits, or otherwise, of pugilism, but included in the opening speech of a 'Mr M' is a tribute to Egan's pugilistic writing: 'BOXIANA is a work which, in genius, is not inferior to the Iliad itself; for the great poet of the ancients has not given more pleasing and diversified descriptions of feats' (*Boxiana III*, p. 579). The speaker's acknowledgement of the 'pleasing and diversified descriptions' implies a partiality for Egan's blend of slang and idiosyncratic phraseology.

Ultimately, *Boxiana I* was a departure from the staid reports of *Pancratia*, fighters being portrayed as individuals with background information. They were also alluded to in elevated terms befitting classical heroes, or in explicitly favourable comparisons, imbuing the action with a sense of the gladiatorial amphitheatre. Analogies would be made between pugilists and contemporary military leaders, thus augmenting the heroic image of the sport and its participants. Essentially, these were humorously exaggerated, and accentuate the light-hearted air that was a fundamental ingredient used by these pugilistic writers. Detractors may have dismissed it as a 'low' form of literature involving 'vulgar sports', but it was welcomed by many:

The reading public immediately singled out *Boxiana* as being different [...] It was racy and intimate, telling personal stories of the boxers [...] It mixed italics, capitals and bold text into a unique cocktail that gave the reader the stresses [...] and it used the Fancy's own slang. It was almost as if you were standing shoulder to shoulder with them at the ring side.[42]

Evidence of a softening in attitude also appeared in periodical publications, *Blackwood's Edinburgh Magazine* producing a string of articles brazenly entitled 'Boxiana' (nine numbers appearing between July 1819 and October 1822).[43] This series was orchestrated by John Wilson ('Christopher North', 1785–1854), politically exploiting *Boxiana*'s popularity as he devised satiric gibes against the 'Cockney school' of poets. These articles also contained boxing-based parodies such as a Wordsworth lampoon 'On the Battle between Mendoza and Tom Owen, at Banstead Downs [4 July 1820]' (Egan's report of the fight appeared in *Boxiana III*, pp. 65–9).[44]

Unsurprisingly, Bee claimed that *Blackwood's* apparent endorsement of Egan's writing was intended to be ironic, which he dubbed 'Ironing':

> Blackwood was *ironing* when, speaking of Egan's boxing reports, he said, 'the historian of the prize-ring excels in language, and his learning is conspicuous'; many fools *took in* this [...] whereas that writer '*excels* only in meagre threadbare *language*, and his want of common *learning* is conspicuous in every page'. (*Bee's Sportsman's Slang*)

There appears nothing ironic, however, in *Blackwood's* statement of March 1820 (reproduced by Egan): 'BOXIANA is a book we never tire of [...] it puts us into immediate spirits'. The writer proceeds to extol Egan's brand of flash writing: 'his style is perfectly his own, and likely to remain so, for it is as inimitable as it is excellent. The man who has not read *Boxiana* is ignorant of the power of the English language'.[45] Thus, Egan, ostensibly a 'middling', non-political writer, was championed by 'the most brilliant

42 Radford, *The Celebrated Captain Barclay*, p. 197.

43 *British Satire, 1785–1840*, ed. by John Strachan and others, 5 vols. (London: Pickering & Chatto, 2003), V, ed. by Jane Moore, p. 184.

44 *Blackwood's* (October 1820) in *Parodies of the Romantic Age*, ed. by Graeme Stones and John Strachan, 5 vols. (London: Pickering & Chatto, 1999), IV, ed. by John Strachan, p. 114.

45 Quoted in *Egan's Life in London, and Sporting Guide*, No. 4 (22 February 1824), p. 25.

satirical journal of the period', one that 'espoused an iconoclastic brand of mordantly effective satire and ultra Toryism'.[46] I believe that the political implication of this potentially controversial endorsement should not be overstressed, as Egan appears to have been a 'convivial creature' who welcomed praise and publicity from any quarter. A century later, one subjective view of *Blackwood's* complimentary article is unequivocal: 'If ever responsible overstatement reached the border-line of sheer dementia it is here'.[47]

Pugilistic Interest Peaks and Declines

The periods covering the Cribb v Molineaux fights (1810 / 11), and Bill Neate v Hickman contest (1821), proved to be highpoints in the history of pugilistic writing. The ramifications relating to national morale of Cribb's title defence had rarely been encountered, and the aftermath prompted journalistic adulation as well as a degree of candid philosophical reflection on the jaundiced conduct of the spectators. Hazlitt's 'The Fight' yielded more publicity for the sport (and the individual fighters) than might have been expected, albeit a major contest. He aligned prize-ring activities squarely with those masculine attributes that the *Boxiana* volumes were so eager to ascribe to the archetypal pugilist.

It is ironic that at the same time as publication of Hazlitt's essay (1822), a correspondent for *The Sporting Magazine* was focusing attention on one of the sport's inherent problems; fighters' susceptibility to bribery, complaining that when greed and chicanery intruded into 'the spirit of manly combat' then 'the art of boxing is made a trade'.[48] It was almost inevitable that corruption would occur in a sport that induced large amounts of

---

46   John Strachan, in *British Satire, 1785–1840*, ed. by Strachan and others, I, p. xvii.
47   Bohun Lynch, *Knuckles and Gloves* (London: Collins, 1922), p. xxiv.
48   Quoted in Radford, *The Celebrated Captain Barclay*, p. 245.

money to be wagered. Egan reported an enticement offered to Dutch Sam and, on this occasion, its contemptuous dismissal: 'SAM was once *tampered* with by the offer of A THOUSAND POUNDS to *lose* a battle [...] but he spurned such a base attempt to degrade his character' (*Boxiana I*, p. 322). Hefty financial stakes increased the pressure on the referees, and there were fewer volunteers prepared to risk incurring the wrath of the losers in contentious fight outcomes. In a period of increased industrial and economic strain the number of bank holidays was reduced from forty (1825) to four (1834) and, in this social climate, unlimited leisure time was frowned upon. This proved detrimental to the prize-ring and it lost many of its backers. In *Bell's Life in London* (2 October 1825), its editor Vincent Dowling (1785–1852) stated: 'The Corinthians [...] have ceased to grant either the light of their countenances, or the aid of their purses towards the encouragement of the Ring, and [...] when honour and fame cease to influence the combatants a system of low gambling is substituted'.[49]

Brailsford records some crucial factors in the wane of pugilism and the incidental effects on its literature:

> An illegal sport was bound to spend most of its energy maintaining its position [...] The ethics of pugilism and society were being pulled further apart [...] The *Sporting Magazine*, at the up-market end of the specialist press, had already rejected bull-baiting and was becoming apologetic over cock-fighting. Robert Surtees was to rank pugilism along with both and to bar it from his *New Sporting Magazine* in 1831.[50]

The dawning of the Victorian era saw the sport's credibility severely damaged, with a decreased demand for pugilistic news. It can be argued that the period 1812–29 was the true 'Age of *Boxiana*'.

49　Quoted in John Ford, *Prizefighting: The Age of Regency Boximania* (Newton Abbott: David & Charles, 1971), p. 189.

50　Robert Smith Surtees, author (1805–64). Brailsford, 'Morals and Maulers: the Ethics of Early Pugilism', p. 141.

Aspects of Egan to Consider

John Reid quotes a review of *Boxiana I*: 'We see no reason why the author of the celebrated work should remain anonymous any more than the author of Waverley' (*Blackwood's*, July 1819).[51] This extravagant comparison is closely followed by a promotion of Egan's abilities as a sporting journalist, claiming that he was a 'wholly individual writer [...] and having access to inside information no other journalist could pretend to'.[52] Amidst this general admiration towards what Reid perceives as a harshly uncelebrated author, it is made clear that Egan had no pretensions to contribute towards public inquiry. Looking at Egan's limited understanding of social reality, the man's optimistically simplistic viewpoint is summarised:

> The Corinthian is always to be differentiated from [...] those with a contemptuous attitude towards other classes; he is a true gentleman who respects and delights in the diversity of society and who sees it as a [natural] hierarchy whose base is the honest working man. Each class has its own duties, its own pleasures [...] Egan views all this with a generous tolerance, without a trace of social indignation or indeed any awareness of the extent of the misery and poverty of his day.[53]

This corresponds with a general impression of Egan as a 'natural', 'middling', conservative, inclined to support the monarchy, aristocracy, and constitution.[54] Reid highlights Egan's vision of sport as a social phenomenon, but is also keen to focus attention on Egan's possible influence on the writing of Dickens. The fact that Dickens appeared eager to downplay any such connection emphasises a changing sensibility, and reinforces the literary transience of Egan's *Boxiana* and *Life in London* (serialised 1820–21) that might be sequestered in a 'Flash and Fancy' voguish period somewhere between 1810 and 1830.

---

51   *Waverley* was published anonymously in July 1814. Walter Scott (1771–1832) was being identified as the novel's author (in reviews) by the end of 1814 (*DNB*).

52   Reid, *Bucks and Bruisers*, pp. 1, 2.

53   Ibid., p. 68.

54   Iain McCalman and Maureen Perkins, 'Popular Culture' in *An Oxford Companion to the Romantic Age*, ed. by McCalman, p. 220.

Brailsford cites Egan's publications as 'necessary', but it is a conditional endorsement which warns of 'the flights of fancy to which his pre-Dickensian linguistic flourishes frequently led him'. His objective appraisal of the journalistic efforts of the period favours Dowling as 'one of the most important influences on nineteenth-century popular sport'.[55] Whilst John Marriott asserts that *Boxiana* was 'recognised at the time and subsequently as one of the finest writings on the sport', he proceeds by stating it was Egan's metropolitan fiction that 'secured his reputation'.[56] There is a dialectic division of Egan's texts into areas of sporting, social, literary, and historical interest and, whilst in-depth studies of the pugilistic writing dimension are non-existent, profiles of sporting figures from the period often include points on pugilistic characters and issues as a natural by-product.[57]

This book concentrates on, primarily, Pierce Egan and the *Boxiana* series. Egan's other pugilistic writing, including his 1820s newspapers, are treated as *Boxiana*-style work, with Jon Bee's *Boxiana IV* forming an integral part. Egan has been treated as a poor relation in the field of nineteenth-century literature, and the (very) limited coverage devoted to his work consistently foregrounds his 1821 metropolitan novel, the *Boxiana* volumes being viewed as peripheral texts. The issue of Egan's flamboyant, hyperbolic, *Boxiana*-style descriptions constitutes a major theme, the language and narrative style deployed by Egan frequently displacing reality. The prizefighting action is often a secondary concern within the author's desire to entertain and, consequently, language and stylistic devices could supplant actual events. As a predominant feature of contemporary sports writing is a concentration on incidental intrigues, and speculation surrounding an event, this theme is a key element in the discussion of Egan's possible long-term influence.

One of the factors in *Boxiana*'s apparent banishment from earnest critical attention is its distinctive slang-laden style. Egan's ebullient metropolitan work, *Life in London*, suffered censure for the inclusion of flash

---

55 Brailsford, *Bareknuckles: A Social History of Prize-Fighting*, p. 165.
56 *Unknown London: Early Modernist Visions of the Metropolis, 1815–45*, vol. II, ed. by John Marriott (London: Pickering & Chatto, 2000), p. vii.
57 A prime example is Peter Radford's biography of Captain Barclay (previously cited).

language, but this element was accentuated in the pages of the *Boxiana* series through the preponderance of pugilistic jargon, particularly in the fight commentaries, which was in addition to the more common metropolitan slang. This trait surely contributes to *Boxiana*'s reputation as some abstruse branch of sporting literature, and accordingly treated as a curio. I look at how the flash language was identifiable with the Fancy, and the social implications of this counter-culture that was regarded with suspicion. Egan and Bee's slang dictionaries augment the discussion in this linguistic area that appears to perpetuate notions of exclusivity attached to the pugilistic world, these contemporary glossaries serving to render the argot knowable, and hence less threatening.

Egan derided foreign ways, but there is a difficulty reconciling the espousal of English superiority, whilst still propagating notions of rivalry, even bitterness, between cities, counties, and countries within Britain. There also remained a distinct lack of the supposed class equality fostered by the pugilistic environment. Egan's accounts often betray a romanticised view of a sporting environment where different social gradations, ethnic backgrounds, professions, and sexes intermingled effortlessly. Certainly, Egan exhibited an impartial mode of reporting that emphasised an individual's attributes irrespective of status or origin. The sense of spectacle that Egan bestowed on the prizefights is one aspect which promotes the concept that his pugilistic 'players' created an appeal that transcended social divisions. Egan instilled this theatrical dimension into accounts of the negotiations, journey, and entrance of the combatants' parties that preceded the drama of the fight commentary. The style supports a philosophy that wished to represent a unified pugilistic community performing, and appreciating, sporting entertainment. Incompatible material emerges in reports of crowd bias exhibited against 'outsiders', and the erosion of class barriers fails to materialise, with little or no development in the status-defined roles of patron and pugilist. In addition, the commentaries are couched in flamboyant, jargon-filled language that risked alienating the non-Fancy reader, and certainly not nurturing a potential new audience.

The xenophobic drift in some of the *Boxiana* writing is a crucial element, and it is not only Egan who constantly cites the military benefits to be derived from men undertaking pugilistic training, or sparring exercise.

Once honed, it is envisaged that the places where this 'manly' science will prove vital are the battlefields of Europe. Occasionally, the recommendation that sporting precepts should be extended to a disadvantaged adversary in the confusion of an armed melee appears fanciful. But, this aversion to dubious tactics receives supporting evidence from accounts of naval conflict in the Napoleonic wars:

> The British despised the French practice of having sharpshooters in the rigging to pick off individual officers and men during close skirmishes. It was one thing for a row of cannon to fire a general broadside [...] But for a marksman to take deliberate aim at his opponent and shoot him was not an honest form of combat.[58]

When the pioneering captain Thomas Cochrane (1775–1860) formulated an unconventional plan to destroy the sheltering French fleets that involved the deployment of explosion ships and poison gas, his superiors dismissed the stratagem as shameful. This demonstrates the readiness to consign anything perceived as underhand to the sphere of foreign dissimulation. In the *Boxiana*-style writings, the championing of English fortitude, and the antipathy towards 'foreign effeminacy', is often simplistically expressed in terms of the Englishman openly standing his ground whilst adopting a pugilistic stance, and the sinister foreigner skulking under the cover of darkness brandishing a dagger. In short, it is ethical tactical acumen allied to bravery versus the concealed manoeuvring of the assassin.

Again, these sweeping attitudes are problematical, and are not uniformly maintained. *Boxiana*'s stout defence of the black American fighters, some admiration of the French general and emperor Napoleon (1769–1821), and domestic regional rivalry are issues that cloud the question of a single, harmonious national spirit, or identity. For instance, Lancashire fighting methods are consistently denigrated, and Walter Scott's *The Two Drovers* (1827) reinforces the discrepancy between prevailing concepts of pugilistic and national qualities amongst the English and Scottish peoples. There was also the embarrassing procession of rowdy English tourists to Europe in the wake of Napoleon's eventual defeat in 1815, and the dandies

---

58   Thomas, *Cochrane: Britannia's Sea Wolf*, p. 36.

were an undeniable feature in fashionable English society, steeped in the 'effeminacy' that Egan abhorred. Egan and Bee constantly derided dandy affectation and language, but this concerted revulsion cannot expunge the group's Englishness.

Such inherent contradictions prevents a simple reading of the *Boxiana* writings, at times smacking of nationalistic rhetoric, but also preaching a romantically humanitarian message that the sporting community is amalgamated by the principles of the prize-ring. Egan's 'Sporting World' was unmistakeably England with London perceived as its core. One such incompatibility, in Egan's writings, occurs between the much vaunted discipline promoted by 'the art' of pugilism and the dissipated, riotous lifestyles of typical Fancy members. The incongruous collocation of conflicting episodes involving valour, generosity, brutality, and deceit, displays an authorial awareness of shortcomings in pugilistic 'heroes', and the essential sporting mantra. The virtual celebration in *Life in London* of frequently dissolute and mischievous protagonists grates with the *Boxiana* espousal of austere pugilistic precepts and temperance.

The influence of Egan's writing is a moot issue. In addition to the evidence of pugilistic or flash-related material in snippets of correspondence from Byron, Scott, and Moore, whole pieces inspired by the *Boxiana* volumes provide testament to its legacy. Egan's sphere of influence extends to the realms of political satire, in Moore's *Tom Crib's Memorial* (1819) and advertising-related parody, in William Frederick Deacon's (1799–1845) *Warreniana* (1824). Egan's 1821 metropolitan tour was one of 'the popular sensations of London life', and the observation that pugilism was 'a popular, if ephemeral, subject in the periodical press during this period', reinforces the notion of an 'Egan moment'.[59] It does not require a gigantic leap of imagination to recognise the *Boxiana* style employed in the satiric works of Moore and Deacon. It forms the bedrock of these pieces, and prizefighting could certainly be regarded as one of the preoccupations in nineteenth-century popular culture. This is amplified by Egan's style

---

59   *Parodies of the Romantic Age*, ed. by Stones and Strachan, IV, ed. by Strachan, pp.
      xxx, 114–15.

of reporting being appropriated by others, but a more onerous task is to determine Egan's position as a 'transition figure', a writer who acts as an enabling force for others to produce mordant political satire, advertising-related parody, or simply to follow the lead in blurring distinctions between spectacle and sport. To some extent, Egan's versatility vitiates his literary reputation. I consider Egan's role, together with other *Boxiana*-style writings, in stimulating awareness of the pugilistic world, and rousing interest in the fortunes of the principal fighters. Ultimately, it is possible to gain insights into the cult of sporting celebrity or, on occasion, notoriety, and Egan's place in its creation.

This book does not seek to endorse Reid's claims for Egan as a direct inspiration for Dickens, but an examination of the period's pugilistic writing encompasses Reid's general advice: 'That Dickens surpasses Egan in every respect should not lead us to overlook the contribution the latter made towards the final effect'.[60] Although this statement relates specifically to the supposed links between Egan's *Life in London* (1821) and *The Life of an Actor* (1825), and Dickens's *Sketches by Boz* (1836) and *The Pickwick Papers* (1837), the sentiment can be transferred to the realm of subsequent pugilistic reporting. Whether the evolution from the formal tones of late-eighteenth-century fight reports, to the above-mentioned flash satire, to the polished comedic prose of Dickens's *Hard Times* (1854), could have occurred without Egan's intervening contribution is debatable.

The novel *Cashel Byron's Profession* (1886), by Bernard Shaw (1856–1950), appears particularly indebted to Egan's work for its pugilistic-based social commentary, as well as jargon. Shaw's comments on the Victorian boxing scene sustain the recurring theme of language and imagery being deployed to camouflage dreary episodes. An overall argument emerges that pugilism created a metaphorical style which evolved over time, and that one sports journalist would not necessarily have been greatly influenced by predecessors. A keystone of the pugilistic writing issues discussed in the book is the concept of a literary response, a naturally recurring reporting strategy. Egan's contribution in this area is consequential and enduring.

60   Reid, *Bucks and Bruisers*, p. 217.

CHAPTER 2

Flash!: The Language of the Metropolis and the Prize Ring

It may be useful to consider this modern view of the linguistic categories that feature heavily in the works under discussion:

> *Slang* is usually short-lived, and often belongs to a specific age group or social clique. It is used, like fashion, to define in-groups and out-groups. *Jargon* is the specialized language of an occupational or interest group, and functions as often to exclude as to include. *Cant* is the secret language of thieves and beggars, and is used for deception and concealment. *Flash* is used with specific reference to the fashionable slang of London's eighteenth- and nineteenth-century demi-monde. The boundaries between these types of language cannot be clearly defined, and individual terms move easily between categories.[1]

Flash is associated with the 'demi-monde', emphasising the term's rather dubious connotations. Presumably, the upper-class individuals who embraced the flash style would not share that particular perception, but Egan's tales about low-life escapades of disguised corinthian impostors imply that they did, intermittently, form part of this underworld community. *Egan's Grose* (1823) yoked the 'showy, ostentatious' sense of 'flash' with the 'shrewd' or 'stylish' one, whilst *Bee's Sportsman's Slang* (1825) suggested a 'Flash-man' may have originally been a 'highwayman', and that he was now 'the favourite, or protector, of a prostitute'. Perhaps the definition that most severely undercuts the desired ideal of 'flashness' is delivered, presumably inadvertently, by its champion himself: 'to appear a knowing person: to be *fly, down,* or *awake*; one not to be had' (*Egan's Grose*). Here,

---

1   Julie Coleman, *A History of Cant and Slang Dictionaries: Volume II 1785–1858* (Oxford: Oxford University Press, 2004), pp. 1–2.

the word 'appear' assumes a conspicuous ambivalence. Arguably, the fiercest denigrators of the Fancy could not have 'exposed' the group's alleged shallowness with more trenchant subtlety. Thus, to be flash could mean to be adept at deception, or simply a charlatan, a natural progression from the term's association with fashion and affectation. The equivocacy of the term could also be channelled in a positive manner to exploit a certain expressive licence, or 'a kind of enabling ambiguity'.[2]

An extract, exhorting the new arrival in London to be wary, from Bee's own metropolitan 'tour', suggests that there was still a vast discrepancy between vying notions of flash:

> Scarcely any stray single gentleman will take a hand at cards with strangers at late hours nor, in flash parlours, much less in confessedly 'flash-houses', where flash-men to flash-whores flash their money, whilst they talk flash, and flashily *do* all they come near.[3]

A further problem was that the bedrock for Egan's brand of flash, the pugilistic sport, was illegal and denied 'the opportunity of developing any formal organisation'.[4] Egan and Bee's lexicons reiterated some of the same issues addressed by Francis Grose's prototype:

> Grose's dictionary was a shrewd appeal to the concerns of its time. The out-of-towner coming to London, as so many did during this period, needed to understand the language used there. Customers wanted to be alert to tradesmen's tricks [...and] those enjoying the dynamic fast-moving world liked to be up-to-date in their speech and manners as well as their clothes.[5]

---

2   Gregory Dart, '"Flash Style": Pierce Egan and Literary London 1820–28', *History Workshop Journal*, 51 (2001), pp. 180–205 (191).

3   Jon Bee, *A Living Picture of London, For 1828, And Stranger's Guide Through the Streets of the Metropolis* (London: Clarke, 1828), reprinted in *Unknown London*, ed. by Marriott, IV, p. 250.

4   Brailsford, *Bareknuckles: A Social History of Prize-Fighting*, p. 19.

5   Coleman, *A History of Cant and Slang Dictionaries*, p. 18. Grose's *Provincial Glossary* (1787), including dialect, proverbs, and superstitions, augmented his position as a pioneering lexicologist.

Essentially, the inauspicious pedigree of the word 'flash' did not stymie the evolution of this controversial idiom. In fact, plurality of meaning was a prominent aspect.

Uncertainty surrounding the accessibility of flash language was exacerbated by the indeterminate nature of many of its definitions. This multiplicity was often accompanied with an ambiguity that was not confined to abstruse words, being prevalent in some of the foremost denominative terms for elements within the Fancy's culture. 'FLASH – Knowing. Understanding another's meaning' (*Lexicon*, 1811) coincides with this group's conceited view of themselves as perceptive men-about-town.[6] The image of the 'Flash-Man' becomes tainted when attention is focused on alternative definitions, such as that of 1785: 'Dashing, ostentatious, swaggering' (*OED*). Also, the flash argot is dubbed 'cant' and 'relating to the underworld' (*B/P*), thereby reinforcing criminal undertones. But, Egan's promotion of the respectability of flash phraseology is demonstrated in 'the fact that George IV should have had no trouble in accepting the dedication' in *Life in London*.[7]

Believing his own glossary to have been anticipated, Bee alleged that *Egan's Grose* was published 'in great haste', and borrowing heavily from *Lexicon*. This latter point is justifiable, as Coleman numbers the entries taken from *Lexicon* as 4972 (87 per cent), and states: 'fewer than 4 per cent of his [Egan's] entries were entirely new to the slang dictionary tradition'.[8] John Ford is unequivocal in his dismissal of Bee's dictionary, calling the work 'as hysterical and unbalanced as its title' (see List of Short Titles), and claiming that Bee was probably 'mentally unstable when it was written'.[9] Bee certainly appears to have harboured an antipathy towards Egan (professional or otherwise) and continued his excoriating condemnation of his rival's lexicographical capabilities, claiming the *Lexicon* 'contained a few misprints or errors of the press', which Egan had reproduced 'with Simian

---

6   *Lexicon Balatronicum* (1811) could be regarded as a fourth edition of *Grose*, although Coleman views it as a dictionary 'based on' Grose's. Ibid., pp. 74–8.

7   Dart, '"Flash Style": Pierce Egan and Literary London 1820–28', p. 190.

8   Coleman, *A History of Cant and Slang Dictionaries*, p. 176.

9   Ford, *Prizefighting: The Age of Regency Boximania*, p. 185.

servility'. Bee concluded that Egan was 'wholly incapable of undertaking a work requiring grammatical accuracy' (*Bee's Sportsman's Slang*, p. ix). However, Reid claims that Egan's edition resisted the challenge of competitors because of its 'comprehensiveness and liveliness [which] won it wider acceptance', adding that it was reprinted 'until late in Victorian times'.[10]

Linguistic Factors: Authenticity and Illicitness

Flash slang was sometimes referred to as 'St Giles's Greek', which could also mean 'unintelligible speech or language' (*OED*). Egan's aspiration to promote a wider understanding and acceptance of flash vocabulary could only suffer by an association with St Giles, 'the grand head-quarters of most of the thieves and pickpockets about London' (*Lexicon*).[11] Its capacity for use as a secret language was a disturbing dimension that rendered it suspect amongst government officials guarding against subversive activities. In his preface to *Tom Crib's Memorial* (1819), Thomas Moore brackets flash and 'St Giles's Greek' together and explains its modus operandi:

> As this expressive language [...] is still used, like the cipher of the diplomatists, for purposes of secrecy, and [...] eluding the vigilance of a certain class of persons, called, *flashice, Traps*, or in common language, Bow-street-Officers, it is subject of course to continual change [...] It resembles the cryptography of kings and ambassadors, who by a continual change of cipher contrive to baffle the inquisitiveness of the *enemy*.[12]

The indeterminacy of this protean language meant that it could encroach into previously restricted areas, and Coleman observes that one feature that made flash both 'dangerous' and 'appealing' was that it could introduce a

---

10   Reid, *Bucks and Bruisers*, p. 102.
11   Tobias George Smollet (1721–71) refers to a 'St Giles's huckster' in his 1771 work *Humphrey Clinker* (London: Penguin, 1985), p. 153.
12   *British Satire, 1785–1840*, ed. by Strachan and others, V, ed. by Jane Moore, p. 194.

'disreputable' and 'enticing' dimension into parlour conversation: 'Cant respected class [...] its speakers knew not to use it outside its proper sphere; flash had no such respect'.[13] Nevertheless, claims that 'drawing rooms were turned into *chaffing cribs*, and rank and beauty learned to patter flash *ad nauseam*' appear fanciful.[14]

Illicit conduct involving slang was more liable to occur in the swindles perpetrated by London fraudsters, as illustrated by W T Moncrieff's theatre production *Tom and Jerry: or, Life in London in 1820* (first performed at the Adelphi, November 1821):[15]

> Just as government spies knew the radical haunts, Bob Logic's brain archives a counter-cartography whose key is explained in the hidden discourse of the lower class. Logic is 'a complete walking map of the metropolis – a perfect pocket dictionary of all the flash [...] in which the knowing ones conceal their roguery'.[16]

Bee also aligns himself with the notion that fraud, and even civil unrest, could be countered by the intricacies of the language being divulged: 'where secrecy is sought for a cant language, whose existence is dangerous, the necessity of disclosure must be obvious' (*Bee's Sportsman's Slang*, p. xiv).

Egan conceded that the Fancy contained an undesirable element of sharpers, thieves, and worse. Negativity is encountered when dealing with some of his primary 'players', although the eighteenth-century use of 'buck' augured well: '[it] indicated rather the assumption of spirit or gaiety [...] than elegance of dress', shaking off the damaging links to 'dandy and fop' (*OED*). But, an air of superficiality recurs as notions of fashion, ostentation, robbery, and assumption of false personas dominate an 1830 *Sporting Magazine* sketch of the last days of the Fives Court: 'the rouged and

---

13   Coleman, *A History of Cant and Slang Dictionaries*, p. 260.

14   Charles Hindley, *The True History of Tom and Jerry* (London: Reeves & Turner, 1888), p. i.

15   This opportunistic dramatisation was 'performed ninety-three nights in succession'. Ibid., p. 76.

16   David Worrall, 'Artisan Melodrama and the Plebeian Public Sphere: The Political Culture of Drury Lane and its Environs, 1797–1830', *Studies in Romanticism*, 39, 2 (2000), pp. 213–27 (224).

villainous countenance of the brothel-bully, the saloon girls' fancy-man, or the wary and well-dressed figure of the swell pickpocket. These, with a few dirty-looking mechanics and butchers [...] compose the present audience'.[17]

Like Egan, Bee avoided prurience, but included social realities such as 'cyprians' (prostitutes). Entertainment is one of the primary considerations, and even short-lived terms are valued, thus perpetuating the principles of Grose, who 'saw the mutability' of language: 'The more novel, the more transient terms are, the more reason there was for recording them'. Coleman also suggests that *Grose* was 'in some way an antidote to Johnson: its contents are neither uplifting nor educational; its purpose is to amuse and entertain'.[18] Egan endorses these points, and highlights Grose's data-gathering 'nocturnal sallies' into the St Giles's district, where '*slang* expressions continually assailed his ears' (*Sporting Anecdotes*, 1825, p. 77). Using 'assailed', Egan, surprisingly for a flash advocate, ascribes a harsh quality to slang diction. His own 'nocturnal sallies' should probably be classified as tavern carousing, rather than research, but such creative measures were evidently being practised long before Dickens's well-chronicled night-time walks.

Bee also stressed the authentic nature of his sources, his publication containing 'recent information, obtained *viva voce* from some eschewed walks of *life*; together with a moral inculcation here and there [...] Aptly *drawn* from the mouths of *downie coves*, phrases over-heard in the market-place [...] in the coffee-panny, around *the ring*, and at other verbal sources' (*Bee's Sportsman's Slang*, pp. iii, x).[19] Bee also challenged the perceived literary unworthiness of 'slangery', and the dismissive reaction it incited:

> What a host of enemies will not this one little word engender? How will every repetition and inflection of *slang* raise the ire [...] of those who imagine, that because they may have ascended the montalto of universal erudition, none else shall mount the bases of those literary glaciers. (p. iv)

17   Quoted in Brailsford, *Bareknuckles: A Social History of Prize-Fighting*, p. 123.
18   Samuel Johnson (1709–84). 'Johnson's Dictionary' published in 1755. Coleman, *A History of Cant and Slang Dictionaries*, pp. 4–5.
19   The ubiquitous 'cove' is defined as 'any body whatever, *masculine*' (*Bee's Sportsman's Slang*). A 'panny' was flash for 'small house' or 'room'.

The mountain-scaling imagery, ironically, sees Bee identifying with the same frustration (struggling against literary prejudice) as Egan, and an unexpected lexical entry exorcises some of his resentment in typical satiric style:

> *Literary pursuits* – subscription to a library and access to talking company; the production of a scrap or two occasionally in a favourite paper, busy intercourse (monthly) with a magazine, and the announcement of a volume once in ten years. Of such quacks and their admirers we find there are two classes, 'those who have erudition without genius, and those who have volubility without research'. (*Bee's Sportsman's Slang*)

Although mocking anti-slang bias, Bee is sufficiently aware not to proffer an unconditional recommendation for the flash genre. In his entry for 'Slang-whangers', he applies a figurative check-rein, warning against those who introduced 'inappropriate' words that 'possess no recommendation by freshness and impertinence'.

Although Egan and Bee proved inconsistent in their logging of sporting terms, their dictionaries are much more than superficial diversions, providing a useful service to a public wary of the street-swindler's patter. Egan heralds the principal aim of his lexical work: 'To remove *ignorance*, and put the UNWARY on their guard; to arouse the *sleepy*, and to keep them AWAKE [...] and to cause every one to be *down* to those tricks, manoeuvres, and impositions practised in life' (*Egan's Grose*, p. xxviii). In this period, any transposable terms between criminal and sporting worlds were detrimental to the latter. Continuing to remark upon the roguish aspect of Regency life, Bee advocated the role of his glossary as a countermeasure:

> The acquisition of *flash* puts many a man *fly* to what is going on, adversely or otherwise [...] They were invariably thieves and gamblers who used *flash* formerly; but other kinds of persons, now-a-day, who may be rippishly inclined, adopt similar terms and phrases, to evince their uppishness in the affairs of life; especially those of the less honest part of the community, who, in this particular, run the risque of being foiled at their own game by means of this dictionary of modern *flash*. (*Bee's Sportsman's Slang*, pp. 79–80)

Part of Bee's lengthy definition of 'slang' pronounces that all such secret language 'is here exposed to the uninitiated', and claims that a transition can be attained through his dictionary: '*Novice* – one not initiated in the affairs of town [...] all inexperienced persons are *novices*, until they peruse this Volume'.

Egan's account of John Thurtell's trial (1824), for the murder of William Weare, partially corroborates a linguistic preconceptions theory. Thurtell was a morally suspect figure operating on the periphery of Fancy circles, trying to make money from dubious fight promotions and gambling. Recording the events at Hertford Assizes (5 December 1823), Egan notes the alleged dialogue between Thurtell (1794–1824) and William Probert (eventually acquitted):

> [Thurtell] 'I have blown his brains out, and he lays behind a hedge in the lane'. 'Nonsense, nonsense', said Probert, 'you have never been guilty of a thing of that kind [...] if you have, and near my cottage, my character and my family are ruined for ever; but I can't believe that you have been guilty of so rash an act'. (*Trial of Thurtell*, p. 9)

The language is melodramatic and consciously circumspect, as if aware that any lapses into slang might be personally incriminating. When the trial resumed (7 January 1824), Probert, under examination, claimed that Thurtell distributed the money stolen from Weare, saying '"that's your share of the blunt"'. When fearing discovery, Probert reports Thurtell's exclamation '"then I am booked"' (p. 60). This expression features in *Boxiana II* (1818, p. 113), referring to a betting 'certainty' (i.e. 'destined'). Bee clarifies the semantics: 'any event being already settled [...] so certain that 'tis already set down in the *book* of history' (*Bee's Sportsman's Slang*). Later, Egan relates details of a private prison interview with Thurtell, in which the accused man recalled his dalliance with the prize-ring whilst expressing indignation at adverse press coverage: 'I will give some of the papers *pepper* [physical punishment] for what they have said' (*Trial of Thurtell Appendix*, pp. 27–8). In this environment, flash forms a natural element of conversation. There is no evidence, in this account, that any emphasis was placed on the accused men's way of speaking as a means of implying guilt.

A fictional scene from *Real Life in London* (1821) reinforces the notion that a more widespread familiarity with the argot could expedite certain situations:

[Charles Sparkle]:[20] 'A learned Judge once, examining a *queer covey*, a *flash customer*, or a *rum fellow*, asked him his reason for suspecting the prisoner at the bar of stealing a watch, (which among the lads is scientifically termed *nimming* a *tattler*, or *nabbing* a *clicker*), replied as follows: "Why, your honour only because you see as how I was *up* to him". – "How do you mean, what is being *up* to him?" – "Why, bless your heart, I was *down* upon him, and *had* him *bang*". But still perceiving the learned Gentleman's want of *nous*, he endeavoured to explain by saying, that he was *up to his gossip*, – That he *stagged* [observed] him, for he was not to be *done* [...] Had the learned Judge been up himself, much time and trouble might have been saved; and indeed the importance of being *down* as a *nail*, to a man of fashion, is almost incalculable; for this reason it is, that men of high spirit think it no derogation from their dignity or rank, to be well acquainted with all the *slang* of the coachman'. (*Real Life in London*, pp. 206–7)

Bee wished to lessen the language's dishonourable connections, seeking to mobilise classical writers as 'props' and 'unpaid auxiliaries' in support of the flash cause (*Bee's Sportsman's Slang*, p. xvi). He advanced London as a modern seat of learning: '[*Attica*] the place in Greece where people were most *up* to wit and learning [...] Cockneyshire, with all its faults, is the present *Attica* of the world – Paris a second rater'. Bee's efforts may have offset or masked the negativity surrounding slang writing, but the air of suspicion remained.

Fancy Connection: The Metropolitan Slang of *Life in London*

Egan's use of sporting and fashionable argot, especially those terms peculiar to members of the Fancy, is a pervasive feature of his writing. This trait would excite widespread popularity and censure when it played a major part in *Life in London* (1821): 'No writer has been more generous in capitalised and italicised words [...] nor as prolific in exclamation marks [...]

---

20   Sparkle is the counterpart to *Life in London*'s Bob Logic.

and once the reader becomes accustomed to this idiosyncrasy, he finds that the typographical oddities impart a colloquial tone and colour'.[21]

Life in London featured some of Egan's prime players in the 'Sporting World', bucks and corinthians, and as flash was not confined to sporting circles, the text provides an insight into the general parlance and lifestyles of typical characters within Egan's depiction of the principal city in pugilistic affairs. The fact that the *Life in London* narrative did not revolve around the prize-ring precluded the extensive use of pugilistic terminology, but Egan appears to distance himself from the Fancy argot amongst his rambling, philosophising introduction that addresses 'BOXIANA':

> Take off the *gloves*, quit the prize ring, put down the *steamer* [pipe], and for awhile dispense with thy DAFFY [gin], but above all, steer clear from the *slang*, except, indeed, where the instances decidedly call it forth, in order to produce an effect, and *emphasis* of character. (*Life in London*, pp. 13–14)

This exculpatory declaration sees Egan symbolically shedding his pugilistic persona, and adopting the role of a 'serious', discerning author who can filter out discordant slang. In his later urban peripatetic work Egan sidestepped the issue by including a qualifying clause: '*Obscenity* ought to be avoided in all instances', but 'effective humour' and 'character' should 'never to be *marred* [...] by far-fetched *squeamishness*' (*The Pilgrims of the Thames*, 1838, p. 138). Arguably, its flash content earns *Life in London* the status of being considered a formative text in metropolitan fiction, which had predominantly assumed the form of cautionary guides to the unscrupulous activities of sharpers and other nefarious characters.[22] The roving *Life in London* adventures include visits to sporting establishments, where the mainstream metropolitan and Fancy worlds coalesce. Significantly, it is the flash language that augments this common ground.

A typically florid passage occurs as Egan recounts details of a 'spree' in the company of one of his main protagonists, Bob Logic: 'I was *gammoned*

---

21   Reid, *Bucks and Bruisers*, pp. 19–20.
22   A selection of such works can be found in *The Metropolitan Poor: Semifactual Accounts, 1795–1910*, ed. by John Marriott and Masaie Matsumura (London: Pickering & Chatto, 1999), I.

to be one of the *squad*. Mixed liquors and *steamers* were the order of the *darkey* [evening...] A glass or two had been *sluiced* over the *ivories* of the party, which made some of them begin loudly to *chaff*' (p. 276). Notwithstanding Egan's ornate footnotes, an obvious drawback is that, in the absence of a comprehensive glossary, a flood of elaborate passages could have rendered the work virtually impenetrable to the reader not apprised of the flash language. Yet, the far-reaching impact of the book is undeniable, and by 1828 Egan was 'able to list the titles of sixty-seven dramatisations, parodies and sequels'.[23] Egan employed a series of London's low-life locations as backcloths for his 'players' to perform, and the proliferation of slang terms was a natural by-product.

Another principal character, Jerry Hawthorn, learns much of city ways by overhearing conversations, adding a level of intrigue for the reader, who, in addition to being guided through a morass of uncharted streets, has their interest further piqued by access to a language shrouded in secrecy. Throughout the text, Jerry benefits from Bob's encyclopaedic knowledge. Bob's conversation, with its significant aspect of disclosure, accentuates a correlation between the analysis of people and the gossip column. Logic justifies the narrator's claim that he was 'UP to *every thing*' (*Life in London*, p. 74), and the conspiratorial tenor is reinforced when the reader accompanies the protagonists on clandestine visits to low-life locations. Egan's narrative grants the reader access to previously concealed areas, enhancing the enthrallment of such episodes. Overall, the inclusion of flash language plays a significant role in this process, and the technique sharpens the sense of reader participation as they listen in to receive a 'members only' guided tour.

Egan's position as a prominent member of the sporting fraternity underpins the linguistic authenticity of his work, as opposed to 'the bland, all-purpose "literary" style of most of his contemporaries'.[24] Egan's journalistic instinct is exhibited in a digressive, episodic style, but this fitted the serialised form. The reportage element complemented Egan's prioritisation

---

23   Louis James, review of the *Unknown London* series (ed. by Marriott). *Times Literary Supplement*, 5152 (28 December 2001), p. 4.

24   Reid, *Bucks and Bruisers*, p. 198.

of accuracy, which naturally included slang discourse. This approach, following the covert escapades of his 'heroes', gleaned insights: 'It is only by means of free and unrestrained intercourse with society [...] that an intimate acquaintance is to be obtained with Englishmen'; 'it is necessary to view their pastimes, to hear their remarks, and from such sources, to be enabled to study their *character*' (p. vi).

Such sentiments are directly transferable to Egan's sports writing. It is this genre, and the *Boxiana* series in particular, that proved most receptive to the heterogeneity espoused by Egan, and offered scope for exploitation of the flash language. Its linguistic elements promoted *Life in London*'s popularity beyond the world of the Fancy. Despite his irregular style, there is a degree of continuity supplied in Egan's portrayal of London as the capital of the universe, and references to a looking-glass philosophy. The capital contained the Fancy's (unofficial) headquarters, and this placed Egan in a favourable position to merge into, and oscillate between, the various social gradations that it comprised, honing the knowledge that would enable him to instil the vim of colloquial language into his writing. Egan savoured the prospect of the Metropolis's 'luxuriant, variegated [...] landscape', with which he would 'embellish' the 'canvass' (p. 17) of his work. The word 'embellish' is an apt choice when considering his verbose digressions, and this is not an isolated analogy of himself as an artist capturing the alternating hues of metropolitan sporting life on a blank canvas.

The level of disapprobation, preventing the text achieving durable acclaim, may be attributable to public preconceptions regarding the social group portrayed and its argot. Both were perceived as distasteful, and there was existing unease about witnessing young males emulating *Life in London* 'sprees' and language. There was also this complaint from James Harley: 'Egan astounds with civic slang our ears'.[25] The word 'flash' harboured undesirable connotations of superficiality, ostentation, and general ephemerality, and these, alongside associations with the criminal underworld, were obstacles that Egan intended to circumnavigate:

---

25   James Harley, 'The Press, or Literary Chit-Chat. A Satire' (1822), in *British Satire, 1785–1840*, ed. by Strachan and others, III, ed. by Benjamin Colbert, p. 374.

I am aware that some of my readers of a higher class of society may feel [...] that I have introduced a little too much of the *slang*; but I am anxious to render myself perfectly intelligible to all parties. Half the world are up to it; and it is my intention to make the other half down to it. LIFE IN LONDON demands this kind of demonstration. A kind of *cant* phraseology is current from one end of the metropolis to the other. (p. 84)

Byron, in a letter 27 September 1813, urged Thomas Moore to 'go to Matlock [...] and take what in *flash* dialect, is poetically termed "a lark", with Rogers and me for accomplices'.[26] It is a moot point whether Egan could have used this morally suspect figure to endorse his quest for a wider acceptance of sporting argot. Certainly, Byron's use of the word 'accomplices' implies a sense of mischief, even unlawfulness, but Harley appears to partially contradict his claim that Egan's slang 'astounds', when he terms Fancy jargon as 'slang-vital',[27] evoking thoughts of a vibrant, useful language, something that thrills the ear rather than grating.

From his position deep within the sporting preserve of the Fancy, Egan enjoyed greater licence to practise his animated, sporadic style, complete with this singular strain of flash. If sports writing was deemed an inconsequential discipline with pugilism commanding only minority interest from uncultured society, and if the genre was conveniently sequestered into a marginal literary category then it derived the benefit of being relatively free to function in this peripheral world of 'low' literature. Sport, and more particularly pugilism, was to evolve a literary life of its own, and the principal proponent would be Egan with his innovative fusion of spectacle and slang which would, in turn, be moulded by the characteristics of the sport itself. Egan functioned as a formative influence that adapted, improvised, and manipulated to produce a 'thick verbal texture [...] a kind of classless language'.[28]

26 Samuel Rogers, poet (1763–1855). *Byron's Letters and Journals*, ed. by Marchand, III, p. 122.

27 Harley, 'The Press, or Literary Chit-Chat. A Satire', in *British Satire, 1785–1840*, ed. by Strachan and others, III, ed. by Colbert, p. 292.

28 Dart, '"Flash Style": Pierce Egan and Literary London 1820–28', p. 191.

Early *Boxiana* Volumes

Although its primacy would be regularly challenged by pugilistic hotbeds such as Bristol, Egan's brand of sporting religion and nationalistic fervour always retained the spirit of the self-proclaimed flash capital (London). This raises further queries relating to the comprehension, and acceptance, of Egan's more slang-laden pieces nationwide. Conversely, there is the notion that flash could become a universal, 'classless' language for sporting men. It would be incompatible with his reputation as 'Lexicographer and Chronicler to "the Fancy"' (*Book of Sports*, p. 75) if his sports writing achieved limited understanding within a supposedly unified pugilistic society.[29] The widespread appeal of their events is underscored by Egan's claim that his sporting newspaper (printed on a Saturday afternoon) 'may be had by Post, on Sunday, Two Hundred Miles from London'.[30]

It could be argued that Egan had little to lose by the extensive use of flash terms in *Boxiana I* (1813), as his detractors already harboured an antipathetic attitude towards '*vulgar Sports*' (p. iv). At first, the tenor is relatively subdued, and there are frequent instances where an opening to insert slang terminology is rejected in favour of a colourful turn of phrase or unusual simile. Nevertheless, it is with this text that the gradual transmutation of flash begins as the language absorbs an influx of pugilistic jargon, some of it improvised from extant terms. An early extract sees Egan extolling the sport's heritage:

> [Doctor Johnson] was another *striking* proof of pugilism being a national trait, by having a regular set-to with an athletic brewer's servant, who had insulted him in Fleet-street, and gave the fellow a complete milling [...] Smithfield and Moorfields [fairs] also sported booths and rings [...] where many a good bit of stuff has *peeled*.[31] (*Boxiana I*, p. 19)

29 Egan is quoting the writer, Samuel Maunder (1785–1849).
30 This wording was printed beneath the newspaper's title (*Egan's Weekly Courier*).
31 'Peeling' – The removal of outer garments before commencement of a prizefight (*OED*).

'Milling' was firmly appropriated by the Fancy as a verb to denote fighting, or as a noun signifying a beating. It is a well-used term by Egan, and its alternative eighteenth-century meaning 'to rob' (*Lexicon*) was suppressed.

Boxiana I tells of the supposedly insolent Venetian Gondolier threatening to '*take the shine* out of Englishmen' (p. 23), and the '*milling* coves' searching for a suitable champion to '*serve him out*'. To 'serve out' is an example of the tendency for an action to possess several alternative expressions, here being the verbs 'mill', 'punish', 'hammer', or 'quilt' – 'To inflict heavy damage, blows, or injury' (*OED*). In this episode, 'BOB WHITAKER', a fighter possessing 'true *bottom*', is selected to defend English prestige and duly 'punished' the challenger so severely that 'the *conceit was so taken out of him*' (*Boxiana I*, p. 25). The term 'bottom' signified endurance, and was usually associated with pugilists and racehorses, whilst the second phrase, essentially, expresses the action of knocking the arrogance, or the 'overweening self-opinion' (*OED*), out of an opponent. It occurs frequently enough in the *Boxiana* series to be regarded as a staple expression in sporting circles: '*Great Jacobs*, challenged WARD [...] but JOE was not to be intimidated [...] and soon took the conceit out of this vaunting blade' (*Boxiana I*, p. 427). It is endorsed by Byron, who remarked to Moore: 'Half of the Scotch and Lake troubadours, are spoilt by living in little circles and petty societies. London and the world is the only place to take the conceit out of a man – in the milling phrase'.[32]

When Egan writes about 'scarcity of the *rhino*' (*Boxiana I*, p. 82) or 'blunt', he is using well-established terms for a general item – money. But, when he describes a pugilist as 'possessing *bottom*' and 'did not know how to *shift*' (p. 84), he is deploying terms synonymous with prizefighting.[33] Egan's definition of 'shifting' adds a sense of deception ('Shuffling. Tricking', *Egan's Grose*), presumably from the belief that something that involved retreat was, at least in part, dishonourable, and this is clearly implied when he reports

---

32   Letter of 3 August 1814. *Byron's Letters and Journals*, ed. by Marchand, IV, p. 152.
33   'Shifting' is directly applicable to the pugilistic skill of avoiding blows by movement about the ring.

that Cribb 'had recourse to shifting' (*Boxiana I*, p. 199).[34] These reservations supply an insight into Egan's predilection for words that convey a sense of positive motion, or urgency. Egan consistently assigned a pugilist with 'impetuosity', rating it a valuable attribute. The word is denuded of negative connotations entailing haste or recklessness and, instead, assumes the vigour of forceful rapidity. Similarly, a 'desperate' hit is not one that is administered in a rash or frantic manner, but one that wreaks devastation. Some terms emerged directly from pugilistic encounters, devised to reflect types of blow, and instances where fighters delivered a simple 'hit' or 'punch' would diminish.

Some apparently complimentary terms, relating to agility or cunning, only remain praiseworthy when practised in moderation. Egan generally privileged references to courage, stamina, and strength, hence his querulous comments on any performance he deemed '*too scientific*': 'so much *shifting* appeared more like a deficiency in *bottom*' (p. 117). Egan was prone to fluctuate from the heavy use of slang terms (the latter extract featuring three in part of one sentence) to paragraphs virtually devoid of such idiom: '[Jem] BELCHER'S style was original – the amateur was struck with its excellence; his antagonists terrified from the gaiety and decision it produced; and the fighting men [...] confounded with his *sang-froid* and intrepidity' (p. 121). Here, Egan reverts to another of his mainstays, 'gaiety', to confer the sense of a fighter endowed with mobility and dexterity. The fact that it is expressed as a quality that terrifies underscores the shedding of its mirthful connotation.

Given the veneration that Egan accorded to the quality of composure (e.g. 'coolness' is consistently mentioned), in and out of the ring, it is puzzling to find a dearth of flash terms for poise and imperturbability. Egan consistently used 'sang-froid' to encapsulate the sense of equanimity he rated so highly, the choice of a French phrase being slightly incongruous considering the general antipathy to foreign influences in some of his

---

34   It is possible that its pugilistic use contributed to the developing definition of 'shifty'. Although its application to expedient manoeuvring had long existed, the earliest recorded associations with evasiveness and artifice are cited as 1837 and 1864 (*OED*).

nationalistic outbursts. Again, this casts doubt on Egan's thoroughness as lexicographer of the flash language. It would surely have benefited the Fancy's cause if Egan's dictionary contained terms denoting calmness, moral probity, charity, philosophical reflection, and so forth. Many of the complimentary phrases only deal with physical prowess and sartorial flamboyance, and terms relating to acumen focus on wiliness rather than wisdom. This order of precedence is not unexpected in a language dominated by such an aggressive sport, but the scope existed to make flash a richer, more balanced, idiom, simultaneously benefiting from the flexibility that an increased range of expressions would have supplied, and enabling it to enjoy a less circumscribed social existence.

At this stage of his development as a sports writer, Egan's work was not fully exploiting Fancy vocabulary, and he appears to be restraining that particular linguistic flourish in favour of relatively rudimentary slang. Combined with his expansive and stately mode of expression, Egan's fight descriptions often yield conflicting qualities, being compelling yet stilted: 'Gregson's strength was manifest to his opponent, who endeavoured to ward off its potent effects by his thorough knowledge of the *science*, and Gulley put in another dreadful *facer*, which made the *claret* fly in all directions' (*Boxiana I*, pp. 176–7). Egan's paradoxical style, replete with slang and fustian, would remain, but the balance evolved as greater vent was given to the diverse and expanding range of sporting argot. Crucially, if Egan could enjoy free rein anywhere, it would naturally be in the detached literary territory of pugilistic reporting. A pattern emerges that the appearance of flash terms, predominantly, occurs within fight commentaries, and these can be regarded as almost exclusively pugilistic, tending to be concerned with the fighters' actions. There was greater scope for Egan to include more general slang in his observations about events and conversation taking place on the journey to a fight, or amongst the spectators and betting men. The hotchpotch of characters that attended Fancy gatherings was especially liable to fall under his scrutiny, raw material for his aim of reflecting 'REAL LIFE' (p. 302).

The round-by-round bursts of action suit the journalistic immediacy that Egan relished, and he could deploy much of his repertoire:

[Caleb Baldwin v Dutch Sam, 7 August 1804] The spectators were extremely anxious to witness on which side the first advantage appeared – great expectations were placed upon Caleb, whose experience, well known *bottom*, and scientific accomplishments, rendered him a finished Pugilist, – and Dutch Sam, was an object of considerable attraction among the *Fancy* in general; after some display of the art, Sam made a *hit*, which did not tell; but Caleb, eager for the fray, returned the compliment extremely sharp, and put in a desperate facer, that *levelled* his opponent. Three to one in favour of Caleb. (p. 309)

In his profile of Dutch Sam, Egan's statement that the man is 'a *hard hitter*' appears a singularly unremarkable observation to make of a champion pugilist, with italics failing to imbue extra panache. Egan expands on the perfunctory opening comment, declaring Sam to be a fighter unsurpassed for 'force' and 'ponderosity', and 'whose blows are truly dreadful to encounter' (p. 321). Stripped of flash terms, the sketch lacks colour, but it does establish a tone that is compatible with a sense of remorseless pressure.

The theme continues in Egan's account of a contest against Tom Belcher (21 August 1807): 'The ferocity of Sam was tremendous in the extreme; he followed his opponent to all parts of the ring, putting in dreadful *facers* and body-blows, dealing out death-like *punishment*' (p. 330). This appears relatively staid in comparison with the sprightly style adopted to portray the fighter's cognitive abilities, Egan pronouncing that 'SAM is *flash* to the very ECHO', also observing that 'in the *slang chronicles*', the fighter would be classified as 'a GAMMONER of the first brilliancy, *down* to all the tricks of life, and not to be *had* upon any *suit* whatever' (p. 323). The picture of mental dexterity is convincing, but again the onus is placed on the practical nous of someone not easily duped, rather than possessing discernment. The emphasis is on being 'leery' when dealing with suspect characters.[35] Here, 'flash' concerns the preventive aspect of using knowledge as a safeguard against swindlers, rather than a means of, say, exercising Solomonic judgement or advancing academic research. Use of the term 'GAMMONER' augments an impression of a capable, almost vulpine, figure amidst various city tricksters – in fact, an archetypal flash-man roaming London streets. Overall, the term fosters an untrustworthy image.

35   Leery (Leary) – Knowing, 'fly' (*OED*).

Boxiana I's climax was reserved for Cribb's defence of the championship against the American Molineaux (December 1810):

> Desperation was now the order of the round, and the rally re-commenced with uncommon severity, in which CRIB shewed the most science, although he received a dreadful blow [...] and exhibited the first signs of *claret*. Four to one on CRIB. Third – After a short space of sparring, *Molineaux* attempted a good blow on CRIB'S *nob*, but the Champion parried it, and returned a right-handed hit under the *Moor's* lower rib, when he fell rapidly in the extreme. (*Boxiana I*, p. 403)

In future volumes and newspaper reports, by both Egan and Bee, the teeth would often be referred to as 'ivories', and blows to the 'nob' and 'ribs' shortened to 'nobber' and 'ribber'. Their initial absence could be construed as a symptom that Egan considered an understated approach appropriate to prepare the way for more intricate explorations of flash. Nevertheless, the phrasing of 'fell rapidly in the extreme' appears particularly cumbersome, and would be superseded by 'levelled', or 'floored'. Pugilism was a catalyst in such linguistic development.

Even in the midst of particularly momentous contests, the gambling element was ever-present, and in such conditions the acuity of the flash men is discernible. When Cribb appears to be struggling, it is those spectators not truly 'down' or 'up' to the state of battle that begin to lay their wagers:

> The battle had arrived at that doubtful state, and things seemed not to prove so easy and tractable as was anticipated [...] On CRIB'S displaying weakness, the *flash-side* were full of palpitation [...] and those who were not thoroughly acquainted with the *game* of the CHAMPION began hastily to *hedge-off*. (p. 404)

Both aspects of the adjective 'flash' are demonstrated by those betting men displaying knowledge and conviction, and those whose judgement is governed by external appearance – only seeming to be informed. An additional facet yielded by the gambling element is the introduction of a flamboyant range of expressions to articulate uneven odds, an example being '*Lombard Street to a China Orange*' (*Boxiana I*, p. 412).[36] These

---

36   Comparing the London street, where many major banks were situated, against a piece of chinaware.

phrases could assume a certain thematic dimension, such as military: 'it was *Chelsea College* to a *sentry-box*' (*Boxiana II*, p. 375). It is possible that creative Fancy minds might have relished devising fresh permutations for such lopsided odds, an apposite one for the sporting fraternity being 'Eclipse to a lame donkey' (p. 311).[37] This imaginative streak is alluded to in a *Real Life in London* footnote:

> Among the *swell lads*, and those who affect the characters of *knowing coveys*, there is a common practice of endeavouring to coin new words and new modes of expression [...] and this affectation frequently has the effect of creating a laugh. (*Real Life in London*, p. 163)

It is apparent that this linguistic creativity is generated by a playful bent rather than lexicographical zeal.

Repeated references to gambling underscore a major aspect of the sporting scene, and raise further questions about the ambiguous nature of 'flash'. When Dutch Sam is unexpectedly defeated by Bill Nosworthy (8 December 1814), Egan notes the disappointment exhibited by the '*soi-disant* Knowing-Ones' (*Boxiana II*, p. 73). In this scenario, it is this flawed group that is identifiable with the 'flash-side'. Originally associated with the horseracing turf, 'knowing ones' only 'profess' to be well versed in sporting matters (*OED*), thus repeating the concept of a façade. There is a further rebuke laced with irony for the '*presumed* Knowing Ones' following another 'unexpected termination', Egan suggesting: 'which ought to operate as a useful lesson in future, by inducing them to prefer the calculation of *capabilities* between the combatants, than to be led astray by the mere greatness of names' (*Boxiana II*, p. 145).

As demonstrated, Egan's writing fluctuated, and greater animation is sustained by those reports possessing some flash content: 'In spite of all his *ruffianism* and knowledge of boxing, his *nob* was instantly placed in *chancery* – his *peepers* [eyes] were taken measure of for a *suit of mourning*' (*Boxiana II*, p. 43). Egan uses a fuller expression than previously ('in *mourning*', *Boxiana I*, p. 327) to signify the blackening of the eyes, and would later

---

37   Eclipse was an undefeated racehorse (at its zenith between 1769 and 1771).

produce a re-wording of a similar situation: 'his *ogles* [eyes] were nearly in a state of darkness; his *frontispiece* [face] all vermilion [blood]' (*Boxiana III*, p. 357). Egan's description of Richmond's victory against Davis (3 May 1814) is analogous to the conflicting characteristics of some of the fighters he portrays, alternately incisive and ungainly:

> Fifth. – The science of Richmond in this round burst forth so conspicuously [...] With his science and courage united, he nobly opposed a rally [...] and planted so severe a teaser on the mouth of Davis that sent him quickly on the grass [...] Seventh. – The manner of Davis was now rather unpropitious towards winning, and he appeared evidently distressed. His temper also forsook him, and he still incautiously kept following Richmond, who *milled* him in every direction. (*Boxiana II*, pp. 128–9)

Egan converts 'teaser' into a blow, which is not inconsistent with its application as something that causes a problem or annoyance.[38] But, saying this particular punch was in its 'severe' form appears unnecessarily awkward, and to formally pronounce Davis's demeanour as 'rather unpropitious towards winning' renders a stilted tone.

In a reminder of the hardiness frequently displayed by the Fancy in their pursuit of sporting spectacle, there is evidence of Egan's ability to articulate the surrounding scene in such a manner that obviates the demand for a ready-made slang expression: 'The unpropitious state of the weather had not the least effect upon the feelings of the spectators, who never shifted an inch of ground in consequence of being so drippingly assailed' (p. 350). Rather than suffering a banal 'drenching', the crowd have encountered a more poetical, if no less wet, experience. Another linguistic stratagem appears in Bee's commentary on the fight between Josh Hudson and 'Caulker' Bowen (5 February 1822):

> They were *bang-up* in *Pepper-alley* [...] The *East-enders* were now dancing with joy, roaring with delight, and offering to sport their *blunt* like waste-paper. In the ecstasy of the moment, 10 to 1, 5 to 1 [...] The combatants now got into a desperate rally, and Josh received the most *pepper*, till he put in a *Gaslighter* in the middle of his opponent's *mug*, that not only sent him staggering some yards, but produced the *pink*. (*Boxiana IV*, p. 127)

38   Previously used, in its pugilistic context, as 'an opponent difficult to tackle' (*OED*).

The 'pepper' term is allusive to the spice's pungent, biting quality as well
as the principle of bombardment, but it is the term 'Gaslighter' that has
plainly originated as a form of homage to the formidable Tom Hickman,
known by the variants: 'Gas-man'; 'Gas-Light man'; and 'the Gas'. Thomas
Fewtrell had stated, in 1790, that 'a *Slack* was commonly used to signify
a blow given with great strength' (*Boxing Reviewed*, p. 52),[39] and Egan
referred to a 'Paddingtoner', in recognition of Paddington Jones (*Boxiana
III*, p. 549). A spurt in this mode of coinage did not materialise and the likely
transience of terms founded on such a treacherous foundation as celebrity
should be considered. It must also be conceded that Egan's expression does
not exactly 'roll off the tongue'.

Claims of trademark qualities also appear somewhat presumptuous.
Egan had a propensity to single out Randall as the master of the 'chancery
suit', which involved securing the opponent's head under one arm and
pounding it (*B/P*), but does stop short of re-naming the tactic. Ultimately,
if the *Boxiana* series writings are accepted as valid accounts, the Fancy
enjoyed the sight of many talented pugilists, and to attribute them all with
a speciality manoeuvre would have been preposterous.

There are sufficient examples in *Boxiana* reports to demonstrate the
lucidity of slang-laden passages. Once the more common expressions have
been introduced to the reader, there appears little requirement for Egan
to ration his idiomatic flair, the reader being conversant with at least the
gist of the narrative. By the latter half of *Boxiana II*, the implication of the
following extract would be relatively clear: '*Frere*, with activity, made two
rallies, but meeting with a *poser* in the mouth, which drew his cork, the
claret ran down copiously' (p. 410). The function of 'poser' is comparable
with that of 'teaser', Egan, once again, employing the term in the spirit of
its existing sense: 'A question that poses or puzzles' (*OED*). The implication
is that, although not a decisive knock-down blow, it constitutes a punch
that causes consternation. These terms consciously lack the 'ponderosity'
of the more brutish slang that pervaded the pugilistic arena at the time,
and raises the question whether this is a deliberate ploy to instil a cognitive dimension to the character of the pugilist, and influence the public's

---

39   Jack Slack, a Norwich butcher, and former champion.

general perception of the sport, ushering it away from notions of being little more than a savage struggle between two ruffians.

Certainly, Egan often pitched his profile of a champion, or depiction of an important contest, around a martial theme, complete with images of the fighters as generals planning strategies. The insertion of terms with connotations of subtlety, such as 'teaser', 'poser', 'scientific', and 'shifting', conferred a degree of guile to even the more brutal encounters. The tacit undercurrent of cerebral capacity supplements the overt military analogies, simultaneously underscoring Egan's penchant for 'coolness'.

Recording the fight between McCarthy and Purcell (27 January 1818), Egan demonstrates the contrasting effect of two terms: 'McCarthy received a precious *snorter*, which produced for the first time the *claret* most copiously, but before he went down, he put in a *bodier*' (*Boxiana II*, p. 444). 'Snorter' is a freshly coined term for a punch on the nose (*B/P*), and aptly encapsulates both the vigour of the blow and a likely reaction (snort) of the fighter suffering such a hit. In comparison, 'bodier' appears insipid and vague.

By 1821, the year that the completed volume of *Life in London* was first published, there was a greater awareness of flash terminology. Egan's London established a reputation as the focal point for Fancy interests and jargon, and this is underscored by Byron's admonishment, when writing to his publisher John Murray (1778–1843), directed at John Cam Hobhouse (1786–1869) for his imprisonment in Newgate: 'I am so provoked with him and his ragamuffins for putting him in *quod*, he will understand that word – being now resident in the flash capital'.[40] *Boxiana III* (1821) promised the greatest scope yet to explore the expanding flash vocabulary, Egan's account of a tavern altercation between Cribb and the volatile Lancastrian Jack Carter uniting slang and imagery:

> Carter's *frontispiece* received such repeated *quiltings* from the fist of CRIBB, that it was like a dashing footman paying away at a knocker in announcing a countess at the door of a rout [...] CRIBB has now added to his former traits and character that of a *dentist*, as it is said he *dislodged* the *ivory* after a mode of his own [...] Carter, upon feeling his mouth, declared the whole of his *rail-way* had departed. (p. 24)

40   Letter of 23 March 1820. *Byron's Letters and Journals*, ed. by Marchand, VII, p. 59.

'Rail-way' appears to be a derivative of *Lexicon*'s 'Head Rails', being another term for 'teeth'. The amusing notion of a pugilistic dentist adds another ingredient, and the incongruous concept of 'dislodgement' being an expert surgical procedure is a subtle touch. The following page sees Cribb 'rather up in the *stirrups*', and this particular expression is consistently employed in the context of someone's senses being 'excited' or, generally, being 'on the alert'. For example, 'upon Randall's being *floored*' we see the supporters of his opponent temporarily 'up in the *stirrups*' (p. 201). It is a sense of sporting anticipation that sparks this condition, although thoughts of betting winnings could enter the equation.

Later, the buckish preoccupation with fashion resurfaces in the form of one of the more colourful pugilistic characters, Tom Owen (1768–1843), who is said to have taken to wearing a white top hat. Egan's footnote gives an insight to prevailing sartorial trends, and is replete with slang: '*White Toppers* have become quite the "*go*" among a great part of the *Milling Coves*, in imitation of this great master of the fist, since Tom has taken to decorate his *upper works* with this *nobbish* feature' (*Boxiana III*, p. 56). The improvised adjective is a typically Eganesque flourish. When the occasion arrives for Owen to temporarily abandon his flash garb and prepare for a pugilistic contest against fellow veteran Mendoza (4 July 1820), Egan describes how this lively stalwart overpowered his adversary: '[Owen] exhibited the advantages of *his stop*; he held Mendoza as firm as if the latter had been *screwed* up in a vice, and pummelled him' (p. 68). Egan conveys the unyielding nature of Owen's checking parry, and his sturdy demeanour is accentuated by the apt vice analogy.

Further evidence of Egan's selective use of slang occurs when Randall injudiciously put his fine record in jeopardy by arriving at a fight (against Wood, 4 October 1819), as Egan quaintly phrases it, possessing 'too intimate an acquaintance with Mr *Lushington*' (*Boxiana III*, p. 202). The aforementioned allusions to excessive drink appear relatively innocuous; less damaging than being labelled a regularly boorish drunkard. And, on the occasion of Randall being arrested, for failing to leave a tavern when 'time' was called, his predicament is attenuated by Egan's deployment of slang, analogy, and italicisation:

[Randall] appeared in tolerable *condition* at Guildhall, before Alderman Smith, to answer the charge of assaulting five constables. One of the *heroes of the staff* said, he believed that RANDALL had mistook his *jaw* for a *drum*, and that the tat-too he had beaten on his mug had set all his *ivory a dancing*, as if they had been *electrified*. (p. 210)

Egan also invites understanding of Randall's bluff, but amicable and generous, temperament away from the ring:

Bluntness is his forte. He is *indignant* at what he thinks wrong; and is not over nice in his expressions, whenever such a subject is the theme of his argument. To the CORINTHIAN or *Flue Faker*, he is equally independent and civil upon their accosting him [...] *Education* has done but little for him; yet *experience* has given him the 'time of day' respecting a more enlarged view and knowledge of society. (p. 213)

And, Egan entreats the readership to visualise a scene where Randall had given away 'the only *bender* he was master of' (p. 213). The 'bender' is a 'sixpence', but its alternative application proves intriguing:

An ironical word used in conversation by flash people; as where one party affirms or professes any thing which the other believes to be false or insincere, the latter expresses his incredulity by exclaiming, Bender! or, if one asks another to do any act which the latter considers unreasonable or impractible, he replies, O, yes, I'll do it – Bender; meaning, by the addition of the last word, that [...] he will do no such thing. (*Egan's Grose*)

This appears prescient of a late-twentieth-century vogue for appending the 'not' tag to a declaration, and also may have borne its connected late-nineteenth-century association with a 'tall' story (i.e. 'to spin a bender', *B/P*). Dickens used a similar expression of incredulity, 'Walker', in *A Christmas Carol* (1843). When instructed, by Scrooge, to buy the prize turkey, a passing boy exclaims 'Walk-ER', and Scrooge is forced to insist 'I am in earnest'.

When reporting on a '*turn-up*' between Carter and Richmond (12 November 1818), Egan stated that Richmond 'planted' such a blow on Carter's '*upper works*' that he 'made a *dice-box* of his swallow [mouth]' (*Boxiana III*, p. 405). The oft-exploited 'dice-box' motif usually appears in conjunction with rattling 'ivories' to convey the sensation of dislodged teeth tumbling around inside the unfortunate pugilist's mouth. Although fully exploiting the vast reservoir of slang terminology available, *Boxiana*-style reports did continue to provide imaginative variation from the norm. In 1820, Egan visited Ireland, dovetailing into the local Fancy. Part of his commentary on the Langan v McGowran fight is couched in routine style, but then comes a fanciful twist: '[Langan] again uncorked the *claret* [...] he then turned lapidary, and changed the cornelian round his eye to an amethyst' (p. 351). The stonework metaphor includes the concept of the fists as workman tools. Bee, similarly, enlivened the act of a fighter being dazed in his commentary of a contest between Paterson and Goldie (13 February 1824): '[Paterson] putting in a tremendous facer that groggified Goldie' (*Annals of Sporting V*, p. 199).

Sports Talk: Reported Speech

One of the chief areas for discussion relating to flash talk, or lack of it, is exhibited in Egan's reproduction of an official reply to a prizefight challenge from Shelton:

> Castle Tavern, Holborn, Feb. 2, 1818.
>
> SIR, – I received your letter of the 29th ult. Respecting your challenge to fight me for £50. Rest assured, it is with extreme regret that I am incapable of accepting it. You are well aware of the defect of eye-sight which I have unfortunately laboured under for some time past; and you must be equally well informed, that I am not recovered [...] But, Sir, should I again enjoy this greatest of blessings, of which I am endeavouring to avail myself, under the assistance of the most eminent oculists in the kingdom, not a single moment shall be lost in communicating to you, that you shall have the preference, as I would sooner enter the ring with you than any pugilist in existence [...] Till then, (which I most earnestly wish was to-morrow) [...] H. HARMER. (*Boxiana II*, p. 493)

Although Egan seizes various opportunities to promote any mental, even literary, accomplishments, of prizefighters, they were predominantly unskilled manual workers or artisans, generally deprived of education. Consequently,

Egan usually confined praise to 'honesty, and rough sincerity' that could be 'acted upon by the most ignorant and inferior ranks' (*Boxiana I*, p. 14). The above extract, reading more like a solicitor's communication, shows that some fighters were able to call on the services of someone to ghost-write their prizefight correspondence.

The reported discourse in the *Boxiana* series fails to substantiate claims made for the flash language. If a cant phraseology was indeed 'current from one end of the metropolis to the other', why did it consistently fail to materialise in the speech attributed to Fancy characters encountered in the pages of these sporting texts? In a tussle between Cooper and Shelton (27 June 1820), after 'some very sharp exchanges' in which Cooper displays generous sportsmanship, the general observations were: '*Bravo! That's noble. Who would not respect true courage, and admire the English charac-ter?*' (p. 52). The language is staid and lacks the vibrancy of Egan's commentaries. Perhaps this stiffness can be partially explained by Egan's earlier observation that the venue (Moulsey Hurst) 'displayed a fine show of the *Corinthians*' (p. 48).[41] If the strong presence of this upper-class section of the Fancy is the cause of such dignified 'banter', the boundless nature of flash is challenged. The implication is that sporting slang has not perme-ated to all levels of the Fancy, and that flash cannot claim to be this group's universal language by which its disparate elements are unified.

Bee also included a curious interjection in the midst of a heated nar-ration of Turner v Tom Oliver (9 August 1821): '*Turner* upbraided him for retreating. "I'll be with you *directly*", said TOM, and parrying some well-intended hits, *grassed* his man' (*Boxiana IV*, p. 243). Contrast this with the remarks attributed to Jem Ward as he delivers another 'doorstep' beating to a 'Knight of the Rainbow [footman]':

> JEM'S *mauley* was constantly *rap tap, tapping* on Johnny Trot's frontispiece, and occasionally *rung the bell* of his ear, until poor Trot did not know whether he had his own hair or a wig on. 'Vy don't you look', says JEM, 'and not *vink* your peepers in that ere vay' (p. 618)

41 Moulsey (or Molesey) Hurst on the Thames – 'for many years a recreational resort, where Garrick had played golf'. Brailsford, *Bareknuckles: A Social History of Prize-Fighting*, p. 42.

This extract contains not only slang, but also a hint of the characterful accent that foreshadows Dickens's loquacious manservant, Sam Weller.

Egan also sought the 'metropolitan' voice in the supposed remarks of two costermongers as the coachman Harry Stevenson passes them on the London to Brighton route: 'Vy, Jem [...] you see *ciwility* costs nothing, and he has got a bag full [...] and he pulls it out as he vants it' (*Book of Sports*, p. 6). Egan had already helpfully stated that a 'swell dragsman' is 'in plain English, a well-dressed Stage Coachman' (p. 2). This scion of the Fancy helped to propagate the flash language, but there is indication that it was a coarser strain than its pugilistic counterpart: 'Young men of fashion found it amusing to litter their conversation with the bawdy slang of the road'.[42] Furthermore, during the Thurtell trial, Egan recorded a witness (William Clark) using 'the ejaculation of whip-men who want to avoid contact on the road' (*Trial of Thurtell*, p. 72), but omitted the unsavoury expression from the text.

As seen, betting odds were a constant feature, and there is further confirmation of this dubious preoccupation from Egan's fictional social commentator, Paul Pry,[43] whose observations are surprisingly candid:

> Sporting chaps *chaff*, as they call it; you cannot be dull in their company; yet [...] there is a great deal of *routine* about their conversation, and they scarcely open their mouths without finishing the sentence with, 'I'll bet you 2 to 1; 6 to 4; and so on'. (*Book of Sports*, p. 50)

A negative, superficial, aspect of sporting conversation is highlighted, and Pry's depressing revelation challenges Egan's past intimations that the Fancy is brimful of characters, whose colourful conversation illuminates everything around: 'Without a *bet* amongst these sort of gentry, any thing like interest seems to evaporate from their minds, and the whole of their arguments become little else than "stale, flat, and unprofitable"' (p. 50). The

---

42   Venetia Murray, *High Society: A Social History of the Regency Period 1788–1830* (London: Penguin, 1998), p. 111.

43   The inquisitive character in John Poole's (c. 1785–1872) comedy *Paul Pry* (1825), possibly 'the most popular single piece on the London stage since *The Beggar's Opera* in 1728' (*DNB*).

inference to be drawn from Pry's comments is that 'sporting chaps' can be somewhat nondescript when deprived the thrill of gambling speculation.

Divergence from London's pugilistic version of flash could be expected to occur as one travelled and encountered regional dialects, or terms introduced from different sporting and occupational fields. The communication issue becomes further entangled when social variants are introduced:

> Whig grandees specialised in a particular drawl [...] a private upper-class slang: they said 'chaney' meaning china, 'yaller' for yellow, went to the 'chimist' and invented a string of nicknames [...] This private language was the password to the inner circle of Whig society; the deb who said cucumber instead of 'cowcumber', laundry instead of 'landry', or failed to realise that when the conversation turned to 'Madagascar' they were talking about Lady Holland, not the island, was branded at once [...] Jane Austen mocks this in *Northanger Abbey* (1818): Catherine: 'I cannot speak well enough to be unintelligible'.[44]

Similarly, the dandies considered themselves as leaders of 'the ton' (fashionable society) and, concurring with Egan's antipathy towards that particular set, Bee ridicules their 'drawl' in a withering lexical entry:

> *Monstrous* – excessive positive. A bon-ton reply renders it a superlative: 'a very pretty girl is that [...] Monstrous pretty *little* creature inde-e-d.' *Monster-ous large* would do better; but dandy cares not: he has it '*monstrous* hot in the house, and devilish cold out': 'I was *monstrously* affected', he concludes; yes, *affected, monster*-like. (*Bee's Sportsman's Slang*)

The entry for 'prodigious' is cross-referenced to 'monstrous', and 'vastly' sees Bee offering some acerbic continuity: 'one of the prodigious fine words so much mis-used by the dandies; who apply it to every thing'. In an entry for 'Cockney Slang', Bee mocks the dandy's snooty diction and squeamishness in pugilistic surroundings:

> As to *the fight*, I have been cursedly disappointed [...] at the entire set of proceedings: my person has experienced extreme inconvenience from the weather and the pressure of the populace; my stomach has been much deranged at the horrid exhibition, and I have been clandestinely deprived of my property by some adept at irregular appropriation.

---

44   Murray, *High Society*, pp. 241–2.

In the familiarity of Egan's sporting environment, the reported speech should acquire an air of authenticity. Yet, this is a debatable point, and Reid, although praising the assured writing and 'inimitable mixture of rhetoric and slang' in the *New Series Boxiana* volumes (1828–9), plaintively remarks upon the 'dignified utterances' attributed to fighters.[45] One offending instance may have been Tom Cannon's remonstrance in a Newbury street with a rogue named Hall, who had 'bilked' him out of a cheese valued at a guinea:

> 'I shall expect, before we part, that you will *tip* up my half of the prize. You behaved very *foul* to me, in *bolting* off the ground […]' 'If you touch me', answered *Hall*, 'I'll take out a warrant for you, and lock you up'. TOM had made up his mind; and, without any more delay, *planted* a rum one on his *nose*. 'That's good', said TOM, 'for *four* bob!' CANNON gave him another on his box of dominoes, which produced the *claret*: '[…] But stop, *Mr Hall*, I have not done exactly with you yet – I must give you *one* for *yourself!*' and then *floored* him. (*New Series Boxiana II*, p. 13)

We see the alternative 'dominoes' used for 'teeth', which represents a colour contrast to 'ivories', and a more realistic expression, implying discolouration instead of the pristine creamy-white of a valuable commodity. However, there is no evidence to suggest that the terms were ever used discriminately according to social status. Egan consistently claimed that mirroring 'real life' remained a priority, and he qualifies his earlier recognition of 'plain English' by insisting: 'The character of the thing must be preserved – and a driver of four "good-uns" ought not to be described with any thing like the gravity of a parson' (*Book of Sports*, pp. 2–3). The issue of how people really spoke is often subservient to dramatic satisfaction, and a degree of artistic licence is often perceptible. However, it should be considered that Egan's journalistic background, and access to a wide range of social company, implies a truthful recording in this area. Egan stressed oral history and it is almost inconceivable that the flash writing of Bee, a staunch Fancy member, would coincide so closely with his rival's if he had not deemed it to be an accurate reflection.

---

45   Reid, *Bucks and Bruisers*, pp. 127, 135.

Incisive conversational sparring, laced with slang, added spice to descriptions of the fighting action, and piqued the reader's imagination, but there was also a danger that too much information, as in the faithful recording of spoken remarks, might explode any air of quixotic mystery elicited by the flash fight commentaries. Which utterances are genuine and which manufactured is debatable, but by channelling attention onto the flash-laden prizefight activity, Egan and Bee portrayed the 'spectacular' side of the Fancy. Ultimately, it was '*yawning* and *ennui*' (*Boxiana III*, p. 559) that these writers wished to avoid, and flash was one of their prime tools to promote interest, colour, and, failing these, controversy.

Egan's Sporting Newspapers and *New Series Boxiana*

Despite the unplanned hiatus between the appearance of *Boxiana III* (1821) and *New Series Boxiana* collected volumes (1828–9), Egan's output was only curtailed. He countered the 1824 publication of Bee's *Boxiana IV* by producing his own continued reports, in weekly format, promoted as *The New Series of Boxiana; containing all the Fun, Life, Anecdotes, and Spirit of the Prize Ring*. This time it was Egan who displayed irritation at the literary efforts of his main rival, urging Fancy members to exhibit a degree of brand loyalty: 'The Amateurs are particularly requested to ask for the NEW SERIES'; 'foul play is attempted to impose on the Sporting World, a spurious Edition of the above Continuation.'[46] In addition, Egan established a printing and publishing concern at his new premises, 113 Strand, and exploited this opportunity to provide a further outlet for his sports writing.

Accordingly, on 1 February 1824, the publication commenced of *Egan's Life in London, and Sporting Guide*, priced 'Eightpence Halfpenny'. Each

46   *Egan's Life in London, and Sporting Guide*, No. 2 (8 February 1824), p. 9, & No. 15 (9 May), p. 113.

issue consisted of eight pages containing regular items such as 'London Markets', 'Fashionable Movements', 'Female Fashions', and 'Hunting Intelligence', in addition to reports of court proceedings, parliamentary debates, and news of forthcoming attractions at the theatre and Vauxhall Gardens. The front page was the place to find miscellaneous advertisements for newly published books and exaggerated 'puffs' for health and beauty products. Not dwelling on more onerous subject matter, the newspaper achieved the diverting tone that Egan sought for 'a lively journal'. In the 'Sporting Guide' section, slang was subservient to reportage in biographically dominated tales. At this incipient stage of the newspaper's development, the fight reports displayed a condensed aspect, with no segmentation of the commentary into rounds. Nevertheless, an increase in slang terminology arose naturally from the pugilistic arena, and although Egan's accounts do not possess the uninhibited feel of florid *Boxiana III* descriptions, they can be distinguished as belonging to the school of sporting flash.

Egan gradually devoted more column space to his sporting priorities, featuring round-by-round reports, but it is likely that the titles of these publications, making no attempt to conceal their sporting roots, would not have enticed purchases from non-Fancy individuals. It might be argued that the entire newspaper could have been written in the flash style, which reinforces the argument for a less specialised vocabulary. The slang lexicons generated in the period were a hotchpotch of diverse elements, including thieves' and beggars' cant, haut monde expressions, and coachman's ribaldry, as well as sporting terms. But, there remained a dearth of refined terms for the cultured sensibilities of prospective enlightened readers.

Egan's newspaper commentaries continued to demonstrate his linguistic spontaneity and innovative flair. The liberating quality of a pugilistic report allowed him scope to insert ad hoc expressions and adapt existing terms, and this, in turn, reflected the unconstrained ethos of a typical Fancy sportsman. Such extemporisation occurs in an exchange between Ward and Samson, who 'received such a *snorter* that put the *botherums* on duty in the *brain country*'.[47] The suggestion is that a forceful punch has set 'a noisy party' in motion within the fighter's head, 'botherums' denoting 'convivial

---

47   Ibid., No. 49 (2 January 1825), p. 389.

society' (*B/P*). A similarly whimsical description is contained within the report of a fight between Johnson and Pat Halton, where 'a *teaser* on the *capitol*' was 'graciously acknowledged by an instantaneous *prostration*', and Halton got his '*dexter ogle* obnubilated by a discharge from Johnson's *maniple*'. In due course, the fighters become '*turfish*'.[48] The humorously inflated phraseology employed confers a ceremonial feel to sustaining a black eye. Similarly, the subsequent deployment of the adjective 'turfish', to convey that the fighters were knocked to the ground, dramatically switches the descriptive tone from verbose and orotund to minimal. Describing a series of punches that 'were more of the *buttery* sort than of the *anvil*' is a further example of Egan inventively relating the action.[49] Throughout his sports writing, Egan veered from documented flash idiom, often producing phrases that straddled registers of elevated diction and slang. The resulting playful hybrid found a receptive medium in the pugilistic-writing genre.

Not deterred by the eventual commercial failure of this first effort, Egan resurrected his newspaper venture with the four-page *Egan's Weekly Courier* (seven pence). The back page was the location for sports writing throughout its short-lived existence (January–April 1829), and pugilism dominated with commentaries continuing to revel in the *Boxiana* style:

> [Young (The Sun Yard Swell) v Lamb (The Whitechapel Sticker)] Lamb put on the *stopper* in style, and the left hand of his opponent was baulked. The Swell's *listener* received an ugly wisty-castor [blow...] Lamb, with great celerity, put in a right-handed hit on the Swell's nob. 'He'll understand that', said Dick [Curtis], 'a very explanatory hit indeed'.[50]

The humorous description of a hit as 'explanatory' compares favourably with the sporting jargon that preceded it. The sardonic remark, attributed to the fighter's second, exudes the spirit of a Fancy expression. Later, *New Series Boxiana* demonstrated Egan's well-honed style, but little new flash

---

48 *Egan's Life in London, and Sporting Guide*, No. 59 (13 March 1825), p. 53. 'Dexter' signified something that was situated on the right side (*OED*).
49 Ibid., No. 150 (10 December 1826), pp. 477, 781.
50 'Sticker' signified a horse or person with staying power (*OED*). *Egan's Weekly Courier*, No. 3 (18 January 1829), p. 12.

jargon emerged. However, one particularly apposite term that appeared was 'chopping-block' (*New Series Boxiana II*, p. 240) denoting a fighter that takes heavy punishment.

Post *Boxiana* Series

In 1832, almost twenty years after the publication of *Boxiana I*, Egan demonstrated his versatility by producing a text devoted to the multifarious aspects of sporting life. Aptly titled *Book of Sports, and Mirror of Life*, it offered material as diverse as that in Bee's *Annals of Sporting*. It should be noted that some of the pugilistic commentaries were reproductions of reports that originally featured in *Egan's Weekly Courier*. The format and vocabulary had become relatively standardised but, in occasional bursts, the sporting argot's mutability is evident. One of the main fights recorded is Dick Curtis v Perkins (30 December 1828):

> Dick like an auctioneer's catalogue, came ditto, ditto, ditto – but it was of no use, the 'Cove was *leary*' and not to be *gammoned* [...] Severe counter hits again occurred, and the left *Peeper* of Perkins napt it, and the *claret* followed [...] In a rally, spirited on both sides, the *chaffing-box* of Dick had the worst of it. (*Book of Sports*, pp. 24–5)

The commentary produces a proliferation of flash, which contrasts with the relative moderation of the pre-1821 *Boxiana* volumes.

The theme of losing money, by one method or another, is continued when Egan imagines an excursion taken 'by the inhabitants of the first city in the world to witness the great Derby Stakes' (p. 60). The phrasing underscores the pre-eminence that Egan accords London, and the piece follows the misadventures of the Twankey family at Epsom. Significantly, any move away from the prize-ring environment was usually accompanied by a severe watering down of the flash content. The family acquire an urban guide, again presaging the advent of the Sam Weller 'type', who forewarns of the chicanery to which strangers are susceptible, and the alien terminology. In this instance, a Mr Smithers supplies counsel:

'The *conveyancers*', said Mr S., laughing, 'are a set of men who convey property [...] without the use of parchment, or the aid of lawyers; by other intelligent persons they are styled artists, being in the drawing profession [...] but by the vulgar sort of folks they are ignorantly alluded to as pick-pockets'. (p. 61)

It is interesting to note that 'conveyancers' is hailed as a more genteel word than the 'vulgar' plain English of 'pick-pockets'. The implication is that a slang façade can veil the base act of petty theft, but bluntness explodes such cosmetic manipulation. Egan later reproduced an 1828 sketch of Newmarket races by 'A GERMAN PRINCE', in which the social equality of the flash language is foreground: 'Dukes, lords, grooms, and rogues, shout, scream, and hallo together [...] in a technical language, out of which a foreigner is puzzled' (p. 128). It might be conceded that any newcomer to pugilistic surroundings would experience a similar language barrier.

Egan consistently portrayed the prizefighting arena as the spiritual home of flash, conveying the sense that its pervasive presence was natural. The emphasis placed on the London scene invalidates the notion of a nationally homogenous sporting language, but Egan and Bee's efforts achieved progress towards that aspiration as well. Certain articles on cock-fighting and horse-racing were not lacking in dramatic imagery and points of interest, but Egan's treatment of 'Doings And Sayings In The Prize-Ring' underscores the sporting area where flash truly formed an integral dimension.

The dawning of the Victorian era hastened the abatement of flash sports writing, in the mould established by Egan and Bee, as elements of society sought to distance themselves from the raffishness of the 1820s. Sport and flash language had been major tools in the erosion of class barriers, but now there was a move to slough off what was perceived as the immoral ethos they nurtured. The reinforcement of the dividing lines between 'high' and 'low' cultures inevitably affected this supposed class-less language. In fact, it is suggested that the Victorians employed flash terms to '*reintroduce* a sense of social hierarchy'.[51] This forms only part of the shift in approach, and the fact that pugilistic affairs were on the wane

---

51   Dart, '"Flash Style": Pierce Egan and Literary London 1820–28', p. 205.

was also a crucial factor in the vanishing flash content. Egan himself, in *A Lecture on the Art of Self-Defence* (1845), focused on the moral and fitness benefits to be gleaned from the pugilistic 'science', and the boost it provided to Britain's 'national feature' (p. 15). A little jingoistic in places, there are only fleeting reminders of the flash repertoire.

Ultimately, it is the enthused inclusiveness with which Egan and Bee instilled their pugilistic writing that most promoted the ideals and language of the Fancy, and contributed to the transitory popularity of flash.

CHAPTER 3

Sporting Theatre: Spectacle and Social Dynamics

Whether describing a snaking convoy of spectators journeying to an illegal prizefight, or conveying anticipation of the pugilists' gladiatorial-like entrance, Pierce Egan's reports embodied the theatricality that the writer associated with this colourful sporting subculture. He reasserted his belief that the English were not 'automatons' by animating the pages of his pugilistic pieces with innovative imagery and linguistic verve, and his distinctive scene-setting accentuated the dramatic uncertainty of the prize-ring environment. By foregrounding the spectacle surrounding a prizefight Egan intrigued a potential new audience, transcending preconceptions harboured by a readership that mirrored the class and race fusion involved in sporting events. The manner in which the *Boxiana* texts sought to erode social barriers might be compared to the appeal of a stage production to a mixed collection of early-nineteenth-century theatre-goers at Covent Garden: 'The dress boxes, pit, and lower gallery were the domain of various middling groups, while artisans, craftsmen, labourers, and servants occupied the upper gallery. The pit especially contained an audience of mixed social background'.[1] Significantly, this degree of segregation was not present in the sporting assemblies described by Egan.

Although its illegality meant that contests were not advertised openly, wealthy patrons boosted pugilism's status and it is ironic that, for a supposedly spectator sport, public crowds were originally considered unnecessary. Receiving funding from its upper-class supporters, prizefighting did not rely on revenue in the form of admission monies, and the Fancy viewed

---

1   In this period, the word 'theatricality' was regarded as 'either neutral or favourable in connotation', rather than associated with artificiality. Marc Baer, *Theatre and Disorder in Late Georgian London* (Oxford: Clarendon Press, 1992), pp. 11, 48.

onlookers as unwelcome outsiders; many pugilistic contests were promoted 'primarily for the purpose of gambling'.[2] This attitude is underscored by the reaction of those who had followed Captain Barclay's pedestrian feat (one thousand miles in one thousand hours, on Newmarket Heath, July 1809), and were irritated by the inundation of spectators, enticed by 'almost incessant' newspaper exposure, for the climax: 'the Fancy [...] probably regarded this event as "theirs", and would have been happy if the other spectators had stayed away'.[3] One conclusion is that pugilism was inexpensive to attend, even if one was not always encouraged to do so. It should also be appreciated that labourers and merchants did not enjoy the leisure time of upper-class followers and were often unable to attend events such as the Ward v Hudson contest (11 November 1823): 'many mercantile amateurs had [...] again to lament that *Tuesday* should be selected for holding this species of exhibition, – when they cannot attend [...] its being foreign-post day' (*Boxiana IV*, p. 620). This may have been a deliberately exclusive policy practised by wealthy patrons and organisers seeking to curtail spectators inundating a fight venue in the same manner as they flocked to a holiday fair. Pugilism's social status was unstable, but any sustained system of manipulated exclusion would have generated only greater demand for Egan's reports.

What was it about Egan's 'Sporting World' that prompted men to consider themselves 'one of the Fancy', attend gatherings, and seek out the latest accounts of major pugilistic battles? Egan regularly commented on the social diversity of spectators rubbing shoulders ringside, '*Corinthians* and *Coster-mongers* in rude contact; *Johnny-Raws* and first-rate *Swells* jostling each other' (*Boxiana I*, p. 366), or in popular sporting meeting places such as the Castle Tavern, Holborn: 'The *groupes* to be met with in the coffee room [...] are highly *characteristic* of the different grades of life – abounding with ORIGINALS of all sorts – a kind of Masquerade' (*Book of Sports*, p. 73).

2   Ford, *Prizefighting: The Age of Regency Boximania*, p. 89.
3   Radford, *The Celebrated Captain Barclay*, pp. 2–4.

Such excerpts underscore the social ambiguity, and charade, around Regency metropolitan life which found upper-class bucks donning shabby clothing in order to 'live low' in insalubrious drinking and gaming haunts. Conversely, the lower classes regularly assumed a respectability of dress to parade on the more fashionable walks, or to merge into large gatherings with criminal intent. An episode set in Hyde Park demonstrated the prevalence of counterfeit characters amongst the crowd in a commotion caused by the activities of some pickpockets 'dressed in the first style of fashion' (*Life in London*, p. 169). Egan's intimate knowledge of the low-life environment supplied his narratives with a diverse collection of venues and characters. His priority was to entertain, and he articulated the enthralment of the performance: 'It is a debt of pleasure we owe to those persons who have so forcibly elicited our tears [...or] dispelled our ennui' (*The Life of an Actor*, p. 12). This indicates Egan's estimation of the emotional influence wielded by stage actors, and the potential for his characters to emulate them. There was a public preoccupation with most forms of exhibition, as indicated by the 1809 re-opening of Covent Garden Theatre: 'the design and size of the new theatre [over 3,000 seats...] reflected the interest of that era in spectacle'.[4]

Disguise, an integral part of the low-life 'sprees' in *Life in London*, augmented a sense of theatre costume. The resultant social confusion was related (in 1771) by Smollet: 'There is no distinction or subordination left – The different departments of life are jumbled together [...] rushing, justling, mixing [...] and crashing in one vile ferment of stupidity and corruption – All is tumult and hurry'.[5] When comparing this with Egan's coffee-room scene, Don Herzog stresses a fundamental variance in outlook: 'Masquerades make Smollett uneasy; he wants to know who people really are, where they stand in the status hierarchy. Masquerades make Egan jolly'; 'For Smollett, "no distinction or subordination" summons up

---

4   Baer, *Theatre and Disorder*, p. 21.
5   Smollett, *Humphrey Clinker*, p. 119.

frightful disorder. For Egan [...] convivial egalitarianism'.[6] Blurring of
social distinctions is a theme that Egan often probed in his writing, on this
occasion highlighting the routine of a '*Sporting Tailor*' who appreciated the
influential 'weight' of a 'good appearance': 'He therefore, in his relaxations,
dressed himself for the part – left the tradesman at home – assumed the
gay, lively, sporting *character*, and entered into the spirit of the *scene* [my
italics]' (*Book of Sports*, p. 98).

The lower classes, or 'the Mob', had another motive for invading upper-
class gatherings: 'levelling distinctions, and parodying wealth or rank'.[7] The
overall social interplay could be considered 'a shatteringly promiscuous riot
of status confusion'.[8] Egan was heavily influenced by *The Beggar's Opera*,
and its theatrical presentation of the city's criminal underclass, replete
with popular ballads and tunes.[9] He identified with the tacit sentiments
of this burlesque production: 'the gaiety and exuberance [...] are in part
based upon the implicit denial of all distinctions of rank and class. It is the
egalitarian [...] instinct of the London populace, represented upon the stage
in a colourful and spirited form'.[10] Egan exercised a similar eclecticism in
the construction of *Life in London*, intermingling quotations, allusions,
comic verse, and ballads, adroitly exploiting the reader's ingrained awareness of popular cultural models to generate widespread appeal. In this
metropolitan novel, Egan explored social difference and ambiguity in an
untrammelled view of the classes:

> *Life in London's* major achievement [...] was to throw itself into this experience of
> social indeterminacy, and to turn it into a source of pleasure. It rejoices in the role-
> playing nature of modern urban existence [...] viewing class society as a repertoire
> of possibilities [...which] has a lot to do with the sporting culture out of which *Life
> in London* emerged.[11]

6   Don Herzog, *Poisoning the Minds of the Lower Orders* (Chichester: Princeton
      University Press, 1998), p. 141.
7   Ackroyd, *London: The Biography*, p. 168.
8   Herzog, *Poisoning the Minds of the Lower Orders*, p. 140.
9   Written by John Gay (1685–1732) and first performed in 1728.
10   Ackroyd, *London: The Biography*, p. 279.
11   Dart, '"Flash Style": Pierce Egan and Literary London 1820–28', p. 185.

This underscores the reciprocity between Egan's primary works; *Life in London* and *Boxiana* capturing the role-playing and sporting ethos of the period, as well as the pervasive presence of the city's gambling and drinking culture. Entertainment also proves a classless concept, Egan manipulating the universally attractive side of a prizefight – its spectacle. For the literate, *Boxiana*-style writing encouraged the visualisation of prizefights and the Fancy characters in attendance.

Drama *Boxiana*: Accentuating Spectacle in Pugilistic Affairs

[9 January 1788] The newspapers teemed with anecdotes concerning them – pamphlets were published in favour of pugilism – and scarcely a print shop in the Metropolis but what displayed the *set-to* in glowing colours, and portraits of those distinguished heroes of the fist. HUMPHRIES and MENDOZA were the rage – the Modern comedies glanced at their exploits – and the *sporting hemisphere* was quite charged with it. (*Boxiana I*, p. 110)

Egan highlighted the development of public interest in the pugilistic exploits of principal exponents, and the sport's easy transition from one recreational platform to another. Although an event's cachet could be accentuated by suggesting the antagonists were eager to settle some personal feud, Dennis Brailsford states that 'long-term animosity' was (unlike modern boxing promotions) 'rare enough to be conspicuous'.[12] Much of the widespread interest in the above fight concerned money, the east-End Jewish community losing money heavily on the vanquished Mendoza. The release of a black pigeon to signify his defeat carried a symbolic resonance which complements the scenic aspect as Egan focussed on the fervour surrounding the fight. But, Egan's use of 'the rage' expression might suggest a transient popularity.

12   Brailsford, *Bareknuckles: A Social History of Prize-Fighting*, p. 67.

Despite advocating accuracy, it is understandable if the sport's principal chronicler chose to embellish his accounts in order to mask the mundanity and repetition of many encounters: 'It would be superfluous to detail the remainder of the rounds [...] A complete *sameness* pervaded the whole of them'; 'Twenty-sixth to thirty-third [...] there was a great deal of *sameness* as to the mode of fighting' (*Boxiana II*, pp. 70; 444). Egan did not claim that a prizefight offered constant excitement and variation, but his commentaries attempted to wring out any drama, vividly describing the punishing nature of the blows and relating the accompanying betting. He also exploited any pantomimic incidents or diverting badinage. Peter Ackroyd reinforces the prioritisation of spectacle:

> The London visionaries [...] are not necessarily ethical or moral artists. They are not necessarily concerned with the minutiae of the human psyche, or with debates about values and beliefs. They tend to favour spectacle and melodrama and the energetic exploitation of whatever medium they are employing. As city writers are more concerned with the external life, with the movement of crowds, with the great general drama of the human spirit. They have a sense of energy and splendour, of ritual and display.[13]

Part of Egan's 'visionary' approach was the use of sporting jargon to supplement the verve of his reports, as in a glowing profile of Tom Belcher:

> Whenever he puts himself in an attitude, there is not a *peeper* absent from the stage. In an amateur, it would, indeed, betray as great a piece of neglect in omitting to witness *Tom's* one, two, put in, as for indifference to be felt by a lover of the drama, in *Kean's out-and-out* effort [see below...] Upon these two subjects, *yawning* and *ennui* cannot occur. (*Boxiana III*, p. 559)

It was a natural progression for Egan to weave the linguistic flourish of the flash argot into the dramatic picture. In *Life in London*, the slang discourse forms part of the element of disguise as Tom, Jerry, and Bob integrate themselves into the low-life haunts: 'it suggests a modish enthusiasm

---

13   Peter Ackroyd, 'London Luminaries and Cockney Visionaries', in *The Collection* (London: Chatto & Windus, 2001), p. 350. Perhaps it is fair, given his imaginative flair, to classify Egan as a visionary, rather than a luminary (source of intellectual or moral inspiration).

for two closely-linked concepts, firstly of fashion as a kind of flash (over) statement, a sort of sartorial italics, and secondly of flash language itself as a species of fancy dress'.[14]

Although promoting the sport's use as a safety-valve for social frustrations, and as a vehicle for ingraining militaristic principles into the formative male population, Egan conferred a theatricality upon pugilistic events that underscores their function as public entertainment. This association could be considered as out of kilter with the supposed benefits, but it again highlights that even when traces of a political message might be faintly discernible in Egan's writing (i.e. encouraging national unity and manliness could be interpreted as the discouragement of dissent and reform), they were quickly subsumed by the prioritisation accorded to spectacle and entertainment. Egan displayed an insouciant attitude to contentious issues, never pretending to be contributing to the field of social inquiry, and he addressed an effusive dedication to his acting ideal, Edmund Kean (1787–1833), in *The Life of an Actor*. This can be rated as a morally questionable connection: 'the private life of Kean – accused of being both a drunk and an adulterer – led to four nights of violent rioting in the playhouse of Drury Lane'.[15] Egan's dedication (penned in December 1824) demonstrates either admirable loyalty or intractability, refusing to be prejudiced by public opinion. Again, it expresses a sporting attitude of fair play. Paradoxically, the 'OP riots', at Covent Garden in 1809, supported a 'safety-valve' theory: 'Theatre as a form of entertainment for plebeians confirmed and sustained disorder, but it did so theatrically, i.e. fostering non-revolutionary discontent'.[16] In short, being part of a vocal audience provided an opportunity to vent grievances.

Egan's metropolitan fiction made no attempt to engage in an examination of a character's psyche or social hardships. Whenever the principal *Life in London* characters delve into the underground world, there

---

14   Dart, "'Flash Style": Pierce Egan and Literary London 1820–28', p. 190.
15   Ackroyd, *London: The Biography*, p. 173.
16   OP riots – Public demands for a return to the 'Old Prices' and seating arrangement of 1808 (the theatre had been destroyed by fire in September 1808). Baer, *Theatre and Disorder*, pp. 13, 14.

is always the awareness that they can jettison their assumed guises and return to the comfort of Corinthian House. This convenient escape route is made evident in the narration of their visit to the 'Condemned Yard' of Newgate Prison, Egan averring that it was 'a truly afflicting scene'. When pressed for time, however, the trio 'hastily quitted the gloomy walls [...] to join the busy hum and life of society' (*Life in London*, p. 282). They are interested but uncommitted observers, and there is no onus necessitating more direct intervention on their part. Essentially, the low-life episodes are imbued with a light-hearted spirit of adventure, but Egan touched upon conflicting elements of metropolitan life that 'confirm two of the city's most permanent images: the world as a stage and the world as a prison'.[17]

Boxiana profiles of individual pugilists did not attempt to conceal instances where a decline in fortunes was attributable to drink abuse. Enthusiastic socialising was an integral part of Fancy life, and the gentleman's club atmosphere one where Egan felt comfortable. Consequently, his writing tends to grant room for manoeuvre in the lifestyles of certain fighters, and this attitude coincides with Hazlitt's justification for the intemperate conduct of talented actors when exposed to the fluctuating extremes of public acclaim and censure:

> An actor, to be a good one, must have a great spirit of enjoyment in himself, strong impulses, strong passions [...] A man of genius is not a machine. The neglected actor may be excused if he drinks oblivion of his disappointments; the successful one, if he quaffs the applause of the world. (*The Examiner*, 31 March 1816)[18]

Hazlitt's sentiment corresponds with Egan's about Englishmen not being 'automatons', and it was difficult to preach moderation to hard-training pugilists, regardless of whether they were bankrolled by a wealthy patron. It was the ring-dominance of 'colourful' characters that contributed to the public's fascination with fight accounts, and this, for Egan and his contemporaries, would have been preferable to a sterile atmosphere in keeping with the upper-class etiquette of duelling.

---

17   Ackroyd, *London: The Biography* p. 279.
18   *The Selected Writings of William Hazlitt*, ed. by Duncan Wu, 9 vols. (London: Pickering & Chatto, 1998), III, 'A View of the English Stage', p. 125.

The *Boxiana* series often involved the reader in the preamble to contests, including pre-fight correspondence and meetings, procession of spectators to the venue, and the customary showmanship of the fighters throwing their hats into the ring and fastening coloured neckerchiefs to the stakes. Egan further assisted the reader's visualisation of the unfolding scene by providing information on the state of the weather, notable figures in attendance, as well as observations on the physical condition of the two combatants as they 'peeled'. Just as a theatre audience member might temporarily escape immediate concerns, the avid *Boxiana* reader vicariously experiences fight day from the perspective of one of the Fancy, eventually being transported ringside. Egan's description of the interest excited by the impending arrival (at Cribb's tavern) of Irish champion John Langan, simply to draw up an agreement to fight English champion Tom Spring, is revealing:

> The taproom might be compared to a MOB – the parlour crowded to excess – the first floor crowded almost to suffocation – the second floor, where Spring *perched* himself, to receive his opponent, much worse [...] and the stairs were filled from the top to the bottom. So great was the curiosity excited by the event of making the above great Match [...] They were all so *jammed* together, that they could not have got their hands up to their mouths.

Egan conveys the congested atmosphere, and then there is the drama of Langan's arrival: "*He's come*". This sentence was conveyed through all the rooms like an electric shock [...] Spring, on being informed Langan had arrived, sent word [...] that he was ready with the *blunt*.[19] Spring is portrayed in terms of a reigning monarch granting an audience to a visiting dignitary. So many spectators had been eager to witness the first contest between the two fighters (7 January 1824) that some intrepid viewers clung to the rigging of advantageously placed ships on the River Severn adjacent to the venue, Worcester racecourse.[20]

---

19   *Egan's Life in London, and Sporting Guide*, No. 6 (7 March 1824), p. 41.
20   This detail is captured in a print, 'Spring and Langan', by James Clements (c. 1787–1840) and John Pitman (1789–1850). See Fuller, *Noble Art*, p. 56.

In the above excerpts, the spectator is treated as a participant in a sociable experience, which is in contrast to the frustration of reading long-winded speculation on prospective fights, a practice condemned by Bee: 'Editors of other contemporary publications, finding that the tortuous lies about matches [...] are inquired after [...] speak of challenges and challengers as if the men actually meant fighting, and had backers to support them' (*Annals of Sporting VII*, 1825, p. 287). Reflecting on an avalanche of 'milling correspondence' following the aforementioned Worcester prizefight, Henry Downes Miles complained that it proved particularly 'weary reading', which 'became as verbose and inconsequential as diplomatic circular notes' (*Pugilistica II*, 1880, p. 31). And, Bee was eager to warn against wild conjecture, as in the boasts made for Neate before a proposed 1823 fight against Spring:

> The torrent of opinion was previously so strong in favour of *Neat*, both in Bristol and London, on account of his *tremendous* hitting, as to carry away, like a flood, all moderate *calculation* [...] SPRING was to have been *smashed*; SMASHED – and nothing else but SMASHED!!! One hit was to have spoiled the *science* of SPRING; TWO taken the *fight* completely out of him! And the THIRD operated as a *coup de grace.* Yes! And so they would, if the *chaffing* over some *heavy, light blue,* or *black ink*, could have done it. (*Boxiana IV*, pp. 331–2)

Spring was victorious whilst Neate sustained a broken arm. Far from increasing anticipation, Bee felt that rival journalists had indulged in a mode of superficial hysteria.

Prevaricating correspondence and unseemly predictive claims aside, spectacle was an overriding concern in the *Boxiana* commentaries. Reporting on the battle between Spring and Bob Burns (16 May 1820), Egan follows the day's proceedings from the Fancy member's first waking moment: 'The morning was truly forbidding [...] and the heavy torrents of rain informed the *kids*, upon opening their *peepers*, that their *game* would again be put to the test' (*Boxiana III*, p. 334). The spectators' hardihood is eventually rewarded by a picturesque and convivial scene that conveys the mood of anticipation:

The glorious sun shot forth its brilliant rays of life and light, illuminating the extensive and picturesque prospect of Epsom Downs. The long string of carriages [...] increasing the animation and interest of the scene, till the *Fancy* reached their grand climax – the *Ring*. This object once gained, the pleasures are *tasted* of taking a *drain* of *Daffy* – meeting with *Old Pals* – with the *chatting* of 'who's to win? – what's the odds?' (p. 335)

The following month, the weather is again a significant factor, and Egan conveys the haze of a sultry scene awaiting Cooper and Shelton (27 June 1820):

Burning rays seemed positively to pour forth liquid heat. Many of the spectators were compelled to quit the ring, in order to avoid fainting; and nothing but an anxiety on the part of the writer of this article to give a faithful and accurate report of this most interesting scene, could have induced him to have kept his situation. (p. 51)

Egan explicitly invites visualisation with the concept of 'liquid heat': 'Let the reader then, for one moment, picture [...] what must have been the *distressed state* of the combatants' (p. 51). The closing scene exudes the animated anxiety of the seconds exacerbated by the torrid conditions:

Spring and Randall, with the greatest alacrity, *dragged* Shelton up [...] he had no *movement* in him. This was a most interesting moment – Cooper was on Harmer's knee, and Belcher was wiping him with the handkerchief, also half turned round, watching the appearance of Shelton, and with a part of his eye directed towards the umpire [...] Belcher's face was a perfect *study* (and we seriously regret that our friend CRUIKSHANK was not present).[21] (p. 54)

Egan's evocation of the almost palpable mental anguish means that the wished-for accompanying illustration is unnecessary.

Public fervour for witnessing spectacle had been demonstrated when Cribb's title was threatened: 'The *Fancy* were not to be deterred from witnessing the *mill*; and who waded through a clayey road nearly knee-deep for five miles, with alacrity and cheerfulness, as if it had been as smooth

---

21   Brothers Robert Cruikshank (1789–1856) and George (1792–1878), who were illustrators, and frequent Egan collaborators.

as a bowling-green' (*Boxiana I*, p. 402). When a major fight, between Oliver and Painter, took place near Norwich (17 July 1820), Egan sustains the exhilaration surrounding what promised to be a novel spectacle. He highlights the event's drawing power to the Fancy, as well as hinting at its suitability for female onlookers:

> This combat engrossed the whole of the conversation, even amongst the most polite and *tender* circles. (*Boxiana III*, p. 139)
>
> Every vehicle in Norwich was engaged to go to the scene of the action. People were in motion by four o' clock in the morning; [...] the doors and windows of the houses displayed numerous groups of inhabitants eager to witness the departure of the *Fancy*. (pp. 140–1)

The excitement of the local population could be likened to that generated by the arrival of a theatre troupe on a provincial tour. The practice of circus companies moving into town, with the attendant bustle generated, is comparable to the Fancy cavalcades that accompanied major prizefights. For observers, 'the parade through their town of all the performers, wagons and animals was not only the chief advertisement for the show but also one of the highlights'.[22] These essential qualities are encapsulated in the account of the Hickman v Oliver fight (12 June 1821):

> The Grey-hound, at Croydon, was the rallying-point for the *swells*, and *the fight* is ever a good *turn* for this road; the lively groups all in rapid motion – and the *blunt* dropped like waste paper, and no questions asked, made all parties pleasant and happy. The delicate *fair ones* were seen *peeping* from behind their window-curtains; the tradesmen leaving their counters [...] *ould* folks hobbling out astonished; the *people of propriety*, with all their notions of respectability and decorum, stealing a *look*. Indeed, it might be asked, how could they help it? Who does not love to see a 'bit of life', though they can't enjoy it. A *peep* costs nothing. The fun met with on the road going to a *mill* is a *prime* treat; and more *good* CHARACTER is to be witnessed than at a masquerade. (*New Series Boxiana I*, p. 34)

Class, gender, commerce, and performance combine in this animated description.

22   Paul Schlicke, *Dickens and Popular Entertainment* (London: Allen & Unwin, 1985), p. 155.

Such influxes of people provided a boost to local economies, and Egan builds this profiteering philosophy into the scene at a contest between Martin and Hudson (24 October 1824): 'Moulsey Hurst, that delightful spot for a scientific contest, was again the appointed place to muster, and the *Bonifaces* [innkeepers] along the road [...] were seen rubbing their hands' (*Boxiana III*, p. 257). Egan asserts that the consensus is 'that no persons spent their money so freely as sporting men' (p. 575). However, this freehandedness could be exploited and Egan captured the mercenary aspect, as well as the all-consuming desire to witness a major fight between Gregson and Gully, on the Newmarket Road (14 October 1807):

> The anxiety manifested by the *sporting men*, and the *Fancy* in general, was so great to witness this second combat, that numbers left London on the Monday, to prevent meeting with any disappointment, in order to be in readiness to follow the cavalcade [...] (The impositions practised upon this occasion by the landlords of the various inns in the country towns near the scene of action, were of the most gross nature). (*Boxiana I*, p. 181)

The differing means of transport reported to be 'in rapid motion', 'from the splendid barouche to the jolting taxed-cart' (p. 182), supplies tacit comment on the social diversity of the spectators.

Egan's account of the second Cribb v Molineaux fight underscores that, when commercially expedient, a blind eye could be turned to illegality: 'All the towns upon the North road gained considerably by this contest, particularly those of Grantham and Stamford. No interruption was offered to the *mill*' (p. 414). Egan suggests that there was even some competition to host the event: 'it is said, that the Corporation of the principal towns in the North solicited that the battle might be fought on their own domains' (p. 414). Towards the close of the *Boxiana* era, Egan's build-up to the Curtis v Perkins contest (30 December 1828) demonstrates an enduring interest in the foremost battles: 'although it was uncommonly dark, dreary, and *foggy* [...] such was the interest manifested by the Fancy [...] that every inn in the route to Maidenhead was overflowing' (*Book of Sports*, p. 24). The commercial sector evidently believed that pugilistic reports still enjoyed a sufficiently wide circulation to be profitably exploited. Here, having stressed the difficult conditions, Egan brazenly offers the remedy:

> Owing to the assistance we derived from Ben Black's improved carriage lamp [...]
> we trotted along towards the scene of action with as much ease and security as if
> it had been broad daylight. We have no hesitation in recommending them to the
> *Fancy*. (p. 24)

This unsubtle 'advertisement' is not in keeping with the concept of pure
sports reporting, but it displays a mercenary resourcefulness and it is interesting that a presumably reputable firm are prepared to have their name
associated with an illegal activity. More importantly, it demonstrates that
pugilistic writing was still regarded as an influential medium.

The air of performance that pervades Egan's commentaries is augmented by the readiness of certain Fancy characters to assume an ostentatious demeanour, paving the way for direct allusions to figures from the
acting world. The arrival of the fashionably attired Tom Owen, complete
with 'white topper', foreshadows the showy behaviour of one of his backers
who, as a prelude to the fight, delivers a recital:

> [*Hinckley*] appeared in the ring, in a most splendid rich waistcoat [...] The feelings
> of the Orator were rather overcome, but a *drain* of DAFFY relieved his exertions
> and soon gave fresh *spirits* to his argument. After smacking his lips at the excellence
> of the *nectar*, he then, with a sort of *Siddonian* look upon the *fogle*,[23] burst forth
> after a manner of one of *Kean's* irresistible touches:
> 'Behold its proud colours are now floating in the air!' [...] (*Boxiana III*, pp. 65–6)

Bee depicts similarly sartorial preliminaries in the contest between Dick
Curtis and Jack Lenney (28 October 1821), where Curtis appeared donning 'a new white upper *tog*, that would have given a sporting appearance
to a *pink* of Regent-street, with a prime *yellow-man* round his *squeeze*, and
a *rum* white *topper*' (*Boxiana IV*, p. 478). For pugilistic chroniclers, flash
dressing and pre-fight posturing boosted the piquancy of their reports.
Owen's overall 'prepossessing appearance' marked him as the archetypal
Fancy buck; 'full of fun and anecdote' (*Boxiana II*, p. 197). This veteran
embraced the Fancy's philosophy of performance and conviviality. One

---

23   Refers to Sarah Siddons, actress (1755–1831). A 'fogle' was a neckerchief ('the colours'
      to represent a fighter). One was often tied to the stakes.

description of Owen (on his way to a cockfight) highlights more fashionable ambiguity as the sportsman tweaks his appearance: 'well fitted to rival a horse-dealer [...] yet with a loose hung gentility about him, that just left it a matter of doubt whether you ought to ask him into your drawing-room or your stable' (*Book of Sports*, p. 150).

Flamboyance and raucous socialising are factors which Egan used to herald the main event, the onus being placed on the performance aspect. Whilst all fighters did not 'play to the gallery', there was at least a consciousness that they were objects of sporting display. Cribb's entrance for the rematch with Molineaux (1811) contains a sense of 'curtain up': 'they mounted the stage [...] CRIB springing upon it with great confidence and bowing to the spectators' (*Boxiana I*, p. 410). It should also be remembered that, in some contests, the loser relied on spectator donations. In such situations, I suggest, it would not pay to play the steely-gazed, enigmatic type.

Social Conflicts

Fame and fortune was an intoxicating combination for those who ascended the pugilistic ranks. The class interaction of the sporting world meant that some would be involved in a social whirl where they, ostensibly, were accepted into the company of high-profile figures such as the Prince Regent and his 'Carlton House set', who dictated much of the Regency social trend. Although the pugilistic writing of the period perpetuates a preoccupation with recognition, Egan applies a check by using astral imagery to imply that the cult of celebrity is transient: 'A star has now and then, for a short period, appeared in the pugilistic hemisphere with uncommon brilliancy; but whose light has soon faded and all its resplendency sunk into a mere glimmering' (*Boxiana I*, pp. 200–1). The theme is repeated by Bee when calling Hickman 'this Meteor of the Prize Ring' (*Annals of Sporting III*, p. 44).

There was an indication that the fostering of influential 'friendships' should be treated with caution, as patronage could prove temporary, and connections with prizefighters sloughed off when inconvenient. Reciprocity did exist, the wealthy supporters deriving sporting and gambling thrills from their charges. Egan highlights the proliferation of affluent participants: 'Numerous *sporting men* rallied round PUGILISM, and the Professors of the Science were not without high and noble patrons [...] and men of the first distinction felt not *ashamed* of being seen in the *ring*, or in acting as UMPIRES' (*Boxiana I*, p. 104). The comment that their aristocratic cohorts are 'not ashamed' to associate with the pugilistic fraternity appears condescending. Although there is evidence of umpiring duties being undertaken and participation in sparring bouts, there is little to support the notion of inter-class prizefights. The prevailing attitude is captured in Walter Scott's *The Two Drovers* (1827), where the judge's summing-up, in the trial of Robin Oig, includes the following remarks:

> Will it be contended that a man of superior rank and education is to be subjected [...] to this coarse and brutal strife, perhaps in opposition to a younger, stronger, or more skilful opponent? Certainly, even the pugilistic code, if founded upon the fair play of Merry Old England [...] can contain nothing so preposterous.[24]

The incredulity expressed at the notion of inter-class bouts is significant.

Bee highlights the prejudicial behaviour displayed amongst a supposedly interacting hotchpotch of spectators descending upon Crawley Downs for the Sampson v Belasco fight (19 August 1823):

> Rich and poor, high and low, and these, with the SHARPS and *flats* from all quarters of the town, filled up the scene; and made, for those persons who are fond of searching after it – an abundance of *character*. The *Corinthians*, however, the great and titled ones, kept aloof; *they* love not the *extreme* of association. (*Boxiana IV*, p. 556)

This echoes the dismay of a correspondent complaining about the number of private boxes at the re-opened Covent Garden: 'There is something aristocratical and supercilious [...] in the idea of separate apartments, separate

---

24   *Walter Scott: Chronicles of the Canongate*, ed. by Claire Lamont (London: Penguin, 2003), p. 144.

channels of communication, and separate entrances [...] as if there were pollution in one Englishman brushing close to another'.[25] Such segregation was not in keeping with Egan's promotion of the Fancy as a tolerant community relaxed about its broad base of members, Barclay being one who immersed himself in the world of prizefighters: 'He preferred their rough and ready ways and in their company he could slip out of his gentlemanly coat with ease'.[26]

It was, primarily, in sparring sessions undertaken through private tuition where the upper classes gleaned pugilistic skills, and Vincent Dowling alludes to some crucial benefits of attending Jackson's rooms in Bond Street:

> Gentlemen of the highest rank did not disdain to take the gloves [...] In after life, they acknowledged when the roar of battle, or the death-struggle with the foes of their country, by land or by sea, required the exercise of those energies which the preparative practice of Jackson's Rooms had nurtured. (*Fistiana*, p. 38)

This underscores the notion of pugilistic exercise as a masculine activity, promoting vitality and hardihood. Essentially, however, the upper-classes wished to arrange prizefights for their entertainment, not participate. Attitudes had not evolved from episodes such as that reported in the *Protestant Mercury* (January 1681): 'Yesterday a match of boxing was performed before His Grace the Duke of Albemarle between the Duke's footman and a butcher'.[27] Despite the supposed rules for all, being 'seen in the ring' usually referred to posturing patrons revelling in the publicity surrounding a major contest. An assumption that pugilists were being treated simply as rich men's pawns might be misplaced, as there is an element of escapism for lower-class men enduring an otherwise bleak existence. Egan depicted the sport as something more than an ephemeral amusement for the privileged, and his intuitive remark that 'the love of *claret* levels all distinctions' is simplistic but valid.[28]

---

25 Letter to *The Times* (7 November 1809) by a 'Gentleman'. Baer, *Theatre and Disorder*, p. 202.
26 Radford, *The Celebrated Captain Barclay*, p. 115.
27 Quoted in Fuller, *Noble Art*, p. 53.
28 *Egan's Life in London, and Sporting Guide*, No. 59 (13 March 1825), p. 53.

One negative aspect of upper-class sponsorship was that impression-
able young men might be exposed to dissolute company: 'one of the fashions [...] was for the hooligan aristocracy to hire pugilists as bodyguards on
their rampages'.[29] Egan recounts the history of Bill Hooper ('the Tinman'),
stating that the Earl of Barrymore's patronage 'proved his complete destruc-
tion' (*Boxiana I*, p. 187). As the tale unfolds, however, Hooper's part in his
own downfall is accentuated:

> Much attached to dress; and rather illiterate, his vanity was too conspicuous, and, not
> bearing in mind the real character in which he stood as a *dependant*, he considered
> himself of equal importance with the *principal* – who, had caressed and noticed him
> *merely* from his intrepidity and knowledge as a scientific pugilist. (p. 193)

Here, a talented fighter had allowed the gesturing side of ring affairs to
displace the moderation that Egan advocated. Such occurrences highlight
a social reality, which Egan understood. In his dramatisations featuring
mixed-class spectators at the dog-pit, or groups enjoying sporting chat in
the coffee room, he portrayed contrasts between such venues 'where people
are relatively free to ignore status distinctions, with other social settings
in which those distinctions have ominous clout'.[30] Herzog also rationally
points out that the boxer could not afterwards expect to 'swing by' an
upper-class residence, gain admittance, and resume a tavern conversation.

Similarly, prize-money earned by pugilists could be frittered away by
attempting to keep pace with the excesses of wealthy Fancy cohorts. When
the Irishman Dan Donnelly travelled to London to fight Oliver, in 1819, he
was 'caressed in the most flattering manner by all ranks of the *Fancy*', and
taken 'to view the tricks and fancies that are continually played off in "*Hell*"
upon its inmates' (*Boxiana III*, pp. 95–6). The ramifications are felt upon
his eventual departure, his purse of 100 guineas being somewhat depleted:
'DAN went off *loaded* with FAME; but [...] had only a TWO-POUND
NOTE left in his pocket-book' (p. 97). Bee clarified the derivation of the
slang term: '*Hell* – Gambling-houses are thus politely denominated, by
reason of the colours *here* and in the *regions infernales* being the same,

---

29   Birley, *Sport and the Making of Britain*, p. 145.
30   Herzog, *Poisoning the Minds of the Lower Orders*, p. 141.

(red and black)' (*Bee's Sportsman's Slang*). It can also be claimed that such establishments contributed to the concept of disguise in the metropolis, Jane Rendell suggesting they provided a form of architectural masquerade in order to 'create an aura of respectability [...] By "imitating" social forms of club organisation'.[31]

In fairness to Egan, he occasionally reproduced attacks on the sport, such as one concerning the vast sums gambled on the outcome of Cribb's rematch with Molineaux (1811):

> The Editor of the *Edinburgh Star* [...comments] 'When the amount of money collected for the relief of British prisoners in France, now suffering for the cause of their country, scarcely amounts to £49,000, there is – Blush, O Britain! – there is £50,000 depending upon a *boxing match!* [...] What will the starving manufacturers of Scotland say, when they read this?' (*Boxiana I*, p. 416)

Cribb, under the training regime of Barclay, spent some weeks in Scotland but the reporter is indignant: 'as if he, the *meritorious* CRIB, did honour to the city of Aberdeen by his presence' (p. 416). This may simply reflect a lack of identification with 'their' champion, an Englishman. In fact, Barclay (a Scot) had received similar censure over an extravagant bet of five thousand guineas on one of his pedestrian challenges: '*The Edinburgh Evening Courant* carried the story [...] alongside news of a sermon by Dr Jamieson in Nicholson Street, Edinburgh "for the benefit of the destitute and sick". The collection amounted to £23'.[32] The moral points being made may have increased English distrust of a home nation that had not embraced prizefighting (despite exhibitions and the existence of an Edinburgh branch of the Fancy) but do reflect more widespread concern about the social repercussions of profligacy. This disquiet cannot be branded as anti-English rhetoric, but foreshadows reservations expressed about an ambivalent attitude, in the *Boxiana* writings, towards the dissipation prevalent in Fancy circles.

---

31   Jane Rendell, *The Pursuit of Pleasure* (New Jersey: Rutgers University Press, 2002), p. 83. The gambling-house employees who assisted in the duping of clients included 'flashers', 'puffs', and 'squibs' (see Appendix). A 'contemporary list of staff' can be found in Blyth, *Hell and Hazard*, p. 53.
32   Radford, *The Celebrated Captain Barclay*, p. 85.

As indicated, some successful fighters were capable of earning enough money to ease their elevation up the social scale. John Gully was an exceptional case, but more modest ambitions could be satisfied by some:

> CANNON, in leaving the Prize Ring, may be said to be one of the bravest as well as one of the *luckiest* men that ever entered it, owing to the very liberal and gentlemanly patronage of *Mr Hayne* [...] He left London [29 November 1824], with *seven hundred and fifty pounds* in his clie, with an intention to open a tavern at Windsor. (*New Series Boxiana II*, p. 47)

Egan provides confirmation of this pugilist's fruitful transition, stating that, in February 1828, Cannon was 'comfortably situated as the landlord of the *Castle* in Jermyn-Street' (p. 60). But, Egan laments that, generally, pugilists were 'not altogether unlike the Jack Tars of Old England, "who earn their money like horses, and then spend it like asses"' (*Boxiana III*, p. 160).

Egan indicated that the prevention of a prizefight, through magisterial interference, united pugilistic followers across class and political spectrums:

> [Martin v Hudson, 14 December 1819] This interruption rather *screwed* the *Corinthians* as well as the *Coster-mongers*. 'Vy, blow me', says the latter, 'vat use is it *sarving* us so; ve are not *Raddycals*; ve only meet to *preserve* the true courage of Englishmen, and to improve the breed; ve have nothing *polly tickle* about us, blow me; and I'm *sartain* if my Lord Castlereagh vas here, he'd say let us have a *mill*'. (*Boxiana III*, p. 247)

This reflects government wariness of large gatherings in this period, fearing radical agitation. However, the citation of the generally unpopular Castlereagh as pugilism's supporter is surprising, and strengthens the concept that energetic activities could assuage civil unrest and deflect attention from domestic hardship. The melodramatic dimension is also a factor, as theatre audiences proved to be remarkably self-regulating: 'the self-control exhibited by the Covent Garden rioters [...] reveals a society at the same time contentious yet unwilling to move to the level of insurrection or revolution'.[33]

---

33   Baer, *Theatre and Disorder*, p. 85.

For pugilists who found themselves in trouble with the law, there were some compensatory benefits of possessing a degree of sporting celebrity. At the Old Bailey trial of Ned Turner (1 November 1816), charged with 'wilful murder' over the death of John Curtis in their fight (22 October), the jury's verdict of manslaughter is accompanied by a plea for leniency. As well as receiving a merciful sentence (two months imprisonment in Newgate), Turner's confinement does not appear to have been as arduous as it might:

> He conducted himself with so much propriety and decorum, as to merit the attention of the head keeper, who granted him every indulgence consistent with the rules [...] in order to render his privation of liberty less irksome and oppressive to his feelings. He was also visited by many of the highest patrons of pugilism. (*Boxiana II*, p. 155)

William Batts was also a beneficiary of a relaxed judicial view of prizefighting fatalities when tried over the death of Thomas Clayton (April 1817), yet, in this same volume, Egan speaks of a partiality against fighters when John Crockey is found guilty of highway robbery and sentenced to 'transportation for life' (July 1817): 'It is [...] feared, from his rough appearance, united with the alarming ideas held by some individuals as to the terrific characters of *scientific* or prize-fighters in general, that an overwhelming prejudice might have operated against him' (p. 408). Perhaps a pugilist's death was considered no great loss, hence the relatively light punishments in the other two instances. A general sympathy does appear to have existed despite pugilists being negatively grouped with reviled social elements, such as those recruited to quell the OP riots: 'The pit has been metamorphosed into a pugilistic arena where all the blackguards of London, the Jew prize-fighters, Bow Street runners, hackney-coach helpers, and vagabonds returned from transportation have ranged themselves on the side of the managers.'[34]

The comfortable conditions enjoyed by Turner when imprisoned, partially through public renown, are comparable to those procured by society's upper echelons. Venetia Murray states that William Cobbett, Leigh Hunt (1784–1859), and John Hobhouse were given luxury quarters, and treated

---

34 *Examiner* (15 October 1809). Baer, *Theatre and Disorder*, p. 216.

like celebrities: 'There was no disgrace about being sent to gaol during the Regency, provided it was for an acceptable "crime" [debt or libel]'.[35] Court proceedings often reflected the inconsistency that enabled prize-fights to sporadically go unchecked. In the episode where Randall appears before Alderman Smith, answering a charge of assaulting five constables, the supposed crime is 'winked at' in a sporting spirit: 'The worthy Alderman wished to look at the constable's *frontispiece*, observing that a BLOW from RANDALL generally, he understood, left a mark, but he certainly saw nothing *legible*' (*Boxiana III*, p. 210). The relaxed attitude suggests that Egan may have, based on hearsay, exaggerated events, but the result is an entertaining description of establishment toleration.

There does appear to have been benevolent conduct by some of the gentry towards selected fighters, and even if the motivation was not completely altruistic then the promise of a sporting spectacle to savour could work in a pugilist's favour: '[October 1805] GULLEY was so great a favourite [...] that it was agreed he should be immediately liberated from *durance vile*, and his debts discharged, that he might fight the *Chicken*' (*Boxiana I*, p. 161). This scenario foreshadows Byron's previously mentioned willingness to intercede, and his interest in the world of the Fancy is evident in his journal entry of 23 November 1813: 'Jackson has been here: the boxing world much as usual [...] I shall dine at Crib's to-morrow. I like energy – even animal energy'. Here Byron's 'animal' reference assumes a complimentary aspect, not implying brutishness but, rather, a vitality that he feels is preferable to an enervated state of over-indulgence. During his 'audience' with Cribb (it is debateable which of them would be considered more famous), the drink flows freely, and his record of 25 November is almost unstinting in appreciation of Cribb's stature: 'Tom has been a sailor – a coal-heaver – and some other genteel profession [...] and is now only three-and-thirty. A great man! Has a wife and a mistress, and conversations well – bating some sad omissions and misapplications of the aspirate'.[36]

---

35   Murray, *High Society*, p. 277.
36   In 1813, Cribb was landlord of the King's Arms, Duke Street. *Byron's Letters and Journals*, ed. by Marchand, III, pp. 216, 221.

Although playful, the entry is infused with an air of affectionate admiration, and even the quibble over Cribb's lack of eloquence is not demeaning. Egan commented that Byron had 'been seen with several other first-rate characters in the veteran *Tom Cribb's* house enjoying his glass of wine, and conversing upon subjects connected with the sporting world in the most animated style'. He then elaborates on the creative benefits gained: 'His lordship was well aware that an author whose intentions were to display something like ORIGINALITY in his writings, ought to view everything in the different walks of life' (*Book of Sports*, p. 14).

Another person depicted as participating in all aspects of the sporting world is the Prince of Wales's godson, Harry Mellish. Egan transports the reader to the scene: 'I think I see him now on a Race Course [...] communicating life and spirits to the circle [...] a complete hero on the box; and an "out-and-outer" in every other point of view upon the Turf' (*Book of Sports*, p. 3). And, elaborates on his popularity:

> Many persons take to themselves, that they are better than other folks, and not like those wicked fellows who frequent horse-races, hunting, and prize-fights [...] The Lord Chancellor Thurlow, on being told that 'Mr Mellish was a great favourite of the populace', observed, 'They like him as a brother blackguard: I am of their opinion'. (p. 69)

This strengthens Egan's argument that a mutual interest in sporting matters existed across a broad spectrum of society, and that distinctions of rank were temporarily shelved at such heterogeneous gatherings. Such interaction appears possible if perceptions of superiority remained unthreatened, and only when sensing this security could the upper echelons '*pretend* [my italics] that social divisions had evaporated in the [...] alchemy of sport'.[37]

---

37   Radford, *The Celebrated Captain Barclay*, p. 29.

Different Perspectives on the Performance

In considering alternative scene-setting methods it is useful to look at different accounts of the same contest. The fight between Randall and Martin (11 September 1821) is included as an excursion for the three 'heroes' (Charles Sparkle, Bob Tallyho, and Tom Dashall) in *Real Life in London* (1821). The episode offers a convenient means of amusing the reader in much the same manner that clowns and acrobats would be introduced into a contemporary play performance. The degree of excitement and nervous anticipation is apparent: 'All alive and leaping. Mirth and merriment appeared spread over every countenance, though expectation and anxiety were intermingled' (*Real Life in London*, p. 397). Bee's *Boxiana* account confirms the anticipation from an insider's vantage point: 'Long before day-light [...] the roads leading into Sussex were covered [...] so great was the interest excited throughout the sporting world to witness the *Nonpareil* once more display his superior stratagems' (*Boxiana IV*, pp. 388–9).

Intriguingly, the 'Amateur' commentary is couched in a tone closely resembling the *Boxiana*-style:

> Martin's *nob* was completely in a vice; and while in that hopeless condition Randall *fibbed* away [...and] then with a violent swing, threw Martin to the ground, falling on him as he went with all his weight. The Ring resounded with applause, and Jack coolly took his seat on the knee of his second. All eyes were now turned to Martin, who being lifted on Spring's knee, in a second discovered that he was done. His head fell back lifeless [...] water was thrown on him in abundance, but without effect [...] Poor Martin lay like a lump of unleavened dough. (*Real Life in London*, pp. 400–1)

This particular 'Amateur' had supplied a meditative analysis of the fight action. For his part, amidst the engrossment of the spectators, Bee devoted attention to the physical and mental state of the combatants:

> [Both] watching the minutest motion of each other's *iris* – the eyes of Randall, which are uncommonly small, being almost ready to start from their sockets. Martin was mildly anxious [...] and, at each new position, we thought he stepped less firm than usual [...] His back also showed signs of dampness, whilst the whole skin of Randall was suffused with a tinge of red that increased with each effort [...] The combatants

closed on Randall's decoying Martin to follow him to his favourite corner of the ring; and in this situation, often as the Nonpareil had astonished the amateurs with his *forte* for *fibbing*, he now put forth such a 'bit of good truth' as positively to electrify the spectators with the terrible execution he was capable of administering. (*Boxiana IV*, pp. 391–2)

Whilst *Boxiana* reports accentuated spectacle, diversity, and novelty amongst the skill and bravery observed, they were the product of authors steeped in the ritualistic enthusiasm of a communal Fancy spirit. Therefore, it is interesting that *Boxiana IV* supplied an opportunity to ascertain a relatively impartial viewpoint from another uninitiated 'amateur' correspondent.[38] Bee appears to welcome this alternative perspective: 'as it contains a few particulars and incidents little known to non-professors, besides some characteristic sketches […] usually passed over or misrepresented' (p. 395). The writer relates his curiosity and the extent to which fellow first-time spectators are relishing a glimpse of a prizefight. He is not unaware of the sport's intricacies however, having read some of the pugilistic writing of the day, and reveals a hint of justifiable scepticism:

> The intense interest excited in our minds by the *sporting intelligence conveyed by the London press*, and the difficulty of discriminating the plain, simple, unvarnished fact, amidst the eloquence and *metaphorical colouring* in which battles are narrated, renders it necessary that we ourselves should, once at least, see a prize-fight, *in order to understand* the events of the day and be able to converse rationally on matters which are the subject of discussion in every body's mouth. (p. 395)

These initial impressions contain both positive and negative connotations for the *Boxiana* style, reflecting its inherent contradictions. The observer's yearning for simple fact constitutes a reprimand for Egan and Bee's flamboyant approach, also suggesting that their reports are lacking in clarity. However, the remark that pugilistic affairs are being widely discussed testifies to the success of the very same accounts in increasing the sport's appeal.

---

38   This 'amateur' should not be confused with the 'Amateur' author of *Real Life in London*.

It is the spectacle and drama with which Egan and Bee imbued their pieces that excited public interest. Contrary to the correspondent's reproaches, *Boxiana*-style imagery enhanced the reader's ability to envisage events, such as the compelling analogy reflecting the rugged nature and volatility of a bare-knuckle battle: 'both of their *nobs*, like two flints, almost struck fire' (*Boxiana IV*, p. 498). Another conveys the exhausted state of two combatants supporting one another: 'they were actually in a position like a couple of bears about to waltz' (p. 459). Any comment that a writer wishes to witness and 'understand' the prizefight rationale is a reasonable one however, as such metaphorical representations merely complement the visualisation process, and entertainment value.

The 'amateur' does not breeze into a description of the physical onslaught but, rather, intensifies the suspense: 'the men stripped and set-to. They stood before one another, with their eyes directed forwards, watching every move' (p. 397). This imparts a sense of tactical judgement combined with trepidation. Once the fight commences, a convincing condensation of the crucial action follows:

> At last they exchanged hits. Randall put in a blow on the breast, which made it appear red; he had a blow under the eye and on the nose, but made a most dreadful return, and came in on his man, caught him in one arm, and his other went to work so fast, it seemed like the motion of a *mill-wheel* in full speed. Both fell and were picked up; but Martin's head hung down like an apple on its stalk. The seconds put it in its proper place, but it dropped again. They moved it backwards and forwards, like a baker rolling about a loaf in the flour; they threw water on him, waved their hats to cool him, but all was not enough; and when thirty seconds were elapsed, time was called, but his senses were gone. Thus was the battle lost. (p. 398)

In contrast to his description of the fighters' earlier jockeying, the writer stimulates visualisation of proceedings by including his own 'metaphorical colouring' of mill-wheels, apple-stalks, and dough-rolling (a common reference to Martin's occupation of baker). The supposed journalistic tyro concludes by recounting the immediate aftermath: 'The conqueror walked about the ground, and enjoyed the admiration in which he was held by the spectators, and a flight of carrier pigeons was let off to convey the intelligence to town' (p. 398).

Bee's version is privy to the subsequent reception of Randall; the mood struck being that of the homecoming warrior:

> The house of RANDALL was literally besieged, at a time when the fight could have been scarcely over at Crawley, 31 miles off; and, towards the evening, great crowds were collected round all the other sporting-houses [...] and a sight of the *hero* of the day was as much in request as that of any conqueror of ancient or of modern times. (p. 394)

Militaristic language is also prevalent in the description of Cribb's reception, following his 1811 triumph over Molineaux, the public response amplified to reflect the national pride at stake: 'Cheered through all the towns he passed, after the manner of an officer bearing dispatches of a victory, so much was it felt by the people of England' (*Boxiana I*, pp. 414–15). Egan renders the mixture of joy and relief almost palpable, and underscores that, to many, the opportunity to share sporting glory was more gratifying than news of distant military success. A similar clamour for information is highlighted in the aftermath of Randall's victory over Turner (5 December 1818):

> The interest excited in the Metropolis [...] to those persons *'out of the ring'* may appear like a romance. Hundreds were waiting at the turn-pike gates along the road [...] The sale of newspapers was as great as if some important victory had been achieved on the continent, so much anxiety was expressed upon this battle. (*Boxiana III*, pp. 185–6)

The pugilistic event is effectively extended, onlookers seeking to claim a degree of participation in the performance.

Egan consistently depicted a dynamic relationship, between spectacle and audience, which affirms a temporary mutual interest. Egan had indicated this communion-like atmosphere when describing the intensity of spectators at the Humphries v Mendoza contest. 'their attentions were so completely riveted [...] an awful silence, as if by one impulse, instantly prevailed' (*Boxiana I*, p. 105). The divergent handling of the Randall v Martin reports occurs only a few months prior to Hazlitt's celebrated essay 'The Fight', but whether they influenced his own thoughtful appraisal of a prizefight is unclear. David Higgins suggests that Hazlitt's attendance of the Hickman v Neate fight (11 December 1821) is represented as 'a sort of pilgrimage to a shrine of manly English virtue'. The sociological concept of Hazlitt affirming his gender identity through involvement with pugilism is supported by Herzog's intriguing picture of spectators as 'vampires, greedily sucking in the potent masculinity', suggesting that Hazlitt's desire, to imbibe some of the latent masculinity associated with a prizefight, was far from an isolated sentiment.[39] As with Egan's pugilistic writing, considerations of manliness and patriotism were prioritised.

Hazlitt's style of fight commentary diverged radically from Egan's flash verve, relying more on descriptive similes and imagery, but parallels do occur:

> After making play a short time, the Gas-man flew at his adversary like a tiger, struck five blows in as many seconds, three first, and then following him as he staggered back, two more, right and left, and down he fell, a mighty ruin. There was a shout, and I said 'There is no standing this'. Neate seemed like a lifeless lump of flesh and bone, round which the Gas-man's blows played with the rapidity of electricity or lightning [...] It was as if Hickman held a sword or a fire in that right-hand of his, and directed it against an unarmed body. They met again, and Neate seemed not cowed, but particularly cautious. I saw his teeth clenched together and his brows knit close against the sun.[40]

There are no slang terms, but the 'electricity' metaphor is familiar from the *Boxiana* series, and the concept of Hickman as a potent force is successfully conveyed. The *Boxiana* spirit flickers when Hazlitt recounts the moments when the contest swings in Neate's favour: '[Neate] planted a tremendous blow on his cheek-bone and eye-brow, and made a red ruin of that side of his face. The Gas-man went down [...] This was a settler'. Hazlitt then conveys the singularity of the situation:

> It was the first time he had ever been so punished; all one side of his face was perfect scarlet, and his right eye was closed in dingy blackness, as he advanced to the fight, less confident, but still determined. After one or two rounds, not receiving another such remembrancer, he rallied and went at it with his former impetuosity. But in vain.[41]

---

39 Herzog, *Poisoning the Minds of the Lower Orders*, p. 334.
40 *The Selected Writings of William Hazlitt*, ed. by Wu, IX, p. 69.
41 Ibid., p. 70.

A 'remembrancer' blow occurs in *Boxiana II* (e.g. p. 129), sardonically mirroring its conventional definition as 'a reminder of something' (*OED*). The proximity of 'settler', 'remembrancer', and 'impetuosity' is a salient feature amidst the essay's overall tone. It is as if Hazlitt, to add a dash of flash authenticity to his commentary, has read some *Boxiana* reports and inserted pugilistic terms almost en bloc.

Hazlitt soon resumes his earlier style, and provides a compelling version of the contest's dramatic conclusion, culminating in Hickman's bloody defeat:

> Neate just then made a tremendous lunge at him, and hit him full in the face. It was doubtful whether he would fall backwards or forwards; he hung suspended for a second or two, and then fell back, throwing his hands in the air, and with his face lifted up to the sky. I never saw any thing more terrific than his aspect just before he fell. All traces of life, of natural expression, were gone from him. His face was like a human skull, a death's head, spouting blood. The eyes were filled with blood, the mouth gaped blood. He was not like an actual man, but like a preternatural, spectral appearance.[42]

Presumably, this would be a suitable juncture for any 'tender' reader to recoil at Hazlitt's 'masculinist' imagery. Whatever Hazlitt's motivation, Bee expressed appreciation: '*the Ring* is much indebted for many home facts (for support) from men of *letters*, who may be considered *outside its vortex*' (*Boxiana IV*, p. 416).

Bee's version reflects on the journey to the fight of the 'milling troops' that were 'descending' and 'ascending' the country (*Boxiana IV*, p. 68), but military imagery is swiftly discarded as he depicts a poetical scene preceding the fight:

> Anxiety beamed in the faces of the *privileged* classes, for on the event depended whether a quarter of a million sterling should belong to this or to that side [...] At this time, too, the rays of the sun being compressed between two large clouds, threw its bright beams right upon the spot, and enlivened the immense assemblage of nearly 30,000 persons, many of whom were taking NEAT for choice, with five to four on his winning; whilst the sun-beams danced in unison with their wishes, and Hungerford church spire, in the distance, seemed, as the clouds now and then passed its apex, to nod assent to their undertakings. (pp. 70–1)

---

42 Ibid., p. 70.

Despite his romantic reverie, Bee conveys practical information regarding the size and class mixture of the crowd and economic implications of the wagers. The notion of a heavenly blessing being conferred upon what, in many ways, were violent and unrefined proceedings might be construed as faintly ridiculous by a non-Fancy observer.

Bee's fight report is liberally peppered with flash, and he presses his view on a misconception concerning Neate's fitness ('roarer' signified lack of stamina):

> Neat planted such a severe left-hander on Gas's gob, as again astonished his weak understanding, and his teeth *chattered* like a *dice-box* [...He] returned blow for blow, until he received a grasser, when Neat also went down. Shouts of 'Gas' followed by several abortive offers of 6 to 4 [...] Neat being none such a *roarer* as had been given out. (pp. 71–2)

The non-stop nature of the fighter's exertions is communicated by the relentless commentary:

> [Hickman] again tried his rushing-in manoeuvre, bored Neat to the ropes, hammering away in all directions; but the latter administered heavy punishment at every step that he fell back, jobbing, nobbing, and pinking, alternately, then giving *Gas* a terrible *belly-go-firster*,[43] then a ribber, another of them, and *ditto* [...Seventh. He] staggered off, but came on again, and was greeted with a straight left-hander on his upper ivories that uncorked his konk, whence the claret now streamed profusely. (p. 73)

The streaming claret of Bee's seventh-round account tallies with Hazlitt's, but the pace and slang of Bee's commentary offers a more knockabout sketch than Hazlitt's cerebral interpretation.

Egan's own account was prefaced by a review of crucial information, such as the contest is 'for 200 Guineas a-side' (*New Series Boxiana I*, p. 42), and 'The GAS weighed twelve stone, and *Neat* nearly fourteen' (p. 47). Once the action commences, Egan conveys the ferocity of the 'punishment': 'Hickman went in resolutely to smash his opponent, but he was met [...]

---

43   The little-used 'jobbing' refers to sharp, cutting hits, which is highly suggestive that the term generated the contemporary 'jab' (c. 1850, *B/P*). 'Belly-go-firster' – an initial blow to the body (*OED*).

with one of the most tremendous right-handed blows ever witnessed [...
Fifth] Gas came up an altered man; indeed, a bullock must seriously have felt
such a blow' (p. 49). Egan's analogy ascribes Hickman with a combination
of savagery and strength, and the ensuing description of defiance echoes
portrayals of a contemptuous figure. The sixth-round commentary continues
the animal motif whilst corresponding with Hazlitt and Bee's recollections:

> The mouth of the Gas was full of blood, and he appeared almost choking with it – when
> time was called. He was getting weak; but he, nevertheless, rushed in, and bored Neat
> to the ropes [...] Neat punished Gas in all directions, and finished the round by *grassing*
> him with a belly puncher [sic] that would have floored an ox. This hit was quite enough
> to have *finished the pluck* of two good men. The *long faces* from London were now so
> numerous, that 100 artists could not have taken their likenesses; and the Bristolian *kids*
> were roaring with delight, and *chaffing* one to another. (*New Series Boxiana I*, p. 49)

This assists the visualisation of Hickman as a persevering fighter, or less
flatteringly, an obstinate one. But, his resistance was soon breached: 'Neat
again put in a tremendous blow on his mouth that *uncorked* the *claret* in pro-
fusion [...Eighth] The *Gas*, laughing, commenced the attack, but received
such a giant-like blow on his right eye, that he was instantly convulsed'
(p. 50). The ensuing drama, and concern for a 'motionless' Hickman is then
communicated: 'The whole ring seemed panic-struck. Spring vociferating
almost with the voice of a Stentor to awake him from his stupor [...] *Gas!*
Gas! Gas!' (p. 50).

Egan's account of the fourteenth round supplies a vivid, and horrific,
image of a fighter 'distressed beyond imagination', as his seconds guide him
back to face his opponent 'the blood dropping from his eye in torrents,
and his other *peeper*, starting, as it were, from the socket, staring wildly'
(p. 52). Here are 'masculine' scenes that might 'offend the delicate', and
the battle correlates with the brutality of the cockpit, being watched in
much the same way by anxious gamblers. The combination of blood and
animal terminology, as well as Neate's profession of butcher, inadvertently
underscores the moral argument pursued by the sport's opponents, that of
desensitisation: 'The uniform Ring-goer witnesses the human butchery of
a Prize Fight with indifference' (*RIPM*, 1824, p. 15). Following the eventual
moment of defeat, when Hickman is 'insensible to the call of TIME', Egan's
concluding remarks, ironically, focus on the defeated man, and a rebuke

contains a degree of admiration: 'His fault was he thought himself, like Achilles, INVULNERABLE' (*New Series Boxiana I*, p. 54).

A year later, there was much public sorrow exhibited upon news of Hickman's death (in a road accident), and at his funeral (19 December 1822):

> Crowds pressed around the Adam and Eve; and the adjoining houses, wherever a glimpse might be caught of the procession, were filled with persons of respectability who maintained their station notwithstanding the cold damp air that prevailed. The funeral, as a spectacle, was singularly imposing and neat; the mourners [...] followed the remains of a man whose achievements had occupied the thoughts of all. (*Boxiana IV*, pp. 208–9).

The concept of a sporting 'celebrity' funeral is not a modern phenomenon, and this report accentuates the social 'spectacle' aspect of proceedings as well as reinforcing the idea that pugilistic concerns could permeate 'the thoughts of all'.

Hazlitt's essay provided a sympathetic overview of sporting circles, without seriously grappling with the flash language. He enjoyed playing the role, in the knowledge that he could speedily retreat to familiar territory. For the casual pugilistic follower (and I treat Hazlitt as a sympathetic, yet uncommitted, observer), the availability of Egan's publications supplied a welcome alternative, particularly in forbidding conditions: 'He dislikes encountering the rude blasts of winter, the pelting showers, and also being pushed about by a coarse unmannerly crowd'.[44] Hazlitt sought to participate in an affirmation of maleness by travelling to a prizefight, and when his coach eventually delivers him home, the writer wistfully states: 'I got out, resigned my coat and green silk handkerchief [...] and walked home in high spirits'.[45] Despite claiming to be loathe to give up 'these ornaments of life', and apparently energised by the excursion, it appears that his first fight also represented his last. Herzog explains one potential philosophy:

> [Spectators] consoled themselves in their undead languor by capitalising on the cultural force of the mind / body distinction. Perhaps, that is, the very physicality

---

44   Egan, *Every Gentleman's Manual. A Lecture on the Art of Self-Defence* (London: Sherwood and Bowyer, 1845), p. 147.

45   *The Selected Writings of William Hazlitt*, ed. by Wu, IX, p. 73.

of these triumphant displays of masculinity let the spectators console themselves in their superior status. The fighters' brute energy, quintessentially male or masculine, placed them close to animal nature.[46]

As a man possessing 'high' sensibilities, Hazlitt, unlike Byron, may have been content to distance himself from 'animal' pugilists. It should be remembered, however, that this major prizefight presented an opportunity to address a new subject; then, as a seasoned essayist and journalist, he would move on to other topics. The fact that Hazlitt was not a devoted sportsman does not diminish the power of his reflective essay which engaged with the Fancy's showpiece event in an expressive and earnest manner.

Ultimately, Hazlitt's aspiration to explore the sporting world of the Fancy appears to have been sincere. Perhaps he wished to absorb a degree of what he perceived as an uncomplicated attitude towards life, and it is worth reflecting that sport constituted 'an honourable and unbiased field of conflict, possessing, for Hazlitt, an unquestionable clarity'.[47] Despite their differing styles, Hazlitt's account touches sufficient mutual points with the *Boxiana* reports to underscore the affinity with pugilistic events for a wide-ranging social blend.

The Arts, and Further Classical Connections

At times, Egan supplemented dramatic tension with overt references to the Arts:

> [Randall v Martin, May 1819] It might be compared to the numerous steps cut in the air, by the celebrated *Duport*, at the Opera; for in the very short space of time that Martin was falling to the ground [...] Randall planted three tremendous blows.[48] (*Boxiana III*, p. 196)

46 Herzog, *Poisoning the Minds of the Lower Orders*, p. 334.
47 I am grateful to John Strachan for this unpublished reference.
48 Louis Duport, French ballet dancer (c. 1781–1853).

[Dick Curtis v Perkins, December 1828] Hopes and fears were seen in the counte-nances of the Backers [...] THE LONDONERS WERE PANIC STRUCK [...] and all manner of colours, *summut* like the incantation scene in Der Freischütz.[49] (*Book of Sports*, p. 26)

The theme continues in comparisons made with a stage-coach driver, Stevenson: 'His start was a first rate thing altogether a *Taglioni* move-ment: and he handled the ribbons with as much ease and confidence as *Paganini*' (*Book of Sports*, p. 5).[50] Egan had previously commented on the aesthetic quality of the metropolis: 'the contrasts [...] so marked with light and shade' (*Life in London*, p. 36), and interspersed specific references in his account of a clash between Donnelly and Oliver (21 July 1819):

It was expressed, that if *Flaxman* [...] had wished to select a living model on the beauty of the action of the muscles, a finer subject than Donnelly could not have been found [...] Smiling confidence appeared to sit on his brow; his eye was sharp and penetrating; his face clear and animated. (*Boxiana III*, p. 84)

John Flaxman was a sculptor, designer, and illustrator (1755–1826). An intriguing footnote is that Donnelly's supposed vitality was at a time when he acknowledged that he had been drinking heavily and succumbed to a sexually transmitted disease whilst 'poaching for petticoats' in the 'preserves of Croydon' (*Pugilistica II*, p. 155).

Egan reported episodes where pugilists, such as the 'truly conspicu-ous' Tring, were used as models (*Boxiana I*, pp. 297–9). Egan's claims for Bob Gregson tally with other records comparing the physiques of Classical antiquity and pugilists of the day:

Six feet one inch and a half, and weighing about fifteen stone [...Gregson] has been considered so good an anatomical subject to descant upon, that Mr CARLISLE, the celebrated Professor of Anatomy at the Royal Academy, has selected BOB to stand several times [...] Possessing good intellectual faculties, his general deportment is above all absurd affectation. (*Boxiana I*, p. 355)

---

49 Opera by German composer Carl Maria Von Weber (1786–1826), first performed in June 1821.

50 Filippo Taglioni, Italian dancer and choreographer (1777–1871). Niccolo Paganini, Italian composer and violin virtuoso (1782–1840).

There was a major pugilistic influence in Thomas Lawrence's 1797 exhibition at the Royal Academy, an enormous painting of 'Satan Summoning his Legions' being based upon a giant portrait of John Jackson. The physical presence of Jackson must have been impressive as Lawrence considered this to be the only work in which he had 'justified his reputation'.[51] Egan highlighted the benefits enjoyed by home-grown artists in a speech attributed to 'Mr M' in the debate at the Society for Mutual Improvement: 'A remarkable instance of the ignorance of foreigners of ancient Grecian and modern British science may be seen in the statues of the four Pugilists, by Canova [...] So completely do they lay themselves open' (*Boxiana III*, p. 580).[52] The technically inept marble stances allow Egan the opportunity to decry foreign knowledge of the sport, 'Mr M' suggesting Canova's fundamental deficiency being that he 'had not had the benefit of a journey to London' (p. 580).

It should also be noted that the engravings by George Sharples (in *Boxiana* and *Annals of Sporting* volumes) depicted pugilists in fashionable attire, and there were the imposing figures of Jackson and Gully captured on canvas by Benjamin Marshall (published in 1810). These portray dapper gentlemen, standing next to Classical sculptures, emanating quiet dignity and respectability.[53] This imagery jars with the staginess of some prizefighting rituals and behaviour which challenged Egan's championing of the sport's honesty and simple philosophy. There was a risk of the demarcation between showmanship and affectation becoming confused, and certain vainglorious pugilists wallowing in public acclaim. Significantly, the popularity of renowned actors could be fleeting if their adoring public detected signs of arrogance: 'Even the hint of pretentiousness or dictation could swing an audience from idolatry to violent opposition'.[54] But, Egan appears to differentiate between entertainment to advance the sport's profile, and 'absurd affectation'.

51 Kenneth Garlick, *Sir Thomas Lawrence* (London: Routledge & Kegan Paul, 1954), p. 7.
52 Antonio Canova, Italian sculptor (1757–1822).
53 Benjamin Marshall, painter and racing journalist (1768–1835). See Fuller, *Noble Art*, pp. 26, 29.
54 Baer, *Theatre and Disorder*, p. 71.

The American Tom Molineaux, a relative newcomer to the Fancy, understood that a certain swaggering style was beneficial to gaining publicity and increasing earning power:

> [He] was remarkably fond of entering a country town in a post-chaise and four, ordering the drivers to gallop as fast as possible to the best inn [...] MOLINEAUX was quite aware that that sort of *dash* created an interest and curiosity. (*Boxiana III*, p. 494)

Of course, attaining a shining position of prominence in the 'pugilistic hemisphere' was partly reliant upon wealthy connections, but it is apparent that some fighters relished the opportunity to mount the sporting platform. Individuals switching between the roles of man-about-town and pugilist were not assuming a part when entering the prizefight arena, and this performance, or ring showmanship, might be interpreted as a manifestation of a natural (Fancy) gregariousness. The presence of entertaining fighters contributed a welcome aspect to pugilistic pieces, and the Fancy community thrived on anecdotal entertainment which, in turn, favoured embellishment and a degree of bluster. The part of the pugilistic press in creating public heroes, or prompting widespread discussion of sporting deeds, was significant. Bee proclaimed a journalistic doctrine that has endured:

> The Biographer of the Fancy does not descend to the haunts of the private individual, there to inspect his acts, for they are not worth recording, and would fail of exciting interest [...] but when individuals, leaving common life [...] render themselves prominent features on the canvass of the age, they and their acts, their achievements and failures, and even motives to action, become public property. (*Boxiana IV*, p. 53)

The pugilist seeking fame was subject to scrutiny in and out of the ring, and Egan regularly administered moral censure.

In addition to the art-world, Classical allusion is an enduring thread and Egan recreated the melodramatic tension of vivid scenes when eulogising Fancy favourites. Egan (quixotically) conveyed the message that pugilists could arouse grandiose visions connected with ancient tradition, whilst retaining even nobler spiritual virtues. He commented on a dilemma faced by Bill Stevens ('The Nailer') with a flattering comparison: 'he sat down like the great ALEXANDER, *weeping that he had no more heroes to overcome*' (*Boxiana I*, p. 70). And, 'Mr M' endorsed the epic value of the first two *Boxiana* volumes: 'Nor do the heroes of the fist enjoy merely fugitive fame, like Achilles and Hector, they have obtained their honour' (*Boxiana III*, p. 579). Hazlitt, too, proclaimed: 'If Neate was like Ajax, "with Atlantean shoulders, fit to bear" the pugilistic reputation of all Bristol, Hickman might be compared to Diomed'.[55] The perception of fighters as mythical-style heroes was intensified in portraits by Thomas Douglas Guest (c. 1779–1839) depicting 'Thomas Cribb' and 'Thomas Belcher' in fighting attitudes. Their striking nature can be attributed to the fact that Guest's speciality was 'historical and mythological subjects' (*DNB*).[56] These paintings feature the pugilists in front of louring skies, evoking a sense of the men as elemental forces themselves.

Egan reported that his French journalistic counterparts, whilst abjectly failing to appreciate the subtleties of the sport, were capable of discerning the superhuman qualities of British pugilists, and reproduced their assessment of sparring exhibitions at Aix-la-Chapelle (October 1818):[57]

> In one of the Paris journals [...] 'Yesterday there was a grand exhibition made by the English boxers. This hideous spectacle attracted but few spectators. The two champions, built like a Hercules, and naked to their waists, entered the lists [...] One might imagine that we beheld the ancient athletic games of Greece'. (*Boxiana III*, pp. 35–6)

The French may have considered this pugilistic exhibition 'hideous' (their objections are not explained) but they acknowledge the 'spectacle' of the activity.

---

55 In Greek legend, the *Iliad*, described Ajax as being of great stature and second only to Achilles in strength and bravery. Diomed was another Homeric hero, King of Argos (*EB*). Lines from *Paradise Lost* (Book II, 305–7). *The Selected Writings of William Hazlitt*, ed. by Wu, IX, p. 69.

56 Published in 1811. Fuller, *Noble Art*, pp. 33, 40. In 1805, Guest was awarded the gold medal for historical painting for 'Bearing the Dead Body of Patroclus to the Camp, Achilles's Grief' (*DNB*).

57 Aix-la-Chapelle Congress was held in September at which ministers from the 'Holy Alliance' (Britain, Austria, Prussia, and Russia) negotiated the occupation of post-Napoleonic France.

Egan encouraged contributed pieces vindicating pugilism, and one by 'a Young Gentleman of the Fancy' extols the merits of a 'plethora' of contemporary fighters against Classical models:

> We hear talk of heroes [...] but we must confess that we never thought much of any of the feats of antiquity, until we read that Milo had knocked down a bull with his fist [...][58] Was Ajax braver than Gregson? – was he bigger than Perrins? – No. was Achilles to be compared to the Game Chicken? Pshaw! Hen would have threshed Mars himself [...] Molineaux, bating his colour; would have been a match for Hercules; and Cribb gives one no unfavourable idea of the great god Pan [...] Gentle readers, weigh these men in their fair scales of your opinion, before ye prefer other heroes to the fighters of your native country. (*Book of Sports*, p. 124)

This piece endorses a complaint raised by Egan 'that most minds labour under a kind of fascination in their respect towards antiquity [...] that it obtains an undue preference, to the manifest injury, and even neglect of modern achievements' (*Boxiana I*, p. 202). As with many sports, a particular generation were / are prone to believe that present 'heroes' surpass all challengers, or to harbour idealised recollections of past performances. Generally, however, these nostalgic leanings only extend to periods from within one's lifetime. This was a tack pursued by Thomas Fewtrell in 1790 when he stated that, although previous pugilists had advanced the sport: 'we have made still greater improvements [...and] so successfully has invention been in our days exerted, that little more can remain to be done for the science' (*Boxing Reviewed*, p. 46). This evaluation constitutes a premature dismissal of any impact to be made by future fighters.

Egan's crambo, 'The Battle of Birdham Bridge', which tells of the Spring v Langan rematch, endorses the worthiness of pugilistic heroes to be eulogised, albeit in the *Boxiana* style: 'Old Homer may prattle / Of many a battle / Betwixt Agamemnon and Troy's mighty King – / We'll sing of a fight / By two moderns of might – / The valorous *Langan* and Champion *Spring*'.[59] The humorous implication is that Egan's jargonic commentaries contain greater literary merit than Homeric 'prattle'. Egan later

---

58   Milo – Greek wrestler who was the most renowned athlete in antiquity (*EB*).
59   *Egan's Life in London, and Sporting Guide*, No. 28 (8 August 1824), p. 224.

published a piece of folkloric verse, by Charles Sloman, that contributed to the ring's heroic ideals:

THE PUGILIST. IN THE OSSIANIC STYLE.[60]
His eye is lightning, and seems to pierce the inmost recesses of the soul – his arm's the thunderbolt – it sends to the earth all 'gainst which it comes in contact – and now he's matched to fight, his heart beats high, e'en as the soldier's, 'fore he enters battle. He *trains*, that, like the tiger, he may be active as well as strong – the *Ring* is enter'd [...] eye meets eye – the arm is ready to defend its master, even as the battery defends the fortress – a *blow* is struck – 'tis *parried*, 'tis *return'd*, and now ensues a *rally*, then a close – they're down – and now they're seated on their *seconds'* knees, ready again for active contest – again they're face to face – the left leg forward, and the body bent – a *blow* is stricken – the force came from the *shoulder* – 'tis a decisive blow – he who receives it falls to earth, like the gnarled oak beneath the stroke of the woodman's axe. (*New Series Boxiana I*, p. 636)

Ultimately, Egan and Bee established a set of sporting legends whose exploits could be followed through pugilistic publications instead of ancient tomes, and many lower-class readers would be more inclined to identify with this jumble of fighting labourers and artisans rather than remote mythical figures.

The *Boxiana* series provided a rarefied atmosphere for pugilists to ascend to heroic status, and Egan successfully united artistic metaphors to pursue his egalitarian message that 'low' tradesmen could aspire to fame, and higher sensitivities, through pugilism. Considering the intense interest focussed on leading fighters it is, perhaps, a natural progression for the spheres of acting and Classicism to intertwine, and for such pugilists to assume the mantle of actor-hero. Egan suggests that this is a welcome form of escapism, providing they do not confuse their role with reality, and that the pity of 'gentlemen' is spurned:

The heroes of the fist want none of it, and feel that [...] they are playing a glorious part; and that the eyes of all that are *noble, heroic*, and *scientific* in the kingdom, are fixed on them; that the nation awaits the event of their glorious enterprise. (*Boxiana III*, p. 591)

---

60 Ossianic ballads – Irish and Scottish narrative poems, as rendered by James Macpherson (1736–96).

Typical Egan overstatement is not conducive to a level-headed approach but, as their journalistic champion, he emphasises: 'The hero, whose valour has gained his life a place in *Boxiana*, goes down to deathless renown' (pp. 591–2). Naturally, Egan does not understate the role of his own writing in perpetuating their talents.

Racial Neutrality: *Boxiana*'s Pugilistic Unity

In *Boxiana*'s impartial tone, black and Jewish fighters were acclaimed or censured according solely to their dexterity or conduct in pugilistic affairs. Egan defended the right of Mendoza to scale the heights of fame, again using planetary imagery:

> MENDOZA was considered one of the most elegant and scientific Pugilists in the whole race of Boxers, and might be termed a complete artist [...] He rose up like a phenomenon in the pugilistic hemisphere, and was a star of the first brilliancy. (*Boxiana I*, p. 255)

Later, Egan offers a flattering analogy: 'In his contests with *Bill Ward*, his excellence was so superior, that it was like a *diamond* in contact with paste' (p. 257). The public attitude may have been different; there was 'much rejoicing when Jackson relieved Mendoza of the title [1795...] and if Jackson's repertoire included grabbing Mendoza by his long hair [...] surely that served the Jew right'.[61] A rant by the character Tom Dashall in *Real Life in London* is certainly antagonistic: 'The Jews are altogether a set of traders [...] and establish a system of mischievous intercourse all over the country [...] The pliability of their consciences is truly wonderful' (pp. 308–9). But Egan permits Mendoza column space to challenge the intentions of the revered pugilistic figurehead, reproducing his plaintive letter:

---

61   Birley, *Sport and the Making of Britain*, p. 156.

> I waited on him, upbraided him [...] Jackson proposed to fight for one hundred
> guineas; and upon that sum being procured, declined fighting under five hundred
> guineas!! Here was courage! Here was consistency! Here was bottom! And yet Mr
> Jackson is a man of honour, AND OF HIS WORD!!! (*Boxiana I*, pp. 269–70)

This extract highlights the acrimonious nature of some published correspondence complete with claims and counter-claims. The histrionics of
Mendoza's protestations are accentuated by the intended irony of 'man of
honour', which resembles the Shakespearian rhetoric of Marcus Antonius
addressing the Roman citizens: 'For Brutus is an honourable man / [...]
And sure he is an honourable man' (*Julius Caesar*, III, ii. 84, 89, 101). Egan
cannot be accused of ignoring Mendoza's grievance, which is in defiance
of pugilism's internal social hierarchy where Jackson is portrayed as the
'fixed *star*', and other pugilists: 'the many satellites revolving around the
greater orb, deriving their principal vigour and influence from his domin-
ion' (*Boxiana I*, p. 287).

Pugilism acted as a levelling device, aiding cultural assimilation, and
Michael Scrivener stresses that although Mendoza may have been referred
to as 'the Jew', he was not caricatured. He argues that the national sport
'becomes Jewish, and the Jews become British. Mendoza's specific contributions to boxing – defensive tactics, scientific training, reliance on balance,
quickness and strategy [...] transform the sport, thus making a cultural
hybridization'. There is no sense of resentment in *Boxiana* commentaries
over any Jewish success, and it is certainly 'not counteracted by Gentile
retribution'.[62] Accordingly, Egan heaps praise on Abe Belasco, as well as the
much-vaunted Randall, in his account of their contest (30 September 1817):
'The spectators were lost in amazement; and their optics were completely
tired in watching the feints [...] contrasting the manoeuvres, stratagems,
and snares' (*Boxiana II*, p. 276). Egan also privileges the more discerning
section of spectators:

---

62   Michael Scrivener, 'British-Jewish Writing of the Romantic Era and the Problem
     of Modernity', in Sheila A Spector (ed.), *British Romanticism and the Jews: History,
     Culture, Literature* (Basingstoke: Palgrave Macmillan, 2002), pp. 160, 162.

> From the admirers of scientific efforts [...] who appreciate the advantages of *hitting*,
> and *getting away*, of *giving* instead of *receiving*, and of seeing a fight won without
> ferocity, gluttony, and copious *streams of claret*, the fight between RANDALL and
> *Belasco* has been pronounced one of the most perfect specimens. (p. 278)

Throughout the report, Belasco is portrayed as an almost equal contributor to the spectacle although, for Egan, Randall was always accorded
precedence.

Bee's overview of the Belasco brothers strikes a discordant note. After
questioning the extent of the stamina of 'the breed', he claims that 'they
make up for this physical defect by the perfections of *Art* [...] that serves
instead of *courage*' (*Boxiana IV*, p. 537). This is hardly an objective appraisal,
and the underhand connotations of this application of 'Art' is underscored
by Bee's assessment of their powers of '*Activity*', being a further area in
which the three Jewish fighters are portrayed as deficient: 'making up for
any deficit [...] by much *leariness*, or sly-fighting' (p. 537). This stereotypical
depiction of the 'crafty Jew' is atypical of *Boxiana* treatment, Egan preferring to advance the principal of an all-inclusive, unified 'race of Boxers'
(*Boxiana I*, p. 255).

Some spectator hostility was exhibited towards the black fighter
Molineaux, but pro-English partiality against any foreign challenger was
a fact. Arguably, Molineaux was subjected to no more antagonism than
the Venetian pretender of 1733. Egan was sympathetic, depicting an enterprising voyager:

> Unknown, unnoticed, unprotected, and uninformed, the brave MOLINEAUX
> arrived in England – descended from a warlike hero [...] he felt all the animating
> spirit of his courageous sire [...] in quest of glory and renown – the British nation,
> famed for deeds in arms, attracted his towering disposition like the daring adven-
> turer. (*Boxiana I*, pp. 360–1)

The tone implies that the nation should extend humanity and hospitality.
An earlier account also adopts this tack: 'It should have been considered,
that Molineaux was a stranger, that he stood indisputably a man of courage,
that he came to the contest unprotected and unsupported' (*Pancratia*, 1812,
p. 369). The fact that English possession of the pugilistic championship

was in jeopardy heightened sporting interest and emotion, not racial issues. Egan explains the significance of a newly discovered public concern over the 1810 fight, and the identification with Cribb: 'Even those persons who had hitherto passed over Boxing, in general, as beneath their notice, now seemed to take a lively interest [...] It appeared somewhat as a national concern, and ALL felt for the honour of his country' (*Boxiana I*, p. 401).

Egan certainly participated in the national attention devoted to 'the fate of their Champion' (p. 401), but genuine disappointment is evident when reporting bias against the American in the rematch:

> The *Black* had to contend against a prejudiced multitude; the pugilistic honour of the country was at stake, and the attempts of MOLINEAUX were viewed with jealousy, envy, and disgust – the national laurels to be borne away by a foreigner – the *mere* idea to an English breast was afflicting, and the *reality* could not be endured. (p. 367)

Pancratia suggested that Molineaux would have expected to encounter some spectator favouritism 'upon a principle of nationality', but as pugilism is 'merely' a sport, the animosity displayed 'was carried beyond all reasonable limits' (p. 370). Again, the principal concern is not Molineaux's colour but, rather, that he constitutes a threat to English dominance.

Egan later expresses the ambivalence of a society that accepted Molineaux amongst them and defended his right to challenge home-grown pugilists, but not to supplant them:

> With *togs* of the best quality and fashion, the *Man of Colour* soon appeared as a *blade* of the first magnitude, and many a proud CORINTHIAN felt no degradation in recognizing this renowned *milling* cove. To be the CHAMPION OF ENGLAND – he could not – *would not* be allowed! (*Boxiana II*, p. 334)

Egan emphasised that he provided 'an impartial statement of a contest' (p. 368), and was eager to chronicle the pugilistic skills of any fighter. The previously mentioned Richmond was also the recipient of generous praise in the pages of *Boxiana*, earning sufficient prestige to, like Jackson, offer sparring-room tuition: 'not only from his superior knowledge of boxing, but from his acquaintance with men and manners, and civility of deportment' (*Boxiana III*, p. 404). Some verses penned by Bob Gregson (who had been 'unanimously voted [...] to the honourable situation of poet-laureate to the Prize Ring', *Book of Sports*, p. 66) did contain inflammatory sentiments. His crambo, entitled 'British Lads and Black Millers', claimed that 'every slave' who arrives in Britain's 'garden of freedom' is permitted to 'impose' and 'pollute' native soil (*Boxiana I*, p. 358). However, Egan's tone is generally one of reconciliation and pugilistic camaraderie. Brailsford places the negative comments directed at black and Jewish fighters in context, stating that these were less malicious than those 'directed at politicians or the royal family': 'The typical attitude was patronising and condescending rather than antagonistic'.[63]

Evidence of Egan's Irish blood and sympathies can be discerned in his anxiety to direct attention to incidents where Irish fighters were maligned. It did not require the occasion of a major prizefight for English antipathy to manifest itself, Egan irately describing the reception accorded to Donnelly during a benefit night (6 April 1819) as 'rather *foul*': 'It was very unlike the usual *generosity* of John Bull towards a stranger – It was not *national* – but savoured something like *prejudice*' (*Boxiana III*, p. 79). But, here again, animosity was borne predominantly from concern over the Irishman's fighting prowess, and Egan underscored the combination of resentment and overwhelming interest when reporting Donnelly's 1819 fight with Oliver: 'The English amateurs viewed him as a powerful opponent [and...] jealous for the reputation of the "Prize Ring", *clenched* their fists in opposition, whenever his growing fame was *chaunted*' (p. 82). Unsurprisingly, Bee did not share Egan's respect for Irish fighting qualities, and he dismissed the pretensions of another touring fighter, Halton, in terms that evoke the acting platform: 'he should not have come out on the *London boards*, if he meant to preserve his celebrity' (*Boxiana IV*, p. 545). Generally, it was an amalgamation of apprehension, at an interloper's power, and a patriotic protectiveness towards their representative that generated public bitterness.

In such contests, it is only the challengers' foreignness that provokes partisanship, not racist contempt. English newcomers attempting to break into the established prizefight circuit could also encounter resentment,

---

63   Brailsford, 'Morals and Maulers: the Ethics of Early Pugilism', p. 138.

even future 'greats': '[7 January 1805] CRIB, being a stranger, had to contend against much ill-usage' (*Boxiana I*, p. 391). Overall, I would say that, despite his obvious relish in describing Irish prizefighting successes, Egan viewed himself as: 1st) A member of the Fancy; 2nd) A Londoner; and 3rd) An Irishman (whether true-born or antecedently). Irrespective of this speculative order of allegiance, Egan does appear to have observed an explicitly stated desire: 'BOXIANA will do its duty [...] neither colour, strength, patronage, or any other consideration, shall tempt it to swerve from IMPARTIALITY' (p. 449).

The Human Equivalent of the Cockpit

The notion of a large middle-class following regarding the pugilistic ring as a form of human cockpit is compatible with pugilism's class-driven hierarchical structure. Wealthy patrons and promoters funded, and exercised a controlling influence over, the matching of opposing working-class fighters for the entertainment of a far from decorous crowd whose baying support was predominantly dictated by wagers. In this atmosphere, prizefighters might be regarded no higher than animals as a means of financial gain, or temporary diversion. A cynical interpretation might be that naïve and needy pugilists were manipulated to provide a vicarious form of entertainment for the massed spectators. In this possessive environment, and lust for spectacle, any eligible pugilists 'were soon pitted, like two GAME COCKS' (*Boxiana I*, p. 94). Vasey claimed the driving force behind this manipulation, and debasement, of fighting men were the 'Gamesters', who permitted 'the heroes of the Ring' no more influence on their destinies 'than two dogs' (*RIPM*, p. 13). Again, this emphasises a persistent thread – gambling dictated the codification of pugilism.

Egan turned to the cockpit motif when describing the emergence, into the ring, of Young Dutch Sam:

> [April 1829] The anxious moment had now arrived, and all the *peepers* were on the stretch to view the *condition* of the men. On *peeling*, Sam appeared as fine as a star [...] laughing and full of confidence. In short, SAM might be compared to a handsome game *cock*, crowing almost to himself, that victory was in his grasp. (*Book of Sports*, p. 200)

The comparison is merely an effective method of conveying the vitality and confidence of a pugilist in prime condition, but the sense of performance remains, Egan capturing the anticipation of an audience straining to see the action. The supporters' delight is possibly a superficial emotion that would not vary whether they were watching a backed racehorse or cockerel. Egan also referred to the dog-pit as 'this Dog-Fanciers' theatre' (*Life in London*, p. 225), and the opinion that moments of great sporting spectacle were to be viewed there is communicated by the reaction of those unable to gain admittance: 'numerous persons went away *grumbling*, as if they had lost the finest sight in the world' (p. 224).

Livestock resemblances appear less demeaning when studying a piece by John Hamilton Reynolds (1794–1852), entitled 'The Cockpit Royal', originally published as one of 'Edward Herbert's Letters to the Family of the Powells' (*The London Magazine*, November 1822). It was reproduced by Egan as 'The Cockpit', the venue being described as 'a large, lofty, circular building with seats rising, as in an amphitheatre' (*Book of Sports*, p. 150). The article continues in its general aggrandisement of the surrounding scene comparable to a Roman coliseum, and the appearance of the first bird (red and black) is treated with the reverential awe befitting a renowned gladiator:

> His neck arose out of the bag, snakelike, – terrible – as if it would stretch upward to the ceiling; his body followed, compact, strong, and beautiful [...] His large vigorous beak showed aquiline, eagle-like; and his black dilating eyes took in all around him, and shone so intensely brilliant, that they looked like jewels. Their light was that of the thoughtful, sedate, and savage courage. (p. 152)

The bird is described in masculine terms throughout (never referred to as 'it'), and the expansive style of this awe-filled description is drastically reduced for the second (yellow) bird: 'seemingly rather slight, but elastic and muscular. He was restless at the sight of his antagonist, but quite silent' (p. 153).

Both birds are ascribed with human-like sensibilities of trepidation, resolve, and arrogance, and the fight itself forms a dramatic 'act' in this sporting study:

> The first terrific dart into attitude was indeed strikingly grand and beautiful – and the wary sparring, watching, dodging, for the first cut, was extremely curious. They were beak-point to beak-point, until they dashed up in one tremendous flirt – mingling their powerful rustling wings and nervous heels in one furious confused mass. The leap, – the fire, – the passion [...] The parting was another kind of thing every way. I can compare the sound of the first flight to nothing less than that of a wet umbrella forced suddenly open. The separation was death like. The yellow [...] staggered out of the close – drooping – dismantled – bleeding [...] The brave bird thus killed, dropped at once from the 'gallant bearing and proud mien', to the relaxed, draggled, motionless object that lay in bleeding ruin on the mat. (p. 153)

The sparring replicates the opening moments in pugilistic encounters, and the triumphant bird's reaction is portrayed in terms resembling the emotions of a leading prizefighter, gladiator, or even principal actor, puffing out their chest in a state of post-performance, adrenalin-fuelled vigour: 'The victor cock was carried by me [...] slightly scarred, – but evidently made doubly fierce and muscular by the short encounter' (p. 153).

The piece exudes the admiration inspired by brave competitors, in whatever guise. In this respect, the confusion of fighting man and beast is more palatable, and Reynolds's observations on subsequent bouts are insightful and poignant: 'The cocks showed all the obstinate courage, weariness, distress, and breathlessness, which mark the struggles of experienced pugilists. I saw [...] the tongue palpitate – the wing drag on the mat. I noticed the legs tremble [...] the eye grow dim' (p. 153). A sense of compassion is discernible, but the underlying feeling remains that both sports are simply satisfying an innate clamour for spectacle and gambling thrills. This base desire accentuates the unifying properties of sporting events, providing common ground for divergent social strands.

Theatricality, and Re-packaging the Sport for Wider Appeal

The entertainment principle attached to pugilism is reinforced by sparring bouts that encapsulated the spirit of display. Egan reproduced the
promotional placard for one particular benefit night (8 November 1819):

> OWEN, the FANCY does invite,
> T' his BENEFIT, on Monday night:
> At the MINOR THEATRE, near the STRAND,
> To view the *Movements*, prime and grand.
> [...]
> SEVEN's the TIME, the Lads engage,
> In a Rop'd Ring upon the Stage;
> Roars of laughter, fun and raillery,
> From the Boxes, Pit, and Gallery.
> Then come along, be not too late,
> Or OWEN can't accommodate.
> (*Boxiana III*, p. 58)

It is evident that a diverse array of spectators are welcome, but the advertisement's tack does not appear to extend beyond Fancy circles. When more
general public displays were initiated, theatres were deemed apt venues to
demonstrate the finesse and showmanship that pugilism permitted. Some
considered a stage-based philosophy an integral part of the nation's genetic
makeup, and this melodramatic bent is underscored by Egan's description
of Thurtell's final plea to the jurors at his trial:

> '*Gentlemen I have done. I look with confidence to your decision*'.
>   Thurtell pronounced this last sentence in the most emphatic manner. He raised
> his eyes to Heaven, and extended his arms a little, then drew them back and pressed
> his hands closely to his heart. (*Trial of Thurtell*, p. 86)

Egan's interview in Thurtell's cell (4 December 1823), sees the prisoner
'fashionably attired in a blue coat with gilt buttons; a yellow waistcoat [...
His irons] tied up with a silk handkerchief' (*Trial of Thurtell Appendix*,
p. 27). Even when facing the hangman, Thurtell is preoccupied with vanity
and ostentation. Overall, theatricality formed a prominent accessory to
nineteenth-century society.

In the '*Boxiana* period', pugilistic demonstrations appear to have been well attended and universally popular: 'In the summer of 1823, RANDALL sparred at the *Theatre*, Margate, to overflowing houses' (*Boxiana IV*, p. 416), and Egan emphasised the parallels between theatrical and sporting performances:

> [Davis v Ned Turner, June 1819] *John Palmer*, a distinguished actor, felt so much embarrassment in being called to rehearse a part before GARRICK, that his power of utterance totally forsook him for a time, so much was he overawed [...] It might have operated in a like manner with *Davis* when he came into contact with the *darting* eagle-eye of TURNER. (*Boxiana III*, p. 222)

For the public to read Hazlitt's 'The Fight' and then be presented with the opportunity to view those very fighters recreating events must have been an intriguing prospect. With coarse badinage, bloody wounds, and fevered gambling expunged from the simulation, it is evident that the performance was rendered an inoffensive spectacle for a diverse audience. In April 1822 (two months after publication of Hazlitt's essay), the enterprising manager of the Royalty Theatre engaged Neate and Hickman to '*perform*' to a 'mixed' and 'genteel' audience (*Boxiana IV*, p. 94). Unsurprisingly, Hickman proved reluctant to faithfully reproduce the most unflattering aspects of his defeat, but the two men received, what Bee considered, generous salaries of 'twelve sovereigns a week', which was 'amply compensated by the great accession of persons' (p. 95).

Away from this controlled environment, it is evident that the performance aspect featured heavily in major prizefights, and Bee claims that watching crowds would sometimes include individuals seeking to gain insights: '[Hickman v Oliver, June 1821] It was a fine *study* for an artist, and it was a complete *picture* for an actor; and we were glad to witness some first-rate performers viewing' (*Boxiana IV*, p. 169). In much early-nineteenth-century theatre, a plain, unbroken performance of a play was not routine, and an evening programme often included at least one side attraction. Pugilistic set-pieces in productions based on *Life in London* characters could be considered as contextually justified, but they might easily have been inserted arbitrarily. Theatrical entertainment focused on variety and spectacle, and this is imitated in Egan's build-up to a prizefight and the performances of some pugilists. Unlike the grandiosity of the sport's art-world connections, Egan could not realistically claim that fighters were possessed by a fiery muse when entering the ring. Some form of role-playing was often present but this could merely be construed as flamboyance, arrogance, or authorial attempts to enliven reality. Egan argued that performers from the worlds of sport and the Arts, and even military leaders, were unified by baser mutual interests: 'The general and the admiral, the poet and the painter, and the architect and the sculptor are all actuated by one powerful *stimulus* – the love of fame and the sweets of reward' (*Boxiana III*, p. 5). Given the financial and social incentives for pugilists to generate interest in their contests, it was certainly not 'art for art's sake'.

One form of pugilistic 'acting' which was not condoned was manipulation of the result, and Egan was swift to spotlight any hint of a rigged fight. In circumstances where hefty sums of money had been wagered, play-acting was not appreciated. In December 1817 'Jack the *butcher*' is mocked for acting 'intimidated, as if a cannon ball was coming at his *nob*, when Burke merely *touched* him'. The encounter proceeds thus: 'Loud murmurs. Much coaxing [...] He now turned to, planted some good hits – exchanged several sharp blows – had the best of it – got his man down undermost – and then finished in style by *giving in!!!*' (*Boxiana II*, p. 415). Such occurrences coincide with the motives of some characters in Dickens's novels which raised 'unsettling questions about the morality of acting by implying that role-paying is not gesture but imposture'.[64] Despite the controversial circumstances of the above fight, it provided another entertaining episode.

This sense of pantomime is a further device that engenders universal appeal; an area where realism was suspended. Here, Egan deploys hyperbolical flourish to conjure an engaging image: '[Sutton's] head seemed to leave his shoulders for nearly a quarter of a yard, and [...] exhibited the rapid twirl of a *Bologna* [sausage]' (p. 120). Seemingly in a playful mood for his report of Randall v tailor Wood (4 October 1819), Egan records an early shock for the favourite: 'the Nonpareil came in most unexpectedly for a *ground suit*'. This knockdown results in the tailoring fraternity being 'as much up in the *stirrups*, as when a sudden *general mourning* comes upon

64   Schlicke, *Dickens and Popular Entertainment*, p. 45.

them' (*Boxiana III*, p. 201). The jocular suggestion of the profession being excited by a surge in funeral business is followed by a comical account of Randall's revival:

> [Randall] commenced his *shower of hail-stones* upon the nob of his opponent [...] The *fight was all out* of Wood in an instant after this tempest, and, in the terror of the moment, he lustily roared out Murder!! and most piteously placed himself under the wing of the umpire, who smilingly told Wood not to be alarmed, as the contest was at an end. (p. 202)

The subsequent scene sees some 'Thimbleonians' go 'strutting up' to remonstrate over the verdict:

> The umpire's 'potent arm' soon *disposed* of this lot, after the manner of an auctioneer [...] One of the '*needle squad*', who had taken too much '*Perry*' felt so alarmed on reaching the ground, that he literally *crawled on all fours* out of the ring. (p. 202)

The hailstone reference aptly communicates the inflicted barrage, and the slapstick of the tailors' drunken, hopeless defiance eliminates any hint of serious violence. Another particularly reluctant competitor is a fighter named Matthews: 'after the manner of an intimidated youth on his first going into the water, that makes a sudden plunge to get out of his *misery*, [he] rushed in upon his opponent'. This unenthusiastic manoeuvre was countered 'so hard' that it 'drew the *claret* copiously', and the novice's ensuing dismay concludes the scene: 'the ghastly look he assumed, accompanied with such marks of horror [...] would have been a new idea for the *climax* of KEAN'S *Sir Edward Mortimer*' (p. 199).[65]

Even when a gambling scam is suspected, Egan could cloak outrage in resigned sarcasm. Jack Carter 'fought' a declining Molineaux (near Banbury, 2 April 1813), and Egan's heavy irony indicates that the two 'performers' should be regarded disdainfully: 'The articles were read [...] it stated the winner was to have a purse of 100 guineas – when CARTER stepped up,

---

65 Kean played the character, Mortimer, in *The Iron Chest* (first performed at Drury Lane, 1795). This play was written by George Colman the younger, playwright and theatre manager (1762–1836), *DNB*.

enquiring what the "LOSER WAS TO HAVE!!!" *Richmond*, who was his second, gnashed his teeth, and shrugged up his shoulders' (*Boxiana I*, p. 454). One can imagine the bemused second rolling his eyes heavenwards as he turns towards ringside spectators in much the same manner as a mock appeal for commiseration to a theatre audience. When the fight commences Egan conveys a sense of the ludicrous:

> Never was such a *set-to* witnessed; one '*was afraid, and the other dared not*', and two minutes were trifled away in this sort of *caricaturing*, when CARTER touched *Molineaux* on the mouth, who *genteely* returned it [...] It would be absurd to detail by way of *rounds* any more of this [...Molineaux] declared that CARTER '*had bit him on the neck!*' [...] It was with great difficulty *Joe Ward* [umpire] could persuade him that it was the *knuckles* of CARTER, and not his *mouth*. (p. 455)

Egan laments of the 'wretched' Molineaux, '*Could* HE have thus degenerated!!!', before conveying the encounter's finale:

> Twenty-five rounds occurred, in which *coaxing, persuading, drumming*, and *threatening*, were obliged to be resorted to, to make these – (what term, Reader, you please to call them, for BOXIANA feels at a loss for an adequate expression) to perform *something like* fighting. But the grand climax of the performance was left for CARTER to enact, *who*, when *Molineaux* was completely *told out* – overcome, perhaps, with the *sensibility* of his drooping antagonist – *swooned away* in all the style of a modern fair lady. (p. 455)

There is no attempt to conceal or exonerate the sham nature of the episode, which constitutes an example where sporting entertainment is 'associated with exploitation, not amusement'.[66] Egan's mock incredulity at the farcical contest is accentuated by treble exclamation marks, and the suggestion that this is a parody of a prizefight.

Any revamping of pugilism's representation as a form of popular entertainment could lead to the more knockabout exhibitions being classified under the umbrella of circus performance. This form of pugilism had the potential to boast the same raw ingredients (variety, spectacle, and novelty). In fact, such exhibitions did transfer to the circus, such as at the

---

66   Schlicke, *Dickens and Popular Entertainment*, p. 139.

Royal Amphitheatre in 1823. The advertising was eager to emphasise that the sparring would contain 'nothing offensive to delicacy', the pugilistic exhibition serving as 'an interlude': 'Such alternation of different kinds of display in consecutive scenes [...] was wholly conventional, although it was more usual to employ the clown'. The transposable nature of clown and pugilist corresponds to the playful *Boxiana* sections where Egan exploits the absurdity of a situation rather than railing against misdemeanours. Egan regularly privileged the entertainment principle, appearing to fall in with Dickens's position; preferring 'the circus and the theatre, in which didacticism was conspicuously absent'.[67]

When denuded of the gore and gaming elements (and illegality), pugilism could be freely promoted as an entertainment that did not offend refined sensibilities. A preoccupation with protecting a possible female contingent can be viewed as another instance of class differentiation amongst the spectators. Lower-class women were unlikely to be perturbed by violence, and when Egan tells of the coarse behaviour of low-life fraudsters (*Life in London*) he is reporting traits commonplace to either sex. It was the more refined female readers who reviewers of *Tom Crib's Memorial* (1819) believed would be excluded by the flash language employed: '*La Belle Assemblée* (April 1819) announced: "This is a work that is by no means suited to female taste", it being written [...] "in a string of slang expressions".[68] In 'The Fight', Hazlitt pre-empted his tale with a plea for the 'Ladies' to 'notice the exploits of the brave' and to 'listen with subdued air and without shuddering'.[69] It is debatable whether it is his representation of physical violence or the sight of an occasional flash word that would be deemed so repugnant, but the phraseology of his appeal evokes historic images of a medieval tournament.

Presumably, if noblewomen had deigned to view armed competition, and confer their colours to a favoured combatant, then that air of spectacle and chivalry could be replicated in major pugilistic contests:

---

67 Ibid., pp. 179, 216.
68 *British Satire, 1785–1840*, ed. by Strachan and others, V, ed. by Jane Moore, p. 186.
69 *The Selected Writings of William Hazlitt*, ed. by Wu, IX, p. 61.

> With what an air would our boxers strike, did they know that bright eyes were looking on them! How delicately would they '*peel*'! and with what an elegant indifference would they come to '*the scratch*'! The consciousness in question would generate the finest feelings […] It is quite overpowering to think of it – the awful pause – the steadfast eye – the advance – the retreat – the increased motion of the hands – the beautiful play of the muscles about the shoulders – the feint – the preparation to parry – the FIRST BLOW! It is, indeed, a grand sight: it is ever grand and awful; but with thousands of fair ones for spectators, how charming it might become! (*Book of Sports*, p. 120)

This anonymous writer emphasises the spectacle, and mischievously suggests 'They would get accustomed to it in a shorter time than to port-wine' (p. 120). In 1841, Dowling latched on to tournament notions in a bid to revive the sport's reputation: 'superiority of character in the mail clad knights over the shirtless pugilists was owing to situation only; their souls were wrought of the same stuff' (*Fistiana*, p. 12). For Dowling, the essential chivalric principles were already in place and merely required a little emphasis in order for the 'parallel' to inveigle prospective female spectators or readers. The piece in Egan's book stated that a tournament was merely a more 'ostentatious and imposing' form of sparring, pugilism being the credible pursuit:

> The spectators of the Fives court would soon be disgusted, were they to witness so barbarous a proceeding […] two men mounted and armed with spits, each in a sort of cupboard of steel, galloping towards each other, for the sole purpose of the one pushing the other off his horse! The thing is really ridiculous. (*Book of Sports*, p. 122)

Tournament imagery was allied with pugilistic scenes by different writers, but the main thrust of their argument appears that they believed objections to their sport, on the grounds of barbarity, unfounded. Bee also published an Edinburgh correspondent's analogy that is comparable to the teasing 'port-wine' reference:

> Pugilism may be likened unto smoking and Blackwood's Magazine. We at first fight a little shy to them, and are a little blind to their inestimable qualities, but no sooner have we given our acquaintance with them fair play, than their native excellence dawns upon our dazzled daylights. (*Annals of Sporting V*, p. 197)

There is no hint of sexual bias, with a message that if people attended a pugilistic event they may eventually share some of the Fancy's enthusiasm for the sport.

Notwithstanding this encouragement, one ringside reporter's experience voices a harsh reality:

> Positions so close to the ring were not for the squeamish. Charles Knight [1791–1873], the well-known publisher [...] tells us in his memoirs: 'The only exhibition of pugilism I ever saw [...] was on Maidenhead Thicket, where the renowned Pierce Egan, with a considerate regard for a brother of the Press, got me a good place, out of which I escaped as fast as I could when I saw Young Dutch Sam fall across the ropes with a broken arm'.[70]

The physicality of pugilism could not be conveniently disregarded, but a debateable point is whether 'polite society' abhorred or secretly relished the feature.

Regarding pugilism in the late nineteenth century, now involving gloved fighters, Bernard Shaw termed this predilection as 'pugnacity', summarising it thus: 'Sense of danger, dread of danger, impulse to batter and destroy what threatens and opposes'. He then suggests that were this element to be removed interest would wane: 'if a famous pugilist were to assure the public that a blow delivered with a boxing glove could do no injury [...] the sport would instantly lose its following'.[71] Despite this view, the sport offered a more humane display than public executions, which had not been 'loaded with abuse, though *these* spectacles, [are] destitute of the animating and comparatively harmless character of a fair fistic combat' (*Fistiana*, p. 8). It might be considered that, for persons of every class, prizefighting could act as a safety-valve. An activity that provided diverting spectacle could assist the sublimation process.

---

70 Reid, *Bucks and Bruisers*, p. 92.
71 'Muffles' (gloves) had been a regular feature, for sparring and exhibitions, in Egan's era. Their mandatory use was initiated in 1867 when the eighth Marquis of Queensbury gave his name to a new set of rules which included three-minute rounds and other 'innovations' that placed an emphasis on skill rather than 'brute force'. Birley, *Sport and the Making of Britain*, p. 286. Bernard Shaw, 'Note on Modern Prizefighting', *Cashel Byron's Profession* (London: Constable, 1950), pp. 249, 246.

The concept that Dickens 'greatly enjoyed unpolished art' is one that can be extended to Egan.[72] Although mock-heroic associations have been discussed, it is the unrefined élan of such entertainments as circus, pantomime, and variety stage-play that coincided with the spectacle of prizefighting. One common factor is that the *Boxiana* style deployed these elements to promote the visualisation process. Pugilistic events were unequivocally 'unpolished', but the *Boxiana* style rendered the prizefight commentary a literary, and dramatic, art form.

72   Schlicke, *Dickens and Popular Entertainment*, p. 146.

CHAPTER 4

The Nation – Military and Moral

> Pugilism is in perfect unison with the feeling of Englishmen.
>
> — *Boxiana I*, p. 3

Egan's extravagant promotion of pugilism as a sporting panacea, significantly contributing to a British superiority in military prowess and philosophical enlightenment, is a theme consistently pursued in the *Boxiana*
series. His is not an isolated voice, Jon Bee stating: 'the *national sports* of
a people cannot be too sacredly guarded, by those who wish to preserve
[...] its proverbial character for real *generosity*, manly *feeling*, and true *courage*' (*Boxiana IV*, p. v). Prominent supporters, such as politician William
Windham (1750–1810), could be relied on for similar nationalistic rhetoric:
'True courage [...] does not arise from [...] the mere *beating* or being *beaten*
but from the SENTIMENTS excited by the contemplation and cultivation
of such practices' (*Book of Sports*, pp. 11–12). When, in an attempt to assert
some 'middle class morality', a group of abolitionists unsuccessfully argued
for a ban on bear and bull baiting, and cock-fighting (in a parliamentary
vote of 1802), Windham, with a certain effrontery in victory, proceeded
to imply that 'bulls enjoyed being baited' and that 'the Jacobins and the
Methodists (by teaching the lower orders to read) were encouraging much
less socially acceptable habits'.[1]

---

[1]   An Old Etonian Whig MP, Windham had occupied the position of Secretary at
War (1794–1801) and was one of the foremost apologists for pugilism. Birley, *Sport
and the Making of Britain*, p. 157.

A Fancy contributor, Tom Reynolds, claimed that the influence of prizefighting extended beyond the inculcation of martial hardiness: 'exhibitions of this kind have their good effects, which can be traced to us as a nation, and, independent of fighting, influence other actions' (*Book of Sports*, p. 171). Egan does not curtail his recommendation to pugilism alone, and includes: 'all those manly amusements, both in the environs of the Metropolis, and in the country, which strengthen the sinews, summon up the generous blood, and characterise the English-man above the inhabitants of every other nation' (p. 384). The stirring nature of this pronouncement leans towards militaristic benefits, a tack pursued in one dedication to the Duke of Wellington which, essentially, replicates the opening salvoes of *Boxiana II* and *III*:

> [Pugilism] teaches men to applaud generosity, to acquire notions of honour; nobleness of disposition; and greatness of mind: to bear hardships without murmurs [...] to *punish* foul play; to decide impartially; and not to look on and see wrong done to any person. It also teaches men to discountenance *treachery*; not to *stab* persons in the dark; and to become horror-struck at ASSASSINATION. (*New Series Boxiana II*, 1829, pp. iv–v)

Egan consistently maintained that the advantages of pugilism to the nation were manifold, and there is more than a suggestion that the sport was quintessentially British and one that bonded fellow countrymen whilst promoting laudable principles: 'never let Britons be ashamed of [...] a SCIENCE that not only adds generosity to their disposition – humanity to their conduct – but courage to their national character' (*Boxiana I*, p. 2). This supports the theory that 'sportsmanship' was regarded as a 'deeply entrenched ethic', an almost innate national trait that 'derived from custom not instruction'.[2]

An unsophisticated concept of a unified nation inspired by, and following, a civilising pugilistic banner is problematic however. Firstly, the alternating use of the words 'British' and 'English' gives an inkling of the confusion over exactly which 'breed of valiant men' (*Boxiana II*, p. iv) identify with

2   Langford, *Englishness Identified*, p. 152.

the pastime. This is exacerbated by regional rivalries and prejudices, as well as antipathies towards certain classes, or what were perceived as effete generic types. The much vaunted Fancy embodied the contradictory facets of the ring. Egan advocated physical and mental improvement as well as propriety and adherence to the law, but proceeded to celebrate the dissolute, bordering on riotous, behaviour of his *Life in London* 'heroes' as well as underplaying the seamy side of pugilistic affairs. A dichotomy develops, pitting the martial and moral benefits gleaned from pugilism's training and codes of conduct against its unwholesome gambling and drinking culture (as well as the criminal element sports gatherings attracted). Typically, prizefighters could be generous, law-abiding citizens, but still succumb to temptation. Egan sympathised with vulnerable men who, like Molineaux, were inveigled 'into all the glorious confusion of *larks* and *sprees*' (*Boxiana I*, p. 368); 'even the *iron*-like frame of the *Black* seriously felt the dilapidating effects of intemperance' (*Boxiana II*, p. 334). Seemingly incompatible lifestyles highlight a theme of 'Discipline v Dissipation'.

The divergent motivations and language of Egan's 'Sporting World' and mainstream society was not merely a Fancy / non-Fancy division. Contradictions to his putative pugilistic utopia can be found within the *Boxiana* series itself, as well as the overt counter-arguments pushed by the sport's denigrators. Amongst his invective against the sport's damaging moral effects, William Vasey concedes: 'it is to me tolerably evident that something wondrously enticing exists in Pugilism' (*RIPM*, pp. 3–4), before depicting the daily engrossment of its followers:

> When they rise, they think of it; at their work, it forms the topic of their conversation [...and] in the evening, they assemble at the corners of the streets to discuss the beauty of such an attitude, the expertness of such a stop, or the force of such a blow; from thence they adjourn to the tap-room [...] where they try their skill, or consume their time in reading accounts of some pugilistic contest, and in settling their wagers [...] and it is neither extravagant nor unreasonable to suppose that when they retire to their slumbers they will dream of it – that the roped ring, the half-naked and blood-stained combatants, the thousands of spectators, and the loud and furious uproar should continue to dwell in their fancies in all their original character and expression. (*RIPM*, p. 4)

It is the state of utter absorption to which Vasey objects, stating that 'philosophy teaches' the population a 'nobler course': 'There are civil, moral, and religious obligations, imperative on our attention' (p. 4). In fact, this latter point constitutes an area of common ground with the pugilistic chroniclers, who remonstrated that such 'obligations' were an integral part of a sporting outlook. The pugilistic mindset they portrayed embraces these finer sensibilities, which offer a means of shielding against the perceived threat of a national descent into 'foreign effeminacy'.

Reporting on a sporting dinner (December 1818), Egan recorded: 'the chairman, in a manly style of eloquence, expatiated upon the advantages of scientific pugilism, in a national point of view, towards *flooring Dandyism*, and *levelling* that sort of effeminacy which was making such rapid progress' (*Boxiana III*, pp. 187–8). This theme of a 'degenerating' influence is still evident in 1841 when Dowling claims that it was the decline of pugilism that had contributed to the 'growth of luxury' and 'selfishness' (*Fistiana*, p. 2). The remedy advocated is unsurprising: 'even if boxing were the low and barbarous practice some have represented [...] some such stimulus is absolutely necessary to maintain an average degree of manliness amongst the rising generation' (p. 11).

Egan's 1821 dedication of *Boxiana III*, to the Marquis of Worcester, centres upon the contribution made by prizefighting to martial prowess, and dangers posed by its discontinuance:

> It is of the very last importance to ENGLAND as a nation, my Lord, that not one particle of this real greatness should ever be *frittered* away from *squeamishness* of DISPOSITION or EFFEMINACY [...] in order to prevent a WELLINGTON [...] from experiencing the want of a body of brave men to direct. (*Boxiana III*, p. v)

These are subjective viewpoints and, the potential for promoting military hardiness aside, pugilism's supposed position as a nationally exclusive unifying pursuit that fostered sound moral practice, and decried indulgence, can be contested.

As well as the overt rhetoric, there were subtler modes of influencing public opinion, *Boxiana*-style descriptions using figures that injected an element of audience recognition. A prime example of the ring transformed into an imaginary field of battle occurs in Egan's account of Randall v

Belasco (1817), as he describes the manoeuvrings: '[NAPOLEON] never looked upon the advantages of a *move* with greater interest – nor did the competent WELLINGTON ever attempt to *frustrate* any grand design, with more zeal, judgement, and anxiety'. The outcome allowed Egan to extend the metaphor: 'Fifth. – It was now clearly seen that Randall was the great Captain, and he *out-generalled* his opponent with all the accomplishment of the Art of War' (*Boxiana II*, p. 276). Egan heaped further praise on 'the Nonpareil' in a more playful piece:

> In a *twenty-four feet ring*, a better GENERAL, or a more *consummate* tactician is not to be seen. Judgement and decision are to be witnessed in all his movements. His NOB is *screwed* on properly – his OGLES are like two experienced *aides-de-camp* ready to scour the enemy's lines on the slightest hint from the commanding officer – his HEART is in the right place – his PINS are after the manner of a well-disciplined charger, cool and collected, to take advantage in the most prompt style of the disorder of the scene before him. (*Boxiana III*, pp. 211–12)

A comparison with a relatively orthodox fight commentary is interesting:

> [Eales v Hall, 29 October 1818] Hall's backers were electrified – astonished – nay, more, confounded. Their *chaffers* were dry – they could not speak – but viewed in *mournful silence* this unexpected change in war. The line of demarcation was now broken, and the enemy was conquering the country. (p. 129)

On this occasion the betting agitation is abruptly replaced by the figurative action of troops swarming over a bulwark, the formal phraseology supplying the tone of a battlefield dispatch.

Martial references are a consistent feature amidst the various fight commentaries, such as the opening of the Shelton v Burns contest (16 March 1819): 'Burns bored in upon Shelton with all the confidence and weight of a *man of war* running down a brig' (*Boxiana III*, p. 304). And, describing Glossop v Manning (1824): 'It was *broadside* for *broadside*'.[3] In 1820, 'Mr M' equated sport and war as he enthused over the thirst for prizefighting news:

---

3   *Egan's Life in London, and Sporting Guide*, No. 8 (21 March 1824), p. 61.

'The daily public papers, the mirrors of public taste, constantly detail every information on the subject, – of events in preparation, the time of action, the state of the bets
[...] whilst the bulletin of the *battle* itself, and of the conduct of the *warriors*, equals,
in length and accuracy, the Gazette of the battle of Waterloo'. (*Boxiana III*, p. 579)

Egan's account of the combat between Jem Hawkins and Paddy O' Leary
(28 August 1820) underscores the parallel: '[Hawkins] viewed his opponent
with all the *accuracy* and *coolness* [...] to plant his hits with effect, as the
Duke of *Wellington's* penetrating eye scours over the map of an enemy's
country to find out its vulnerable points' (p. 426). An 'amateur' account
of Randall v Martin included: 'Their eyes kept in parallel, marching and
countermarching to prevent surprise. It reminded *military* amateurs [...] of
Wellington and Marmont, before the glorious *mill* at Salamanca' (*Boxiana
IV*, pp. 397–8).[4] The incongruous terming of a major battle as a 'glorious
mill', exhibits a romantic perception of warfare, focusing on laurels to be
gained rather than bloodshed. And, Egan's summary of Tom Cannon's
brief career is couched in terms of a successful battleground operative:
'The *Popper* [...] has proved himself a CANNON; and, indeed, produced
a *loud* report [...] *hit* numbers of persons much *harder* than they expected,
and left the field of battle with the proud title of CONQUEROR affixed'
(*New Series Boxiana II*, p. 25). On this occasion, Egan benefited from a
particularly opportune surname, Cannon unsurprisingly being 'designated
as THE GREAT GUN OF WINDSOR' (p. 4).

Transferring Sporting Attributes into Martial Combat

The association of a pugilist with the principle of a representative warrior
(champion) defending national honour can be traced in eighteenth-century
writings. Christopher Johnson focuses on an apposite term, 'championism',

---

4   In July 1812, Wellington defeated French forces (commanded by Marmont) at
     Salamanca, Spain.

stating that its use predated the *OED*'s first recorded occurrence, and endorses the pivotal concept that it 'clearly implies both martial prowess and moral virtue'.[5] Paul Whitehead, in his epic poem *The Gymnasiad, or Boxing Match* (1744), compared the pugilistic hero to a royal champion defending his monarch against any foreign menace: 'And what *Frenchman* would not tremble more at the puissant Arm of a BROUGHTON, than at the ceremonious Gauntlet'. This is comparable with the *Boxiana I* record of the Venetian challenger's defeat, when the 'blow in the stomach carried too much of the English *rudeness* for him to bear' (p. 25).

The threat posed by foreign pugilistic challengers amplified general fears concerning invasion and effeminate degeneracy, which engendered a degree of nationalistic unity. The Venetian's challenge is couched in archetypal terms: 'he *threw down the glove*' (*Boxiana I*, p. 22). For Molineaux's contest with Cribb the language speaks in terms of a martial meeting of champions:

> The towering and restless ambition of MOLINEAUX induced him to [...] erect his hostile standard among the British heroes, and who dared the most formidable of her chiefs to the chance of war; when it was reserved for the subject of this memoir to chastise the bold intruder, in protecting the national practice and honour of the country. (p. 387)

There is a gladiatorial feel of the pugilist as a national representative with greater issues at stake than personal renown: '[it was] by no means unusual to imagine the figure of the boxing "champion" as the embodiment of brave moral independence, whether individual or national'.[6]

The qualities imbued by pugilistic training are depicted as being inextricably bound up with naturally occurring national traits that, when marshalled, provided the raw ingredients to mould an effective military force. Egan promoted the idea that the pugilist honing his fighting potential would become a potent presence on the battlefield. This ethos contradicted Vasey's adamant contention:

---

5   Johnson, '"British Championism": Early Pugilism and the Works of Fielding', p. 332.
6   Ibid., p. 341.

It is said that the milling art is necessary to the excitement of courage and the preservation of our national character [...] But, a century ago, Englishmen knew not
Pugilism [...] and yet we are told, however fabulously I do not pretend to say, that,
many centuries since [...] courage was a striking part of the British character and has
continued to be so. (*RIPM*, p. 7)

Significantly, Vasey does not seek to diminish British military feats, only
to discredit the role claimed for the sport: 'It is not by Pugilism, but by
the policy of councils, and the movements of fleets and armies, that a
nation's glory is sustained. It was not by the fist that Nelson was renowned,
or Waterloo so wonderfully won' (p. 7). Egan agreed that military for-
midableness was borne from longstanding tradition, but emphasised his
preferred reason: 'Britons have always been characterised as a [...] robust
race of people, inured to hardship and fatigue, and, by the exercise of those
manly sports [...] which rendered them so decisive in their warlike com-
bats' (*Boxiana I*, p. 14).

An overriding theory is that pugilism 'served to form a manly population, and breed them up to contempt of danger [...] the man who could
beat another with his fists would never scruple to meet him with a gun and
bayonet'.[7] Around the period of the Napoleonic wars, special pugilistic
exhibitions were considered respectable fare for the variety of royalty and
statesmen in London celebrating the latest allied victories: 'On 15 June 1814
Viscount Lowther hosted a sparring exhibition at his home on Pall Mall
for the Tsar of Russia, General Platov and Marshall Blücher'.[8] And, John
Jackson 'continued to be in demand to demonstrate his sport to visiting
grandees' (*Bell's Life in London*, 19 June 1836).[9] The impression is that a
pugilistic bout was regarded as an exemplar of an exclusively British talent.

Throughout the *Boxiana* series there is an unconcealed disdain
towards the clandestine methods supposedly employed by foreigners in

---

7   Langford, *Englishness Identified*, p. 46.
8   Blücher, Prussian military leader (1742–1819). *British Satire, 1785–1840*, ed. by
     Strachan and others, V, ed. by Jane Moore, p. 187. Byron referred to this period as
     'the summer of the sovereigns'. *Byron's Letters and Journals*, ed. by Marchand, IX,
     p. 171.
9   Brailsford, *Bareknuckles: A Social History of Prize-Fighting*, p. 74.

disputes, often categorised as 'assassination'. In a swipe at foreign tactics, Egan exhorted pugilists to 'discountenance *treachery*; not to stab persons in the dark; and to become horror-struck at ASSASSINATION'. He pronounced: 'these maxims [...] are felt and acknowledged by the mass of the people' (*Boxiana III*, p. 4). A fundamentally different ethos appeared to predominate abroad: 'Europe offered no parallel. Where plebeian systems of honour did seem to prevail [...] as in Italy and Spain, they were associated with inherited tribal enmities, a vengeful mentality, and brutally underhand forms of combat'.[10] Such unfavourable perceptions abounded well before any *Boxiana* diatribes, and a piece by Robert Southey (1774–1843) articulated some stereotypical notions:

> In England a boxing match settles all disputes among the lower classes, and when it is over they shake hands, and are friends. Another equally beneficial effect is the security afforded to the weaker by the laws of honour, which forbid all undue advantages; the man who should aim a blow below the waist [...] would be sure to experience the resentment of the mob, who on such occasions always assemble to see what they call fair play, which they enforce as rigidly as the Knights of the Round Table did the laws of chivalry. (*Letters from England: by Don Manuel Alvarez Espriella*, London, 1807)[11]

Puzzlingly, Southey applies the quality of medieval honour to 'the mob'.

The somewhat idealistic concept that all disputes can be settled without lasting acrimony was refuted by Vasey: 'It is unnatural that two men, each having hatred enough in his mind to prompt him to do the other all manner of personal injury, should in one hour undergo a miraculous change from enmity to affection' (*RIPM*, p. 10). Thus, Egan's quotation of pugilist Tom Shelton, 'I like fighting [...] but I hate animosity', expresses naïve expectations of unwavering equanimity.[12] Even a staunch advocate of the sport, Thomas Fewtrell, had conceded that resentment was to be expected when two men 'free from enmity' fought one another: 'without any cause for passion, without any motive for vengeance [...] they assault each other

---

10 Langford, *Englishness Identified*, p. 150.
11 Quoted in Christopher Johnson, 'Anti-Pugilism: Violence and Justice in Scott's *The Two Drovers*', *Scottish Literary Journal*, 22, 1 (1995), pp. 46–60 (54).
12 *Egan's Life in London, and Sporting Guide*, No. 59 (13 March 1825), p. 53.

with all the appearance of deadly hatred, and determined revenge. The ties of humanity are broken, and Nature revolts at the sight' (*Boxing Reviewed*, 1790, pp. 10–11).

Egan's record of the speech made by John Emery (1777–1822) of the Theatre Royal, when making a presentation to Cribb in celebration of his victories over Molineaux, included aspersions on foreign dissimulation and lack of spirit: 'You gave proof that the innovating hand of a foreigner, when lifted against a son of Britannia, must not only be aided by the *strength* of a lion, but the heart also' (*Boxiana I*, p. 419).[13] Byron, writing from Pisa, told of a tussle with an Italian dragoon: 'he got his paiks – having acted like an assassin.'[14] Byron selected this Scottish term for blows to describe the physical admonishment meted out, which echoes the 'English peg' that had so discomfited the Venetian a century before. Byron also supplied a condensed view of the motivating principles throughout Europe: 'The French courage proceeds from vanity – the German from phlegm – the Turkish from fanaticism & opium – the Spanish from pride – the English from coolness – the Dutch from obstinacy – the Russian from insensibility [...] the *Italian* from *anger*.'[15]

The consistent accusation, explicitly posed by Egan, is that a foreign foe is reluctant to 'meet our brave sons on equal terms in the field or on the wave' (*Book of Sports*, p. 172). The message promoted is that a street altercation abroad might result in a concealed dagger being produced to inflict a lethal revenge, but an argument between two Britons could be resolved in the ring in a somehow pugnaciously civilised expression of national character.

These stereotypical traits could be extended to the battlefields of Europe, and the notion of British forces acting as a pugilistic avenger, inflicting punishment on persecuting nations, is articulated by Byron: 'As

13   In keeping with the Fancy's dubious preoccupations, Emery 'drank to excess' (*DNB*). A silver cup worth eighty guineas was presented at the Castle Tavern (2 December 1811).

14   Letter of 4 May 1822, to Scott. *Byron's Letters and Journals*, ed. by Marchand, IX, p. 154.

15   Letter of 31 August 1820, to Murray. Ibid., VII, p. 169.

for the Scoundrel Austrians they are bullying Lombardy – as usual. – It
would be pleasant to see those Huns get their paiks'.[16] Referring to the
Napoleonic wars, Egan depicted an otherwise rampant French army intimidated by the prospect of facing the British, and the author is adamant that
it is a pugilistic ethic to which the nation is 'indebted':

> Are not the English superior to any other nation in the junction of active and passive
> courage and is it not a fact that, the French, during the late war, frequently charged the
> troops of all the continental nations with whom they were engaged, with the bayo-
> net; while they scarcely ever ventured to cross one with ours? (*Book of Sports*, p. 31)

This impression corresponds with the sentiments of 'Mr M', who articulated
the mixture of awe and fear felt by foreign adversaries on the battlefield:
'They dare not await the assault of the British battering-ram preparing to
put in motion'; 'a Briton, trusting in native strength, moves amongst them
like Achilles amongst the Trojans' (*Boxiana III*, p. 580). The idea that a
typical British pugilist constitutes an intimidating presence is comically
underscored in 'Appendix No. 1' of Thomas Moore's *Tom Crib's Memorial*
(1819), as a 'Grand Pugilistic Meeting' considers sending their own rep-
resentatives to the Aix-la-Chapelle Congress. Veteran Joe Ward suggests
that a heavyweight delegation may prove disturbing for the supposedly
enervated foreigners: 'a *few*, at first, should go, / And those, the *light-weight
Gemmen* chiefly; / As if too many "*Big ones*" went, / *They might alarm the
Continent*!!'.[17]

The unbalanced ascription of covert and unscrupulous tendencies
to foreign armed forces, in this period, displays a distorted perception of
British moral superiority: '[c.1808] Spanish troops were known as guerrillas
even when uniformed and in regular formations'. And, in naval skirmishes,
the British abhorred the 'French practice' of employing sharpshooters: 'It
was one thing for a row of cannon to fire a general broadside [...] But for a
marksman to take deliberate aim at his opponent and shoot him was not
an honest form of combat'. However, the British interpretation of a 'code

---

16   Letter of 17 October 1820, to Hobhouse. Ibid., VII, p. 206.
17   *British Satire, 1785–1840*, ed. by Strachan and others, V, ed. by Jane Moore, p. 211.

of honour' appears to have been flexible: 'When Sir Sydney Smith sailed into Brest harbour in 1795, flying French colours and hailing his enemies in their own language, no-one thought he had acted otherwise than honourably'. Such acts were rated as 'minimal deceptions'. When recruited by Greece to coordinate their naval campaign against Turkey, Thomas Cochrane witnessed the fragile 'courage' of the Greek sailors:

> He arranged a magic-lantern show for them. The 'dissolving views' filled them with an obvious and child-like delight. Then Cochrane put on a slide of a Greek being pursued by a Turk [...] The audience broke into wild panic, some jumping over the ship's side, others barricading themselves in the hold.

At one point Cochrane refers to Greek forces as 'bands of undisciplined, ignorant, and lawless savages', and throughout his stint of 'authority' the threat of treachery was rife, hence 'the loaded pistol he carried under his coat'.[18]

In a more light-hearted vein, the fictional character, Charles Sparkle, scoffs at the degeneration of that nation's reputation for Classical warriors. He states that present-day Greeks can only be said to possess the '*cunning and wariness*' of their illustrious antecedents: 'no modern Greek can be said to have any resemblance to Achilles, Ajax, Patroclus, or Nestor, in point of courage, strength, fidelity, or wisdom' (*Real Life in London*, p. 191).[19] Chronicling his own experience in Greece, Byron reported a fusion of deceit and avarice contributing to a general unreliability: 'the Greeks appear in more danger from their own divisions than from attacks of the Enemy. – There is talk of treachery – and all sorts of parties amongst them [...] and a desire of nothing but *money*'.[20]

Paradoxically, when Cochrane proposed the use of explosion ships and gas (1809), he was 'dismayed to find that Lord Gambier [commander-in-chief of Channel Fleet] had a pious objection to fire-ships [...] on the

---

18   Thomas, *Cochrane: Britannia's Sea Wolf*, pp. 126, 36, 308, 315.
19   Patroclus was a Greek legendary hero (*Iliad*), slain at Troy. Nestor's role was 'largely to incite warriors to battle and tell stories of his early exploits'.
20   Letter 11 September 1823, to Hobhouse. *Byron's Letters and Journals*, ed. by Marchand, XI, p. 24.

ground that they were "a horrible mode of warfare".[21] The decision by Gambier (1756–1833) 'reflected his awareness that the fleet was the mainstay of national defence and not to be put at hazard' (*DNB*). Clandestine tactics were viewed as 'unsporting', and hardly conformed to Egan's concept of replicating the open engagement of the pugilistic ring. This more extreme mode of strategic cunning was tainted and, in this instance, one could not imagine Egan celebrating 'the Cochrane touch'.

One of the soldiers killed at Waterloo, John Shaw (1789–1815), had been an acclaimed member of the pugilistic ranks: 'He was speedily taken up as an emblem of English manliness [...] as proof of the beneficial effects of boxing. His glorious death demonstrated the heroism of British, and more specifically English, manhood'.[22] Egan describes Shaw as 'upwards of six feet in height, and above 15-stone in weight' (*Boxiana II*, p 114), which is comparable to the aforementioned 'model' dimensions of Gregson. Whilst Egan's tribute does not attempt to yoke Shaw's pugilistic and battlefield exploits together, there is a sense of contesting for both military and sporting laurels: 'On April 18, 1815 [...] he entered the lists with that brave hero of the fist *Ned Painter*. Victory again crowned his efforts' (p. 379); 'After having performed his duty towards his country in a giant-like manner [...] he fell on the 18th of June' (p. 381). The proximity of the two dates adds an extra poignancy. The veneration of Shaw's bravery was not confined to Fancy circles, and Scott, writing to the Duke of Buccleuch, accords Shaw the status of national, as well as sporting, champion:

> Officers and soldiers all fought hand to hand without distinction; and many of the former owed their life to the dexterity at their weapon, and personal strength of body. Shaw, the milling Life-Guardsman [...] among the Champions of the Fancy, maintained the honour of the fist.[23]

21 Thomas, *Cochrane: Britannia's Sea Wolf*, p. 148.

22 Johnson, 'Anti-Pugilism: Violence and Justice in Scott's *The Two Drovers*', p. 51.

23 *The Letters of Sir Walter Scott*, ed. by H J C Grierson, 12 vols. (London: Constable, 1933), IV, pp. 80–1. 'His energy and bravery were of the highest order, although reports that he captured a French eagle standard are contradictory and may be an exaggeration' (*DNB*).

In addition to spotlighting their physical strength and bravery, Scott indicates the mixed-class composition of the British troops. This replicates another Fancy tenet – a heterogeneous united body pursuing an honourable goal.

From the opening pages of *Boxiana I*, Egan had highlighted the transferable nature of sporting attributes, particularly their usefulness in issues of national defence:

> The *cause*, Sir, ought not to be lost sight of in the *effect* – and the alacrity of the TAR in serving his gun, and the daring intrepidity of the BRITISH SOLDIER in mounting the breach – in producing those brilliant victories which have reflected so much glory on the English Nation [...] SPORTS, Sir, which can produce *thorough-bred* actions like the above, will outlive all the sneers of the fastidious, the *cant* of the hyper-critics!!! (*Boxiana I*, p. iii)

The inclusiveness of Egan's claim is noteworthy, not restricting his praise to pugilism alone. One of the more obvious sports that played its part in developing practical skills was sailing, Egan attending many regattas. He recorded, in 1832, that 'numerous Yacht Clubs have been formed', and hinted at the significance of discovering 'some excellent sailors [...] who would do credit to vessels of a much larger size' (*Book of Sports*, p. 354). The seventh verse of the Thames Yacht Club (T.Y.C.) song highlights the members' concomitant gallantry and willingness to mobilise in times of conflict:

> Should e'er Old England's fabled foe, the Dragon, reappear,
> To *spit fire* at our gallant fleet, we've nothing still to fear;
> For harmless would be all his rage, his reign a transient hour,
> For England's Champion, brave St George, would re-display his power:
> For the T.Y.C shall foremost be
> Where courage is the rub;
> And bravery the watch-word be
> Of this – the Thames Yacht Club.
> (*Book of Sports*, p. 105)[24]

---

24   Written by club member Ben Backstay. Nine verses to the tune 'There's nae luck about the house'.

Tom Paulin focuses attention on the ruggedness of the British sailor ('tar') when suggesting that Hazlitt, in 'The Fight' (1822), was portraying the two fighters as symbolic of the fundamental differences between English and French 'matter':

> [Hickman] is 'light, vigorous, elastic' [...] Neate, is a huge, knock-kneed English materialist, a Jack Tar [...] By association – or opposition – this makes Hickman French. Hazlitt compares the French national character to the greyhound in his description of the superior fighting powers of English sailors.[25]

This also emphasises the aforementioned British propensity for open confrontation, whereas the 'Frenchified' Hickman is depicted as relying on movement, which implies evasiveness. Egan was swift to emphasise the moderation exercised by Cribb in '*milling on the retreat*': 'he never resorted to its scientific effects till the necessity of the moment compelled him' (*Boxiana I*, p. 408).

Anything that was deemed '*too scientific*' (p. 117) was likely to be designated 'foreign'. In this respect, Birley chronicles the perception of the Jewish Mendoza: 'he preferred to use footwork', which was 'regarded by traditionalists as un-British'.[26] But, by 1818, there is evidence of the perception of 'shifting' being revised:

> Activity, or *milling on the retreat*, is, at the present period, a greater requisite toward victory than it was formerly considered. Some have censured *shifting* as an unmanly custom, but without reason. If, indeed, mere brutal force were to decide a combat, it might be deemed improper; but, where the mind has considerable share in the decision [...] *getting away* cannot be thought unmanly. (*Boxiana II*, p. 18)[27]

It would, presumably, be an excessive expectation for true sportsmanship to be extended to the battlefield, and Egan confirmed that such notions would be unrealistic: 'would it not be absurd to say to a man, whose only

---

25   Paulin, *The Day-Star of Liberty*, p. 31.
26   Birley, *Sport and the Making of Britain*, p. 155.
27   This is an almost verbatim reproduction of the view espoused in Fewtrell's *Boxing Reviewed*, p. 19.

care is the preservation of his life, – "You must not avoid your enemy's sword by changing your ground; you must not make use of that activity of which you are capable'" (p. 18). Yet, recounted prizefight incidents appeal to high-minded principles, such as when Hickman had been rendered 'utterly *insensible*': 'Neat took no advantage of this defenceless position [...] he acted conformably to the right old English character' (*Boxiana IV*, p. 75). Egan summed up the general pugilistic attitude as a national one: 'An Englishman abhors the idea of inflicting an incurable injury on his antagonist. He endeavours, indeed, to make him *put up his black shutters*, to darken him for awhile, but he never attempts to break the glass or shatter the frame' (*Boxiana III*, p. 594).

Such integrity is prominent in the opening exhortations of *Boxiana III*, claiming that prizefighting 'teaches' men 'invincibility of soul' (p. 4). Later, Egan explicitly stated that pugilism engenders 'a spirit of *humanity*' and that 'every act of generous forbearance' is applauded (p. 584). He conveniently disregarded the tactic employed by ['Gentleman'!] Jackson, who had held Mendoza by the hair in order to increase the effectiveness of his punches, Brailsford stating: 'what Jackson did was common practice'.[28] Nevertheless, Egan claimed: 'No soldiers show so much mercy to a fallen foe as the British'. Exactly what form of mercy is unclear, but it can only be presumed that a soldier is not being advised to endanger himself in the name of sporting ethics. Egan proceeds to offer practical justification for extending restraint: 'in the heat of battle [...] it is the pugilist who keeps his temper, who is able to avail himself of his scientific acquirements' (p. 584). When compared to sentiments expressed amidst future conflicts, the sporting philosophy appears to have been an enduring one: 'the British Army was perceived as playing by [...] rules, evolving from a moral code'.[29]

When Hazlitt reported, in 'The Fight', that there was 'little cautious sparring [...] none of the *petit-maîtreship* of the art', it underscores apparent contradictions. Paulin states that Hazlitt is 'using a term which he often

28   Brailsford, *Bareknuckles: A Social History of Prize-Fighting*, p. 70.
29   Vanessa Furze Jackson, *The Poetry of Henry Newbolt: Patriotism is Not Enough* (Greensboro: ELT Press, 1994), p. 83.

employs in a literary context to characterize a mere professional competence that lacks real force and originality'.[30] This view is certainly corroborated by Hazlitt's ensuing reflections on the 'force' of witnessing 'two men smashed to the ground, smeared with gore, stunned, senseless, the breath beaten out of their bodies'.[31] The term appears in its more pejorative sense, with its connotations of effeteness, when the Lord High Admiral backs the 'hardy' game of cricket 'in preference to lending his countenance to those "petit maître" amusements, which tend to debase' (*Book of Sports*, p. 341). This stance coincides with Egan's warning against a tide of 'effeminacy', correlating with the *OED* definition of 'petit maître': 'An effeminate man; a dandy, a fop'. This still leaves a question over the collocation of 'petit maître' and 'cautious sparring'.

Hazlitt's evident gratitude at the absence of caution might also be interpreted as an ignorance of pugilism's subtleties. It can be conceded that the *Boxiana* accounts of the Neate v Hickman fight substantiate the uncompromising severity and direct approach of the two combatants, but Hazlitt's comment suggests that he could not be included amongst those spectators regularly 'lost in amazement [...] contrasting the manoeuvres, stratagems, and snares' (*Boxiana II*, p. 276), and would not appreciate the tactical qualities relished by Egan: 'NICHOLLS, like a skilful general armed at all points, was not to be deluded by the feints of the enemy' (*Boxiana I*, p. 197). Egan enthused on the merits of wariness and strategy:

> It might be asked, what is an Admiral without tactics? or, a General without scientific precision? And where it has appeared, that downright *force* has succeeded once – *skill*, it will be found, has produced victory a hundred times; courage would degenerate into mere ferocity, if not tempered with judgement. (p. 254)

Whilst not seeking to diminish the courage of Neate and Hickman's onslaught, and the spectacle provided, Egan's accounts emphasise that tactical manoeuvring was a vital attribute for pugilists. Predictably, Egan cited his '*Prime Irish Lad*' Randall as one adept at tactical discretion:

30   Paulin, *The Day-Star of Liberty*, p. 82.
31   *The Selected Writings of William Hazlitt*, ed. by Wu, IX, p. 70.

'RANDALL is a complete *rara avis* [...] His *look-out* in battle is equal to any admiral upon the station; and he turns the neglect of his adversary to account' (*Boxiana II*, pp. 262–3). Despite referring to 'the art', Hazlitt was preoccupied with immersing himself in the physicality of the contest, but Egan emphasised that it is only 'when united' that these qualities 'become truly irresistible' (*Boxiana I*, p. 254).

Egan was consistent in his assertion that bravado and power alone could not prove decisive in military campaigns, and the discipline of pugilistic 'science', instilling strategic astuteness and calmness, is promoted as indispensable:

> *Impetuosity*, when occasioned by *irritation*, not only defeats its original intent, but ultimately, produces consequences so diametrically opposite [...] *Coolness* should be the leading feature of every boxer – it is then that the manifest advantages of the *science* are to be witnessed over the impotent efforts of blind fury. (*Boxiana I*, p. 215)

Foreigners are portrayed as being particularly deficient, and Egan highlighted this disparity in his record of an exhibition (near the Haymarket in London), where a Frenchman 'undertook to prove that *science*, in competition with *strength*, was of no avail' (*Boxiana I*, p. 9). Egan delighted in recounting the dismissive manner in which this foreign argument was disproved:

> *John Bull* soon took the conceit out of him, as he had done many more of his countrymen, in more formidable contests [...] The Frenchman very soon got *milled*, and, shortly afterwards, *mizzled*; so that the science received but little interruption from *his* lectures. (p. 9)

As well as being an alliterative touch, Egan's use of 'mizzled' is unlikely to be random, the term having a dubious association with the action of pickpockets scattering at the sight of a constable: '*Mizzle* – when any number of the light-fingered tribe [...] disperse incontinently' (*Bee's Sportsman's Slang*). The implication is that the Frenchman is a charlatan who is hurried into an ignominious exit from the scene.

Extending this notion, there was a suggestion that French armies would rather beat a precipitate retreat from the field of battle than stand to face British opposition, and Reynolds ridiculed a supposed Gallic predilection for dancing: 'The French dance every night in the week [...] There is no doubt that dancing has an effect on the heels, for Wellington has often scratched his head, and given them a left-handed blessing, for their quickness' (*Book of Sports*, p. 170). Egan attributed similar mocking comments to Cribb in a fictional meeting with Corinthian Tom: 'If they can't use their fists quicker in France than they do their legs, the Lord have mercy' (*Life in London*, pp. 220–1). The author also accredits Cribb with a comical statement of derision couched in hybrid-style language: '[CRIBB] is rather up in the *stirrups*, and somewhat *learnedly* observes, "that he is *toujours prêt* in the defence of his king; and likewise, *sans cérémonie*, will give an enemy of Old England a drubbing *tout sweet*"' (*Boxiana III*, p. 25). The latter misspelling also implies a laboured mispronunciation of the French diction, and Bee proves remarkably exacting when extending anti-French feeling: 'I detest [...] that British amateurs should drink brandy [...] It is a suspicious liquor' (*Boxiana IV*, p. 396). The notion of a 'suspicious' drink tainting unsuspecting Fancy members appears to border on paranoia. Ultimately, Egan's insular view regarding foreign knowledge of pugilism coincided with that of 'Mr M': '[Foreigners] know nothing of it; they handle their arms like the flapping of the wings of a duck' (*Boxiana III*, p. 580).

Whilst encouraging notions of an instinctive English (or British) martial superiority, the pugilistic writers under discussion do suggest that some instruction is required. Pugilism was perceived as a wholly English discipline that advanced the desired blend of pugnacity and acumen. Dowling reported that the valorous Englishman Shaw had to be educated in the 'scientific' subtleties of the art by the sport's 'ambassador':

> [Shaw] told Mr Jackson he was 'a main good un at the goots'; that is to say, he could plant his body blows with finishing effect. 'Ay', said Mr Jackson, 'when you have a *yokel* [inexperienced man] to deal with, but with a master of the art you would find that game a bad one'. Shaw was incredulous. (*Fistiana*, p. 41)

There followed a practical demonstration of 'the art':

> Mr Jackson put on the gloves, and called upon our hero not to mind him, but to do his worst [...] Mr Jackson had him on the head with such severity, as not only to send his head back, but as altogether to set his 'blow at the goots' completely at nought. (p. 41)

A lexical definition, by Bee, acknowledged the necessity of multiple attributes, but stressed the difference that elevates the more dexterous fighter: '*Millers* – second-rate boxers, whose arms run around in rapid succession [...] they seldom win against equal strength in a scientific opponent' (*Bee's Sportsman's Slang*). Egan again used Reynolds's 'defence' of pugilism to highlight the Briton's capacity for combining strategy with bravery whilst, simultaneously, questioning the foreigner's: 'Theirs is not the frenzied courage like that inspired by brandy [...] but 'tis that kind of round-after-round courage which will admit of thinking and command and knows no abatement' (*Book of Sports*, p. 172).

On the theme of doggedness, a recurring quality attributed to the Fancy was their resistance to extreme weather. Egan regularly registered the imperturbability and perseverance of fighters and spectators alike whilst withstanding an elemental battering. For the contest between Spring and Burns (Epsom Downs, 16 May 1820), Egan described the Fancy's inauspicious preparation for a customary matutinal trek:

> The morning was truly forbidding for the *Swells* to leave their *downy dabs*; and the heavy torrents of rain informed the *kids*, upon opening their *peepers*, that their *game* would again be put to the test; but *delicacy* of *canvass* [skin] is not one of the features of the Ring, and those *lads* who delight in witnessing a *Prize mill*, value not *distance* – fear not *weather* [...] and the *drag* is *shoved* forward with as much indifference, as if the most perfect serenity of climate prevailed. (*Boxiana III*, pp. 334–5)

And, Egan ascribed the greatest fortitude to the pugilists themselves:

> [Holt v O'Donnel, 26 March 1817] The combatants stripped with the utmost *sang froid* [...] notwithstanding the rain descended in torrents, the combatants seemed insensible to its chilling effects, and opposed each other with the utmost gaiety. (*Boxiana II*, p. 349)

> [Purcell v McDermott, 31 August 1819] Such an *out-and-out* shower has not been experienced; it operated on the frames of the spectators with that sort of deluge, as if one of the dykes had given way in Holland. It was almost impossible to withstand its driving qualities [...] but the combatants, with hearts like lions, unmindful of the

'pelting pitiless storm', stood up to each other [...] as if they were promenading the walks of Vauxhall.[32] (*Boxiana III*, pp. 356–7)

Although not explicitly stated, the inference is that a weather-beaten pugilist will possess the necessary resilience to endure the deprivations and brutality of the front line. Egan certainly valued this form of endurance, and provides a cogent argument for the advantages, to the nation, of possessing fighting forces filled with men steeped in pugilistic lore, rather than those preferring *'assumed refinement* to rough Nature [...] whom *a shower of rain* can terrify' (*Boxiana I*, p. iv). Considering the various commentaries that indicate a flow of 'claret', the natural progression is to assume that pugilists inured to gore can better endure a pitiless battleground: 'How should a man [...] be able to do his duty as a soldier, or a sailor, or a surgeon, if the mere sight of another's blood appals him' (*Fistiana*, p. 7).

Despite the supposed incompatibility of English and French sporting attitudes, Egan reported an Englishman, Fuller, to be 'happily passing his time among the French, at *Valenciennes* [1818]' (*Boxiana II*, p. 470). The local inhabitants displayed a willingness to participate in a range of pastimes, with Fuller ensconced in a co-ordinating position:

> He presides at the races, as *clerk of the course*. He also keeps a sort of subscription house, and has two billiard tables constantly in use, besides a room elegantly fitted up for the instruction of self-defence [...His] hotel is much frequented both by French and English gentlemen; and many of the former [...] have a trial, (*à la Anglaise*), with the *gloves!* (pp. 470–1)

As with many successful foreign relations throughout different eras, compromise is crucial and Egan recognised the most significant contribution to Fuller's successful adaptation: 'his industry', and ability to 'acquire an excellent knowledge of the French language' (p. 471). This provides a more balanced picture amidst the explicit nationalistic rhetoric of *Boxiana*-style reports and expansive dedications extolling a natural British supremacy. Such enlightened snippets appear out of kilter with prevailing jingoistic

32   The phraseology appears to be inspired by a Shakespearian line – 'That bide the pelting of this pitiless storm' (*King Lear*, III, iv, 29).

notions. There is a feeling that the pugilistic chroniclers were naively pandering to a set of comfortable, but unrealistic, partisan myths, and this might be construed as a simple courting of popularity.

In some quarters, there existed a romanticised view of the defeated Napoleon as a bullied hero. The crux of *Tom Crib's Memorial* was 'to condemn the Napoleonic witch-hunt that was the Holy Alliance'.[33] Even Cochrane, when overseeing the navies of Brazil and Chile, admired this former enemy, and planned to install Napoleon as sovereign of a merged South American empire. This typical 'secret' admiration reflected 'a sympathy with the prevailing intellectual fashion'.[34] Holland House in Kensington 'was somewhere where Whigs could admire Napoleon, damn the Tories, scoff at God and preach progressive liberalism'.[35] It would have been easier, however, for these gatherings (often including Byron) to acclaim the 'audacious rapidity' of the French general when his threat had been extinguished.[36] There had been a genuine state of panic about possible invasion (1803–4) when 'terror gripped the southern coastal areas', and 'an exhilarating effect at home' at news of Nelson's naval victories. Following the ratification of a peace agreement at Amiens (March 1802), the primary emotion amongst the British public was a 'craven sense of relief'. It appears that, to many, 'the enemy was always Bonaparte rather than the French', and that once this obstacle had been removed the English people felt eager to 'hurry over to Paris' to spend some time amongst a people they regarded as 'civilised' and with whom they had 'more in common politically, culturally, and ideologically [...than] erstwhile allies'.[37]

In another pugilistic comparison, Egan complimented the martial prowess of selected non-Britons: 'But who can rule the uncertain

33   *British Satire, 1785–1840*, ed. by Strachan and others, V, ed. by Jane Moore, p. 185.
34   Thomas, *Cochrane: Britannia's Sea Wolf*, p. 346.
35   Home of Lady Elizabeth Holland (c. 1771–1845). Boyd Hilton, *A Mad, Bad, and Dangerous People?: England 1783–1846* (Oxford: Clarendon Press, 2006), p. 206.
36   Another literary admirer of Napoleon was the playwright Richard Brinsley Sheridan (1751–1816).
37   Hilton, *A Mad, Bad, and Dangerous People?: England 1783–1846*, pp. 88–91, 103, 239.

chance of war? Napoleon was *floored*! MARC ANTONY was defeated! SUWARROW *licked*! [...] All great masters in the art of war [...] have been compelled to surrender in turns to superior TACTICS' (*Book of Sports*, p. 27). Here, Egan refers to Russian Field-Marshall, Aleksandr Vasilievich Suvorov [Suwarrow] (1729–1800), but his praise is subtly (intentionally?) undercut by the implication of strategic deficiency. In *Don Juan* (1823), Byron initially projected Suwarrow as an inspirational leader: 'great joy unto the camp! / To Russian, Tartar, English, French, Cossacque, / O'er whom Suwarrow shone like a gas lamp, / Presaging a most luminous attack' (Canto VII, verse 46). The tone changes however, focussing on his ruthlessly mechanical efficiency: 'the greatest Chief / That ever peopled hell with heroes slain, / Or plunged a province or a realm in grief' (VII, 68). There is no anti-foreign tone present, rather a world weariness with the harshness of armed conflict.

Boxiana's ambivalence towards Napoleon is exacerbated by comparisons featuring one of the era's most controversial pugilists, Tom Hickman. This fighter split opinion, and identification of him with military figures provides one of the more curious aspects within the series. Pugilistic writers were quick to condemn any exhibitions of conceit from fighters, but Hickman was frequently adjudged guilty of exceptional brashness, and Hazlitt effectively conveyed this unfortunate trait: 'the gas-man came forward with a conscious air of anticipated triumph [...] He strutted about more than became a hero'. Hazlitt also offered an amusingly hyperbolic analogy:

> A boxer was bound to beat his man, but not to thrust his fist, either actually or by implication, in every one's face. Even a highwayman, in the way of trade, may blow out your brains, but if he uses foul language at the same time, I should say he was no gentleman.[38]

Again, the strutting, preening fighter underscores notions of the cockpit. But, this fighter was the recipient of some flattering comparisons: 'HICKMAN possesses all the *confidence* of a NELSON, united with the

---

38 *The Selected Writings of William Hazlitt*, ed. by Wu, IX, pp. 68, 69.

desperation of a *Paul Jones*' (*Boxiana III*, p. 291).[39] Significantly, Egan focused on the audacity of military leaders rather than their tactical knowledge. Given the blunt nature of Hickman, this appears a conscious choice by the author to celebrate the hardihood of the pugilist whilst not claiming a shared aptitude for strategic subtleties. Where Hickman is concerned, there appears no room for a generous interpretation of arrogance as 'confidence' and, following a victory against Crawley (16 March 1819), Egan conjured some appropriately militaristic imagery: 'The *gas-light* blade seemed as well *primed* as a four-pound burner, and eager to eclipse his opponent' (*Boxiana III*, p. 293). And, does not overlook the victor's hubris: 'he *burnt* brighter in his own opinion than before' (p. 295). Egan had propounded the merits of retaining a level-headed approach well before publication of Hazlitt's strictures.

Bee apportioned some blame for Hickman's demeanour to the Fancy, who 'exalted him' (*Boxiana IV*, p. 174), and almost replicated Egan's earlier comparison: 'he comes up to the *scratch* with all the determined resolution of a Paul Jones, to obtain conquest, united with the courage of a Nelson' (p. 200); 'his confidence is *out-and-out*, and he goes up to the head of his opponent to commence the fight with as much certainty of success [...] as Nelson entered Aboukir-Bay' (p. 171).[40] Further to these military connections, Bee's subsequent lengthy analogy of the fighting careers of Hickman and Napoleon might be deemed somewhat tenuous: 'Both were *fighting-men*, irascible, pugnaceous [sic], and abusive [...] *Boney* had his encomiasts, up to flummery; so had *Gas*. Both obscurely born, early initiated in affrays, fulsomely bespattered by fools [...] losing themselves during their elevation' (pp. 203–4). The perplexity at such extravagant comparisons is echoed in an exchange between two upper-class characters in Bernard Shaw's novel *Cashel Byron's Profession* (1886), as Lucian Webber explains the term prizefighter to his cousin, Lydia Carew:

---

39   John Paul Jones (1747–92). Born in Scotland, but was 'the most successful American naval commander to date'. He preyed on British ships during the American War of Independence (*DNB*).

40   The mouth of the Nile, in Egypt, where Nelson's fleet routed the French (1798).

'He is simply what his name indicates [...] A man who fights for prizes'.
'So does the captain of a man-of-war. And yet society does not place them in the same class'.
'As if there could be any doubt [...] There is no analogy whatever'. (*CBP*, p. 125)

Yet, to the pugilist Cashel Byron, discrimination between the two appears equally strange. Upon looking at the new biographical dictionary, he remarks: 'This is a blessed book [...] Here's ten pages about Napoleon Bonaparte, and not one about Jack Randall: as if one fighting man wasn't as good as another' (*CBP*, p. 122). It might be argued that a sporting man of any social level would not regard such associations as inappropriate.

Although tenuously linking the audacious quality of Napoleon and Hickman, Bee's piece highlights further contradictions in the desired model of an archetypal British pugilist. Bee referred to Egan as an 'apologist' for Hickman (*Boxiana IV*, p. 177), but this appears unfair. Egan was consistent in his condemnation of Hickman's contemptuous attitude, and the only charge against the author that might be substantiated is his neglect of reporting unsavoury incidents, such as in the 'Bear and Staff' after hours where Hickman was reprimanded by the landlady for 'abusing the persons present in coarse and repulsive terms':

> Unable to bear a *check*, GAS hereupon seized *the poker* and broke the back of a dog that slept before the fire [...] As a *public man* he deserved the most public reprehension in some honest public print. He received it not, however, although one of the party present was *the Sporting Editor* of a weekly print [...] One single goodly paragraph, sufficiently keen and castigatory, in the last column of *the Dispatch*, would undoubtedly have operated as to prevent the *death-blow* given to ould *Joe Norton*. (pp. 161–2)

The elderly Norton died a week after being 'pitched into' by Hickman, in response to some teasing. One question prompted is to what extent cognitive preconceptions would have been triggered, in readers of Hazlitt's essay, by such information, and would they have been predisposed to reject the noble and heroic imagery. Bee stated that 'the man who denies the value of *intellect* in pugilistic encounters, must be [...] a mere slobberer' (p. 155). Yet this is one of the much vaunted 'breed' of English pugilists; a high-profile fighter who generated publicity and inspired pugilistic chroniclers. The inconsistency is discernible, and the perpetuation of a simplistic concept revolving around a uniform ethos of British sporting superiority appears unsound.

Notwithstanding his shameful actions, the applicability of Hickman's resoluteness to the battle environment could not be overlooked:

> He grapples with danger as one to be disarmed of its terrors, till it is overthrown [...] He prefers the ponderous charge, in order to confound, route, and dismay the feelings of his opponent. His attack is truly terrific. His head and body seem as if secured by a coat of mail, insensible to *punishment*. His *game* is unquestionable; and his course not to be impeded. (*Boxiana III*, p. 287)

Egan veiled Hickman's lack of subtlety under 'a sort of *Nelson-like touch*, "nothing venture, nothing win"' attitude, claiming that this approach was 'the touchstone of all exploits' (*Boxiana III*, pp. 306, 307). One notion that could undercut the reported bravery of a pugilist is that the motivation for enduring severe punishment may have been rooted in betting concerns rather than thoughts of honour: 'anxious that his backers should not find fault [...Oliver] contended for victory as if the fate of an empire hung upon the event' (*Boxiana III*, p. 280). This preoccupation is underscored by the pleadings of Cashel Byron's trainer, Mellish: 'Every man oughter do his dooty. Consider your dooty to your backers' (*CBP*, p. 58).

Ultimately, Egan championed the cause of pugilism in many areas, but it is the sport's collateral military benefits which proved most straightforward to proclaim:

> It was the true British stuff, under the *training*, and *seconded*, on the day of battle, by the genius of Wellington, that checked the insolent career of the enemy. Unequalled as are the *milling* tactics of the great hero – the saviour of Europe [...] would be the first to avow, that it was the sound *stamina*, the genuine *game* and *bottom* of the British soldiers, and their insatiable *gluttony* in fight, that enabled him to take the conceit out of all the marshals of France. May Britons ever have such a *second* to direct the operations of the battle, and [...] such well-prepared material to do justice to his science. (*Boxiana III*, p. 591)

The 'material' refers to soldiers honed in a prizefighting tradition, the use of flash pugilistic terms rendering the allusion unmistakable. When relating details of Hudson's contest against Ward (11 November 1823),

Egan conveyed his determined state of mind: 'It was, mentally speaking, "I cannot be defeated"', an attitude that the Duke of Wellington would have 'fastened on [...] when he *floored* the great Prize Fighter of Europe' (*New Series Boxiana I*, p. 434).

Fight chroniclers' repeated use of the word 'battle' endorsed the oft-pursued military theme, and Egan advanced claims for significant fights to be revered in a similar manner to the nation's martial triumphs: 'Historians and poets have been mighty fond of scribbling at large about soldiers, as if there were half the merit in annoying your adversary, or defending yourself, *with* weapons as without' (*Book of Sports*, p. 123). This jocular tone aside, the sport was consistently portrayed as a metaphorical aide or, in this context, adjutant, in successful military campaigns.

Native Enmities: Rivalry Between Britons

The issue of possessing, or attaining, 'scientific' fighting proficiency is one where discrepancies can be detected in the nationalistic rhetoric of the pugilistic writers. Dowling maintained that inherent deficiencies in Frenchmen's genetic make-up precluded their acquiring necessary skills: 'they never will be a pugilistic nation; to become so they must cease to become French' (*Fistiana*, p. 7). In fact, Dowling's later remarks were scathingly dismissive of a number of unspecified foreign peoples when he defends the sport from the ever-present accusation that it is brutal: '[brutality] is clearly inapplicable; for the monkey tribe [...] do not box, neither do certain nations who form the connecting link between monkeys and human beings' (pp. 9–10). Similarly, Egan reported a John Palmer, in his 'travels of 1817', declaring that '*Prize-boxing* is unknown in the United States'. Also, the Kentuckian mode of fighting is depicted as particularly vicious, the combatants striving to '*pull, bite, kick*', and '*gouge*' (*Sporting Anecdotes*, p. 81).

The implication is that of an international deficiency owing to a lack of pugilistic tradition, and inaptitude for instruction. Egan's lyrics to 'The Lads of the Fancy' song read: '*country* or *colour* to us are the same, / Only anxious are we in preserving the GAME' (*Boxiana II*, p. 557). And, as discussed, the 'game' is repeatedly depicted as exclusively British. In his essay 'Merry England' (1825), Hazlitt declared: 'the noble science of boxing is all our own. Foreigners can scarcely understand how we can squeeze pleasure out of this pastime; the luxury of hard blows given or received [...] the perseverance of the combatants'. This implies that a certain satisfaction, can be derived from physical exertion, and the sense of achievement is beyond 'the Parisian' who is content to be 'stewed in his shop or his garret', but suited to 'the Londoner' who is 'glad to escape from them'. In a footnote, Hazlitt stated: 'The English are fond of change of scene; the French of change of posture; the Italians like to sit still and do nothing'.[41] When Frenchmen did exhibit an awareness of this 'English' sport, its idealistically pacific principles were misconstrued. Dickens, in a letter (June 1846) to literary advisor John Forster (1812–76), reported witnessing an argument between a French innkeeper and customer: 'After various defiances on both sides [...] "Je vous boaxerai" [...] "Voulez-vous boaxer? [...] Boaxez-moi donc!"'. He stated that the two men 'goaded each other to madness with it'.[42] The basic sporting sentiment appears to have been 'lost in translation'.

A retrograde attitude was also reported as prevalent within certain British recesses, the fighting methods practised in Lancashire being recorded as a form of savagery: '*Kick, boloc, and bite* – Lancashire brutality, which they call fighting' (*Bee's Sportsman's Slang*); '[*Purring*] its most hideous form [...] consists in running the head against the adversary's belly, upsetting him, and, if possible, biting off his nose or ear' (*Annals of Sporting III*, p. 130). An early allusion to this lack of subtlety is evinced in an ironic report of '[Heskin] Rimmer bringing down his man by Lancashire ingenuity' (*Pancratia*, p. 356). Similarly, Dickens, in *Hard Times* (1854), described the scenario imagined by the rakish James Harthouse of being confronted by a blustering Mr Bounderby seeking physical retribution, for Harthouse's dishonourable attentions towards Louisa Bounderby, in

41   First published in *New Monthly Magazine* (December 1825). *The Selected Writings of William Hazlitt*, ed. by Wu, IX, pp. 123, 125.

42   *The Letters of Charles Dickens*, ed. by Madeline House and Graham Storey et al., 12 vols. (Oxford: Oxford University Press, 1965–2002), IV, ed. by Kathleen Tillotson, p. 560.

the form of 'an impromptu wrestle [...] in the Lancashire manner'.[43] Here, Dickens effectively deploys the laughable idea of a rotund, if irascible, Bounderby, advanced in years, overwhelming Harthouse in a violent frenzy of kicking and gouging.

Looking further north, attempts were made to cultivate a more receptive approach to prizefighting in Scotland. A correspondent attending a contest between Goldie and Paterson (February 1824) reported a 'strong muster of the Edinburgh Fancy' (*Annals of Sporting V*, p. 198). The existence of this branch of pugilistic followers, as well as the staging of the actual fight, is partly a result of the aforementioned sparring tours; in 1791 Mendoza had 'demonstrated his skills to the Gymnastic Society in Edinburgh'.[44] Such exhibitions excited interest, Egan reporting: 'patrons of pugilism anxious [...] to witness a prize-mill in Scotland, entered into a subscription purse [...] to be fought for by COOPER and *Molineaux* [Lanarkshire, 10 March 1815]' (*Boxiana II*, pp. 354–5).

This apparent enthusiasm might be regarded as an isolated demonstration by a minority group of supporters if Egan's surprisingly disdainful comment is to be believed: 'SCOTLAND is not a *milling* country; it seems entirely opposite to the genius of the people. In Aberdeen, one might as soon hear of a meeting for reform, as of a stake or prize-fight' (*New Series Boxiana II*, p. 704). When an interest was shown a 'Young Gentleman of the Fancy' proved protectively resentful:

> Our brethren of the North would fain monopolize the 'ring' [...] We have no objection to our smart brethren availing themselves of what is peculiarly Edinburgh-*ish* [...] but be the muffles ours [...] No name of eminence has arisen north of the Tweed to give a colour to usurpation. The fame is ours: be ours the task of maintaining it. (*Book of Sports*, pp. 120–1)

Such an attitude was discordant with Egan's tub-thumping claims for combined British forces, and Vasey ridiculed the necessity for such 'teaching':

> Scotchmen and Quakers, among whom Pugilism is out of all question, are as firm, undaunted, and brave, as the proudest Pugilists among them all. And as to national

---

43   Charles Dickens, *Hard Times* (London: Penguin Books, 1994), p. 204.
44   Radford, *The Celebrated Captain Barclay*, p. 72.

character, it is obvious that no man [...] could ever perceive any connexion between the preservation of a nation's honour and the practice of Pugilism. (*RIPM*, p. 7)

This mocking of the link promoted between pugilism and the formation of national character produces a credible point.

Although Irish fighters were consistently portrayed as a pugnacious set, there was a strong suggestion that English pugilists possessed greater finesse and tactical awareness; as in Bee's general denigration of the Irish style, which he claimed 'seldom succeeds' when pitted against English science (*Boxiana IV*, p. 545). Egan, despite previously describing English trepidation at the threat posed by Donnelly, conceded that the Irish champion's form on his 1819 visit to London had been conspicuously unimpressive:

He did not raise himself in the estimation of the English amateurs [...] nor did the *Irish* FANCY in London, it is said, think half so much of his capabilities, as they had previously anticipated, and those gentlemen who also came from Ireland to witness the fight, expressed themselves *astonished* at the *deficiency* of boxing talent. (*Boxiana III*, pp. 124–5)

It transpired that Donnelly had succumbed to temptation in London. It was 'acknowledged' that his stamina was impaired by a fondness for a 'small drop' of drink, and by contracting, as euphemistically phrased, 'a disease in the promiscuousness of his amours' (*Pugilistica II*, p. 155).

When Tom Belcher travelled to face Dogherty at the Curragh of Kildare (23 April 1813), Egan's commentary implies that the 'home' fighter was outclassed by the London Fancy's hero:

Twentieth. – Belcher now seemed perfectly at home, and felt convinced how things were going. The length of his arm, added to the advantage of superior science, enabled him to *serve out* Dogherty about the head with such severity of manner, as to occasion the latter to fall at his feet. – A bet could not be obtained, from the offer of any odds.

Twenty-first. – Dogherty still at his post contended with the utmost bravery to prolong the fight, but it appeared only to receive additional *punishment*. His head and face exhibited a rueful aspect – he was covered with blood, and in the event was *milled* to the earth. (*Boxiana II*, p. 34)

Egan's summary emphasises the emphatic nature of the Englishman's victory:

> The dexterity, the ease, and perfect *sangfroid*, with which Belcher defeated Dogherty, surprised even those persons who were somewhat acquainted with the art [...] it excited universal astonishment – to view one man (and a scientific professor too) nearly *smashed* all to pieces – his head so *transmogrified* [...] and perfectly insensible as to his fate; while, on the contrary, the other combatant [...] driving away from the Curragh, with all the gaiety of a spectator. (p. 36)

An interesting footnote is that Belcher later defeated an English hero with similar ease: '[Shaw, the Life-Guardsman,] a Hercules in appearance, with arms like two May-poles [...] was also *dead-beat* with the *gloves* by TOM', and Egan cited this meeting as establishing 'the superiority of ART over *strength*' (p. 39).[45]

Generally, Egan treated fighters according to their respective merits, and produced a profile of John Langan, which was continued over several editions of his newspaper. Egan recounts an episode from Langan's time at sea: 'In Bull Bay, Lisbon, in spite of the *stiletto* used by two Portuguese, he made the cowards run before him [...] although he was attacked in such an assassin-like manner'.[46] This firmly accredited the Irishman with the national quality of bravely confronting adversaries. Langan is unequivocally depicted as a British pugilist. The fighter's popularity amongst English pugilistic circles appears to have transcended the taint of reported resentment encountered by Molineaux.

It is evident that Langan commanded respect, not merely spectator curiosity, as he attended English Fancy events in the months leading up to his second championship fight against Spring: '[Fives Court] The name of Langan had the desired effect; and Bob Purcell had a most excellent Benefit'.[47] Egan's coverage of the eventual fight (8 June 1824, at Birdham Bridge near Chichester) devoted more attention to Langan than the English champion. If ever Egan's Irish sympathies are evinced it is in his sentimental, and possibly apocryphal, recounting of a pre-fight occurrence:

---

45 The use of 'gloves' indicates that this encounter was 'merely' a sparring bout.
46 *Egan's Life in London, and Sporting Guide*, No. 1 (1 February 1824), p. 5.
47 Ibid., No. 3 (15 February 1824), p. 24.

> A black silk handkerchief was placed loosely round Langan's neck, which we under-
> stand was tied by the delicate hands of the lady of a gallant Irish Colonel [...] Mrs
> O' B– offered him a green handkerchief, as a token of his country; but Langan
> politely refused, saying, 'I am not of importance enough to make it a national affair
> [...]' Mrs O' B– romantically exclaimed, 'You are Irish: colour is immaterial to a
> brave man: glory is your only object'.[48]

The chivalric notions of a tournament resurface, and although Spring was
'received with loud huzzas', Egan reported that 'Langan was also cheered'.
Following a titanic struggle (one hour forty-nine minutes), Spring prevailed,
but Langan dominates Egan's closing analysis: 'he has risen in the estimation
of his countrymen; he has also risen in the hearts of all brave Englishmen;
and twenty thousand or more spectators'.[49] Prizefighters usually fought
until physically unable to walk to 'the scratch', and fights of over one hour
were not exceptional. Nevertheless, the duration of this contest is one of
the longest recorded in the *Boxiana* period.

The inference is that the English public viewed the prospect of this
Irish pugilist prevailing as a palatable scenario, perhaps no more irksome
than past Bristol fighters taking the title away from London. In 'A New
Song on Spring and Langan', the concept of British camaraderie is underscored as the Irishman was eagerly adopted as a representative of British
unity against foreign invaders:

> While such heroes as those are Britannia's boast,
> We might still bid defiance to each foreign host;
> And should our proud foes dare assault Britain's shore,
> They might get as good millings as they've had before.
> Then Britons rejoice and make the air ring,
> In praise of our heroes, brave Langan and Spring.[50]

In his accounts, Egan consistently reflected the pugilistic worthiness of
various fighters, avoiding stereotypical depictions. But, this pugilistic objectivity was not always maintained.

48   Ibid., No. 20 (13 June 1824), p. 157.
49   Ibid., No. 20 (13 June 1824), pp. 156, 160.
50   Ibid., No. 21 (20 June 1824), p. 165.

As with the scathing condemnation of Lancastrian fighting methods, prejudices were noticeable against non-London prizefighting communities. Bee warned that 'random' hitting and hauling did not make a positive impression, and that 'countrymen ought to be aware how they appear in the London Ring' (*Boxiana IV*, p. 469). The city of Bristol was an exception, and Egan acknowledged its longstanding tradition without rancour, observing that the championship had often found itself 'in the *unsullied keeping*' of a Bristol 'native' (*Boxiana I*, p. 112). In the preface to *Tom Crib's Memorial*, when considering the Classical precedent of competing cities gaining prestige from their victorious athletes, Moore declared: 'Bristol has been rendered immortal'.[51] Although the worth of Bristol pugilists, and London's dependence on such regional hotbeds, was not questioned, victories obtained outside the dominant Fancy 'circuit' were only 'fitfully recorded'.[52]

Egan suggested that, to triumph, a non-London fighter must prove successful in 'divesting himself of those *provincialities* in which he has been reared' (*Boxiana I*, p. 356). This could be construed as a condescending attitude involving relativity – a district champion is only pre-eminent amongst his own restricted environment. The capital city was depicted as the proving ground for those worthy of pugilistic acclaim: 'every thing in London must be excellent to gain eminence [...] the exalted Champion of a County [...] ranks *only* with Champions of Counties [...] till he soars above those comparisons, and some great event places him upon *that* elevated seat' (p. 356). Dowling elaborated on how 'the generic and individual courage of men' varied domestically: 'Tom, a hero in his own county, and judged invincible, if brought up to town [...] shrinks into insignificance' (*Fistiana*, p. 16).

Bernard Shaw commented on the emphatic manner of victory that later provincial fighters felt they needed to achieve when encountering the bias prevalent at St James's Hall exhibitions: 'Birmingham, sent up a new race [...] whose sole aim was to knock their opponent insensible [...] knowing

---

51 *British Satire, 1785–1840*, ed. by Strachan and others, V, ed. by Jane Moore, p. 193.
52 Brailsford, *Bareknuckles: A Social History of Prize-Fighting*, p. 38.

well that no Birmingham man could depend on a verdict [...] for any less undeniable achievement'.[53] When a visiting fighter entered the metropolis, there is a sense that he was invading the pugilistic citadel, a representative challenging the capital's dominance. Welshman Ned Turner's homecoming saw Egan indulge in some archaic, overstated, imagery:

> [NED] was hailed with all the respect due to a hero in a more important cause [...] Admirers of pugilism among the Ancient Britons, caused a congratulatory peal to be rung upon the bells [...] The Welsh bards who were mustered upon this occasion composed and sung some extempore verses in praise of the brave and the exploits of the ring. (*Boxiana II*, p. 173)

Notwithstanding the acknowledgement of the existence of weightier matters, a major prizefight victory is being treated as would news of a military conquest. It appears that sporting success conferred a comparably significant amount of local prestige, with or without Egan's quixotic touches.

Conversely, travelling London fighters assuming the guise of pugilistic tyros, in order to inveigle local men into money-fights, were regarded with hostility. Such a fraud occurred at Bath races (July 1823), 'where numerous Bristol men attend expressly for Pugilism' (*Boxiana IV*, p. 613). Bee recorded the aftermath: 'a sad lamentation was made about it in the Bath papers [...] and the appalling circumstances of a man's going by a *misnomer* excited *the chaff*' (p. 613). Bee, a member of the London fraternity, remained unsympathetic: 'the *Fancy* writers in the Bath papers wince and whine' (p. 616), but there was a stark warning for such infiltrators: 'if they catch a "*cockney*" astray", there is no place in the world where they can *punish* him better' (p. 613).

A cynical interpretation towards some of the disputes supposedly sparked by pride is that it was only the money wagered on the local man that generated support and celebrations. When an Irish fighter, O' Donnel, defeated Wilson, in October 1812, Egan reported that his expatriate supporters 'carried their hero off in triumph' (*Boxiana I*, p. 316). When overcome, in a subsequent fight, however, there were a distinct lack of

---

53   Shaw, 'Note on Modern Prizefighting', *Cashel Byron's Profession*, p. 242.

comforting devotees: 'MARK THE DIFFERENCE!!! – *no smiles! no shouts! No shoulders offered to support the drooping hero!* But placed in a hackney coach, to groan and reflect upon the reverse of fortune! Any comment is unnecessary!!!' (pp. 316–17). Again, the analogy of a backed cockerel would be appropriate.

Overall, the pugilistic chroniclers convey a sense of community pride and satisfaction gleaned in sporting achievement, as well as resentment at defeats. Shaw encapsulated this attitude in the expression 'local patriotism', stating that the 'average' late-nineteenth-century pugilist 'is a violent partisan.'[54] This inadvertently undercuts one of *Boxiana*'s repeatedly propounded arguments; that pugilism engendered a sporting ethos which, in turn, drove a fundamentally unified national spirit. This idealistic ambition is exploded by such rivalries and jealousies, an opinion articulated in Hazlitt's essay 'On the Pleasure of Hating' (*The Plain Speaker*, 1826): 'Does any one suppose that the love of country in an Englishman implies any friendly feeling or disposition to serve another, bearing the same name? No, it means only hatred to the French.'[55]

Looking at a more contemporary example of prejudicial attitudes, it appears that 'internal' schisms were liable to be perpetuated with an even greater ferocity than international differences. George Orwell (1903–50) suggested that an 'intelligent man [...] who would have nothing but contempt for nationalism in its ordinary form' would exhibit less rationalism on domestic matters: 'Put to him some such proposition as "One Britisher is worth three foreigners", and he would repudiate it [...] But when it is a question of North versus South, he is quite ready to generalise.'[56] This underscores that the concept of a prizefighter as a disparate national entity often foundered on persistent 'tribal' enmities.

54   Shaw, 'Note on Modern Prizefighting', *Cashel Byron's Profession*, p. 240.
55   *The Selected Writings of William Hazlitt*, ed. by Wu, VIII, p. 120.
56   George Orwell, *The Road to Wigan Pier* (London: Penguin Group, 2001), p. 103.

Conciliation and Integrity v Revenge and Dissipation

> Such are the triumphs of boxing [...and] the principles of honour, justice, and humanity, it never fails to produce and support. Where it is known a man is safe from the violence of superior numbers, from the poisonous draught, and the dagger of the assassin. It is a safe and salutary cure for the violence of human passion and, as such, is deserving of admiration and applause.
>
> — 'MR M', *Boxiana III*, pp. 595–6

> As to those miserable ruffians, whether the ornaments of a gaol or the disgrace of a noble house, who [...] call fighting for a few guineas English-spirit, they are most probably out of the reach of literary ridicule, which must be read before it is felt: but we shall use our strongest endeavour to hold up them and their admirers to the contempt of others who might not take their murderous business for manliness. What! Shall English noblemen croud the highways to admire the exploits of a few thieves and butchers [...?] What an amiable vivacity!
>
> — LEIGH HUNT, 'Prospectus', *The Examiner*, 3 January 1808[57]

Such antithetical quotes are illustrative of the contradictory reactions stimulated by prizefighting, and those who reported on the world of the Fancy. 'Mr M' proposed pugilism as a 'cure' for social unease, using a 'steam-engine' analogy: 'We must allow passion to work itself off [...] We must have a *safety-valve*' (*Boxiana III*, p. 581). Prizefights supplied a cathartic outlet for spectators, who identified themselves with the fighters, and it appears that this therapeutic concept could be applied to sparring in the upper classes, Byron recording: 'an hour's exercise with Mr Jackson [...] has given me spirits & fatigued me into that state of languid laziness which I

---

57   *The Selected Writings of Leigh Hunt*, ed. by Robert Morrison, Michael Eberle-Sinatra et al., 6 vols. (London: Pickering & Chatto, 2003), I, ed. by Greg Kucich and Jeffrey N Cox, p. 33.

prefer to all other'.[58] In reality, this is an overly simplistic attitude, and any touting of pugilism as a socially calming influence appears equally flawed as counter-claims involving thievery and butchery.

Hunt went on to mete out further condemnation in a 'dreamingly speculative' poem, *The Choice*: 'as for prize-fights, with their butchering shows, / And crowds of blacklegs, I'd have none of those; / I am not bold in other people's blows' (lines 197–9).[59] Hunt felt disinclined to try the 'emulation' prescribed by Egan, contesting the notion that spectating at prizefights 'calls forth a continued admiration of prowess and hardihood' (*Boxiana I*, p. 284). In turn, Egan refuted Hunt's aspersions:

> Although that classic *sprig* of literature, LEIGH HUNT, has with the *flourish* of his pen, completely condemned the manly and national practice of Boxing, as debasing the finer feelings of our compositions [...] it by no means decides, that PUGILISM is a barbarous trait, because it does not accord with his imperative notions! Nor is the old intuitive English spirit of Boxing to be suppressed, or the nation suffered to become effeminate, because the *refined* pages of a newspaper (the *Examiner*) are not to be sullied. (*Boxiana I*, pp. 301–2)

Egan enjoyed the support of other publications, *Blackwood's* endorsement of *Boxiana* writing being fuelled by Hunt's aversion to it: 'Mr Leigh Hunt would be entitled to complain of the cruelty of boxing, were Little Puss to tip him a stomacher while meditating a crisp sonnet in some farmy field'.[60]

Egan also included a piece by Charles Sloman that specifically countered Hunt's allegation: 'Would they repress the rising feelings of courage [...] Would they suppress that science, which has become mathematically precise, and raise to its exalted station brutality?'[61] Another piece

---

58 Letter 8 April 1814, to Lady Melbourne. *Byron's Letters and Journals*, ed. by Marchand, IV, p. 90.

59 First published in *The Liberal*, no. 4, 1823. *The Selected Writings of Leigh Hunt*, ed. by Morrison, Eberle-Sinatra et al., VI, ed. by John Strachan, p. 27.

60 The fighter Henry Abrahams was 'better known' as 'Little Puss' (*Boxiana III*, p. 491). *Blackwood's* (March 1820). *Parodies of the Romantic Age*, ed. by Stones and Strachan, IV, ed. by Strachan, p. 124.

61 *Egan's Weekly Courier*, No. 3 (18 January 1829), p. 11.

of dialogue in Shaw's novel illustrates the prejudicial views harboured by some, as Webber attempts to explain the 'low' social background of a typical pugilist:

> 'Possibly a discharged soldier, sailor [...] But he is generally a common labourer [...]'.
> 'Do they never come from a higher rank?'
> 'Never even from the better classes of their own [...] Gentlemen are not likely to succeed at work that needs the strength [...] of a bull and the cruelty of a butcher'. (*CBP*, p. 126)

This particular fictional preconception coincides with Hunt's perceptions.

Part of the moral ambiguity surrounding pugilistic matters is rooted in the portrayal of the men-about-town in *Life in London*. This text, and its imitations, depicted reprobate behaviour amidst a hedonistic philosophy: 'PLEASURE was their idol; it was the creature of their imagination: and no heroes ever offered more sacrifices at its attractive *shrine*' (*Life in London*, p. 246). Certain 'libertine elements' contributed to the work's popularity:

> It took the drawbacks of bachelor life, namely its lack of status and respectability [...] and transformed them into positive virtues, open invitations to freedom and mobility [...] It reinterprets the insecurity and isolation of the lower middle-class male as an invitation to overleap all bounds.[62]

The philosophical core of such 'early-nineteenth-century rambles' was male-orientated, as Jane Rendell explains: '[Rambling] can be defined as the pursuit of pleasure, or the exploration of urban sites of leisure and entertainment by men'. Thus, issues of sybaritic indulgence and exclusion of women coalesce, and are detrimental to the moral perception of Egan's metropolitan and pugilistic writing, which may be justifiably interpreted as an anti-domestic portrayal of a limited London locale with its 'multiple sites of desire'.[63]

Confusion is compounded by a blurring of the distinction between generic types, Egan asserting of Corinthian Tom: 'Although *One of the FANCY*, he was not a *fancy-man* [...] our hero was no *Dandy*' (*Life in London*, p. 42). Notwithstanding his declared abhorrence, the conduct

---

62   Dart, '"Flash Style": Pierce Egan and Literary London 1820–28', pp. 198–9.
63   Rendell, *The Pursuit of Pleasure*, pp. 4, 6.

of Egan's heroes sometimes coincides with that very same group. How far removed is dandy ostentation from the exhibitionism of Tom, Jerry, and Bob on their 'struts' through the metropolis? Similarly, there are instances of the trio's tardy hours: 'The clock had announced *three* before TOM and his COZ were able to lift their *damaged* heads from the pillow' (p. 290); 'It was late in the day before our heroes took their breakfast at *Corinthian-House*' (p. 339). Although these belated movements can be attributed to nocturnal 'sprees', they do little to distance the trio from a lifestyle strongly associated with dandies, who 'rarely left their rooms before noon'.[64] This illustrates another contradiction, some dandy traits being compatible with the amoral ramblings of Fancy members, but pugilistic principles categorically not. A street-disturbance allowed Egan the opportunity to convey events in the style of a pugilistic contest, with the collateral bonus of deriding the dandy as he describes how the miscreants are summarily dispatched by a Fancy buck (Martin):

> The Dandy went down as if he had been *shot*; the second shared the same fate; the third was no better off; the fourth came in for *pepper*; the fifth got a severe *quilting* [...] It was truly laughable to see the ridiculous way in which the *Dandies* appeared; – the *claret* trickling down. (*Boxiana III*, p. 253)

The scene is imbued with the feel of a *Life in London* incident.

The chorus to 'Milling, a New Song to an Old Tune' warned: 'RUN, dandies, run, all London now are milling it' (*Boxiana IV*, p. 658), and Egan and Bee ridiculed those guilty of extreme affectation:

> [The EXQUISITE] can talk of military manoeuvres and of an affair or two in defence of his country [...] He is *made* up, but so well *finished*, that his appearance at an evening party brightens up many an eye. – His composure of countenance, however, is such as to prove that he is too much a man of fashion to love *any thing*; and his conduct is such as to leave no doubt as his always being ready to sacrifice *every one* at the shrine of his selfish vanity. His dressing-room and other apartments are filled with a rare collection of pipes and snuff-boxes [...] and his wardrobe the *ne plus ultra* of what [...] expensive tradesmen can afford to give credit for. – His conversation is *agreeably* unintelligible. (*Sporting Anecdotes*, p. 60)

---

64 Murray, *High Society*, p. 35.

Exquisite (an) – another name for Dandy, but of more *refined* or *feminine* manners. The *Chronicle* says, '[...] an *Exquisite* fainted [...] in Bond-street, and was assisted into a shop [...] Medical aid being sent for, it was ascertained that his valet had laced his stays too tight'. (*Bee's Sportsman's Slang*)

Yet these are 'pure' Englishmen, some with military service, contradicting the nationalistic rhetoric of pugilistic writing. Shaw commented on the influence exerted by such works, claiming that a typical reader 'gradually persuades himself that all Englishmen can use their fists'. But, he instantly underscores the risible nature of Eganesque stereotyping: 'which is about as true as the parallel theory that every Frenchman can handle a foil and that every Italian carries a stiletto'.[65]

More disconcerting for the moralist detractors was the lack of condemnation for dissolute, or illegal, actions. Instead, Egan pinpointed the 'jollity of the *Cadgers*' (*Life in London*, p. 346), and the general fun of drinking late into the night. In addition, the fictitious Sparkle recommended 'continual practice' in the dubious 'art' of 'Greekery': 'The professor should frequently exercise himself in private with cards and dice, in order that his digits may be trained to a proper degree of *agility*' (*Real Life in London*, p. 192). 'Greeking' meant cheating at cards (*OED*), which also implied that it was somehow a form of foreign immorality. Advocating such deception conflicts with the honourable ideals of the ring, and when a 'fashionably dressed' friend of Dashall communicates details of a recent 'spree', there is an impression of wild lawlessness: 'We now sallied forth, like a pack in full cry, with all the loud expression of mirth and riot' (p. 219). A footnote goes as far as to claim such unrestrained mischief 'is a proof of high spirit [...] and serves in many cases to stamp a man's character' (p. 90).

Life in London depictions cannot be blamed for the city's degenerate behaviour, but more the prevailing culture in which alcohol 'coloured daily life at all levels': 'At the beginning of the nineteenth century, according to one estimate, there were 50,000 pubs [open all day] to cater for a population of 9 million'.[66] The ramifications for prizefighters could be

---

65   Shaw, 'Preface', *Cashel Byron's Profession*, p. xvi.
66   Murray, *High Society*, p. 197.

extreme: '[Power] was a most distinguished favourite of the *Fancy*, and much caressed [...] It was this circumstance that caused his ruin' (*Boxiana II*, p. 91). Egan reveals that Power died in June 1813, aged 23. Such accelerated deaths were not isolated, and Egan had attempted to forewarn that: '*stamina*, once undermined [...] will never again arrive at its pristine purity' (*Boxiana I*, pp. 475–6). Egan's metropolitan work attempted to demarcate the boundaries of acceptability, and offered a fulsome behavioural guide to those wishing to 'See Life':

> IT WAS NOT that 'sort of LIFE', that encouraged individuals to drink very hard [...] to appear *learned* in every thing allied to obscenity and lewdness [...] IT WAS NOT to frequent places of fashionable resort, and to *keep it up* all night in drinking, swearing, and singing; and when fair morn makes her approach, then heroically to sally forth into the street, *reel* about like a RAKE of the first magnitude, insult all you meet [...] break a few windows, stagger to another tavern [...] and finish your glorious frolic in being sent home in a hackney-coach, senseless. (*Life in London*, pp. 127–8)

Overall, Egan espoused noble sporting precepts, decried affectation, and highlighted 'an afflicting portrait of the rapid degradations from virtue to vice' (p. 179).

Regardless of whether he thought that the censure elicited by *Life in London* was unjustified, Egan adopted a penitent tone in his somewhat purgative sequel *The Finish to [...] Life In and Out of London* (1828). Revealingly, Egan had broached the idea of retribution for his idlers in an 1821 draft for a proposed Covent Garden production: 'portraying that LIFE IN LONDON without the check-string is a rapid trot towards Death'.[67] Rather than thinking that dissipated behaviour was incited merely by its representation, it can be argued that Egan's metropolitan tour quenched such urges by relating the trio's escapades: 'for the benefit of *fire-side* heroes and sprightly maidens, who may feel a wish to "see Life" without receiving a *scratch*' (*Life in London*, pp. 19–20). Egan filtered the risks and, having the metropolis placed before them, the reader was vicariously satisfied.

---

67 Reid, *Bucks and Bruisers*, pp. 71, 149.

Widespread attention devoted to major trials sheds further light on the ambivalent attitudes that prevailed in the Regency period: 'the career of Thurtell can be fairly taken as a paradigm of the lives of one section of the Fancy who would claim distinction because they had once shaken John Thurtell by the hand'.[68] The curious moral ambivalence of the age was underscored by observations made by judge Justice Park, concerning: 'an appetite for this species of intelligence' (*Trial of Thurtell*, p. 1). Thurtell's statement of defence invoked the conflicting national and moral traits under discussion: 'The country which is dear to me I have served, I have fought for her [...] I have been a gambler'; 'If I have erred [...] half of the nobility of the land have been my examples' (*Trial of Thurtell*, p. 80). Unfortunately, his association with the Fancy fortified the arguments of its opponents: 'it shall suffice to state, that the felon and fiend THURTELL was one of the chief supporters, and greatest ornaments of the Prize Ring' (*RIPM*, p. 13).

Sports corruption involving bribery and betting scams reflected a street culture rife with sharpers and prostitutes. Egan candidly reported a pugilist, Tom Cropley, to be 'a *protector of the naughty dickey birds*' (*New Series Boxiana II*, p. 520), thus corroborating an earlier accusation made by Vasey: 'it is no extraordinary thing for the members of the Milling Profession to depend chiefly upon the earnings of street-walkers for their support' (*RIPM*, p. 14). General corruption was also prevalent within the armed forces (illicit trading in army commissions), and certain life-endangering 'economies' were practised by dockyard manufacturers in shipbuilding practices: 'Men who had political influence or held offices of state were milking the revenues quite as assiduously as their rivals in private commerce'.[69]

Issues of sporting, and national, integrity were equally tangled. Distrust of foreignness extended to language, and Langford focuses on the positive perception of English: 'The English had no word [...] to match "naïveté" [...] because they did not need a pejorative term for describing innocence. German "Einfachheit" came closer but did not quite convey the implied

68   Ford, *Prizefighting: The Age of Regency Boximania*, p. 165.
69   Thomas, *Cochrane: Britannia's Sea Wolf*, p. 44.

benevolence of English simplicity'.[70] In a journal entry (28 September 1823) that echoed the concerns voiced by Cochrane, Byron lamented the duplicity of his Greek colleagues-in-arms:

> There never was such an incapacity for veracity [...] One of them found fault the other day with the English language – because it had so few shades of a Negative – whereas a Greek can so modify a No – to a Yes – and vice versa – by the slippery qualities of his language – that prevarication may be carried to an extent and still leave a loop-hole through which perjury may slip without being perceived.[71]

One of the quibbles directed at Egan, by Bee, is the writer's predilection for words with French origins, such as 'sang froid'. On one occasion, complaining about the choice of 'nouvelle', Bee categorically stated his belief concerning pugilism's unadulterated national heritage: 'as *Jack Frenchman* is no boxer, we dislike the applying his language to a sport *wholly* ENGLISH' (*Boxiana IV*, p. 388).

It is somewhat ironic to find evidence of honourable precepts applied to the financial dealings of gamblers. In upper-class circles, profligacy was generally regarded as an acceptable vice with an absence of disapproval over domestic or commercial debts. Moreover, such insolvency was considered 'not only normal, but somehow rather chic'. The onus of repayment was transformed, however, when transferred to the sphere of sporting wagers, where delay was not an option: 'voluntary exile or even suicide was preferable to dishonour. The rationale [...] seems to have been that interest was not involved between gentlemen: therefore it was obviously incumbent upon the creditor to pay them at once'.[72] There is an incongruity about a moral code being, ostensibly, adhered to in the shady business of gaming debts, and the shame associated with reneging. One dubious reason for settling promptly may have been that it maintained credit worthiness, thus enabling one to continue gambling. Questionable motives aside, it aids understanding of why conduct in pugilistic circles was promoted as

---

70   Langford, *Englishness Identified*, p. 87.
71   *Byron's Letters and Journals*, ed. by Marchand, XI, p. 33.
72   Murray, *High Society*, pp. 61, 64.

self-regulating. Where arbitration was required, there were 'enough experienced men of authority, gentry and pugilists, on hand to make sure that the accepted modes of behaviour prevailed'.[73] Nevertheless, Egan felt it necessary to publish a warning against a spiralling gambling culture: 'precipitate ruin, is too often the serious consequences' (*Book of Sports*, p. 57).

Nationally, pugilism was considered to be performing an important cultural function, and could be regarded as a civic necessity. Egan's pugilistic writing attempted a degree of moral inculcation extending beyond the regulation of wagers. Dowling endorsed the theory that witnessing honourable conduct engendered emulation: 'Any attempt at *treachery* or *foul play*, meets with reprehension [...] The spectators, however numerous, are impressed with the value [...] of these rules, and whenever violated are prompt in expressing their indignation' (*Fistiana*, p. 20). A sporting code encouraged public conformance to a general law-abiding attitude, upon which a Middlesex magistrate, Barber Beaumont, elaborated:

> It is further objected that a boxing match draws together a vast number of thieves and blackguards. This is very true; and so does an execution, a lord mayor's show, a court-day at St James's, and every interesting sight which is open to the public at large. (*Fistiana*, p. 77)

Arguably, the most compelling aspect of prizefighting spectators' conduct, occurred when frustrated by judicial interference:

> They suffer themselves to be driven from the scene of their much-loved amusement, like a flock of sheep, at the bidding of some clerical or meddling magistrate [...] It seems to show that the lessons of patience under suffering, and the command of temper and submission to authority taught by the laws of the Ring, extend beyond it, and influence the habits and manners of the people connected with it in their general demeanour. (p. 78)

This particular magistrate champions pugilistic supporters, and his assertion of general public compliance with law-enforcement is viewed as another area of British superiority. It is implied that only a light-handed

---

73   Brailsford, *Bareknuckles: A Social History of Prize-Fighting*, p. 50.

approach is required in matters of crowd control, and this is noted by an eminent German visitor: 'The Saxon Heinrich von Watzdorf was amazed to see the crowds enjoying Vauxhall without any sign of a grenadier or a fixed bayonet'.[74] When the disruptive behaviour of a Frenchman at Drury Lane Theatre is ridiculed by Egan (who mockingly labels the Frenchman's offences as 'certain manifestations of mischievous magnificence'), the subsequent remarks made by the magistrate allude to the more oppressive treatment necessary abroad: '[Sir Richard Birnie] said, "had you so conducted yourself in a *French* theatre, you would have been quickly dragged away by certain gentlemen with fixed bayonets"'.[75]

The issue of self-policing is a confused one, pugilism being advanced as a means of settling disputes, without legal intervention, in addition to its superiority over lethal foreign 'revenge' practices. The prospect of a wronged party, trained in the pugilistic art, meting out summary justice to a bullying braggart is an appealing theory. Bee claimed that societal control was, in fact, pugilism's prime role: '[Never] has it ever entered our noddle that pugilism, as an art, should be encouraged for its own sake alone [...] Without "the science", which all young men are desirous of attaining, would our streets be filled with rampant bravoes' (*Annals of Sporting VIII*, p. 375). In this vein, Egan reported the intervention of a passer-by thwarting a drunken assault on an innocent couple: 'with the swiftness of a feathered Mercury, [he] flew along the pavement, and with one blow, laid the foremost of our assailants in the kennel' (*Book of Sports*, p. 12).

Vasey pronounced that a pugilist's inability 'to discriminate between a proper and an improper occasion for the exercise of his powers, must be instantly acknowledged' (*RIPM*, p. 8). But, this statement is as flawed as the idealistic claims made by the sport's chroniclers, and the comments of the eponymous hero in *Cashel Byron's Profession* endorses Bee's point about the reticence of genuine pugilistic men to wantonly exercise their powers: 'any one who is used to being paid for a job is just the last person in the world to do it for nothing' (p. 134). Also, Fewtrell stated his conviction

74 Langford, *Englishness Identified*, p. 65.
75 *Egan's Life in London, and Sporting Guide*, No. 1 (1 February 1824), p. 3.

that because 'the science is universally understood [...] the strong are taught humility, and the weak confidence' (*Boxing Reviewed*, p. 11). One of the most fanciful claims, relating to the conduciveness of pugilism to restoring harmonious relations, was made in another contribution by Tom Reynolds:

> Only the BOXING GLOVES can give the true polish of civilisation to the world. And, I am confident, if Adam had been *fly* he would have taught his sons to box; then the club would not have been used, and murder prevented. Cain would have given Abel a good *milling*, perhaps *queered* his *ogles*, or spoiled his *box of dominoes*; but they would have been found next morning supping porridge as comfortably as lord mayor's sons. (*Book of Sports*, p. 171)

Although whimsical, this imagined scene of concord displays typically creative persuasiveness.

A more realistic concept, than having instilled an honourable code throughout Fancy circles, is that an imposing pugilistic 'presence' acted as a deterrent. This can be detected in the influence exerted by the formidable bearing of Jackson: 'a newcomer to the boxing crowd described him "moving like one of Homer's heroes" [*Sporting Magazine*, 12 July 1823]'.[76] Jackson appears to be the commanding figure alluded to in the 'amateur' report on Randall v Martin (1821), the writer observing the degeneration of behaviour for the subsidiary bouts following his departure:

> The Commander-in-Chief, it seems, was absent, and republican government will never do [...] Individuals exerted themselves to keep a wider ring, by laying on the whip, but there was no system for acting in concert; and if such confusion were commonly the case, few people would be induced to go to see fights. (*Boxiana IV*, p. 198)

It was amidst such congested scenes that petty crime flourished. At the above fight, there is reference to the 'daring outrages of an immense gang of pickpockets' (*Real Life in London*, p. 393) and, in the vicinity of Drury Lane, such warnings as 'the *Divers*, are all upon the lay' (p. 149). This expression formally translates as 'pickpockets upon the look-out to exercise their profession', and a subsequent altercation is witnessed by Dashall and

---

76   Brailsford, *Bareknuckles: A Social History of Prize-Fighting*, p. 72.

Sparkle: '"Keep your hands out of my pockets [...]" said a tall man standing near them, "or b— me if I don't *mill* you" [...] and gave him a *floorer* [...] a random sort of fight ensued' (pp. 149–50). This testifies to the use of the fist to extract retribution, but the subsequent mayhem does not correspond to Egan and Bee's concept of justice being swiftly and neatly delivered. Claims that pugilism acted as a regulating device also ignored the prevailing gambling culture.

Egan had previously made idealistic claims for his home country: 'the stiletto is not known [...and] revenge is not finished by murder. Boxing removes these dreadful calamities' (*Boxiana I*, p. 3). Bee supported Egan's championing of pugilism, but a piece he included from 'a correspondent' implicates the other 'home' countries: 'Foreigners affect to consider pugilism as a very low and mean custom [...] but if we came to reason the point, it will be found every way preferable to [...] the malignant dagger; the unrelenting shillelagh, or the maiming claymore' (*Annals of Sporting III*, p. 12). The 'Young Gentleman of the Fancy' confirms a very English outlook: 'Blows and the shaking of hands are the alpha and omega: – the life and death [...] of dispute' (*Book of Sports*, p. 121).

Egan had ventured the doctrine that men would always quarrel, but it was preferable for them to do so in 'a way that will bear reflection' (*Boxiana I*, p. 12). However, Vasey claimed that this promotes a 'palpably false principle that we are *incapable* of improvement', and argues that society will eventually become more enlightened and recognise 'the inutility of quarrelling'. He proceeds to argue that it was nonsensical for the pugilistic advocate to cite foreign methods as 'more dreadful and deadly' than sporting jurisdiction: 'It can avail him nothing [...] by the imbecility of its argument, in citing a greater abuse in order to effect the toleration of a less' (*RIPM*, p. 9).

Such complications inform the debate on civilised means of settling disputes, and lead to consideration of duelling. Byron, writing to Murray, set out its heritage: 'They prate about assassination – what is it but the origin of duelling [...] it is the fount of the modern point of honour – in what the laws can't or *wont* reach'.[77] This emits a mixed message, linking the activity with both murderous and honourable aspects, and hints at its usefulness in circumnavigating the vagaries of the law. Bee dismissed the practice in some sardonic pieces, his causticity encapsulated in a lexical definition: '*Duel* – two testy chaps firing at each other, until they are tired, or one drops' (*Bee's Sportsman's Slang*). He also alluded to the dangers involved in frequenting the gaming haunts, citing '*hellish gambling*' as the cause of duelling, and belittling such dubious motives: 'If a man cannot quietly put up with the loss of £3000, at roley-poley, of a night, he ought to have his head perforated in the morning' (*Annals of Sporting II*, p. 63). The depiction of duelling as the preferred practice of the French was also ridiculed:

> Two law-students of Paris fought a duel in the Bois du Boulogne [...] On arriving at the wood they drew lots for the first fire. He to whom good fortune proved favourable, judiciously fired in the air; his opponent fired on one side, and, most fortunately, killed one of the seconds. (*Annals of Sporting I*, p. 423)

In a similarly acerbic swipe, Bee described duelling as '*War with French Manners*', reporting: 'M. Grange, an advocate at Bordeaux [...] has been killed in a duel by an English physician. Several other duels have taken place, with less fortunate results' (*Annals of Sporting II*, p. 347).

In the aforementioned episode of drunken assailants being denied by a pugilistic passer-by, Egan offered an alternative scenario:

> Had my friend been as little *knowing* in the *science* as his adversaries, *very dreadful might have been the consequences*, because might in that case would have overcome right, unless the fellows would have had patience to wait till he ran home for his sword [...then] he might have *killed* them in a *gentleman-like* manner. (*Book of Sports*, p. 12)

Egan mocks the fatal repercussions of a more 'gentlemanly', and in this case impractical, means of administering justice. It should be noted that this successful application of the pugilistic method is one where a crime is being committed and the perpetrators are morally indefensible. The emotional

---

77   Letter of 28 September 1820. *Byron's Letters and Journals*, ed. by Marchand, VII, p. 184.

ramifications of preventing, or punishing, a vindictive criminal act are minimal. But, in a pugilistic bout that purports to be an activity that exorcises animosity, Vasey makes a valid charge; that a wondrous transformation from 'enmity to affection' is an 'unnatural' expectation (*RIPM*, p. 10).

The 'safety-valve' theory espoused by 'Mr M' was an omnipresent theme in various pugilistic writers' encomiums on the sport, and can be used as a touchstone for the usual *Boxiana* perspective, incorporating class and nationality issues:

> Common people, in settling their disputes by the fist, act much more wisely, humanely, and philosophically, than the nobility and gentry [...] If we look abroad [...] we shall see the desperate and fatal effects of human passion, for want of a regular and innocent mode of working itself off. (*Boxiana III*, pp. 582–3)

However, none of the rhetoric against 'deadly' practices acknowledges the occasional fatality in the ring, as recorded by Byron: 'I hear that the fancy has had a sad reality in somebody being killed in a fight – which will turn the pugilistic uniform to sackcloth.'[78] Sensitivity to such tragedies is evident when Bee firmly rebuked Hickman for some thoughtless bragging: '*Gas* is reported to have declared his intention of "killing *Oliver* in ten minutes" [...] The words are to be reprobated' (*Boxiana IV*, p. 164).

Whilst advancing the notion of a national aptitude for the sport, Dowling touched on social restrictions, and adversities, rarely engaged by Egan:

> The increasing commercial habits of the country, the growth of luxury following thereupon, and the selfishness and effeminacy, unhappily their constant attendants, at length occasioned many of these pursuits to be abandoned by the higher classes for more sedentary and enervating occupations, and caused most of those exclusively followed by the common people, to be discouraged. (*Fistiana*, pp. 2–3).

Dowling then highlighted one of the pernicious effects of this sporting decline: 'Large cities arose [...] The population were forced into those hives of men so inimical to the health of body or mind' (p. 3). The theme

---

78 Letter of 10 April 1817, to Scrope Berdmore Davies. *Byron's Letters and Journals*, ed. by Marchand, XI, p. 166.

is pursued when launching an excoriating attack on a typically myopic stance adopted by those seeking to marginalise, or eradicate, the sport:

> 'Demoralizing' is another 'good mouthfilling', vituperative epithet, which has been applied [...] The Ring is demoralizing is it? Is it more so than the cotton-mills of Manchester, the tender-hearted owners of which, actually formed a society for the suppression of pugilism? Would not a Briton of the olden time sicken with disgust and amazement, could he see those dens of misery, and hear them appealed to as specimens of the greatness and glory of his country, whilst its hardy and invigorating exercises are stigmatized as its disgrace? (p. 13)

This constitutes yet another national division.

Unsurprisingly, an activity that relied on the sufferance of those who judged it to be militarily expedient was prone to no longer be condoned following the end of the Napoleonic Wars (1815): '[Peace] put pugilism quite out of favour and gave free reign to the incipient antagonism of all the governmental, magisterial, and respectable classes'.[79] The fragile, and fickle, basis of the toleration shown towards pugilism is exemplified by the furore created by the death of Sandy McKay. *The Times* (5 July 1830) commented on 'public indignation and alarm [...] "The claims of justice, the blood of the murdered, and the well being of the country alike all call for an example"'.[80] This is an extreme reaction, and objections raised against pugilism were more frequently typified by the following: '*Prize-Fights* were [...] the means of collecting numerous blackguards together' and tended 'to encourage a spirit of *gambling*, and *ferocity* of disposition' (*Boxiana III*, p. 586).

Vasey concluded his attack against the Prize Ring scene with claims that it was 'composed of members so truly depraved, and kept in being by individuals so fully fitted for the lowest kinds of infamy' (*RIPM*, p. 13). Egan's views tallied with magistrate Beaumont's; that undesirable elements did not require pugilistic events to congregate, or participate in gambling:

> Is there a horse-race, a fair, or any other public sight [...] where bad characters are not to be seen? [...] Persons who are not connected with pugilism [...] will lay wagers

---

79   Brailsford, *Bareknuckles: A Social History of Prize-Fighting*, pp. 51–2.
80   Radford, *The Celebrated Captain Barclay*, p. 260.

on the election of any particular parson, who is considered the *favourite* to obtain a *rectorship*, with as much *sang froid*, if it requires judgement, or produces *gain*. (*Boxiana III*, p. 6)

And, Egan openly welcomes any curious person who feels 'anxious to take a peek at the resort of the Fancy', defiantly declaring: 'The Castle Tavern is most respectably conducted [...] in spite of the calumny which is continually heaped on such places by hypocrites and canting knaves' (*Book of Sports*, p. 72).

Some of Egan's own connections were dubious, further demonstrated by his fulsome recommendation for 'Beardsworth's Repository', touted as 'unquestionably the best conducted establishment of the kind in the United Kingdom and consequently in the world'. Beardsworth is proclaimed as a person who 'has "worked his way" with industry [...] and integrity, to his present eminence'.[81] It might be cynical to suggest that this 'advertisement' was not simply an appreciative gesture (the Repository staged Fancy 'Sparring Benefits'), and that Egan received some financial incentive to publish such a glowing piece. In 1830, amongst racing successes, Beardsworth was 'sued successfully [...] and barred from his Warwick winnings because he was in arrears for both stakes and forfeits'.[82] The stigmatic nature of gaming obligations renders Beardsworth culpable of contravening unwritten Fancy tenets.

Ultimately, accusations of pugilistic barbarity, and the dissipated behaviour of the Fancy, could be rebuffed or minimised by positive associations. Economically profitable ring enterprises were tolerated, and English victories over foreign challengers greeted as a boost for national morale, thus augmenting the militaristic benefits connected with pugilistic training. Just as an under-pressure government has been re-elected amidst the euphoria of a military victory, or economic reforms rendered palatable, a prizefighting scene associated with success forestalled interference and cushioned, or nullified, censure. Accusations levelled by the *Edinburgh Star*, regarding profligate wagering, underscore the slim margin between

81 *Egan's Weekly Courier*, No. 9 (1 March 1829), p. 36.
82 Beardsworth's horse, 'Birmingham', won the St Leger Stakes at Doncaster in 1830. Brailsford, *Bareknuckles: A Social History of Prize-Fighting*, p. 123.

acceptance and denunciation of an event 'poised somewhere between public adulation and official condemnation. If Cribb lost his fight [...] condemnation would surface everywhere'.[83] Crucially, the champion won, and general rejoicing drowned out the denigrators.

Pugilistic events became increasingly less likely to be 'winked at', and Reid provides a snapshot of changing attitudes as the 1820s advanced: 'there was a growing reaction against the looseness of regency living [...] A new temper of moral seriousness, associated with a more responsible sense of national purpose and destiny, was invading society'.[84] To some extent, pugilism had become 'anachronistic'. Robert Surtees had barred pugilistic reports from his *New Sporting Magazine*, and occasions when notable prizefights provoked widespread interest evaporated. The primetime of the Fancy and flash language was compacted into a relatively brief *Boxiana* period (approximately 1812–32). There was a later (genuine) endorsement of sporting influence: 'moral education, in spite of all the labours of direct instructors, is really acquired in hours of recreation. Sports and amusements are [...] means by which the mind is insensibly trained'.[85]

Questions remained concerning which pastimes were beneficial to society, and whether they could adequately replace supposedly 'barba-rous' means of sublimating aggression: '"Rational Recreation" sought by progressives could embrace [...] such "striking instances of refinement" as the substitution, at Engton, in Staffordshire, of the Easter bull-baiting by a performance of the *Messiah*'.[86] This dilemma persisted well into the Victorian era and, in his essay 'Open-Air Entertainments', journalist George Augustus Sala (1828–95) ruefully commented upon 'the striving fancy that there is in most of us, which even a lecture or a steam-engine will not always satisfy'.[87] Sala's sarcasm finds its mark in a manner that Jon Bee would, doubtless, have applauded.

---

83   Radford, *The Celebrated Captain Barclay*, p. 169.
84   Reid, *Bucks and Bruisers*, p. 137.
85   William Cooke Taylor, *Notes of a Tour in the Manufacturing Districts of Lancashire* (1842), quoted in Schlicke, *Dickens and Popular Entertainment*, p. 214.
86   *Sporting Magazine*, 2 April 1793. Brailsford, *Bareknuckles: A Social History*, p. 93.
87   *Household Words* (8 May 1852), quoted in Schlicke, *Dickens and Popular Entertainment*, p. 205.

Enlivening Reality: The Egan Touch

I invoke Shakespeare, Kipling, Keats, Shelley et al. in my reports oftentimes to paper over the cracks in what has been a totally negative, dull,
featureless game. I search for the beautiful, the witty, the *charmant*, the
stimulating. I want to bond with fellow bizarre spirits.[1]

I could describe the scene [...] Content yourself with fancying who first
drew claret [...] who put out cleverly with his left; whose face bore severe
marks of punishment, hit out wildly, hung like a mass of butcher's meat
on his second's knee; and, failing at last to come up to time, fell down
senseless on the turf [...] What need is there for me to state who officiated [...] how there was a cry of 'Foul!' and how the swell mobsmen
robbed right and left.[2]

These extracts encapsulate the essence of Pierce Egan's *Boxiana*-style
accounts, as well as highlighting the problem of reporting on pugilism's
repetitiveness. It appears to be an unavoidable truth that Egan embel-
lished proceedings in a bid to mask, or 'paper over', frequently uninspiring
sporting action. Despite Sala's endorsement that sports were an intrinsic
constituent of English life, his comments cast doubt on the consequence
of Egan's pugilistic reports. Sala implies that the action which he 'could'
recount, is relatively inconsequential as events have followed a predict-
able course. A natural progression might be to surmise that the language

---

1   Stuart Hall, *Heaven and Hall: A Prodigal Life* (London: BBC Worldwide, 2000),
    pp. 41–2.
2   G A Sala, 'The Sporting World'. *Gaslight and Daylight* (London: Chapman & Hall,
    1859), p. 388.

that chronicles such happenings was, likewise, stale and dispensable. This supports the concept that Egan's linguistic style compensated for a short-fall in excitement.

When analysing *Boxiana* accounts, a more extreme interpretation is that the language displaces, even replaces, actual events, and that the reporter merely renders a likeness or sketch. This can be observed in later sports writing, and places Egan as a forerunner in jettisoning reality for the sake of spectacle and entertainment. Regarding the influence of sporting newspapers, Sala said: 'Instanter we become denizens if not habitués of the sporting world',[3] and the American journalist A J Liebling (1904–63) would later declare: 'Part of the pleasure of going to a fight is reading the newspapers next morning to see what the sports writers *think* [my italics] happened'.[4]

Egan appears to have merely enlivened his pugilistic accounts, rather than invented false intelligence. However, the scope for abuse existed, and this is alluded to in Thomas Moore's journal entries (of 4, 5 December 1818) relating to Randall's defeat of Turner:

> Heard, while at dinner, 'an account of the battle, by express', crying in the streets. Sent to buy it, and found it anticipated victory on the side of Turner [...] The Sunday papers all placarded with 'true', and 'genuine', and 'best' accounts of the battle.[5]

This contemporary record supplies cogent evidence to the existence of a well of routine, transposable, and certainly non-committal phrases that could be inserted into the 'firsthand' reports of those wishing to achieve early sales. Obviously, this mode of attempting to pre-empt rival publications was a gamble, but was in keeping with the general Fancy spirit of enterprising speculation. Egan's report of the fight conceded that 'to describe minutely the feints – the pauses – dodgings [...] would fill a volume' (*Boxiana III*, p. 177).

---

3   Ibid., p. 375.
4   A J Liebling, 'Sugar Ray and the Milling Cove' (1951). A J Liebling, *Just Enough Liebling: Classic Work by the Legendary 'New Yorker' Writer* (New York: New Point Press, 2004), p. 341.
5   *Memoirs, Journal, and Correspondence of Thomas Moore*, ed. by Russell, II, p. 234.

We can readily imagine that charlatan reporters enjoyed leeway to invent the content of their sketches, complete with general 'dodgings', not revealing (perhaps 'forecasting' would be a more appropriate word) the victor until the last sentence. The issue of linguistic verve and imagery supplanting chunks of more mundane action is a consistent theme, but it was the pugilistic jargon that was immediately appropriated by imitators. Perhaps most noticeably, this element is illustrated in the flash verse of Moore and William Frederick Deacon.

The *Boxiana* Style in Political Satire and Parody

> The Romantic period was saturated in satire. The age saw a torrent of occasional satire: squib, pasquinade, *ad hominem* parody, and lampoon in broadside, newspaper column, and political journal. The political, social, and literary issues of the day resound through the age's satire.[6]

Thomas Moore's squib *Epistle from Tom Crib to Big Ben* was published in *The Morning Chronicle* on 31 August 1815. In a style imitative of a *Boxiana* report, this work depicted Cribb 'milling' Big Ben (a thinly veiled caricature of the Prince Regent) 'over his ungentlemanly lack of sportsmanship in refusing Napoleon sanctuary.'[7] The demand ignited by this piece of political satire resulted in it being reproduced eleven days later, the newspaper describing it as an 'exquisite *jeu-d'esprit*.'[8] Like Egan, Moore was generous in his deployment of italics, although they were not uniformly applied to slang terms. In the lines 'the only one trick, good or bad, / Of the fancy you're up to, is *fibbing* my lad' (20–1), the duality of '*fibbing*' underscores Moore's views concerning the mendacity of European monarchs and governments, which would achieve greater prominence in his sequel.

---

6   John Strachan, in *British Satire, 1785–1840,* ed. by Strachan and others, I, p. xvi.
7   *British Satire, 1785–1840,* ed. by Strachan and others, V, ed. by Jane Moore, p. 115.
8   *Memoirs, Journal, and Correspondence of Thomas Moore,* ed. by Russell, II, p. 80.

Seeking an effective satirical medium to reflect his scepticism about the Aix-la-Chapelle Congress (September 1818), Moore again turned to the *Boxiana* style and formulated 'a series of *flash* letters' from those pugilists selected for sparring exhibitions. Any endorsement of the literary merit of Egan's flash work is somewhat undercut by Moore's ensuing assessment that the task would 'not take long', clearly feeling that his scholarly capabilities would not be extended. This attitude is reinforced in his journal recording the completion of twenty lines of flash verse on each of the days 7 to 11 November. Before the month's end Moore questions his judgement in writing such 'buffoonery' and 'profanation', but does enough to suggest that he is a genuine admirer of Egan's style. His admission that he 'felt rather faint-hearted about the Flash volume [...] as it might be thought too *low* a thing for such great booksellers & poets as we are' appears to merely reveal a natural anxiety combined with playful self-mocking. During its composition, Moore tried various means to increase his slang vocabulary, but it was not until 13 November that he says: 'borrowed Grose's "Slang Dictionary" [...] which will be of much service'.[9]

In December, Moore attended the Randall v Turner fight in the company of Jackson. Egan's account of this fight commenced in a contemplative manner: 'They *eyed* each other with all the acute precision of fencing-masters; and seemed positively almost to look into each others hearts' (*Boxiana III*, p. 176). Rather than describing the fight, Moore focused on the 'very picturesque' scene formed by pigeons being 'let off at different periods of the fight with dispatches'. He does corroborate Egan's claims of the Nonpareil's resilience, stating that 'Turner's face was a good deal dehumanised, but Randall [...] had hardly a scratch'. Egan, with the intense quixotic imagery of the fighters peering into one another's hearts, may have proven a worthy rival for his renowned fellow author. Moore's outing can be regarded as a 'research trip', undertaken to immerse himself in the character and language of a Fancy showpiece event, rather than demonstrating any support for the pugilistic sport. It is likely that Moore derived more practical aid in his attempted mastery of the flash argot from a study

9   Ibid., pp. 212, 218, 252, 216.

of *Boxiana*. In his journal, he dismisses the four-volume *English Rogue* as 'coarse and dull'. First published in 1665, and written by the Irish author Richard Head (c. 1637–86), *English Rogue* was a fictional autobiography of 'Meriton Latroon, a witty extravagant'. In the end, Moore decides a better course is to read *Boxiana*: 'to store my memory with the cant phrases'.[10]

The resultant work was *Tom Crib's Memorial to Congress* (1819), and Moore stated he was compiling a 'voluminous' work that would complement the writing of Egan, 'the elegant author [...and] historian so competent'.[11] The scenario employed for this piece is Cribb's proposal to train the 'Holy Alliance' rulers in 'the myst'ries of *milling*' (23), in the hope that, rather than full-scale warfare, differences can be settled by leaders facing one another in a 'ROYAL SET-TO' (56). Moore's side-swipes at the inherent corruption, arrogance, and general avarice of these major powers is evident throughout, but it is the flash language, combined with Moore's subtle nuances, that renders the satiric message comprehensible to a wider social sphere. Moore's portrayal of the dominant European '*squad*' (1) is fortified by their dialogue being dubbed '*gammon*' (15). Their grasping deceit extends to financially '*diddling*' their subjects and '*gutting* their *fobs*' (6), the phrase meaning 'pick their pockets' (*B/P*).

This prepares the way for the main event, a fight between the Prince Regent (referred to alternately as 'GEORGY' and 'THE PORPUS') and Tsar Alexander I of Russia ('LONG SANDY' and '*the Bear*'). Like Egan, Moore first gives the reader an insight into the surrounding scene of gathering spectators:

> 'Twas diverting, to see, as one *ogled* around, (95)
> How *Corinthians* and *Commoners* mixed on the ground.
> [...]
> While Nicky V-NS-T, not caring to roam,
> Got among the *white-bag-men*, and felt quite *at home*. (100)
> [...]
> Both *peel'd* – but, on laying his *Dandy-belt* by, (141)

10 Journal entry of 4 December 1818. Ibid., pp. 233–4. Journal entry of 14 December. Ibid., p. 240.
11 *British Satire, 1785–1840*, ed. by Strachan and others, V, ed. by Jane Moore, pp. 188–9.

> Old GEORGY *went floush*, and his *backers* look'd *shy*;
> For they saw, notwithstanding CRIB's honest endeavour
> To train *down* the *crummy*, 'twas monstrous as ever!

Moore ridicules the Regent's 'monstrous' body fat (*'crummy'*), which, in turn, affects the odds calculations. The partially omitted name (line 99) refers to then Chancellor of the Exchequer, Nicholas Vansittart (1766–1851), and the earlier embezzlement motif is accentuated by this character's comfort at being ensconced amidst the *'white-bag-men'* (pickpockets). The collateral effect of this reference is that it highlighted the social nuisance caused by the criminal element preying on the crowds at sporting events. The cumulative impact of Moore's tactic is that the statesmen are stigmatised as little more than glorified swindlers.

In Moore's versified commentary, 'Sandy' lands a knockdown blow, 'he *tipp'd* him a *settler*' (163), and his backers appear disconcerted when they saw what a *'rum knack* of *shifting* he had' (172). An upsurge in the amount of slang accelerates the pace of the account:

> Neat *milling* this Round – what with *clouts* on the *nob*,
> *Home hits* in the *bread-basket*, *clicks* in the *gob*,
> And *plumps* in the *daylights*, a prettier treat   (185)
> Between two Johnny Raws 'tis not easy to meet.
> [...]
> And after a *rum* sort of *ruffianing* Round
> Like *cronies* they hugg'd, and came *smack* to the ground;
> Poor SANDY the undermost, smothered and spread
> Like a German, tuck'd under his huge feather bed!   (195)
> 'Twas though SANDY's soul was squeezed out of his *corpus*,
> So heavy the *crush*. – *Two to one on the Porpus!*

The alliterative *'clouts'* and *'clicks'* are additional terms for blows, whilst *'plumps'* appears to be an abbreviated version of 'plumpers', signifying heavier punches. Amusingly, the Fancy classifies these ageing combatants as novices ('Johnny Raws'). The ninth proves to be the pivotal round when the Regent's eventual defeat is expedited:

> One of GEORGY's bright *ogles* was put   (236)
> On the *bankruptcy list*, with its shop-windows *shut*;

While the *other* soon made quite as *tag-rag* a show,
All *rimm'd* round with *black*, like the *Courier* in *woe!*

The imagery of a street-shop's hardship forms an imaginative theme, with its windows representing the troubled fighter's eyes. When a pugilist is placed 'on the bankruptcy list', it is a somewhat sedate method of declaring that he has been 'knocked out' (*B/P*). Moore could be accused of being a little premature, as the 'set-to' continues for a further three rounds. The inspired representation of the fighter's damaged eyes, describing a shop-front being draped in black, alludes to the convention for period newspapers to be published with a black border when reporting the death of a member of the Royal family.[12]

Despite the popularity of the 'Epistle', Moore harboured misgivings about his new flash project, fearing it to be 'too vulgar a subject perhaps for the refined readers, and too refinedly executed for the vulgar'.[13] This appears an overly nervous assessment of a piece that would have appealed to a wide audience receptive to new methods of lampooning the Prince Regent and corrupt statesmen. However, some of the critical reception suggests that no inroads had been achieved in rendering flash universally palatable: 'Wit and humour [...] hold their place, but so concealed that a *masculine* eye alone can recognise them. *We* have had some hearty laughs, but our fair friends can neither understand nor enjoy our merriment' (*Monthly Review*, April 1819). Ultimately, the work was a commercial success:

> A first edition of two thousand copies had all but sold out by mid-March [...] with extracts appearing in *The Morning Chronicle*, on 10 March, and Leigh Hunt's *Examiner*, on 18 April 1819 [...] Moore was first amongst his [Egan's] contemporaries to press the popular subject of pugilism into the service of socio-political satire.[14]

12   *The Courier* was a London evening paper founded in 1792.
13   Journal entry of 13 March 1819. *Memoirs, Journal, and Correspondence of Thomas Moore*, ed. by Russell, II, p. 276.
14   *British Satire, 1785–1840*, ed. by John Strachan and others, V, ed. by Jane Moore, p. 183.

The financial viability of the work proves that the pugilistic content had an appeal, which augured well for further *Boxiana*-style reports, books, and pastiches. A 'success is credibility: credibility is success' philosophy is valid to the argument that the disdain exhibited towards the flash school of writing, borne from either social unease about its subversive potential, or artistic pretentiousness, could be expiated by the prospect of monetary gain.

Overall, Moore's interpretation of Egan's work resulted in a predominantly positive imitation, embracing the true spirit of the slang element. There is no hint of a mocking undercurrent, but it should be accepted that Moore, whilst admiring facets of the sporting argot, was exploiting a modish medium to deride the Alliance and their controversial summit. His ambivalence is neatly summarised in the journal entry for 17 December 1818:

> Twenty lines more. This sort of stuff goes glibly from the pen. I sometimes ask myself why I write it; and the only answer I get is, that I flatter myself it serves the cause of politics which I espouse, and that, at all events, it brings a little money without much trouble.[15]

Nevertheless, some professional esteem was evinced via Moore's explicit acknowledgements to *Boxiana* and the flash language it championed. Egan declared his satisfaction at the publicity accorded to Jack Randall: 'The *Literary World* have outdone the Sporting Hemisphere, from the lively degree of anxiety several writers have shown of emulation [...] in exerting themselves to prevent the *capabilities* and triumphant fame acquired by RANDALL from sinking into obscurity' (*Boxiana III*, p. 205).[16] Later, Egan defiantly presented a statement that could have been adopted as the flash writer's credo: 'We only stand up for the character of the thing [...] We like to express ourselves like "one of the Fancy" [...] We are FLASH, and nothing else but FLASH' (*Book of Sports*, pp. 262–3). For Moore, the flash style was a convenient satiric device, but despite early reservations about literary worthiness he held it in high enough esteem to be ranked

---

15   *Memoirs, Journal, and Correspondence of Thomas Moore*, ed. by Russell, II, p. 240.
16   Egan cites *Tom Crib's Memorial* and *Blackwood's* as prime examples of the 'Literary World'.

by adverse comment.[17] Crucially, the saleability dimension assuaged the creative and moral 'prejudice' that the sporting genre still encountered.

Various publications appropriated the flash style and applied it to their own political agenda. Base economic considerations appear to have clouded those of supposedly 'high' culture, but the role of the periodicals in shaping the ideological awareness of their audience shows how flash language could transcend social barriers and influence a malleable cross-section of supposedly 'status-conscious' readers. The periodicals' readership was partially dictated by a financial factor: 'the quarterlies cost four to six shillings each, monthly magazines two to three shillings'. Thus, even if workingmen 'had been faintly interested in what *Blackwood's* had to insinuate [...] – such reading matter would have cost a member of the "lower orders" an unthinkable full day's pay'.[18]

A different outlook to the deployment of pugilistic slang is demonstrated by Deacon in *Warreniana* (1824). The work operated as a parody on the advertising techniques of the period, in this instance the newspaper promotion of blacking (boot polish). Deacon exploited public familiarity with a popular cultural model, and this device engendered an instant rapport, via recognition, with his readership. In a similar manner, Moore had appealed to certain in-built identification codes, eliciting support from those interested in, or associating themselves with, the Fancy. This exchange, and appropriation, of cultural models accentuates the pluralism of the sports-writing genre. Skilfully employed, this mode of satire could extract a broader appeal, and understanding, for its rapier-like thrusts against the object of derision. Deacon amalgamated both advertising and sports-related material in 'a compendious parodic survey of contemporary writing'.[19]

The fictional premise for the text is that a leading blacking manufacturer, Robert Warren of The Strand, has enlisted the services of several

---

17   See journal entry of 4 May 1819. *Memoirs, Journal, and Correspondence of Thomas Moore*, ed. by Russell, II, pp. 301–2.

18   Jon P Klancher, *The Making of English Reading Audiences* (London: University of Wisconsin Press, 1987), pp. 4, 50.

19   *Parodies of the Romantic Age*, ed. by Stones and Strachan, IV, ed. by John Strachan, p. x.

prominent writers to encourage sales. The result is a collection of specially commissioned 'puffs', which are attributed to a series of distinguished authors (including Byron, Wordsworth, Hunt, Scott, Moore, Southey, and Hogg). Just as Egan profited from the comic misapplication of classical allusion in his pugilistic commentaries, *Warreniana* functions through an incongruity between its elevated style and 'low' subject matter. There had been a penchant for blacking-related squibs, prompting a jocular piece by John Hamilton Reynolds, appearing in the *Westminster Review* (1824), 'upon the unorthodox company which the muse had been keeping':

> [Poetry] was glad to perch wherever she was able, and in her bewildered state, as a scared pigeon flies down a lawyer's chimney [...] she dashed into Warren's blacking manufactory [...] and dipping her wing in an eighteen-penny bottle, took up the cause of boots and shoes. Thus lowered in her and others' estimation, she sat awhile in a solitude of brilliant jet.[20]

The analogy with the low regard afforded to Egan's flash work is striking; when the muse took up the cause of 'mills and mauleys' she was similarly ostracised.

In the *Warreniana* 'advertisement' purporting to be in the style of Samuel Taylor Coleridge (1772–1834), Deacon combined the world of advertising and the *Boxiana* series to achieve a double-edged parodic force. Coleridge (Deacon) explains the circumstances that have generated the piece, 'The Dream, a Psychological Curiosity', by reporting that, whilst pondering Warren's project, he had fallen asleep 'over a provincial paper which detailed the battle between Cribb and Molineaux'.[21] The consequence is that instead of dreaming about Kubla Khan's palace, Coleridge envisages an argument between Warren and Satan over which is the darkest – the waters of the hellish river Styx, or Warren's blacking. To settle the argument, in true British fashion, a ring is formed for the two antagonists to battle it out, and it is the ensuing action that provides the scope for Deacon to demonstrate his own aptitude for the *Boxiana* style.

---

20   *Parodies of the Romantic Age*, ed. by Stones and Strachan, IV, ed. by John Strachan, p. xiii.
21   Ibid., p. 119.

My analysis should be prefaced by noting that Deacon's burlesque does not function as a tribute to Egan. On the contrary, an earlier reference to 'Tom and Jerry' is accompanied by a scathing explanatory note:

> A dramatic non-descript of the same name, which was performed for two successive seasons to the crowded (of course) and enlightened audiences of the Adelphi. I merely mention the thing as a curious specimen of the most singular and superlative stupidity, that the thrice-sodden brains of a hireling scribbler ever yet inflicted on the patience of the public.[22]

It is regrettable that a parodist as skilful as Deacon was less than enamoured with Egan's metropolitan work, but was not averse to applying the *Boxiana* style for maximum authenticity in his parody.

Prior to commencing '*The Fight*' section of his piece, Deacon prepares the reader for the imminent shift in style: 'Now list ye with kindness, the whiles I rehearse / In shapely pugilistic verse, / [...] this desperate *Mill*'. There is a hint of sarcasm present in Deacon's description of such verse as 'shapely', whilst his note to '*Mill*', feigning misapprehension, mocks its appropriation by the patrons of the ring:

> I was for some months puzzled to ascertain the precise meaning of this ambiguous term. My mind first conjectured that it alluded simply to a windmill; and secondly, that it meant a treadmill [...] as a last resource I applied to Mr John Randall, who informed me with prompt politeness, that 'Mill' was the generic denomination of a fight.[23]

Upon the usual 'peeling' ceremonies, Deacon highlighted the distinctive Fancy apparel of '*yellowman*' (yellow silk handkerchief). But, it is in the '*Rounds*' section that the *Boxiana* style is conspicuous:

> 1. [...] Brummagem Bob
>   Let fly a *topper* on Beelzebub's *nob*;
>   Then followed him over the ring with ease,
>   And *doubled him up* by a blow in the *squeeze*.

---

22 Ibid., p. 205.
23 Ibid., pp. 124, 213.

2.   Satan was cautious in making play,
      But stuck to his sparring and pummelled away;
      Till the *ogles* of Warren looked *queer* in their hue,
      (Here, bets upon Beelzebub; three to two).[24]

Deacon's italicisation is applied somewhat haphazardly.

A '*topper*' signifies a 'violent blow to the head' (*Lexicon*), and it is superfluous for Deacon to state that the blow was directed at the 'nob'. This is an 'error' that would surely not be committed by an experienced pugilistic reporter. Deacon's phrasing equates to saying that a fighter 'received a floorer, that knocked him to the ground', implying that the author is not conversant with the idiomatic intricacies, or simply disregarded a tautological blemish as it was poetically expedient. Mimicry of Egan's manner is augmented by reference to the betting odds, and the journalistic feel is underscored by the untrammelled nature of the verses, which are allowed to contract or expand according to the action. This corresponds with typical Egan commentaries, and the climactic round is recorded in detail (by this stage any relation to Coleridge's work appears to be non-existent):

3.   Satan was floored by a *lunge* in the hip,
      And the blood from his peepers, went drip, drip, drip,
      [...]
      His *box of dominos* chattered aloud,
      (Here, 'Go it, Nick!' from an imp in the crowd),
      And he dropped with a *Lancashire Purr* on his back,
      While Bob with a *clincher* fell over him, whack.
      Both men piping came up to the scratch,
      But Bob for Abaddon was more than a match;
      He *tapped* his *claret*, his mug he rent,
      And made him so *groggy* with *punishment*,
      That he gladly gave in at the close of the round,
      And Warren in triumph was led from the ground.[25]

The repetition of 'drip' echoes Egan's treatment of the word 'ditto'.

24   'Squeeze' – a flash term for 'neck'. Ibid., p. 125.
25   Ibid., p. 126.

Despite his apparent antipathy towards the 'hired scribbler', Deacon successfully exploited his style. Humdrum blacking and the degraded genre of sports writing conflate to produce an engaging parodic 'advertisement'. Deacon and Egan did coincide on their viewpoint regarding the observance of character and detail and, ironically, *Warreniana* yields similar collateral potential to Egan's work of 'superlative stupidity', *Life in London* (1821):

> Deacon is much concerned with the social epiphenomena of contemporary life and *Warreniana* might be said to offer a parodic *vade mecum* to late Georgian culture. His text is peppered with references to the fashionable metropolitan preoccupations of a society only recently released from over twenty years of war [...] Deacon's attention to advertising culture facilitates an examination of metropolitan society at large.[26]

Sporting culture, and its language, constituted a noteworthy portion of this metropolitan society, and the 'literary-critical function' of Deacon's work is significant: 'contemporary literary satires on the likes of Wordsworth and Coleridge or Keats and Hunt are important and revealing critical documentation'. Not all literature, be it satire or sporting commentary, purported to address 'the literary spirit of the age or profound issues of state'. Such pieces do, however, constitute 'a mode of social commentary, providing a real insight into English society'. The world of prizefighting formed part of this metropolitan social blend, and John Strachan's comment that verse satire 'languished in an ill-merited neglect' might also be applied to Egan's pugilistic writing.[27] The playful manipulation, by Moore and Deacon, of *Boxiana* language propelled it deeper into public consciousness. But, Egan and Bee remained the formative figures, whose energies maintained and developed the genre.

26 Ibid., p. xxx.
27 John Strachan, in *British Satire, 1785–1840*, ed. by Strachan and others, I, pp. xv, xix.

Boxiana Traces in Selected Nineteenth-Century Literature

In R S Surtees's *Jorrocks' Jaunts and Jollities* (first collected volume published in 1838), although the sporting content is primarily confined to hunting with the Surrey hounds, it is interesting to note the occasional transferral of flash terms from the prize-ring context. In the opening, as the fox's flight becomes desperate, Jorrocks cries 'we shall have a rare teaser up these hills'. The 'teaser' in this case is the circumnavigation of difficult terrain, rather than a troublesome punch. Jorrocks is also requested to keep his 'potato-trap shut'.

Surtees, too, was not averse to a little self-promotion, and a judge drawing on his knowledge of Game Laws during a court case against Jorrocks includes an overt reference to the publication founded by Surtees, stating: 'I derive my information from [...] the bright refulgent pages of the *New Sporting Magazine*'. Incidentally, in the court exchanges, Jorrocks is considered to have been on the receiving end of a verbal 'good quilting'. A further similarity occurs in the scope that slang offers for improvisation, Surtees adapting the term 'gammon', to produce an adjective, in Jorrocks' assessment of a stranger at the George Inn: 'there was nothing gammonacious, as I calls it, about his toggery'.[28] Although not a pugilistic text, the flash terms are seemingly natural utterances blending with the narrative flow.

Ironically, Egan's own 'novel' published that same year, *Pilgrims of the Thames*, is almost devoid of slang despite his bold declaration that such language is justifiable:

> The laughable, rude, yet witty sayings, which so often occur in crowds, are worthy of record [...] *Character* is our decided object – an adherence to truth and nature our constant aim – and let us ask of what value is our description, if we do not relate faithfully the dialogue and manners of all classes? (*Pilgrims of the Thames*, 1838, p. 138)

It should be noted that this is not a sporting text, more of an episodic travelogue in the 'Pickwick' style. But, the dearth of flash language appears to be as artificial as slang overload would have been, thus contravening Egan's

---

28   Surtees, *Jorrocks' Jaunts and Jollities* (London: Dent, 1941), pp. 11, 55, 53, 103.

own stated objective – the reflection of 'character'. Nevertheless, its absence accentuates the author's uneasiness about the perception of the Fancy argot, and its place in literature. This may have been a result of the censure directed at *Life in London*, but Egan certainly modulated the approach of his 'serious' works. In this period, he was still sufficiently self-assured to criticise others: 'Charles Knight quotes him as saying of a certain fashionable novelist of the 1830s [Dickens?], "Ah! He's very clever, but uncommon superficial in slang"'.[29] Again, the vexed question of how people actually spoke cannot be reliably ascertained, but Shaw includes familiar *Boxiana* expressions in *Cashel Byron's Profession* (1886), such as 'it's bellows to mend' (p. 183). This author's observations also provide a clue to linguistic variation:

> I once asked an ancient prizefighter what a knock-out was like [...] He was a man of limited descriptive powers; so he simply pointed to the heavens and said 'Up in a balloon'. An amateur pugilist, with greater command of language, told me that 'all the milk in his head suddenly boiled over'.[30]

The latter expression demonstrates the creative imagery embraced by Egan, but the extract implies that some artistic licence was necessary to enliven discourse.

Shaw contributes a cogent testimony to the influence Egan imparted on a 'typical' reader:

> Though his neighbours are as peaceful and nervous as he; though if he knocked a man down or saw one of his friends do it, the event would stand out in his history like a fire or a murder; yet he not only tolerates unstinted knockings-down in fiction, but actually founds his conception of his nation [...] on these imaginary outrages, and at last comes to regard a plain statement [...] that the average respectable Englishman knows rather less about fighting than he does about flying, as a paradoxical extravagance. (*CBP*, p. xvi)

This statement endorses Egan's scene-setting adeptness, and the convincing nature of his nationalistic rhetoric. Egan's stance could also be bracketed with that adopted by Shaw's fictional defence counsel whose impassioned,

29   Reid, *Bucks and Bruisers*, p. 201.
30   Shaw, 'Note on Modern Prizefighting', *Cashel Byron's Profession*, p. 244.

and lengthy, plea for the merits of pugilism includes a frequently-used *Boxiana* tack: 'it was to our national and manly tolerance of the fist [...] that we owed our freedom from the murderous stiletto of the Italian' (p. 225). At the conclusion of the counsel's speech, Byron is portrayed as: 'awestruck [...] as if he half feared that the earth would gape and swallow such a reckless perverter of known facts' (p. 228). If Egan is branded such a 'perverter', it could be argued that he is a visionary, if idiosyncratic, one.

John Reid pronounces: 'understanding of great writers is enhanced by a knowledge of those they began by imitating and came to surpass'.[31] The various imitations of the *Boxiana* style that captured the ebullient realism of Fancy jargon can be forwarded as evidence that, to gifted authors, Egan's flash style was far from unparalleled in its construction. Even within the very period that Egan was at the zenith of his influence and reputation, fellow pugilistic reporters pressed their claims for equal billing, and rivals sought to topple him from his predominant position within the sporting sphere. Charles Molloy Westmacott (1788–1868), writing as 'Bernard Blackmantle', articulated Egan's precarious tenure in a fascinating little cameo that accompanied a scene set in the Castle Tavern, which, at this time (1825), was under the stewardship of Tom Belcher (see Illustration):

> You will perceive the *immortal typo*, the all-accomplished Pierce Egan; an eccentric in his way, both in manner and person, but not deficient in that peculiar species of wit which fits him for the high office of historian of the ring. The ironical praise of Blackwood he has the good sense to turn to a right account, laughs at their satire, and pretends to believe it is all meant in *right-down earnest* approbation of his extraordinary merits [...] Pierce kept undisturbed possession of the throne; but recently competitors have shown themselves in the field *well found* in all particulars, and carrying such witty and weighty ammunition wherewithal, that they more than threaten 'to push the hero from his stool.' (*The English Spy*, I, p. 337)

Westmacott proceeded to directly allude to Bee and Dowling as the 'fellows of wit' who were Egan's immediate competitors. He could have added his own name to the shortlist of capable Egan successors; *The English Spy*, replete with its own intrepid city explorers, provides a worthy contender to rival *Life in London* for cleverly-written 'flash' metropolitan sketches.

---

31   Reid, *Bucks and Bruisers*, p. x.

This particular tavern snapshot appears to be playfully friendly, nevertheless Westmacott obviously perceived something about Egan that warranted him applying the 'eccentric' label.

The flash style was adaptable to differing ambitions, Deacon and Moore underscoring its transferability to parody and political satire. Pugilism dominated much of the Fancy's energies, and its influence regularly infiltrated metropolitan offshoots. W T Moncrieff's dramatisation *Tom and Jerry; or, Life in London. An Operatic Extravaganza* (1821) included scenes set in Cribb's 'parlour' and Jackson's Bond-Street rooms, where Logic spars with Jerry, whilst Tom advises the former 'mind your pipkin [head]'.[32] Much of *Real Life in London* (1821) is written in an almost indistinguishable style particularly in flights of inflated imagery. Here, the 'amateur' author muses on the resolute philosophy of the true sporting type:

> Ordinary minds, in viewing distant objects, first see the obstacles that intervene, magnify the difficulty of surmounting them, and sit down in despair. The man of genius with his mind's-eye pointed [...] on the object of his ambition, meets and conquers every difficulty [...] and the mass dissolves before him as the mountain snow yields. (*Real Life in London*, p. 7)

One can easily imagine such passages appearing in the columns of Egan's newspaper, or *Book of Sports*. However, an extravagant claim made in the *Dublin Morning Register* (30 June 1838), advertising a benefit night for 'the popular writer of *Life in London*', that Egan's characters were 'the precursors of the "Pickwick Club"', is unrealistic.[33] More admissible is the enduring sporting ethos advanced by Egan's, primarily, pugilistic writing, which permeated later works.

Reid's theories on the extent of Egan's influence upon the writing of Dickens warrant a separate in-depth analysis, but it is interesting to briefly look at more of this celebrated author's allusions to the pugilistic 'science'. In an early episode from *The Pickwick Papers* (1837), an irritated cab-driver commences 'sparring away like clockwork' and then assaults Pickwick's party:

---

32   Reproduced in Hindley, *The True History of Tom and Jerry*, p. 55.
33   Reid, *Bucks and Bruisers*, p. 204.

> [He] knocked Mr Pickwick's spectacles off, and followed up [...] with a blow on Mr
> Pickwick's nose [...] and a third in Mr Snodgrass's eye, and a fourth, by way of variety,
> in Mr Tupman's waistcoat, and then danced into the road, and then back again to
> the pavement, and finally dashed the whole temporary supply of breath out of Mr
> Winkle's body; and all in half-a-dozen seconds.

No flash is necessary for Dickens to provide a comical picture of a frenzied, whirling cab-driver meting out swift, yet relatively innocuous, physical admonishment. The same sense of over-excitable activity is later displayed by Sam Weller's father:

> 'Now Sammy', said Mr Weller, taking off his great coat with much deliberation
> [...] Before Sam could interfere [...] his heroic parent had penetrated into a remote
> corner of the room, and attacked the reverend Mr Stiggins with manual dexterity
> [...] and without further invitation he gave the reverend Mr Stiggins a preliminary
> tap on the head, and began dancing round him in a buoyant and cork-like manner.[34]

Dickens's ploy of applying the image of a bobbing cork to the elderly man is humorous, and should not be attributed to anything other than his own inventiveness.

The notion of pugilistic chastisement being an expeditious means of resolving disputes, or administering punishment, is perpetuated. In addition, it is implied that those holding the moral high ground are most likely to possess some degree of pugilistic ability. Essentially, honourable conduct is being associated with Fancy ideology, and Pickwick's development can be couched in prize-ring terms as he adopts a stance described as: 'neither truculent nor obsequious, neither priggish nor unprincipled, which can withstand the blows of the world. This spiritual stance [...] is analogous [...] with the practical goal of the Fancy'. It is also noted: 'Dickens was consistently in touch with the Fancy [...] His work is filled with allusions to and the diction from boxing, as well as characters who are boxers by vocation, avocation, or evocation.'[35] It is this more general consciousness that might

---

34   *Charles Dickens: The Pickwick Papers*, ed. by Robert L Patten, pp. 74, 551.
35   James E Marlow, 'Popular Culture, Pugilism, and Pickwick', *Journal of Popular Culture*,
      15:4 (1982), pp. 16–30 (18, 21).

be ascribed to the reading of Egan's reports. Dickens's sensitivity, to what he perceived as an unflattering comparison with Egan, is evinced in his letter to Frederick Yates (who was producing and acting in a dramatic version of Dickens's novel *Nicholas Nickleby*): 'would you think me very unreasonable if I asked you not to compare Nicholas with Tom and Jerry?'[36]

In an early scene from *Hard Times* (1854), Dickens portrayed a school inspector in pugilistic terms:

> A mighty man at cutting and drying, he was; a government officer [...] a professed pugilist; always in training, always with a system to force down the general throat [...] ready to fight all England. To continue in fistic phraseology, he had a genius for coming up to scratch, wherever and whatever it was, and proving himself an ugly customer. He would go in and damage any subject whatever with his right, follow up with his left, stop, exchange, counter, bore his opponent [...] and fall upon him neatly. He was certain to knock the wind out of common sense and render that unlucky adversary deaf to the call of time.[37]

This excerpt is unequivocally couched in sporting parlance, but without embracing Egan's flash style. Nevertheless, its effectiveness in conveying the persevering adherence to duty in this governmental official is convincing. The piece succeeds in humorously impugning the unrelenting officiousness of 'a system', thus imparting a degree of weighty social comment whilst simultaneously providing a comic analogy.

It is in such pieces, melding insightful gravitas and entertainment, where, in overall effect and literary worthiness, Egan is surpassed rather than simply imitated. When Dickens advanced the vicissitudes of Pickwick as a reflection of prize-ring fortunes, figuratively parrying and weaving against the blows of life, profound social concerns were thinly concealed behind a metaphorical image. This approach is more compelling than the author's more simplistic deployment of sporting flash, such as that used by the threatening Mr Flintwinch to his wife in *Little Dorrit* (1857): 'You shall have it, my woman [...] Oh! You shall have a sneezer, you shall have a

---

36   Letter of 29 November 1838. *The Letters of Charles Dickens*, ed. by Madeline House and Graham Storey et al., I, ed. by House and Storey, p. 463.

37   Dickens, *Hard Times*, p. 4.

teaser'. And, in the piece 'Main Line. The Boy at Mugby': 'Agitation became awakened. Excitement was up in the stirrups'. Or, to quote two final examples from *Martin Chuzzlewit* (1844): '[Pecksniff] "Sir, you must strike at him through me [...] and in such a cause you will find me, my young sir, an Ugly Customer!"'; 'Martin was not a little puzzled when he came to an end, for the two stories seemed to have no connexion with each other, and to leave him, as the phrase is, all abroad'.[38]

The rhetoric employed by Dickens, in a speech delivered to the Playground and General Recreation Society (1 June 1858) to emphasise his belief of the 'immense importance to a community' of 'children's play', has a familiar ring:

> A country full of dismal little old men and women who had never played would be in a mighty bad way indeed; and you may depend upon it that without play, and good play, too, those powerful English cheers which have driven the sand of Asia before them, and made the very ocean shake, would degenerate into a puling whimper, that would be the most consolatory sound that can possibly be conceived to all the tyrants on the face of the earth.

Similarly, his manner of expression when endorsing the invigorating pursuit of rowing could have been plucked straight from the pages of any *Boxiana* volume:

> Rowing men pursued recreation under circumstances which braced their muscles, and cleared the cobwebs from their minds. He assured them that he regarded such clubs as these as a 'national blessing' [...] They were greatly indebted to all that tended to keep up a healthy, manly tone.[39]

Of course, one can only speculate on the precise extent of Dickens's sincerity as the reported transcripts of his public speeches reveal more than

---

38   Dickens, *Little Dorrit*, ed. by John Holloway (London: Penguin, 1985), p. 752; From the Christmas 1866 number of *All the Year Round*, *Dickens: Selected Short Fiction*, ed. by Deborah A Thomas (London: Penguin, 1985), p. 374; Dickens, *Martin Chuzzlewit* (London: Penguin, 2004), pp. 629, 693.

39   *The Speeches of Charles Dickens: A Complete Edition*, ed. by K J Fielding (Hemel Hempstead: Harvester Wheatsheaf, 1988), pp. 272, 360–1.

a few traces of gushing praise for the hosts whose hospitality he appears to be whole-heartedly relishing (the latter extract is from 'a dinner of the Metropolitan Rowing Club at the London Tavern, 7 May 1866'). Notwithstanding his undoubted sporting sympathies Dickens often appears to be playing to a particular audience for a particular evening, and generally fuelling mass adoration at his sound judgement in supporting their cause.

In *Cashel Byron's Profession*, Shaw's reading of *Boxiana* is exhibited in instances of well-honed rhetoric and visualisation techniques. Firstly, there is the elevated physical imagery of the main protagonist sighted in training:

> [Byron's] arms shone like those of a gladiator [...] Like slabs of marble. Even his hair, short, crisp, and curly, seemed like burnished bronze in the evening light. It came into Lydia's mind that she had disturbed an antique god in his sylvan haunt. (*CBP*, p. 36)

Later, Lydia Carew remarks on the 'novel' aspect of this individual (p. 55), a quality encouraged by Egan's writing. The character Lucian Webber's denigration of pugilists includes a frequently occurring analogy: 'the combatants are trained as racehorses, gamecocks, or their like' (p. 126). In addition, there is Byron's comic appraisal of famous composers using pugilistic terminology:

> 'There isn't one man in a million that ever heard of Beethoven. Take a man that everybody has heard of: Jack Randall [...] This German gentleman, who knows all about music, tells you that many pretend that this Wagner has game, but no science. Well, I [...] will bet you twenty-five pounds that there's others that allow him full of science'.[40] (*CBP*, p. 90)

The latter utterance, made to an upper-class gathering following a lecture by an eminent academic, both underscores previous observations on the omnipresence of a wagering ethos, and its jarring quality when used outside its usual environment. Conversely, it is a similar sense of misapplication, using seemingly immiscible characters and language, which enhances the comedy of certain scenes.

---

40 Ludwig van Beethoven (1770–1827) and Richard Wagner (1813–83).

Shaw's allusion to the exaggerated praise and moral censure elicited by pugilism (*CBP*, p. xi) is displayed in the conflicting doctrines espoused by the sport's supporters and denigrators. William Vasey queried of pugilists: 'What eminence did any of them ever possess in literary and intellectual life? [...] Let those who believe in the moral excellence of the Science search the annals of Pugilism and make a reply' (*RIPM*, p. 5). And later claimed: 'The body of men who compose the Prize Ring may with some correctness be termed *unique* [...] They are the worst men from the lowest ranks of society. Their depraved passions are calculated for the transaction of every thing base' (p. 12). In a partial contradiction of negative assertions, Peter Radford observes that the general principle of exercise was considered a complementary element of the creative process by such 'inveterate walkers' as Wordsworth, Coleridge, and Hazlitt:

> It was an age that discovered [...] a new grandeur in long and tiring physical effort and nobility in experiencing and resisting fatigue. Walking was not merely a backdrop to the self-searching and self-discovery that were a prelude to the creative process. It was part of it.[41]

A collection of pieces inspired by pugilism incorporates much of the connected sentiments alluded to in various commentaries, offering 'glimpses into boxing's storied history, its facts and fables, its social and cultural impact' with the prize-ring 'acting as a place where such traits as character and endurance often overcome wealth and social status'. Commenting upon the contribution made by nineteenth-century 'chaunts' and verse (included in the *Boxiana* series): 'they are typically adulatory in tone and tend to portray their subjects as part of a long legacy of heroic figures, praised for their strength and skill, as well as for their ability to uphold moral virtue and national pride'.[42]

Thomas Fewtrell's 1790 work proposed the credible theory that the perception of brutality was fuelled by a misconception of the archetypal pugilist, thinking 'that the more savage and unenlightened he is, the better

---

41   Radford, *The Celebrated Captain Barclay*, p. 111.
42   *Perfect in Their Art*, ed. by Robert Hedin and Michael Waters (Carbondale: Southern Illinois University Press, 2003), pp. xix, xv–xvi .

qualified he must be to excel in his profession' (*Boxing Reviewed*, p. v). Essentially, Fewtrell provided a pre-emptive refutation of Vasey's 1824 dismissal of a pugilist's supposedly ferocious disposition and lack of cognitive ability, claiming his own volume 'was written for the purpose of vindicating Pugilism from the unjustifiable censures of illiterate and weak minds, and proving its utility on rational principles' (p. vi). Fewtrell inverted the accusations levelled by the sport's opponents who, in turn, are deemed culpable of ignorance.

Sweeping generalisations about pugilists are at odds with one of the principal features attributed to the Fancy environment – its heterogeneity. This is accentuated by Egan in a recapitulation of his *Life in London* snapshot of Tattersall's:[43]

> a *mixture* of persons of nearly all ranks [...] The 'best judge' respecting sporting events is acknowledged the 'best man' here; every person being on the 'look out' to see how he *lays* his *blunt*. The DUKE and *Parliamentary Orator*, if they do not know the properties of a horse, are little more than ciphers [...] The *nod* from a *stable keeper* is quite as important, if not more so to the Auctioneer, as the *wink* of a RIGHT HONOURABLE. (*Book of Sports*, p. 179)

Egan stressed how social barriers could be demolished by the possession of sporting intelligence, or intuition. In this environment, information is power and a new hierarchy of influence established. It is suggested that, far from being 'depraved', 'no man of fashion can be received into [...] polished society, without a knowledge of this place [Tattersall's]' (*Real Life in London*, p. 165).

Accusations of histrionics, however, might be justifiably levelled over Egan's portrayal of Pearce (the 'Game Chicken') rescuing a girl from the attic of a burning shop in Bristol (November 1807):

> He draws his trembling charge from the window, places her safe upon the parapet [...] Universal joy prevailed, and the delighted and astonished multitude were lost in the ecstasy of the plaudits – and the almost lifeless sufferer clinging round the knees of her deliverer, invoking blessings on his name. (*Boxiana I*, p. 152)

---

43   Horse auction mart, founded by Richard Tattersall (1724–95), *EB*.

Egan's closing remark, 'Yet, this was the act of a *Pugilist*', appears an apt
riposte to critics claiming that prizefighting constituted 'a *show* or appearance' of bravery, and was 'calculated to *deaden* in the spectator that *sympathy*
for the sufferings of others' (*RIPM*, pp. 14–15). Perhaps Sala's observations
offer a more accurate appraisal of a typical prizefight gathering at which
he perceived 'all peculiar and distinct varieties of the *genus* sporting man'
amongst a 'locust crowd': 'There are several horsemen, hovering on the
skirts of the ring, well-mounted gentlemen in garb, and apparently half
interested and delighted with the prospect of the sport, and half ashamed
to be seen in such company'.[44] The ambivalent feelings coincide with the
indeterminacy of a pugilistic scene incorporating conflicting senses; deplor-
able yet enticing, degrading yet honourable.

Bee included verse by one of the sporting poetasters, 'Chopstick',
which light-heartedly suggested a widespread philosophical application
of one of the foremost pugilistic terms:

> MILLING HO! A CHAUNT
> Look through the world, observe mankind,
> No more each other killing,
> But, in a friendly way, you'll find,
> Each one his neighbour milling.
>
> CHORUS – For high
> All the world are milling, ho!
> Milling, ho! Milling ho! all the world
> Are milling, ho!
>
> View but the state, see little *Van*,
> With taxes mill us all, sir;
> View chancery's court, the *pun*-ing man,
> Here mills us with the law, sir.
>
> If to the church you bend your way,
> With steps slow and unwilling,
> To hear what clergy has to say,
> Your conscience, then, he's milling.
> (*Boxiana IV*, p. 655)

44   Sala, 'The Sporting World', pp. 386–7.

In the Victorian period, a versified recording of the fight between Sayers and
Heenan [Farnborough, 17 April 1860], by William Makepeace Thackeray
(1811–63), was published in *Punch* (28 April 1860) as *The Fight of Sayerius
and Heenanus, a Lay of Ancient London*.[45] Some excerpts, from a lengthy
piece, convey Thackeray's fascination with the spectacle of the event and
his familiarity with appropriate jargon:

> Adown Heenanus' Roman nose,
> Freely the tell-tale claret flows,
> [...]
> Again each iron mauley swung,
> And loud the counter hitting rung,
> Till breathless all, and wild with blows,
> Fiercely they grapple for the close;
> [...]
> Ah, me! That I have lived to hear
> Such men as ruffians scorned,
> Such deeds of valour 'brutal' called,
> Canted, preached down and mourned!
> Ah! that these old eyes ne'er again
> A gallant mill shall see!
> No more behold the ropes and stakes,
> With colours flying free![46]

Further *Boxiana*-style rhetoric underscores the sport's propensity for promoting gallantry, as well as the perceived injustice of unrelenting moral
censure.

A common characteristic in both forms of writing was the precedence
of entertainment. The impact of the above fight on public consciousness
was extended by Dickens in a piece published the following month. In
'Shy Neighbourhoods', he tells of stumbling across portraits of the two
'illustrious' fighters in a small shop. Dickens stated that they were depicted
in 'fighting attitude', and then playfully suggests that the settings elicit 'the
pastoral and meditative nature of their peaceful calling':

45   Tom Sayers (1826–65), and the American John C Heenan (1835–73).
46   *Perfect in Their Art: Poems on Boxing from Homer to Ali*, ed. by Hedin and Waters,
     pp. 193–5.

> Mr Heenan is represented on emerald sward, with primroses and other modest flowers springing up under the heels of his half-boots; while Mr Sayers is impelled to the administration of his favourite blow, the Auctioneer, by the silent eloquence of a village church. The humble homes of England, with their domestic virtues and honeysuckle porches, urge both heroes to go in and win; and the lark and other singing birds are observable in the upper air, ecstatically carolling their thanks to Heaven for a fight.[47]

This reverie possesses a certain poetical quality and echoes Jon Bee's aforementioned musings on sunbeams dancing and church spires nodding assent at the prospect of a major prizefight (*Boxiana IV*, p. 71).

In the succeeding period, the sporting theme would appear in more onerous issues concerning service to the Empire. In this context, the poetry of John Henry Newbolt (1862–1938) was prominent:

> Newbolt was using words and symbols that would already be familiar and accessible to a broad readership, for sporting expressions and images were in common use during the late-nineteenth and early-twentieth centuries, occurring in parliamentary speeches, in newspaper articles, in periodical literature, in popular novels and poetry, and elsewhere. Many outside the public schools would therefore understand the concept of 'playing the game'.[48]

The latter phrase refers to Newbolt's *Vitai Lampada* (1898), in which the repeated exhortation to 'play up, and play the game' was pivotal. In such pieces, the onus switches to Egan's heavily espoused theory that envisaged sporting tenets, involving honourable conduct and courage, being extended to the battlefield. The title of his collected volume, *The Island Race* (1898), accentuates the sense of British values being placed apart, and above, those of other nations. The poem implies that some form of consolation could be derived, even when facing a hopeless situation, by the recollection of sporting principles: 'The Gatling's jammed and the Colonel dead, / And the regiment blind with dust and smoke / [...] But the voice of a schoolboy rallies the ranks: "Play up! play up! and play the game!"'

---

47 First published in *All the Year Round* (26 May 1860). *Charles Dickens: Selected Short Fiction*, ed. by Thomas, pp. 199–200.

48 Jackson, *The Poetry of Henry Newbolt*, p. 84.

The piece also underscores the belief that the archetypal Englishman possessed noble sporting precepts that separated him from the stereotypical foreigner, but there was a danger that the chivalric element could be contorted: 'dying for one's country; and fighting, as long as one played the game, was seen as a test of individual character and corporate honour: as an entire metaphor for living'.[49] This interpretation of sporting behaviour demonstrates an instance where Egan's playful pugilistic writing might be regarded as preaching a more balanced and realistic outlook. A living embodiment of Egan's ideal hybrid sporting character, complete with its many conflicting qualities, was Lionel Hallam Tennyson (1889–1951).[50] Tennyson excelled in a different sport, cricket, and a later century, but the reputation of Egan's *Boxiana* period endured: 'Many cricket writers dubbed him a "Regency Buck"; a man born out of his time [...] One of cricket's most colourful characters'. It is intriguing to ponder how Egan might have relished recording the exploits of a man conforming to the paradoxical nature of his corinthian prototype, including a 'prodigious appetite for the high life' and 'substantial gambling losses'. Tennyson's biographer maintains that 'scandal was always lurking just below the surface', but that 'his courage in the field of battle during the First World War was beyond dispute'.[51]

If Shaw's fictional work reflected typical attitudes of upper-class individuals, the task facing pugilistic chroniclers would appear almost insurmountable. His character Webber states 'I never read articles on such subjects. I have hardly time to glance through the ones that concern me' (*CBP*, p. 122). Such obstacles are exacerbated by the problems preventing the female contingent understanding, not to mention appreciating, pugilistic writing. Again, the proliferation of flash language would preclude comprehension of a *Boxiana*-style report, Lydia remarking on an overheard Fancy conversation: 'I am a fair linguist; but I did not understand a single sentence of their conversation, though I heard it all distinctly' (p. 82). And, when given the opportunity to witness two pugilists sparring: '[she] thought their

---

49   Ibid., p. 188.
50   Grandson of Lord Alfred Tennyson (1809–92).
51   Alan Edwards, *Lionel Tennyson: Regency Buck* (London: Robson, 2001), pp. 17–18.

pawing and dancing ridiculous; and [...] could distinguish nothing of the leading off, stopping, ducking, countering, guarding, and getting away to which Lord Worthington enthusiastically invited her attention' (p. 158).

Considering that this species of display was pugilism in its more sanitised form, essentially an exhibition of the 'scientific art', it might have been disconcerting for any aspiring sports reporting evangelist to detect such bewilderment. Lydia's concluding query, 'And is that all [...?] It seems as innocent as inanity can make it' (p. 159), prompts further debate. The *Boxiana* series had celebrated the transferral of pugilistic exhibitions to the theatre, attributing their success to the elimination of bloodshed and coarseness. But, the question is raised whether the spectacle had been rendered overly tame, denuded of vitality and risk. It is plausible that the authentic article would have been secretly savoured. Despite criticism directed at the supposed vulgarity of *Life in London*, and claims that Moore's flash pieces were not 'suited to female taste', the possibility for surreptitious appreciation of such works existed:

> Speculation on the female readership of *Life in London* is reinforced by the fact that Frances Burney's *Evelina* was given a new title [...] when it was reprinted [*Female Life in London, being the History of a Young Lady's Introduction to Fashionable Life and the Gay Scenes of the Metropolis Displaying A Highly Humorous, Satirical, and Entertaining Description of Fashionable Characters, Manners and Amusements in the Higher Circles of Metropolitan Society* (London: 1822)].[52]

There is no definitive answer, and the most likely scenario, amongst female spectators would be for a division to emerge. Doubtless the lower-class cadgers and street revellers of Egan's newspaper reports would not be unduly concerned about witnessing a bloody prizefight. Overall, despite attempts to instil chivalric ideals and spectacle, the most frequent scenario for the female population in the vicinity of a prizefight location was that described by Egan at the conclusion of the momentous contest between Spring and Langan: '[Spring] was received by the shouts of the populous

---

52   Frances Burney (1752–1840). *Evelina, or, A Young Lady's Entrance into the World* (1778). Rendell, *The Pursuit of Pleasure*, p. 38.

all along the road [...] And the fair sex were equally liberal in waving their handkerchiefs as Langan passed by their windows'.[53] Fewtrell's earlier pleas for 'the ladies' not to 'declare themselves [...] enemies' of the sport; 'neutrality is only desired' (*Boxing Reviewed*, p. 3), appear to propose more realistic goals.

In 1886, Bernard Shaw declared: 'It is the prizefighter's interest to abolish the real cruelties of the ring and to exaggerate the imaginary cruelties'.[54] This dimension has already been alluded to in terms of increasing interest and earning power in the reporting context. Shaw's dialogue included that it was 'in human nature to go to such a thing once' (*CBP*, p. 190) but, alarmingly for the sport's chroniclers, suggests that it was not merely the curiosity to attend prizefights that could be satiated:

> When after wading through Boxiana and [...] I had written Cashel Byron's Profession, I found I had exhausted the comedy of the subject; and as a game of patience or solitaire was decidedly superior to an average spar for a championship in point of excitement, I went no more to the competitions.[55]

Shaw's comments imply that Egan's brand of pugilistic writing palled through repetition. In *The True History of Tom and Jerry* (1888), Charles Hindley focused on general shifting tastes: 'although LIFE IN LONDON [...] did make our grandfathers so very – *very!* merry [...] we are constrained to admit; that it is a terrible dull and tedious work to read through in the present day' (pp. ii–iii). Its theatrical adaptations helped to make *Life in London* a 'hit', but 'its very intense phase lasted for no more than three years, and the fame of Tom and Jerry for perhaps ten'.[56] This would explain why Hindley's publication comprised various related 'selections' from Egan, or to express it in more modern phraseology – an edited highlights package.

53   *Egan's Life in London, and Sporting Guide*, No. 19 (6 June 1824), p. 160.
54   Shaw, 'Note on Modern Prizefighting', *Cashel Byron's Profession*, pp. 246–7.
55   Ibid., pp. 243–4.
56   Donald A Low, *The Regency Underworld* (Stroud: Sutton, 2000), p. 102.

A Watershed, and Eganesque Sports Reporting

Egan's scenes reinforce the notion that a degree of mystique could increase the appeal of pugilistic reporting (e.g. Classical and artistic allusions). Such imagery could have been exposed if pugilism's 'barren dreariness' was conspicuously present in the accompanying reportage and, in this respect, the absence of casual non-Fancy spectators may have proved a blessing for those wishing to glamorise events. The increase in demand for news of major contests appears a relatively straightforward fact, as illustrated by Bee's assessment of the extra coverage commanded by Neate and Hickman in 1821:

> Not only did most of *the journals*, and more substantial *monthly periodicals* of the metropolis, enter into ample details [...] but all those numerous *hebdomadaries* of the provinces, the *weekly press*, and some *foreign publications*, extracted and reprinted the *red hot intelligence* that emanates ever from *the capital* [...] The sedate editors of the *Edinburgh Magazine* turned aside from their more erudite labours, to enliven their pages with a bit of *the milling* news [...] and those of the *most substantial* of the *London prints*, hitherto devoted to poetry and the fine arts, appropriated several of its bulky pages. (*Boxiana IV*, p. 181)

It is noteworthy that Hazlitt's essay can be added to the boasted coverage of the above contest, but such pre-eminent prizefights were greatly outnumbered by those of a smaller scale. It was these unheralded contests that relied on Egan and Bee for publicity, and on the *Boxiana* style to supply the necessary flamboyance to generate interest.

Away from Egan's quixotic pugilistic reporting, the sport's popularity declined as the thrill of competition became buried beneath economic factors, and legalistic quibbling:

> Dependence on gambling always laid it open to suspicions of corruption and sharp practice [...and] the falling away of gentry support from the 1820s onwards was due as much to the unreliability of prize-fight gambling as to the rising social stigma.[57]

---

57   Brailsford, 'Morals and Maulers: the Ethics of Early Pugilism', p. 134.

Egan himself was compelled to publish a medical certificate to quash recriminations over the withdrawal of a fighter amidst accusations of malingering and fight-rigging:

> The following document, signed by a SECOND medical person, may perhaps prove the best answer: 'This is to certify, that I have examined Dutch Sam for injuries received [...] and found a FRACTURE of the RIBS sufficient to incapacitate him for any vigorous exertion'. (*Boxiana II*, p. 83)

The reproduction of everyday documentation adds an historical authenticity, but when extending its practice to include the 'Articles of Agreement' for various fights, the fluency of the narrative was unnecessarily disrupted. By 1841, Dowling was noting the diminishing appearance of pugilistic reports: 'Since the fifth volume of *Boxiana* [...] the only correct record of the battles [...] is to be found in the columns of *Bell's Life in London and Sporting Chronicle*' (*Fistiana*, p. 70). However, these accounts were abandoning any notion of imitating a *Boxiana* style, being 'written as to excite no painful feeling' (p. 71).

Amidst a revamped outlook towards working life, and reduction of public holidays, any preoccupation with sporting matters was reassessed as 'vulgar licence': 'Increasingly earnest attitudes about the sanctity of work created suspicion of leisure of any sort'.[58] Brailsford introduces the expression 'early Victorian prize-ring' and proceeds to question whether it effectively existed ('Victorian Britain and the prize-ring were implacably at odds'), before stating the fundamental shift in sensibility involved:

> According to the canons of a society that saw itself as serious, industrious, respectable, and religious [...] old sports, inherited from what seemed a barbarous and primitive past were charged with time-wasting, licence, disorder, and disrepute. There was some awareness of working-class leisure needs, but little consensus or realism about how these needs might properly be met.[59]

---

58 Schlicke, *Dickens and Popular Entertainment*, p. 10.
59 Brailsford, *Bareknuckles: A Social History of Prize-Fighting*, p. 93.

The latter problem recalls Sala's humorous suggestions concerning public lectures and grand musical performances. The radical organiser and labour activist Francis Place (1771–1854) promoted the theory of 'gradualist change through ameliorative measures [...] towards the reformation of artisan manners and morals, away from masculine blackguardism and brutality'.[60] More specifically, Place believed that 'self-improvement could be advanced by rational recreations' such as 'visiting museums', 'joining reading circles', as well as the aforementioned sedate activities.[61]

Considering these prevalent attitudes, Egan's lavish praise of huntsman George Osbaldeston (1786–1866) would not have aided an increasingly austere public perception of sporting characters: 'As the ATLAS OF THE SPORTING WORLD [...] the whole of your movements have rendered you conspicuous' (*Book of Sports*, p. iii). This constitutes another dubious association for Egan (gambling was Osbaldeston's downfall; he lost about £200,000 on horses, and was forced to sell his estates in 1848 for £190,000 to pay his debts of £167,000, *DNB*), and it may not be a coincidence that Osbaldeston officiated as referee for the fight, between Caunt and Thompson, that expedited pugilism's fall from, if not favour, tolerance. According to Birley: '[Osbaldeston] brought the long-drawn out affair to an end in doubtful circumstances. *Bell's Life* (14 September 1845) reckoned it "a disgraceful and disgusting exhibition" that had given a blow to "the boxing school" from which it could never recover'.[62]

That same year, Egan lamented: 'however the march of intellect may have done great things for the improvement of the arts and sciences, I must confess that improvements in pugilism have not kept pace'.[63] Although Sala was reluctant to deprecate English sports, he complained they 'are afflicted [...] by the betting blight', and feared that pugilistic activities would be

60   Jonathan Fulcher, in *An Oxford Companion to the Romantic Age*, ed. by McCalman, p. 649.
61   McCalman and Perkins, in *An Oxford Companion to the Romantic Age*, ed. by McCalman, p. 215.
62   Birley, *Sport and the Making of Britain*, p. 209.
63   Egan, *Every Gentleman's Manual. A Lecture on the Art of Self-Defence* (London: Sherwood & Bowyer, 1845), p. 142.

increasingly regarded as 'ruffianly anachronisms'.[64] Overall, a turning-point
had arrived, and pugilistic reporting needed to muster all the techniques
at its disposal, cosmetic if necessary, in order to survive let alone thrive.

According to Egan's comments on the influence exerted by that 'powerful engine', the press, the effect on public consciousness of regularly-
published pugilistic reports should not be understated: 'The proprietor
of a Morning newspaper is a person of some consequence in the affairs
of the world; he possesses that sort of power which is felt, but unknown'
(*Book of Sports*, p. 181). The notion of a sporting monitor for society had
been mooted earlier, at the close of his description of an Epsom race-day:

> A day of feasting, drinking, and chit-chat. In England, it is this sort of saucy inde-
> pendence which makes its inhabitants so happy, and the country so great. Deny
> them not their pleasures; let them say their *say* [...] *grumble* at any thing they do not
> like, and contentment is the result. The name only of oppression and tyranny, in the
> slightest shape, brings forth thousands in an instant as opponents; but whenever the
> country is threatened with danger, the people flock together. (*Finish to [...] Life In
> and Out of London*, 1828, pp. 156–7)

This underscores the self-regulating, or 'safety-valve', element of sporting
activities that aided the channelling of aggression into defensive or useful
activitiy.

An issue which Egan's pugilistic writing had to address was providing the
necessary entertainment to inveigle those uninitiated in sporting journalism,
and to maintain the support of, what Sala dubbed, the 'reading neophyte'.[65]
Egan indicated a prevailing fascination, for persons unacquainted with the
intricacies of sporting circles, 'to take a peep at the resort of the Fancy' in
order to observe 'heroes of the ring; and the persons considered "public
characters" connected with the turf' (*Book of Sports*, p. 72). This viewpoint
is endorsed in another essay by Sala that suggested the viewing of 'a sporting public-house' would prove an intriguing prospect for most, the scene
described hinting at the attraction of being privy to an otherwise concealed
environment 'thronged' by 'members of the Fancy': 'The parlour itself is a

64   Sala, 'The Sporting World', pp. 389–90.
65   Ibid., p. 385.

pugnacious-looking apartment, grimed with smoke, the paper torn from the walls in bygone scuffles [...] Belcher, Mendoza, and Molyneux [...] spar ominously at the spectator from muddled mezzotinto plates in shabby black frames'.[66] The reader is enticed by access to a scene containing vestiges of illicitness, but is shielded from anything 'ominous' by the mediating reporter.

Repeated references to an increase in the popularity of sporting events amongst the public cannot conceal the impression that reality frequently failed to fulfil expectation. The pre-fight excitement generated was often followed by a drab encounter, and this is an area where Egan's pugilistic accounts could embellish. It would be economically expedient to 'create' absorbing reading in order to encourage sales. In Sala's essay, 'The Sporting World', the writer acknowledges an increasing public immersion in this realm by inviting the reader to view *Bell's Life* not merely as a source of sporting information but, rather, as: 'a curiously accurate, but perhaps unconscious mirror of what, from the amusement of the mass of the people, has come to be the engrossing business and occupation of a very considerable section of that people'.

Sala's later description of a supposed fight hints at the transformation necessary to produce this engrossment: 'The heroes peel, and divesting themselves of the grubby or chrysalis-like covering of great-coats [...] appear in the bright butterfly bravery of denuded *torsos*'.[67] Egan's pugilistic writing can be said to perform a similar metamorphosis on events, converting the banal to the engaging. This approach raises questions concerning the extent of enhancement permissible, and a possible dichotomy being established between those attending and those solely reading about events. Perhaps people had become disenchanted with the reality of oftentimes mundane contests. Conversely, there is the viewpoint recorded by Hazlitt when canvassing opinion on the standard of entertainment provided in the Neate v Hickman fight: 'When it was over, I asked Cribb if he did not think it was a good one? He said, "*Pretty well*"'.[68] Cribb's enigmatic retort implies that the high drama provided by this momentous clash was not an exceptional case.

---

66   Sala, 'Phases of "Public" Life', *Gaslight and Daylight*, p. 97.
67   Sala, 'The Sporting World', pp. 381, 387.
68   *The Selected Writings of William Hazlitt*, ed. by Wu, IX, p. 71.

There is evidence suggesting that the *Boxiana* style succeeded in instilling sufficient verve into fight accounts to intrigue readers. Later problems of dwindling attendances might even be attributed, in part, to a preference for reading entertaining portrayals, rather than traipsing about the countryside, braving the elements, to eventually obtain a restricted view. Die-hard Fancy members would, doubtless, have persevered in their customary social ritual, revelling in the fluctuating agitation and ebullience generated by their gambling. For the uncommitted pugilistic follower, however, the availability of Egan's publications supplied a welcome alternative, particularly in forbidding conditions: 'encountering the rude blasts of winter, the pelting showers, and also being pushed about by a coarse unmannerly crowd [...] He prefers the comforts of [...] his own fireside, and *reading* the account of battles'.[69]

This Fancy / non-Fancy divide underscores a 'contradiction' mentioned by Hazlitt, in 'Merry England' (1825). His illustrating scene saw some Englishmen eager only to 'shut themselves up [...] by their own firesides' because 'they cannot do without *their comforts*'. Such men preferred to 'ward off physical pain and annoyance', but others harboured 'the highest possible relish [...] of hard knocks and dry blows, as one means of ascertaining their personal identity'.[70] This endorses the notion of withstanding the blows of worldly life. Hazlitt himself had sought to participate in an affirmation of maleness by travelling to a prizefight but, tellingly, appears to have been reluctant to vacate his own fireside for more than this (token?) attendance. If Egan's embellishment of fight reports is adjudged a form of literary deception, rather than licence, it is also admissible to imagine a sizeable portion of the sporting readership to be receptive to a degree of illusory, or escapist, imagery. Some form of fabrication was still necessary to engage interest, and elicit an affinity between reader and competitor.

The all-consuming attention commanded by certain sporting events is demonstrated by the effect of Barclay's pedestrian feat of 1809 on the British fleet waiting off the Kent coast to sail to Walcheren to oppose Napoleon's forces: 'Lord Huntley could have instructed Captain Barclay,

---

69   Egan, *Every Gentleman's Manual. A Lecture on the Art of Self-Defence*, p. 147.
70   *The Selected Writings of William Hazlitt*, ed. by Wu, IX, p. 130.

his aide-de-camp, to be at Deal too [...] It was almost as if they were waiting there in a state of suspended animation'.[71] Such 'suspended' conditions
can be equated with Egan's attempts to portray major prizefights as awe-
inspiring spectacles, the spectators responding as if by 'one impulse' as the
action unfolds. Episodes where intense interest in a prizefight's outcome
overshadowed news of military conflict are testimony to sport's power to
enthral. Perhaps this can be attributed to the need for diversion in times
of hardship, but the sentiments can be applied through different ages, as
demonstrated by George Orwell's twentieth-century recollections:

> I happened to be in Yorkshire when Hitler re-occupied the Rhineland [...] Fascism
> and the threat of war aroused hardly a flicker of interest locally, but the decision of
> the Football Association to stop publishing their fixtures in advance [...] flung all
> Yorkshire into a storm of fury.[72]

Notwithstanding the intermittent appeal aroused by sporting events, the
issue remains that a certain degree of invigoration appears to have been
necessary to render the resultant accounts attractive to prospective readers
wishing to be entertained.

Regarding the powers of invention required to avoid the banality of
an event being replicated in its commentary, Dowling's enthusiastic promotion of the *Boxiana* series betrays a major difficulty to be surmounted:
'Every battle of importance is given in detail, with memoirs of the heroes
who distinguished themselves in the Prize-ring, interspersed with amusing
and characteristic anecdotes [...] for which the "doings" of the ring have
afforded ample scope' (*Fistiana*, p. 70). It is the extent of the 'detail' which
is problematical. Egan had already announced, in some fight commentaries, that it would be 'superfluous' to detail what has proved to be repetitive
action. The sheer volume of fights covered meant the danger of duplication,
triteness, or monotony seeping into reports remained.

The techniques employed to enliven pugilistic writing included the use
of flash jargon and the general 'spectacularisation' of events. In the preface

---

71   Radford, *The Celebrated Captain Barclay*, pp. 10, 12.
72   Orwell, *The Road to Wigan Pier*, p. 82.

to his own pugilistic novel, Shaw announced: 'the true artistic material of the story is the comedy of the contrast between the realities of the ring and the common romantic glorification or sentimental abhorrence of it' (*CBP*, p. xi). Given his unstinting praise of the supposed courage, honour, and moral probity encouraged by prizefighting, Egan is certainly culpable of 'glorification'. Yet, his methods and objectives cannot be so simplistically assessed and, as Shaw's later comments inadvertently attest, embellishment was necessary:

> The sport was supposed to have died of its own blackguardism by the second quarter of the century; but the connoisseur who approaches the subject without moral bias will, I think, agree [...] that it must have lived by its blackguardism and died of its intolerable tediousness [...] In barren dreariness and futility no spectacle on earth can contend with that of two exhausted men trying for hours [...] for the sake of their backers. (*CBP*, p. xii)

This pivotal sentiment was endorsed in an early-twentieth-century boxing study that clearly distinguishes between what it terms 'knuckles' and 'gloves' periods, and recollects: 'unfortunately, the beginnings of prize-fighting [...] were more romantic than its subsequent career, for it lived on brutality and it died of boredom'.[73] Shaw suggests that the situation was exacerbated by insipid reporting: 'the fight between Sayers and Heenan had been described in The Times as solemnly as the University Boat Race'.[74] It was 'tediousness' or, as Egan termed it, 'yawning and *ennui*' that the *Boxiana* style, primarily, sought to avoid.

In his trawl through some of the major pugilistic contests in the sport's history, Denzil Batchelor applied his own slant on the above fight, including imagery that would have sat comfortably in a *Boxiana* volume: 'The little pinnace comes in with a wet sail, looses its cannonade, and tacks out of the reach of the galleon's thunderclap reply [...] Excited whispers echo through the ranks of spectators'. Later, Batchelor accentuated the concept that an event of great consequence has taken place, whilst simultaneously perpetuating the notion of the 'Sporting World' as a disparate entity:

---

73   Theodore Cook, in Lynch, *Knuckles and Gloves*, p. vii.
74   Shaw, 'Note on Modern Prizefighting', *Cashel Byron's Profession*, p. 237.

The sun is rising in the clear blue sky above the bare hedges and the unruffled stream behind the ring. Two hours are gone by since the first blow was struck. It is half past nine of a brilliant April day: already the men of Farnborough are eating their breakfast bacon, and [...] a top-hatted business man sits reading his *Morning Post* in the special train making its sedate return journey to London Bridge. But Farnborough is a battlefield; Farnborough is earning the crossed swords it deserves to be marked with in every map of England.[75]

Opinion on the import of the day's contest may have been divided, but the style employed in this retrospective account blends the imaginative and quixotic to produce an entertaining yet reflective commentary.

Shaw had reported on the gloved fighters of his generation, and twentieth-century boxing appears far removed from the bare-knuckle prizefighting covered by Egan. In a modern society which boasts an organised outlet for boxing, bare-knuckle 'clubs' have travelled the country and, using subterfuge, hosted illegal bouts.[76] The existence of such activities reinforces the discrepancy between the form of prizefighting reported by Egan and the legitimised, arguably diluted, sport that has enjoyed the spotlight of intense media scrutiny. It appears doubtful that a similar underground correspondent has chronicled the covert fights, and this is corroborated by Bartley Gorman (1944–2002), a leading prizefighter of the 1970s: 'There are no record keepers [...] and I have had to rely on memory'. Gorman says of 'travelling men': 'They would rather settle a row with knuckles than resort to the courts'. And, of their most renowned champions: 'They live on only in oral tradition and family folk memory. To us children gathered around the campfires [...] they were dragon-slayers'.

A cynical slant would be that such contests were merely another means of providing gambling entertainment. Nevertheless, the prizefighting scene does appear to have wielded some form of compulsion or fascination, and

---

75   Denzil Batchelor, *Big Fight: The Story of World Championship Boxing* (London: Phoenix House, 1954), pp. 59, 60.
76   Under the guise of 'Blackpool [...] Horse and Carriage Club', a mixture of Irish travellers and Romany gipsies proposed an 'upmarket equestrian event' for an Easter bank holiday weekend. This was deemed newsworthy not for sporting reasons, but for the panic incited amongst the local community (Kirkham) at the imminent 'invasion'. *Daily Mail* (15 April 2006), p. 35.

these contemporary comments correspond with Egan's treatment of sporting subject matter as mythical legend. The continuation of bare-knuckle fighting beyond the early Victorian period raises the possibility of investigating the existence of accompanying commentaries. The fact that creative, distinguishing labels continued to be accorded to certain fighters' favoured blows (examples of speciality punches include the 'temple-tickler' and 'ox-dropper') encourages the belief that some written records may survive.[77]

Reporting parallels between fundamentally different strains of the sport do occur. In fact, A J Liebling openly acknowledged the *Boxiana* influence in his own boxing articles:

> [Sugar Ray Robinson v Randy Turpin] One more punch like the ones Robinson was throwing might have ended the boxing days of any fighter – even Turpin, who is what *Boxiana* would have called a 'prime glutton'. *Boxiana* is one of my favourite books [...and] I had a refresher glance at it [...] On the night of the fight I started out early, in the true Egan tradition.[78]

Liebling consistently alluded to how Egan 'would have styled' something, and also claimed that, compared to Egan, Hazlitt 'was a dilettante'. Commenting on Byron's sparring sessions with Jackson, Liebling gives the impression that he is bringing the reader into his confidence over a piece of previously concealed information: 'Jackson conned his lordship into thinking he had a hell of a right hand; he advised him never to let it go at a husband or he might have to marry the widow'.[79]

In 1962, Liebling spent some time with an unusually astute and loquacious boxer, Cassius Marcellus Clay, as he prepared for a fight against Sonny Banks.[80] In the subsequent commentary, the *Boxiana* influence is again prominent: 'Standing straight up, he boxed and moved – cuff, slap, jab and stick, the busy hands stinging like bees [...Banks] kept throwing that left

---

77 Bartley Gorman (and Peter Walsh), *King of the Gypsies* (Bury: Milo Books, 2002), pp. 267, x, 60, 7.

78 Liebling, 'Sugar Ray and the Milling Cove'. *Just Enough Liebling*, p. 342.

79 Liebling, 'The University of Eighth Avenue' (1955). Ibid., pp. 385, 386.

80 Later known as Muhammad Ali (b. 1942), this contest was Clay's New York professional debut.

hook [...] but he was like a man trying to fight off wasps with a shovel'.[81] This raises the question whether Liebling inspired the 'float like a butterfly, sting like a bee' slogan that later became associated with Clay (Ali), and suggests that Egan's brand of flash would have been conducive to generating an array of similarly 'snappy' mottos.

A decade later, Norman Mailer's interpretation of the same gifted fighter's mesmerising style arguably surpasses Egan and Liebling's metaphorical playfulness:

> Clay punched with a greater variety of mixed intensities than anyone around, he played with punches, was tender with them, laid them on as delicately as you put a postage stamp on an envelope, then cracked them in like a riding crop across your face, stuck a cruel jab like a baseball bat [...] next waltzed you in a clinch with a tender arm around your neck, winged away out of reach on flying legs, dug a hook [...] a mocking soft flurry of pillows and gloves, a mean forearm, cutting you off from coming up on him, a cruel wrestling of your neck in a clinch, then elusive again, gloves snake-licking your face like a whip.[82]

Mailer produced his own 'mixed intensities' as this thoughtful appraisal accentuates the finer sensibilities that can be discerned in the midst of a frenetic encounter (favoured language including 'tender', 'delicately', 'cruel', and 'mocking'; whilst 'slap' and 'jab' are absent). Also underscored is the concept of language and imagery operating as devices to encourage appreciation of pugilism's less conspicuous elements. Is this wasted on the reading audience? It is apparent from Egan's descriptions of nineteenth-century Fancy spectators that an absence of 'streaming claret' and palpable distress led to a generally unappreciative attitude prevailing, especially amongst losing backers.

To some extent, Egan envisaged the *Boxiana* writings as a form of sporting historical archive, enabling posterity to learn about the exploits of prizefighting legends. Unsurprisingly, Randall is proposed as one whose '*capabilities* and triumphant fame' must be preserved:

81   Liebling, 'Poet and Pedagogue' (1962). *Just Enough Liebling*, p. 409.
82   Norman Mailer (1923–2007). 'Ego', first published in *Life* magazine (March 1971). Quoted in Alan Hubbard, *The Independent* (14 January 2007) <http://news.independent.co.uk/world/ americas/ article2152439.ece> (accessed September 2007).

BOXIANA. This exclamation may perhaps be considered as having something too much of *self* belonging to it; but if the fame of RANDALL outlives the present period, we may sincerely wish [...] that the *Records* of his achievements may be sought after till the end of time. (*Boxiana III*, p. 205)

On the theme of Egan's writings 'outliving' his period, it is intriguing to note that the revered martial artist and actor Bruce Lee (1940–73) included the following advice amongst his detailed, technical guide: 'Success in "milling on the retreat" takes good judgement of distance and the ability to stop in your retreat quickly and unexpectedly'. The application of quotation marks suggests that Lee's reportedly voracious 'studying, analyzing, and modifying' of fighting-related literature (his personal library consisted of over two thousand such books) might have included a *Boxiana* volume.[83] The engaging notion of this popular cultural figure consulting this text should be qualified by the observation that the above quote is an isolated instance amidst his instructional volume, which consists of over two hundred pages.

The existence of an alternative sporting canon was treated as jest by Egan himself when describing the knowledge of 'thorough-bred sports-man', Sir Henry Tally-ho:

The Racing Calendar, he pointed out to his friends with delight: the Stud Book, was also a treat to him, the Sporting Magazine, from its commencement, was his 'History of England', as he termed it; and Boxiana, reminded him of divers blows in sundry places. All the above books he had read so often, that he used to boast, he was as perfect about sporting events, as a clergyman, belonging to a cathedral, with his bible. (*Pilgrims of the Thames*, p. 359)

The latter remarks demonstrate the prior existence of a modernistic cliché regarding the concept of sporting religion: '[25 August 1990] At 2.55 p.m. the Shrine [Old Trafford stadium] was full [...] Forty-six thousand, seven hundred and fifteen supplicants in multicoloured hue basked in euphoria as their gladiators paraded'.[84]

Regarding the place of Victorian writing on the sport, some reports continued to appear in the *Sporting Magazine*, but Reid claims that the

83   Bruce Lee, *Tao of Jeet Kune Do* (Santa Clarita: Ohara Publications, 1994), pp. 150, 4.
84   Hall, *Heaven and Hall: A Prodigal Life*, p. 140.

three volumes of *Pugilistica* (1880), by Henry Downes Miles, were 'coloured by the author's prejudices, particularly his contempt for Pierce Egan'.[85] Within its 'Introduction', however, there can be found familiar national-istic rhetoric, praising the 'Anglo-Saxon race' for its pre-eminence in the 'least dangerous of all forms of the duel' (*Pugilistica I*, p. v), reiterating arguments for the supposedly civilised manner in which pugilism could resolve disputes. Conceivably, these could have been transplanted directly from a *Boxiana* volume, and the fight commentaries include reproductions of accounts by Egan, Bee, and Dowling.

A lack of fresh writing demotes the *Pugilistica* volumes to little more than a methodical assembly of contemporary reports. And, these are fre-quently doctored by Miles to expunge original typographical flourishes, or insert snippets of information that emerged later. Miles's 'contempt' for Egan is intermittently apparent, calling the latter's praise of Owen a demonstration of 'bad English and worst taste', and bemoaning 'the apocryphal rigmaroles which disfigure' the *Boxiana* series (*Pugilistica I*, p. 110). He condemned Egan's playful treatment of one episode as a ram-bling conglomeration of 'slang and ungrammatical "patter"' (p. 350), and ridiculed the labelling of Scroggins as 'invincible' shortly after 'four defeats' (p. 346). Perhaps the latter complaint is an instance of Egan's disregard of 'mere reality'. In addition, Miles's acceptance of Egan's version of events is sometimes grudging: 'So says the reporter' (*Pugilistica II*, p. 40); 'This is the account in "Boxiana", and *faute de mieux* we must adopt it' (p. 139). Nevertheless, Miles regurgitates Egan's commentaries at length.[86]

Throughout different modern sports-writing areas we see the deploy-ment of techniques that can be tentatively dubbed Eganesque, or as Hindley phrased it: 'a *Piercy Egania!!!* style'.[87] Such playful techniques are well within the capabilities of those possessing a degree of inventive flair, and an example of the easily transferable nature of *Boxiana*-style qualities in sports

---

85   Reid, *Bucks and Bruisers*, p. 164.
86   These included accounts of Randall v Turner (*Pugilistica I*, pp. 342–5) and Neate v Hickman (*Pugilistica II*, pp. 110–14).
87   Hindley, *The True History of Tom and Jerry*, p. xviii.

reporting is evinced in a piece by newspaper horse-racing correspondent Michael Henderson recording his impression of unfolding events at an exciting Arc de Triomphe (Paris, 6 October 2002). The report of the afternoon is split into time bands, which fulfil a segmental effect similar to the rounds of a prizefight. The 'Five o' clock' dispatch commences: 'Excitement mounting [...] It's fascinating, this enclosed world, with its rituals and customs. And then there are the horses'.[88] This mirrors Egan's enthralment at the activity surrounding a sequestered sporting kingdom, with the actual fight, ironically, almost an afterthought. The account proceeds by echoing familiar theatrical allusions: 'The prelude is over. The actors take the stage'. At 'Five-thirty', the scene depicted matches the spectacle and sense of yearning conveyed by the *Boxiana* treatment of a major contest:

> The sense of anticipation sharpens the appetite for any top-notch event, and there are 40,000 spectators here, appetites sharpened, hungering for this annual feast [...] When the horses come round the final bend, and the punters respond with one resounding voice, it feels like one of those special I-was-there moments. Frankie Dettori is there, all right, a 16–1 shot nipping in as roars stick in a few thousand throats.[89]

Egan's favoured notion of the crowd propelled by a communal impulse is reinforced. Henderson's concluding instalment of the account is headed 'Postlude', thus accentuating the sense of the event, and the report itself, as an uninhibited, artistic composition. Overall, the piece demonstrates the creative licence typically enjoyed by sports-writing 'visionaries'.

My adoption of the label 'idiosyncratic' to augment the defining of such imaginative reporting, and general creative exuberance, coincides with Stuart Hall's touting of the 'bizarre'. The reproduction of techniques honed by Egan can be discerned in other sporting fields, essentially far removed from pugilism. The television commentator Phil Liggett has, since the 1970s, reported on the Tour de France cycle race and has beguiled viewers 'not least for his habit of lapsing into obscure flights of fancy when

---

88   Michael Henderson, *Daily Mail* (7 October 2002), p. 67.
89   Champion jockey Dettori was riding the Newmarket-trained Marienbard. Ibid., p. 67.

describing the action'. Observe the imaginative slant deployed in these mock-heroic allusions: 'To wear the yellow jersey is to mingle with the gods of cycling'; 'Once you pull on that golden fleece you become two men'.[90] Such flourishes have been dubbed 'Liggetisms', but it might be argued that they are steeped in the tradition established by 'Eganisms'.

Similarly, if we recall Egan remarking on the plight of a frustrated pugilist; '["The Nailer"] sat down like the great ALEXANDER, *weeping that he had no more heroes to overcome*' (*Boxiana I*, p. 70), and compare this imagery to that employed by Sid Waddell at the World Darts tournament in 1985: 'When Alexander of Macedonia was 33, he cried salt tears because there were no more worlds to conquer – [Eric] Bristow is only 27'. The parallel is almost exact. Waddell recalls that this particular virtuosic effusion coincided with a rebuke from his BBC producer for 'getting Moses, Rod Stewart, and Ivanhoe all in five minutes of commentary' – but Waddell was eventually given 'free rein' to continue his engaging style.[91] Continuing in the realm of vocal commentary, and a modern broadcasting medium, the distinctive, often onomatopoeic, summarising of John ('Boom') Madden over decades of big-game American football coverage has been dubbed 'Maddentary'.

In respect of Egan's pugilistic accounts, the comparison provided by some commentary on another classless, popular sport (football) by another latter-day writer and broadcaster, Hall, is striking:

> [Manchester City v Tottenham Hotspur, 15 December 1990] Enter Peter Reid; he inspired; City plundered. Crablike Reid scrabbles all over the park, his legs battered like ancient Roman ruins, his brain as cool as Napoleon's, his spirit that of Olympus [...] The second half was a reprise, full throttle [...] the players' hot breath like steam that rises from New York manholes.[92]

90   *The Independent* (*Extra* supplement) 6 July 2007, p. 5.
91   Sid Waddell, <http://www.sidwaddell.compsyswebdesign.com/q.htm> (accessed September 2007).
92   In ancient Greece, Mount Olympus was regarded as the abode of the gods. Hall, *Heaven and Hall: A Prodigal Life*, p. 142.

Eganesque ingredients are present; Hall intriguing the reader by deploying classical, historical, and military references amidst his linguistic verve. In short, an account featuring such creative imagery to depict the players' exhalation and the cumbersome frame of others ('the City centre forward [...] a bit like a stevedore in a *corps de ballet*')[93] contains the *Boxiana*-style spirit regardless of whether the writer has read, or even heard of Pierce Egan. A possible question arises over whether this is an overly idiosyncratic style, limiting its appeal to other 'bizarre spirits'.

I will not dwell on a catalogue of similar examples of reports from non-pugilistic sources, but such snippets help to highlight aspects of Egan's writing which could be viewed as a model for later sporting commentaries. A common outlook of these writers, towards sporting description, appears to be that one should descant upon the subject. In short, accounts featuring creative imagery can transcend the reality of an event bereft of entertaining incident. An overriding question is to what extent Egan laid the groundwork for such unconventional reporting styles. The appealing tenor of imaginative bursts of sporting commentary, with an accompanying sense that they contain a degree of spontaneity, reinforces the notion of Egan setting a precedent for later writers.

It is feasible that Egan may have trail-blazed a new approach to pugilistic writing without necessarily establishing a style to be adopted as a template or acting as a direct influence on subsequent reporting. A distinct division was established between bare-knuckle prizefighting and its regulated, gloved version. It is difficult to detect any blatant *Boxiana*-style in Bohun Lynch's account of the fourth round between Jack Dempsey and Georges Carpentier (New Jersey, 2 July 1921):

> The sullen giant crouched and attacked Carpentier with all his strength, driving him fast before him round the ring until he had him in a corner [...Dempsey] got him close up against the ropes and sent in a very hot right to the jaw. Carpentier collapsed upon hands and knees. The ring, his antagonist, the faces peering at him from the level of the stage, were misty and vague. There was only one idea in his mind, only one thing that he could hear. He must get up somehow before the referee counted ten.[94]

93   Ibid., p. 201.
94   Lynch, *Knuckles and Gloves*, pp. 187–8.

Lynch briefly adopts the fighter's persona (a ploy repeatedly used by this writer) to provide an alternative aspect of events. Another difference is the technical description of blows, such as during the commentary to Carpentier's subsequent victory over the Australian George Cook (Albert Hall, 12 July 1922):

> Suddenly, as the Australian tried to force him into his own corner, he sent in a right to Cook's jaw, through his guard, at very long range and with extraordinary dexterity [...] For one thing it was exquisitely timed, coming in not straight, but without the elbow being markedly bent, striking the right place, the glove turning over as it struck, and avoiding Cook's guardian left with the most delicate precision.[95]

Lynch proceeds to cite Carpentier as 'the first French boxer of the highest order, the first to make us realise that boxing was not the sole prerogative of the English-speaking races', but was eager not to perpetuate the depiction of fights as national concerns, stating the men are simply 'two boxers', and appearing grateful to report that 'the international habit of thought has largely [...] dropped into the background'.

The scene at this latter contest does highlight an issue of contention that appears to linger from Egan's day – the female spectator: 'The huge hall was full. Large numbers of women were present [...] and these called to mind the amusing discussions in and out of newspapers, before the war, as to the propriety of admitting female spectators to "Gladiatorial displays"'. On this occasion, some interest may have been aroused by physical considerations: 'Carpentier is a Greek bronze, dark-skinned, beautifully proportioned, covered with easy, flowing muscle, a sight to stir the hearts of older athletes with vain regret'.[96]

Contemporary reports on boxing bouts highlight the fundamental changes in the sport's structure, which sees reporters required to instil vigour into a much shorter event of, often, twelve three-minute rounds. It would be unsurprising if Egan and his contemporaries had to conjure a little 'filling' amidst seventy or eighty rounds of an attritional two-hour encounter between two fighters steadfastly refusing to yield. Daniel Herbert's account

95   Ibid., p. 191.
96   Ibid., pp. 164, 167, 190.

of a featherweight title fight between Mathews and Marsh (Bethnal Green, 13 October 2007) is delivered in short, non-digressional sentences, and the commentary reinforces the thought that Egan's flash jargon was the most short-lived element of the *Boxiana* style:

> Marsh lacked nothing in heart or brains. After conceding a close first, he adopted the right tactics to lift the next three sessions.
> Instead of rushing in, he stood off, moved around the ring and timed his incursions expertly. In and out he went, landing jabs and rights as Mathews occupied ring centre, waiting for exchanges that didn't come.

Terming a fighter's attacks as 'incursions' might, initially, appear linguistically formal, but instils the martial sense of an army making forays into enemy territory. As the momentum of the fight shifts, the less expansive range of words deployed for various blows becomes evident:

> By the seventh the champ was landing rights after his jabs and it was clear Marsh was moving less than before.
> 'Work that body!' ordered Eames but Mathews outmuscled his challenger and piled up points with lefts.
> Marsh was driven into a corner in the ninth, and in the next tried to be more aggressive only to walk on to shots.[97]

This typical contemporary fight report has little in common with Egan's accounts two-hundred years before. However, traces of a more general metaphorical style, borne from the nature of pugilistic action, are discernible.

Presentation varies between rival newspaper accounts. For his report on the Super-middleweight title fight between Joe Calzaghe (Wales) and Mikkel Kessler (Denmark), on 4 November 2007, John Rawling recounts:

> As Calzaghe leaned forward and fell into range behind his shots, Kessler was showing the handspeed and power that had made him such a feared puncher, rocking the Welshman with hooks and uppercuts [...] Calzaghe is nothing if not a warrior. With his father having demanded his son use the traditional method of jabbing his

---

97   Daniel Herbert, *Boxing News*, 63, 42 (19 October 2007), p. 14.

way back and with Warren [the promoter] imploring from ringside that his fighter should eschew an inclination to slug it out with the Dane, Calzaghe slowly began to assume control.[98]

This represents a considered approach and, whilst the writer is not saying that the animated promoter has couched his instructions in such formal language (i.e. 'Eschew your attacking inclinations, my son'), the phraseology imparts a dispassionate tenor to the commentary. This account is partially in keeping with the style adopted by Herbert above, but Ron Lewis includes a pronounced round-by-round approach:

> Round 1
> Cagey opening by both. Calzaghe lands to the body, but is caught by Kessler's jab.
> [...]
> Round 3
> Calzaghe lands a left and Kessler slips. The Welshman lands punches repeatedly, forcing Kessler back, while the Dane tries to get Calzaghe to walk on to his right.
> Round 4
> Good start again by Calzaghe but Kessler catches him with a straight right and lands two uppercuts.
> [...]
> Round 6
> Calzaghe lifts his workrate, moving around, beating Kessler to the jab.
> [...]
> Round 8
> Kessler puts all his effort into the round as the bout threatens to run away from him, landing with a powerful straight right. Calzaghe fires back with a body shot.[99]

Despite the segmentation employed, this commentary is more concise than Egan's, and any terminology (such as 'jab' and 'uppercuts') remains relatively simple.

Once more, I turn to a typical Egan extract, recounting the contest between Young Sam and Ned Neal (Newmarket, 18 January 1831):

---

98   John Rawling, *Guardian* ('Sport' supplement, 5 November 2007), p. 2.
99   Ron Lewis, *The Times* (5 November 2007), p. 78. Calzaghe was eventually adjudged the victor.

> There is a sort of magic about his [Sam's] blows; the bat of Harlequin cannot change the scene quicker than the 'bunch of fives' of our hero [...][100] The fine eye of the latter seemed to penetrate into the very soul of his adversary [...] and he positively rallied against the effects of nature [...] until he sent his opponent down amidst the admiring shouts of thousands. (*Book of Sports*, pp. 300–1)

The concept of a pugilist as a mystical figure conferring colour to the immediate scene, and fascinating the spectators, is an apposite one when discussing the *Boxiana* style. It might be said that Egan weaves 'a sort of magic' in his transformation of sporting scenes. It is the skilful unorthodoxy practised by similarly inventive chroniclers that particularly befits the sports-writing genre, and renders it distinguishable by their untrammelled ability to blend multifarious techniques. In terms of their linguistic inventiveness and spirit, they are effectively poets. Ultimately, the scope exists (and existed) for an incongruity to develop where a sport's popularity is artificially created, or prolonged, by the calibre of reporting associated with it, and the extent of its escapist nature. It may also be fair to conclude, from a greater proliferation of imaginatively entertaining pieces, that the term 'maverick reporter' would be an inappropriate tag in an area where the inventive, or 'bizarre', is becoming less exceptional.

The disparity between the critical acclaim accorded to Egan and Dickens is, to some extent, understandable. Reid states: 'that Egan is Dickens stripped of genius and heart and left only with energy and talent', and this is, arguably, a palatable view for admirers of Egan.[101] However, commenting on Egan's contemporaries in the metropolitan writing genre, it is claimed that Egan swayed 'the popular imagination' and, consequently, 'it was virtually impossible for these writers to break entirely from his influence; all their work in the period can be thought as a direct response to his vision'.[102] As mentioned, there were certain illustrious literary figures that sympathised with much of the sporting ethos promoted by Egan, their respective philosophies appearing to overlap.

---

100 A mute character in pantomime, often appearing in varicoloured costume.
101 Reid, *Bucks and Bruisers*, p. 204.
102 *Unknown London*, ed. by Marriott, IV, p. 1.

Egan's influence on the novels of George MacDonald Fraser (1925–
2008) should also be acknowledged. *The Flashman Papers* incorporates
period dialogue, and the character traits ascribed to the central protagonist exploit the adventurous, but sleazy and dishonourable, aspects of a
Life in London buck: '[Harry Flashman] the celebrated Victorian soldier,
scoundrel, amorist, and self-confessed poltroon'.[103] The *Boxiana* connection
is clearly discernible throughout Fraser's historically-inspired pugilistic
novel *Black Ajax* (1997).

It is in sporting journalism where associations with Egan particularly
come to the fore. Frank Keating's obituary of Ian Wooldridge (1932–2007)
describes this respected journalist as 'an undisputed heavyweight champion
of British sports writing', one of a 'luminous handful'. An Egan connection is immediately established by the choice of a pugilistic phrase, but its
admittedly general application is not as significant as a subsequent reference to the 'peripatetic trade, sometimes considered trivial, if not rather
grubby'. This underscores a familiar perception encountered by Egan, and
Keating praises Wooldridge with an artistic analogy that resembles Egan's
outlook: 'he had a singular but always flexible style: he could daub on the
primaries with broad strokes or work with a water-colourist's touch'.[104] Egan
advanced a distinctive narrative approach that helped to avoid sterility. His
successors beyond the mid nineteenth century have only rarely been aware
of Egan's work. Nevertheless, consciously or unconsciously, elements of a
metaphorical style have been perpetuated in fluctuating degrees by writers
sharing the realm of unconventional sports reporting.

---

103   George MacDonald Fraser, *Flashman and the Tiger* (London: Harper Collins, 2000),
         p. 9. 'Captain Flashman, a blustering fellow, a coward' (*Sinks of London laid open: A
         Pocket Companion for the Uninitiated*, 1848), quoted in Coleman, *A History of Cant
         and Slang Dictionaries*, p. 130.
104   Frank Keating, *Guardian* (6 March 2007), p. 36.

CHAPTER 6

Post-Fight Observations

This book has freely acknowledged, and quoted from, pugilistic writing which pre-dates Egan's contributions. Whilst no claim can be made that Egan instigated the reporting of prizefights, he did devise a different literary approach – the *Boxiana* style. I have examined nineteenth-century works, and the treatment of predecessors to the *Boxiana* series has been necessarily brief, but the inclusion of this earlier material establishes the context in which Egan wrote.

Regarding the target audience of the *Boxiana*-style writings, there must be a degree of scepticism applied to the erratically scattered pieces (throughout the primary texts) expressing aspirations for universal accessibility. Concerns over declining masculinity, increasing 'effeminacy', national identity, and martial readiness suggest that idealistic calls to extend the sport's appeal lacked conviction. The evidence implies that such pieces expressed unrealistic pretensions to attract a diverse audience. Looking at Egan's supposedly national newspapers, the inclusion of more general news, fashions, advertisements, and event notices (often culled from other publications) might be interpreted as a token effort at generating a wider audience. It is almost inconceivable that a prospective purchaser of an affordable newspaper would buy something entitled *Pierce Egan's Life in London, and Sporting Guide Connected with the Events of the Turf, the Chase, and the Ring*, or *Pierce Egan's Weekly Courier to the Sporting, Theatrical, Literary, and Fashionable World*, unless they were a member of the Fancy fraternity. There is no attempt to conceal the sporting bent of these publications which the selection of more neutral titles may have, at least temporarily, achieved. Such episodes underscore the unconvincing sincerity of occasional pieces included in *Boxiana* and, particularly, Egan's *Book of Sports*, which promoted pugilism and its writing as attractive for 'ladies' and those possessing refined sensibilities.

What should not be overlooked was that the Fancy consisted of a wide-ranging social blend. Therefore, the readership of Egan's *Boxiana*, *Book of Sports*, and so forth, mirrored 'an emerging "mass" reading public which cut across middle- and working-class boundaries'. Iain McCalman's outline of this 'mass' audience echoes the types that openly or surreptitiously participated in sporting events, and collectively constituted the Fancy. This readership 'included the hordes of not always respectable artisans, clerks, army and navy officers, students, journalists, professionals, businessmen, government officials and tourists who inhabited London and visited its seamy underworld', as well as a 'more respectable middle-class audience'.[1] Whilst it can be acknowledged that Egan produced a hybrid style tailored for the metropolitan, sporting male of Regency London, it might also be claimed that, in respect of the more general audience, where his sporting voice failed to appeal, his metropolitan voice would succeed.

It is interesting to view the perspective of a pugilistic chronicler writing one hundred years after the *Boxiana* period. Bohun Lynch was a writer well aware of Egan's *Boxiana* series, and he delivers an objective viewpoint of Egan's value:

> Pierce Egan made a record of the old Prize Ring which is invaluable. So that we are not concerned with his literary distinction as with his accuracy as a chronicler, and, as other records of contemporary events are either scarce or […] totally lacking, it is not easy to check his accounts. From internal evidence, we know at the first glance at Boxiana that we must be careful; for Egan shouts his praises of almost all pugilists upon the same note. And all of them cannot have been as good as all that! […] It is his passionate zeal (apart from the matters of fact which he tells us) that make him worth reading. For the rest we must regard him as we are, nowadays, prone to regard most historians, and make such allowances as we see fit for inevitable exaggerations.[2]

Lynch highlights issues, raised in this book, concerning the mixture of merit and anomalies to be found in most of Egan's work. It is claimed that the *Boxiana* series and *Life in London* 'inaugurated new forms of cheap, mass-circulating literature', and that his journalistic pieces 'pioneered

---

1   McCalman, *Radical Underworld*, p. 236.
2   Lynch, *Knuckles and Gloves*, p. xxiv.

new modes of sporting, documentary, and crime reporting which looked forward to the work of the young Charles Dickens'.[3] I would accentuate the expression 'looked forward', which implies only a partial influence. Nevertheless, this limited bearing must also have been unequivocally perceptible in order to prompt further enthusiastic advancement of the writer's significance: 'Arguably, Pierce Egan did for urban plebeian culture what Walter Scott did for the rural Scottish peasantry, inaugurating a brand of popular Romanticism which William Hazlitt and the young Charles Dickens were to perfect'.[4]

I do not claim that a direct lineage can be charted from the more colourful elements of contemporary sports writing back to Egan's pugilistic writing. The disappearance of Egan's peculiar brand of flash sporting slang demonstrates one of the more obvious traits that failed to survive in any recognisable form. In addition, the general promotion of the idea that pugilism contributed to the defence of the nation was particularly relevant during the lengthy Napoleonic wars when invasion was a genuine threat (as opposed to later conflicts in far-flung regions of a Victorian British Empire). Egan's metropolitan writing did not express outrage at the living and working conditions of the urban poor in a newly industrialised society. His was certainly no 'condition of England' work in the mode of Dickens, Benjamin Disraeli (1804–87), Elizabeth Gaskell (1810–65), or Henry Mayhew (1812–87). Nor did Egan's *Boxiana* profiles follow the pugilists back into their, generally, impoverished societies, or question the motives of the sport's aristocratic organisers, rarely alluding to the possibility of exploitation. The dawning of the Victorian age appears to have been one of those historical periods of discontinuity, or rupture, which Egan's virtuosic style failed to withstand.

Possibly, the transmutation of sports writing would have progressed at a similar rate without the existence of Egan and the *Boxiana* series. Distinctive flair has been, and continues to be, evinced by talented authors,

---

3   McCalman and Perkins, in *An Oxford Companion to the Romantic Age*, ed. by McCalman, pp. 217–18.

4   McCalman, ibid., p. 493.

but the increasingly dominant role assumed by news of sporting events in society, and its burgeoning allocation of space in different journalistic and broadcasting media, could conceivably be borne from a *Boxiana*-style *spirit* typified by Egan's sporting work. Where idiosyncratic writing conflates with popular subject matter, formal evaluation is problematic and, to some extent, rendered inconsequential. Egan's writing created its own literary history, one that sits uncomfortably in the Romanticism category (perhaps 'Regency Literature' would be a more apt tag), and his flash style embraced a virtuoso culture.

The nature of most sporting events produces difficulties associated with repetitiveness and, as has been demonstrated, these are not always successfully circumvented. Metaphorical gilding can only be deployed to a limited extent, and although the inclusion of participants' profiles, alongside quotes, can pique the 'human interest' element of an event, this should merely complement, not displace the sporting action. The linguistic and imaginary guile that Egan deployed could be viewed as a literary response to certain sporting situations. Rather than espousing the existence of an 'Egan tradition', it is possible that Egan's own literary response is one that constitutes a naturally recurrent strategy deployed in the sports-writing sub-genre.

Essentially, the sport of prizefighting / pugilism / boxing (choose your own preference, reader, of these oft interchangeable terms) created a form of reporting that was relatively self-perpetuating. One writer providing commentary on an event could duplicate some stylistic nuances of predecessors without necessarily being familiar with past pieces. Basic recurring aspects of the sport render that dimension almost unavoidable. More difficult to rationalise is the idiosyncratic, or more playful, bent of Egan, Bee, and occasional others (discussed in last section). One theory is that wit and verbal cleverness are quite often used to contain and somehow handle the 'uncontainable'.[5] My study demonstrates that a *Boxiana* style existed, the many imitations underscoring this. Longevity, however, is an area where the style was undeniably deficient. Egan's innovative treatment of sports

5   I am grateful to Claire Lamont for her observations on this aspect of the discussion.

writing was an original and invigorating approach, but one subsumed amidst changing social, linguistic, and sporting conditions and attitudes.

Any individualistic style demonstrated by various writers, recording sporting events other than pugilism, is unlikely to have been directly influenced by Egan's work. Arguably, the *Boxiana* writings can be placed at the beginning of a tradition, whilst acknowledging that, in many ways, subsequent sports writing did not follow any 'Egan style'. Retaining its 'bruising', uncouth image, the modern variation of prizefighting, boxing, still occupies an awkward position in its relationship with different social classes. An alternative theory is that Egan's brand of pugilistic writing was one way to handle these complexities by accentuating any excitement and, simultaneously, deploying distinctive language to diminish awareness of anything that might be considered dangerous or 'low'.

If a transition was accelerated by Egan, the argument might be developed for identifying him as a forerunner of present-day sports journalism complete with its frequent sensationalism and hyperbole. That, however, may be an accreditation that Egan himself would have willingly disclaimed. There are plentiful examples of more contemporary sports writing that exercise a contemplative playfulness and, when allied to inventive imagery and expressiveness, there is more than a similarity between such reports and distinctive *Boxiana*-style pieces.

Ultimately, Egan functioned as an integral factor in pugilism's infiltration of the national psyche, which forms part of the widespread influence of a sporting philosophy on everyday life. In addition, he assumed a prominent position in the development of sports reporting, as well as contributing to more imposing areas of satire, parody, and novel writing. Many of the contemporary imitations, and later pugilistic-inspired pieces, may be regarded as surpassing Egan's original, but his enlivening style expedited the evolvement of innovatory-cum-unconventional sports reporting. Throughout the lengthy time period examined, there is a progression from the somewhat expository, formal tone of Fewtrell's *Boxing Reviewed*, to the cerebral musing of Hazlitt's 'The Fight', the similitude of Bee, comic application of Dickens, and the balance of social commentary and pugilistic authenticity achieved by Shaw.

Although some of the recurring Eganesque features in contemporary sporting commentaries may be inadvertent, and Egan's writing style might be (conveniently) sequestered in a '*Boxiana* period' or 'Flash and Fancy era', there is still enough evidence to sustain a perception of Pierce Egan as a transition figure, and certainly to establish his deserved relevance in literary history.

'The Daffy Club, or a Musical Muster of the Fancy' [at the Castle Tavern, Holborn]
Artist: Robert Cruikshank. Charles Molloy Westmacott ('Bernard Blackmantle'),
The English Spy (London: Sherwood Jones & Co., 1825) I, p. 339
(<http://www. gutenberg.org/etext/20001>)

'The Daffy Club presents to the eye of a calm observer a fund of entertainment [...] To see the place in perfection, a stranger should choose the
night previous to some important mill, when our host of the Castle plays
second, and all the lads are mustered to *stump up* their blunt, or to catch
the important *whisper* where the *scene of action* is likely to be'.
        — 'BERNARD BLACKMANTLE', *The English Spy*, I, pp. 335–6

'[*the* "TEMPLE OF THE FANCY!"]
Milling, "*glorious milling*" was the order of the day. Patrons "came out"
in mobs to give it support [...] He had lots of sporting dinners; numerous
gay little suppers; and always plenty of matches on the board to excite
the attention of the fancy. The *Daffy Club*, a prime hit, also became very
popular in the *Sporting World*; and for a long time crowded to excess
almost every night'.
        — PIERCE EGAN, *Book of Sports*, 1832, p. 71

Glossary of Nineteenth-Century Flash
and Sporting Terms

ABROAD – Senses knocked astray, in distress, pugilistic (*OED*).

ALIVE – Full of alacrity, 1709 (*OED*).

BANG-UP – (adj.) Stylish, in the pink of fashion (*OED*). 'A dashing fellow' (*Lexicon*).

[on the] BANKRUPTCY LIST – Completely knocked out, pugilistic c. 1820–60 (*B/P*).

BELLOWS TO MEND –Winded, short of breath (*OED*). [Bellows – Lungs, *Lexicon*]. 'Bellows to mend' (*Blackwood's*, 1822). Probably originating from street-cry (*B/P*).

BELLY-GO-FIRSTER –Initial blow to body, C19 (*OED*).

BENDER – 'A sixpence' (*OED*). An ironical word expressing incredulity, *Egan's Grose*.

BENJAMIN – Coat, from c. 1815 (*B/P*).

BENJAMIN BOLUS – Apothecary, physician, late C18 (*B/P*).

BIT – Money, C16–19 (*B/P*).

BIT OF STUFF – Boxer, c. 1810–50 (*B/P*).

BLACK STRAP – Pejorative term for thick, sweet port, late C18 (*B/P*).

BLADE – A sharp fellow, c. 1750–1860 (*B/P*).

BLINKER – Eye, 1816 (*B/P*).

BLUE – (adj.) Gloomy, early C19 (*B/P*). Confounded, disappointed (*Lexicon*).

BLUNT – Ready money (*OED*).

BODIER – A blow on side of body; loosely, on breast or belly, c. 1815 (*B/P*).

BONE – (verb) To take into custody, apprehend (*OED*).

BONIFACE – Generic name of innkeepers, 1803 (*OED*).

BOOKED – [e.g. 'was *booked* as the winning man', *Boxiana II*, p. 113] Meaning to be rated in the betting by the bookmakers ('odds men'). Destined (*B/P*).

BOTHERUMS – Convivial society, late C18 (*B/P*). Hence, 'a noisy party'.

BOTTOM – Physical resources, staying power, power of endurance; said esp. of pugilists, wrestlers, race-horses (*OED*).

BOUNCE – (noun) Boaster, swaggerer, c. 1690 (*B/P*). (verb) To bully (*Lexicon*).

BRADS – Money, copper coins, c. 1810 (*B/P*).

BREAD-BASKET – Stomach, c. 1750 (*B/P*).

[well] BREECHED – To have plenty of money (*Lexicon*).

BRILLIANT – Raw gin (*B/P*).

BROADS – Playing cards, from c. 1780 (*B/P*).

BROWNS – Halfpennies, from c. 1810 (*B/P*).

BUBBERY – Senseless clamour, 1818 (*B/P*).

BUCK – A gay, dashing fellow, a dandy, fop, 'fast' man (*OED*).

BUFF IT – To swear to (*Lexicon*).

BUFFER – A boxer, mostly Anglo-Irish, c. 1810–50 (*B/P*).

BUNTER – Low woman, c. 1730–1900 (*B/P*).

BURSTER – Something which 'takes the wind out' of one, 1851 (*OED*). Heavy fall, c. 1860 (*B/P*).

BUSH-COVE – A gipsy (*B/P*). [Or, 'Wandering Cove', *Boxiana III*, p. 421].

BUSTLE – Money, c. 1810 (*B/P*).

CABBAGE – A tailor, late C17–early C19 (*B/P*).

CAG – Irritate, 1801 (*B/P*).

CANISTER – The head, from c. 1790; mainly pugilistic (*B/P*).

CANVAS[S] – Human skin, pugilistic c. 1810–70 (*B/P*).

CASTOR – Hat, C17 (*B/P*).

CATOLLA – A noisy fellow, prating or foolish, or both, early C19 (*B/P*).

CHAFF – (noun) Banter, light raillery, 1648. (verb) To banter, rail at, 1827 (*OED*). To rebuke, but more usually 'to blow up' (i.e. to boast), talk aloud (*B/P*).

CHAFFER – The mouth (*B/P*). Hence, CHAFFING-BOX [e.g. *Boxiana IV*, p. 122].

CHALK FARM – Cant phrase for credit at tavern. [e.g. *Book of Sports*, p. 82].

[in] CHANCERY [suit] – Pugilistic, c. 1815–50. The head under an opponent's weaker arm to be punched with his stronger (*B/P*).

CHAPPERS – Possibly derived from CHAPS –Jaws, cheeks, 1708 (*OED*). [e.g. *Book of Sports*, p. 206].

CHARLEY [CHARLIE] – Night-watchman, 1812 (*OED*).

CHATTERER – A blow, esp. on the mouth that makes the recipient's teeth chatter. Pugilistic, c. 1820. Hence, CHATTERERS – Teeth, C19 (*B/P*).

CHAUNT – Song, c. 1810–90 (*B/P*).

CHAW-BACON – Contemptuous designation for a country bumpkin, *Blackwood's*, 1822 (*OED*).

CHEEKER – Blow to the cheek. [e.g. *Book of Sports*, p. 299].

CHEVY – To chivvy. To shout, cheer, esp. rough or chaffing, c. 1810 (*B/P*).

CHOPPER – Blow struck on the face with back of hand, *Tom Crib's Memorial* (*B/P*).

CHOPPING-BLOCK – An unskilled man that can take punishment, c. 1830 (*B/P*).

CLARET – Blood. Pugilistic slang, 1604 (*OED*). (verb) To draw blood (*B/P*). [Egan occasionally uses CRIMSON and VERMILION as alternatives].

CLEAN OUT – To deprive of money (usually illicitly), c. 1810 (*B/P*).

CLICK – A blow, punch, c. 1770 (*B/P*).

CLIE [CLY] – Pocket, C17–19 (*B/P*).

CLINK – A smart, sharp blow, 1722, 1820 (*OED*).

[blow a] CLOUD – Smoke tobacco, c. 1690 (*OED*).

[consult] COCKER – To calculate, 1818 [re. Arithmetician, Edward Cocker (1631–75)] (*OED*).

COMPO – (Short for 'composition') Stucco, cement, 1823 (*OED*).

[take the] CONCEIT [out of] – Knock the arrogance out of person.

CONK – The nose, 1812. (verb) To punch on the nose, c.1810 (*OED*).

CONVEYANCER – A thief, C18–19 (*B/P*).

CORINTHIAN – Relating to the licentious manners of ancient Greek city Corinth (Johnson). Profligate, in C19 use: Given to elegant dissipation (*OED*). A rake, C16–18. A dandy, hence a fashionable man-about-town, c. 1800–50 (*B/P*).

CORPORATION – The body, abdomen; esp. when prominent, 1753 (*OED*).

COVE – A fellow, 'chap', 'customer', orig. thieves cant (*OED*).

CRACK – Pre-eminent, 1793 (*OED*). The fashionable theme, 'the go' (*Lexicon*).

CRACKER – Heavy punch (*B/P*). [e.g. *Boxiana IV*, p. 458].

CROSS – A contest lost by collusory arrangement; a swindle, 1802 (*OED*).

CROSS-BUILT – Awkwardly built or moving, c. 1820–70 (*B/P*).

CRUMMY – Body-fat, sporting, c. 1818–40 (*B/P*).

CUT – A stage, degree, from c. 1815 (*B/P*).

CYPRIAN – Prostitute. 'A fashionable term in Regency period' (*B/P*).

DAB – Bed, c. 1810 (*B/P*). An adept, *Lexicon*.

DADDLE – The hand or fist, *Grose* (*OED*).

DAFFY – Gin, 1680 (*OED*).

DAFFY PASSAGE – Improvised term for throat? [e.g. *Boxiana IV*, p. 556].

DARKEY – The night, 1789 (*OED*).

DART – A straight-armed blow in boxing (*Lexicon*).

DAYLIGHTS – Eyes, c. 1750. Esp. pugilistic phrase 'darken one's daylights' (*B/P*).

[taking] DEGREES – To be imprisoned, c. 1820 (*B/P*).

DEXTER – Situated on the right side, C16 (*OED*).

[naughty] DICKEY-BIRD – A harlot, c. 1820 (*B/P*).

DING – To throw, or throw away, 1812 (*OED*). To knock down (*Lexicon*).

DISHED – Baffled, disappointed, from c. 1798 (*B/P*).

DIVER – A pick-pocket, C17 (*OED*).

[a complete] DO – Swindle or hoax, 1641 (*OED*).

DOMINOES – Teeth, esp. if discoloured, c. 1820 (*B/P*).

DOMINO-BOX – The mouth and teeth (*Bee's Sportsman's Slang*).

DORSE – The back, pugilistic. Also, 'to send to dorse' is to throw on one's back, *Blackwood's*, 1822 (*OED*). (verb) To knock down, c. 1810–80 (*B/P*).

DOUBLER – A punch that doubles up a person, 1811 (*OED*).

DOUGHEY – Baker, 1823 (*B/P*).

DOWN – Awake, suspicious, aware of (*B/P*).

DOWNER – A knockdown blow. Boxing, c. 1815 (*B/P*).

DOWN [E]Y – (noun) An artful fellow, c. 1820–80. (adj.) Artful, knowing (*B/P*).

DRAGSMAN – Driver of drag or coach, *Sporting Magazine*, 1812 (*OED*).

DRAIN – A drink, 1836 (*OED*).

DRAWING THE CORK – To draw blood, c. 1815 (*B/P*). To give a bloody nose (*Egan's Grose*).

DROOPER – One whose energy or spirit fails, C16 (*OED*).

DROP – To bring to the ground by a blow, 1726 (*OED*).

DUMP – Small coin, 1823 (*B/P*).

DUNG – A workman at less than union wages, C19 (*B/P*).

DUNNY – Dull of hearing, 1708 (*OED*).

FACER – A blow in the face, *Sporting Magazine*, 1810 (*OED*).

FANCY – The Fancy (collectively), 1735. Those who 'fancy' a particular pursuit (*OED*). 'The Fancy', the boxing world, c. 1810 (*B/P*).

FIB – (verb) – To strike, beat, or deliver blows, 1665 (*OED*). Hence, FIBBING.

FILE – A man, chap, 1812 (*B/P*).

FINISHER – Final or decisive blow, c. 1815 (*B/P*).

FLASH – Knowing, smart, 1812. Belonging to, connected with sporting men, esp. patrons of the ring, *Sporting Magazine*, 1808 (*OED*). (noun) Cant; relating to underworld or its slang, c. 1756 (*B/P*).

FLASHER – One of the attendants at a gaming-table whose function was to talk loudly of the bank's heavy losses, 1731 (*OED*).

FLASH-MAN – Dashing, ostentatious, or swaggering 'swell', 1785 (*OED*).

FLASH OF LIGHTNING – Glass of gin, 1789 (*OED*).

FLAT – A person easily duped, simpleton, 1762 (*OED*).

FLIMSY – A banknote, c. 1810 (*B/P*).

FLINT – A worker at union rates, c. 1760 (*B/P*).

FLOOR – (verb) To knock down (*Lexicon*). FLOORER – A knockdown blow (*OED*).

FLUE-FAKER – A chimney-sweep, c. 1810–1900 (*B/P*).

FLY – Knowing, sharp (*OED*). 'Synonymous with *flash* or *leary*' (*Egan's Grose*).

FOB – Pocket, C19 (*B/P*).

FOGLE – Handkerchief (silk) or neckerchief, *Lexicon* (*OED*).

FUNK – (noun) State of fear, 1743; (verb) To fear, 1737 (*B/P*).

GAME – Plucky, spirited, 1765 (*OED*).

GAMMON – (verb) Talk plausibly, 1789 (*OED*). To humbug, deceive (*Lexicon*). (noun) Nonsense, cant, 1805 (*B/P*). Hence, GAMMONING & GAMMONER.

GILLS – The mouth (e.g. *Real Life in London*, p. 123).

GLIM – Eye, c. 1790 (*B/P*). A light of any kind, 1700 (*OED*).

GLUTTON – One who takes a deal of punishment before he is satisfied, 1809 (*OED*).

GLUTTONY – Fortitude in taking punishment, c. 1810–60 (*B/P*).

GNOSTIC – A knowing person, 'a downy cove', c. 1815 (*B/P*).

(the) GO – The height of fashion; the 'rage', 1793 (*OED*).

GO-BY – To go past (*OED*). [As noun: 'gave him the go-by', *Book of Sports*, p. 2]. 'Give him the go-by' also means 'to ignore', C17 (*B/P*).

GRASS – (verb) To knock or throw (an adversary) down, *Sporting Magazine*, 1814 (*OED*). Hence GRASSER and GRASSED.

(St Giles's) GREEK – Unintelligible speech or language (*OED*).

GREEKING – Cheating at cards, 1817 (*OED*).

GRUBBERY – The mouth, c. 1870 (*B/P*). Also, GRUB-WAREHOUSE.

HALF-AND-HALF COVES – Cheap would-be dandies, c. 1820–60 (*B/P*).

HAMMERING – Dealing of hard repeated blows, *Sporting Magazine*, 1811 (*OED*).

HANDLE – Nose, 1790–1910 (*B/P*).

HASH – 'Settle the hash' – to subdue, silence, defeat, 1803 (*B/P*).

HEAVY – Porter and stout, C19 (*B/P*).

HEDGE [off] – To secure a wager by taking the odds on another, 1736 (*OED*).

HELL – A gaming-house, *Sporting Magazine*, 1794 (*OED*).

HOCUS – To drug, esp. with liquor, 1821 (*B/P*).

INDEX – The nose, 1817. [Alternatively, the head, c. 1818] (*B/P*).

IVORIES – Teeth, *Lexicon* (*OED*). 'Sluice the ivories' – to drink, c. 1780 (*B/P*).

JACKY – Gin, 1799 (*OED*).

JALAP – A purgative drug, 1675 (*OED*).

JARVEY [JARVIE, or JARVIS] – A hackney-coachman, 1796 (*OED*).

JOB – (verb) To strike with sharp, cutting stroke, *Sporting Magazine*, 1818 (*OED*).

JOHNNY-RAW – Novice (*OED*). 'A gawky countryman' (*Egan's Grose*).

KIDDY – 'A little dapper fellow' (*Lexicon*). Thieves slang for a professional thief who assumes a 'flashness' of dress and manner, 1812 (*OED*). [To be 'dressed kiddily' (*Bee's Sportsman's Slang*)].

KNIGHT OF THE RAINBOW – A footman, c. 1780–1880 (*B/P*). ['From the variety of colours in the liveries and trimming', *Lexicon*].

KNOWING ONE[S] – Person[s] professing to be well up in secrets of the turf, or sporting matters, 1750 (*OED*).

KNOWLEDGE-BOX – Head, *Lexicon* (*B/P*).

LAG – (verb) To transport as a convict, c. 1810 (*B/P*).

LARK – A frolicsome spree (*OED*). A piece of merriment (*Lexicon*).

LARRUP – (verb) To beat, thrash, c. 1820 (*B/P*).

LEARY [LEERY] – Knowing, fly, 1796 *Grose* (*OED*). On one's guard (*Lexicon*).

LEVEL – Knock person down, 1760. LEVELLER – Knock-down blow, *Sporting Magazine*, 1814 (*OED*).

LICK – To beat, thrash, 1732 (*OED*).

LIKE FUN – Very quickly, vigorously, c. 1815 (*B/P*).

LIKE WINKING – In a flash, rapidly, 1827 (*OED*).

LISTENER – Ear, c. 1805 (*B/P*).

[enter the] LISTS –Enter a place of contest, 1671 (*OED*).

LUMPY – Tipsy, intoxicated, c. 1810–90 (*B/P*).

LUSH – Liquor, 1790 (*OED*). LUSH[Y] COVE – Drunkard, c. 1810 (*B/P*).

LUSH-CRIB – Low public house; a gin shop c. 1810 (*B/P*).

LUSHINGTON – Referring to drink, 1823 (*OED*).

MACE – To swindle, defraud, c. 1790 (*B/P*). ['Mace Cove – A swindler', *Lexicon*].

MAG – (verb) To talk (noisily), 1810. (noun) A halfpenny, c. 1781 (*B/P*). [MAGPIE – Idle or impertinent chatterer, 1632 (*OED*)].

[the] MARK – The pit of the stomach, 1747 (*B/P*).

MAULEY [MORLEY, MAWLEY] – Hand, fist, 1780 (*OED*).

MAW – Mouth, C18–19 (*B/P*).

MAX – Very good gin, C18–19 (*B/P*).

MAZZARD – Head, C17 (*B/P*).

MELLISH – Money, c. 1815–60. Mainly sporting (*OED*) [possible connection with the wealthy Harry Mellish?].

MELT – (verb) To defeat, 1823. Hence, MELTER – One who administers a sound beating. MELTING – (noun) A sound beating, c. 1820–1900 (*B/P*).

MIDDLE PIECE – The chest, c. 1800–70 (*B/P*).

MILL – (noun) Pugilistic encounter, *Boxiana I*. (verb) To beat, thrash, c.1700. Hence, MILLING (*OED*).

MIZZLE – To decamp, depart slyly, c. 1780 (*OED*).

MOLLISHER – Low woman, c. 1810 (*B/P*).

MONKERY – The country, cant 1790 (*B/P*).

MOPPERY – Head, 1821 (*B/P*).

[in] MOURNING – Blackened by fighting, 1814 (*OED*).

MUFF – 'A foolish silly person', 1812 (*B/P*).

MUFFLES – Boxing gloves, 1755 (*OED*).

MUG – Face, 1708 (*OED*).

MUMMER – The mouth, c. 1780–1870 (*B/P*).

MUZZLER – A blow to the mouth, c. 1810 (*B/P*).

NAIL – (verb) To strike smartly, to beat (*B/P*). [Used in sense 'to charge extortion-ately', *Boxiana III*, p. 335]. [tip the] NAILER – Give heavy blow.

NAP [it] – 'Catch it', 1700 (*OED*). 'Get the worst of contest' (*Bee's Sportsman's Slang*).

NECK OR NOTHING – Determined, readiness to venture everything, 1715 (*OED*).

[the] NEEDFUL – The necessary funds, money, 1774 (*OED*).

NIB – 'A gentleman', 1812 (*OED*). 'Person of the highest order' (*Egan's Grose*).

NIPPERED – Arrested, c. 1820–50 (*B/P*). 'Nippers – Handcuffs' (*Egan's Grose*).

NIX – Nothing, c. 1815 (*B/P*).

NOB – (noun) Head, 1700. (verb) To deliver blows to head, 1812 (*OED*).

NOBBER – Blow to the head, 1818. Or, one skilful at head-punches, c. 1820 (*B/P*).

NO GO – No use, impossible or impracticable, 1816 (*B/P*).

NOZZLE – The nose, 1755 (*B/P*).

NUTTY – (adj.) Amorous, fond of person (*OED*). [e.g. *Real Life in London*, p. 145].

[give] OFFICE – Signal, hint, or pass on information, 1803 (*B/P*). [e.g. 'in striking he gave the office so strong', *Boxiana IV*, p. 527].

OGLES – Eyes, 1700 (*OED*). Hence, OGLER – blow to eye [e.g. *Boxiana IV*, p. 126].

ONE-TWO – Two punches in quick succession (*OED*).

OUT-AND-OUTER – 'A person of a resolute determined spirit, who pursues his object without regard to danger or difficulty', 1812 (*OED*).

PADDY-WHACK – Irishman (only if big and strong), *Grose* (*B/P*).

PALINGS – Ribs? [e.g. *Book of Sports*, p. 24].

PANN[E]Y – Lodgings, rooms, c. 1785 (*B/P*).

PATLANDER – An Irishman, *Sporting Magazine*, 1820 (*B/P*).

PEEL – To remove outer garments in preparation (*OED*).

PEEPERS – Eyes, 1700 (*OED*).

PEPPER – (noun and verb) [To inflict] severe punishment, 1500. Allusive to pungent, biting quality of pepper (*OED*). Hence, to 'pay a visit to PEPPER ALLEY'.

PERSUADERS – Spurs, c. 1786 (*B/P*).

PHILISTINES – Drunkards, late C17 (*B/P*).

PIGEON – One who is swindled, a dupe, esp. in gaming, C16 (*OED*). [cf. 'Rook'].

PIMPLE –The nose, c. 1815–60 (*B/P*), or head (*Lexicon*).

PIMPLER – Presumably a blow to head or nose [e.g. *Boxiana II*, p. 120].

PINCH – The critical or crucial juncture, 1489 (*OED*). [e.g. 'at the *pinch* of some of his late contests', *Boxiana IV*, p. 233].

PINK – (verb) To strike with fist to visible effect, *Sporting Magazine*, 1810 (*OED*). (noun) Buckish cant for 'swell' or dandy, 1815–40. (adj.) Fashionable, 1818 (*B/P*).

PINKIFIED – Made pink in colour, 1886 (*OED*).

PINS – Legs, 1530 (*OED*).

PIOUS – Intoxicated [e.g. *Book of Sports*, p. 85].

PIPE – (verb) To pant, breathe hard from exertion, 1814 (*B/P*).

PIPKIN – Head, c. 1820 (*B/P*).

PLANT – To deliver a blow, *Sporting Magazine*, 1808.

PLANTER – A well-directed blow, *Sporting Magazine*, 1821 (*OED*).

PLUMB – Person worth a fortune of £100,000, 1709 (*OED*).

PLUMPER – A heavy blow, 1772 (*B/P*).

PODGER – A stiff blow, 1816 (*OED*) [e.g. *Boxiana II*, p. 457].

[put on the] POLISH – To finish off quickly, *Sporting Magazine*, 1829 (*OED*).

POSER – Blow. 'A question that poses or puzzles', 1793 (*OED*).

POTATO-TRAP – The mouth, 1785 (*B/P*).

POTATO BASKET – Mouth or stomach? [e.g. *Boxiana IV*, p. 540].

POWELL [it] – To walk. Sporting, c. 1810–50, after famous early C19 walker (*B/P*).

PRAD – Horse, 1798 (*OED*).

PREVENTER – A thing that hinders or restrains, C16 (*OED*). [Used to denote 'arm', *Boxiana IV*, p. 71].

PRIG –To plunder, cheat, *Sporting Magazine*, 1819 (*OED*).

PRIME – Used as universal approbative, c. 1810–40 (*B/P*) [cf. 'Bang-up'].

PUFF – A decoy in a gambling-house who played and won with high stakes, 1731 (*OED*) [cf. 'Squib'].

PUNDITS – Learned experts, 1816 (*OED*).

PUNISH – To inflict heavy blows, or injury, 1801 (*OED*). Hence, PUNISHMENT.

PURRING – 'A rushing in, Lancashire fashion, with the head against opponent's guts', c. 1810–50. Causes opponent to '*purr* or grunt' (*B/P*).

QUEER – To spoil, put out of order, 1812 (*OED*).

QUILT – To thrash (*Egan's Grose*).

QUOD – Prison, 1700 (*OED*).

RAILINGS – Teeth, 1910 (*B/P*). Also RAIL-WAY [e.g. *Boxiana III*, p. 24]. [*Lexicon & Egan's Grose* list 'HEAD RAILS'].

RATTLER – A sharp or severe blow, *Sporting Magazine*, 1812 (*OED*).

RECEIVER-GENERAL – A boxer giving nothing for what he gets, early C19 (*B/P*).

REMEMBRANCER – A reminder of something (*OED*). [Used in sense of pugilistic blow (e.g. *Boxiana II*, pp. 129, 339)].

RHINO – Money, C17 (*OED*).

RIBBER – A punch on the ribs, c. 1810 (*B/P*). [Alternative is RIB-BENDER].

RIP – (noun) Worthless, dissolute fellow, a rake, 1797 (*OED*).

ROARER – A broken-winded horse, c. 1810 (*B/P*).

ROOK – A cheat or sharper, esp. in gaming, C16 (*OED*). [cf. 'Pigeon'].

ROSINANTE – Ill-conditioned horse, 1745 (*B/P*).

ROW – (noun) A violent disturbance, 1746 (*OED*). (verb) Assail roughly, 1790 (*B/P*).

RUFFIAN – 'A fellow regardless of the science who hits away' (*Egan's Grose*).

RUM – (adj.) Good, excellent (*OED*). [*B/P* cites *Grose*: 'questionable, disreputable'].

RUMBLE – (verb) Handle roughly, c. 1810–50 (*B/P*).

RUMGUMPTION – Common sense, c. 1770 (*B/P*).

SANDY – Abbreviation of Alexander, as nickname for a Scotsman, C18 (*OED*).

SAUSAGE-BOX – Mouth or stomach? [e.g. *Boxiana IV*, p. 473].

SAWNEY – A fool or very simple person, late C17 (*B/P*).

SCALY – Stingy, c. 1810 (*B/P*).

SCIENCE – Trained skill, esp. pugilism, 1793 (*OED*).

SCONCE – Head, 1567 (*B/P*).

[the] SCRATCH – A line drawn across ring, to which pugilists are brought, 1778 (*OED*).

SCRATCHERS – Hands, c. 1815–60 (*B/P*).

SCREEN – A bank or currency note, esp. if counterfeit, c. 1810 (*B/P*).

SENDER – A severe blow, orig. boxing C19 (*B/P*).

SENSITIVE PLANT – The nose, c. 1815–60 (*B/P*).

SERVE OUT – To punish, *Sporting Magazine*, 1817 (*OED*).

SETTLER – Something that settles an antagonist in an encounter or argument; a crushing or finishing blow, 1817 (*OED*).

SET-TO – Pugilistic encounter, 1743 (*OED*).

SHEENY [pl. SHEENIES] – A Jew, 1816 (*B/P*).

SHIFTING –'Running from adversary, whenever he attempts to strike [...] with a view of tiring him' 1793 (*OED*) [i.e. to evade blows]. ['Shuffling. Tricking', *Lexicon*].

SHINE – ['take shine out of']. Surpass, put in shade, 1818 (*B/P*).

SLAVEY – Female servant, esp. hard-worked, c. 1810–70 (*B/P*).

SLOBBER[ER] – Unsubtle, clubbing fighter. [A possibly connected definition is *OED's* 'To deal with in clumsy manner, 1859'. More likely is that term is forerunner of SLOGGER – One who delivers heavy blows (*B/P*)].

SLUICE-HOUSE – The mouth, 1840 (*B/P*).

SLUICERY – 'A gin-shop or public-house' [e.g. *Real Life in London*, p. 118].

SMASHER – A damaging or settling blow, 1826 (*B/P*).

SNEEZER – Nose, *Sporting Magazine*, 1820 (*OED*).

SNEEZING-TRAP – Nose? [e.g. *Boxiana IV*, p. 473].

SNORTER – A punch on nose, 1818 (*B/P*).

SNUFF-BOX – Nose, 1829 (*OED*). SNUFF-TAKER – Nose? [e.g. *Boxiana III*, p. 199].

SNUFFY – Tipsy, drunk, 1823 (*OED*).

SOFT – (noun) Bank notes, 1821 (*OED*).

SPALPEEN – A low fellow; scamp or rascal, 1815 (*B/P*).

[the] SPANISH – Money, c. 1786 (*B/P*).

SPARKLERS – Eyes. Pugilistic, c. 1805–60 (*B/P*).

SPELL – Playhouse, theatre, 1812 (*B/P*).

SPREAD – Umbrella, c. 1820–50 (*B/P*).

SPREE – A lively or boisterous frolic, 1804. A spell of somewhat disorderly enjoyment frequently accompanied by drinking (*OED*).

SPRINGS – Young men, youths (*OED*). [e.g. 'Nib Springs', *Book of Sports*, p. 194].

SPUNK – Spirit, mettle, pluck, 1773 (*OED*).

SQUEEZE – The neck, 1812 (*B/P*).

SQUIB – A subordinate decoy in a gambling-house, a trainee 'Puff', 1731 (*OED*).

STAG – (verb) To observe, *Grose*, 1796 (*OED*).

STALL OFF – Evasive tactics; to keep the upper hand over opponent, 1812 (*OED*). [*Egan's Grose* adds 'prevarication'].

STAMPERS – Shoes, boots, from c. 1565 (*B/P*).

STEAMER – Tobacco pipe, *Lexicon* (*OED*).

STEEVEN [STEVEN] – Money, 1812 (*OED*).

STICKER – One who persists in a task, 1674. Sporting, a horse or person with staying power, 1860 (*OED*).

[up in the] STIRRUPS – 'A man [...] having plenty of money, is said to be up in the stirrups', 1812 (*OED*). [To be excited, on the alert (e.g. *Boxiana III*, p. 201)].

STOMACHER – A blow to stomach, *Sporting Magazine*, 1814 (*OED*).

STOPPER – A checking parry against opponent's blow. Or, something that brings to a standstill or terminates, 1823 (*OED*).

STRING – A hoax, c. 1810 (*B/P*).

STUMP – Money, c. 1820–50 (*B/P*).

SUCTION – Strong drink, drinking, 1817 (*OED*).

SUIT – Wager, game, method, pretence, c. 1810–50 (*B/P*).

SWAG – A quantity of goods or wares. Or, a trend, in the betting, c. 1810–50 (*B/P*).

SWELL – (noun) A fashionably dressed person, of good social position, 1786. (adj.) Stylish or first rate, esp. dress, 1812. 'To cut a Swell' – behave in swaggering manner, 1800. SWELL MOB – A class of pickpockets who assumed dress and manners of more respectable class, 1836 (*OED*).

SWIP[E]Y – Somewhat intoxicated, 1821 (*OED*).

SWISHED – Married, c. 1810–80 (*B/P*).

SWOONEY – Foolish person. [e.g. *Book of Sports*, p. 70].

TEASER – Something that teases or causes annoyance [A blow]. In pugilistic slang: 'an opponent difficult to tackle', 1759 (*OED*).

THIMBLE – A watch, *Lexicon* (*B/P*).

THROTTLE – The throat (*Lexicon* & *Egan's Grose*). THROTTLER – A punch on the throat, c. 1815–60 (*B/P*).

THWACKER – The term 'thwack' (vigorous blow) already in existence, hence 'thwacker' (same sense) [e.g. *Boxiana IV*, p. 574].

TICKER – A watch, 1800 (*B/P*).

TICKLER – Type of blow [perhaps ironic understatement? (e.g. *Boxiana IV*, p. 127)].

TIC-TAC – Instant? [e.g. 'recover position in a *tic-tac*', *Boxiana IV*, p. 506].

TIE UP – To knock out, c. 1810. (noun) A knockout blow, 1818 (*B/P*).

TILE – Hat, 1813 (*OED*).

TINGLER – A blow that causes tingling; a stinger, 1829 (*OED*).

TINNY – Fire, 1812 (*B/P*). [e.g. 'to leave their tinnies', *Boxiana IV*, p. 355].

TIP – To give, hand over, esp. money, C17 (*OED*).

TIPPY – (noun) An extremely fashionable swell, 1810 (*B/P*).

TIP-TOP – First-rate, prime, C18 (*OED*).

TIZZY – A sixpence, 1804 (*B/P*).

[nap or catch] TOCO – Receive punishment, 1823 (*B/P*).

TODDLERS – Walkers, C18 (*OED*).

TOG – Coat, C18 (*B/P*). TOGS – Clothes, 1779 (*OED*).

TOLD OUT – Counted out, exhausted, 1861 (*OED*).

[the] TON – Fashion, fashionable society, 1760s (*B/P*).

TOPPER – A violent blow on the head (*Lexicon* and *Egan's Grose*).

TOWEL – (verb) To beat, cudgel, thrash, 1705 (*OED*).

TRUMP – Person of surpassing excellence; a first-rate fellow, C18 (*OED*). 'One who displays courage on every suit' (*Egan's Grose*).

TULIP – A showy person, C17 (*OED*).

TURN-UP – Boxing contest, *Sporting Magazine*, 1810 (*OED*).

TWIG – Style, fashion, 1806. Or, condition, spirits, 1820 (*B/P*).

TWISTER – A slanting blow that turns an opponent around, late C18–19 (*B/P*).

[catch the] UGLY – To 'catch' a thrashing [e.g. *Boxiana III*, p. 427].

UP [TO] – Knowledgeable about, early C19 (*B/P*).

UPPER WORKS – Head, or mental capacity, 1809 (*OED*).

VERMILION – (noun and verb) Blood. Besmear with blood; sporting, 1817 (*B/P*).

WALKER – Expressive of incredulity, used in same sense as 'humbug' (*OED*). [cf. 'Bender'].

WAP – To beat soundly, C16 (*OED*). A species of slap (*Bee's Sportsman's Slang*).

WASTE-BUTT – A publican, *Egan's Grose*.

WEAVE – To step into opponent whilst feinting other way, *Sporting Magazine*, 1818 (*OED*). Hence, WEAVING SYSTEM.

WHITE-BAG MAN – Pickpocket, 1923 (*B/P*). [e.g. *Boxiana IV*, p. 486].
WINDER – Blow that 'knocks the wind' out of one, 1825 (*OED*).
WIND-MARKET – Stomach? [e.g. *Boxiana III*, p. 461].
[on the] WINKING LIST – Damaged eye [e.g. *Book of Sports*, p. 45].
WISTY-CASTOR – A blow, punch, c. 1815–40 (*B/P*).
YAPPER – Mouth? [e.g. *Boxiana IV*, p. 329]. ['Yap' is to prate volubly, late C19 (*B/P*)].
YELLOW-MAN – A yellow silk handkerchief, c. 1820 (*B/P*).
YOKEL – Contemptuous term for countryman or rustic, 1812 (*OED*).

Bibliography

Primary Works A

Amateur, An, *Real Life in London*, 2 vols. (London: Methuen, 1905)

Anon., *Pancratia, or a History of Pugilism* (London: Oxberry, 1812)

Badcock, John, ('Jon Bee'), *The Annals of Sporting and Fancy Gazette*, 13 vols. (London: Sherwood, Neely, & Jones, 1822–8)

——, *Boxiana; Or, Sketches of Modern Pugilism*, vol. IV (London: Sherwood, Jones & Co., 1824)

——, *Bee's Sportsman's Slang* (London: 1825)

Dowling, Vincent, *Fistiana* (London: Clement, 1841)

Egan, Pierce, *Boxiana; or, Sketches of Antient and Modern Pugilism* (London: Smeeton, 1813)

——, *Boxiana; or, Sketches of Modern Pugilism*, vol. II (London: Sherwood, Neely, & Jones, 1818)

——, *Boxiana; Sketches of Modern Pugilism*, vol. III (London: Sherwood, Neely, & Jones, 1821)

——, *Life in London* (London: Sherwood, Neely, & Jones, 1821) [Facsimile reprint in: John Marriott (ed.), *Unknown London: Early Modernist Visions of the Metropolis, 1815–45*, vol. II (London: Pickering & Chatto, 2000)]

——, *Grose's Classical Dictionary of the Vulgar Tongue* (London: Sherwood, Neely, & Jones, 1823)

——, *Account of the Trial of John Thurtell* (London: Knight & Lacey, 1824)

——, *Sporting Anecdotes* (London: Sherwood, Jones, & Co., 1825)

——, *New Series Boxiana*, 2 vols. (London: Virtue, 1828–9)

——, *Book of Sports* (London: Tegg, 1832)

——, *Every Gentleman's Manual. A Lecture on the Art of Self-Defence* (London: Sherwood & Bowyer, 1845)

——, *The Finish to the Adventures of Tom, Jerry, and Logic, in their Pursuits Through Life In and Out of London* (London: Reeves & Turner, 1887)

Fewtrell, Thomas, *Boxing Reviewed* (London: 1790)

Miles, Henry Downes, *Pugilistica*, 3 vols. (London: Weldon, 1880)

Vasey, William, *Remarks on the Influence of Pugilism on Morals* (Newcastle: Newcastle Debating Society, 1824)

Primary Works B

Anon., *Lexicon Balatronicum* (London: Chappell, 1811) [Facsimile reprint in: *The 1811 Dictionary of the Vulgar Tongue* (London: Senate, 1994)]

Dickens, Charles, *Hard Times* (London: Penguin, 1994)

——, *Martin Chuzzlewit* (London: Penguin, 2004)

Egan, Pierce, *The Pilgrims of the Thames in Search of the National* (London: Strange, 1838)

——, *The Life of an Actor* (London: Pickering & Chatto, 1892)

Grierson, H J C, (ed.), *The Letters of Sir Walter Scott*, 12 vols. (London: Constable, 1933)

Hindley, Charles, *The True History of Tom and Jerry* (London: Reeves & Turner, 1888)

House, Madeline, and Storey, Graham et al. (eds), *The Letters of Charles Dickens*, 12 vols. (Oxford: Oxford University Press, 1965–2002)

Lamont, Claire, (ed.), *Walter Scott: Chronicles of the Canongate* (London: Penguin, 2003)

Magriel, Paul, (ed.), *The Memoirs of the Life of Daniel Mendoza*, ed. by (London: Batsford, 1951)

Marchand, Leslie A, (ed.), *Byron's Letters and Journals*, 12 vols. (London: John Murray, 1973–82)

Marriott, John, (ed.), *Unknown London: Early Modernist Visions of the Metropolis, 1815–45*, 5 vols. (London: Pickering & Chatto, 2000)

Marriott, John, and Matsumura, Masaie (eds), *The Metropolitan Poor: Semifactual Accounts, 1795–1910*, 6 vols. (London: Pickering & Chatto, 1999)

Morrison, Robert, and Eberle-Sinatra, Michael et al. (eds), *The Selected Writings of Leigh Hunt*, 6 vols. (London: Pickering & Chatto, 2003)

Patten, Robert L, (ed.), *Charles Dickens: The Pickwick Papers* (London: Penguin, 1986)

Russell, John, (ed.), *Memoirs, Journal, and Correspondence of Thomas Moore*, 8 vols. (London: Brown, Green, and Longmans, 1853)

Sala, George Augustus, *Gaslight and Daylight* (London: Chapman & Hall, 1859)

Shaw, Bernard, *Cashel Byron's Profession* (London: Constable, 1950)

Slater, Michael, (ed.), *Charles Dickens: The Christmas Books*, vol. I (London: Penguin, 1985)

——, (ed.), *Dickens' Journalism: Sketches by Boz and Other Early Papers, 1833–39* (London: Dent, 1994)

Smollett, Tobias, *Humphrey Clinker* (London: Penguin, 1985)

Steffan, T G, and Pratt, W W, (eds), *Byron's Don Juan*, 4 vols. (London: University of Texas Press, 1971)

Stones, Graeme, and Strachan, John, (eds), *Parodies of the Romantic Age*, 5 vols. (London: Pickering & Chatto, 1999)

Strachan, John, and others, (eds), *British Satire, 1785–1840*, 5 vols. (London: Pickering & Chatto, 2003)

Surtees, Robert Smith, *Jorrocks' Jaunts and Jollities* (London: Dent, 1941)

Thomas, Deborah A, (ed.), *Charles Dickens: Selected Short Fiction* (London: Penguin, 1985)

Wu, Duncan, (ed.), *The Selected Writings of William Hazlitt*, 9 vols. (London: Pickering & Chatto, 1998)

Secondary Works

Ackroyd, Peter, *The Collection* (London: Chatto & Windus, 2001)

——, *London: The Biography* (London: Vintage, 2001)

Baer, Marc, *Theatre and Disorder in Late Georgian London* (Oxford: Clarendon Press, 1992)

Batchelor, Denzil, *Big Fight: The Story of World Championship Boxing* (London: Phoenix House, 1954)

Beale, Paul, (ed.), *A Dictionary of Slang and Unconventional English, Eric Partridge* (London: Routledge & Kegan Paul, 1984)

Birley, Derek, *Sport and the Making of Britain* (Manchester University Press, 1993)

Blyth, Henry, *Hell and Hazard: or William Crockford versus the Gentlemen of England* (London: Weidenfeld & Nicolson, 1969)

Brailsford, Dennis, 'Morals and Maulers: the Ethics of Early Pugilism', *Journal of Sport History*, 12, 2 (1985), pp. 126–42

——, *Bareknuckles: A Social History of Prize-Fighting* (Cambridge: Lutterworth Press, 1988)

Coleman, Julie, *A History of Cant and Slang Dictionaries: Volume II 1785–1858* (Oxford: Oxford University Press, 2004)

Dart, Gregory, '"Flash Style": Pierce Egan and Literary London 1820–28', *History Workshop Journal*, 51 (2001), pp. 180–205

Edwards, Alan, *Lionel Tennyson: Regency Buck* (London: Robson Books, 2001)

Fielding, K J, (ed.), *The Speeches of Charles Dickens: A Complete Edition* (Hemel Hempstead: Harvester Wheatsheaf, 1988)

Ford, John, *Prizefighting: The Age of Regency Boximania* (Newton Abbott: David & Charles, 1971)

Fraser, George Macdonald, *Black Ajax* (London: Harper Collins, 1997)

——, *Flashman and the Tiger* (London: Harper Collins, 2000)

Fuller, David, *Noble Art: Prize-fighting in England 1738–1860* (Catalogue for an exhibition held in Newmarket by the British Sporting Art Trust, 2005)

Gorman, Bartley, (with Peter Walsh), *King of the Gypsies* (Bury: Milo Books, 2002)

Hall, Stuart, *Heaven and Hall: A Prodigal Life* (London: BBC Worldwide, 2000)

Herzog, Don, *Poisoning the Minds of the Lower Orders* (Chichester: Princeton University Press, 1998)

Higgins, David, 'Englishness, Effeminacy, and the New Monthly Magazine; Hazlitt's "The Fight" in Context', *Romanticism*, 10. 2 (2004), pp. 173–90

Hilton, Boyd, *A Mad, Bad, and Dangerous People?: England 1783–1846* (Oxford: Clarendon Press, 2006)

Jackson, Vanessa Furze, *The Poetry of Henry Newbolt: Patriotism is Not Enough* (Greensboro: ELT Press, 1994)

Johnson, Christopher, 'Anti-Pugilism: Violence and Justice in Scott's *The Two Drovers*', *Scottish Literary Journal*, 22, 1 (1995), pp. 46–60

——, '"British Championism": Early Pugilism and the Works of Fielding', *The Review of English Studies*, 187 (1996), pp. 331–51

Klancher, Jon P, *The Making of English Reading Audiences, 1790–1832* (London: University of Wisconsin Press, 1987)

Langford, Paul, *Englishness Identified* (Oxford: Oxford University Press, 2001)

Lee, Bruce, *Tao of Jeet Kune Do* (Santa Clarita: Ohara Publications, 1994)

Liebling, Abbott Joseph, *Just Enough Liebling: Classic Work by the Legendary 'New Yorker' Writer* (New York: New Point Press, 2004)

Low, Donald A, *The Regency Underworld* (Stroud: Sutton, 2000)

Lynch, Bohun, *Knuckles and Gloves* (London: Collins, 1922)

McCalman, Iain, *Radical Underworld* (Cambridge: Cambridge University Press, 1988)

——, (ed.), *An Oxford Companion to the Romantic Age* (Oxford: Oxford University Press, 2001)

Marlow, James E, 'Popular Culture, Pugilism, and Pickwick', *Journal of Popular Culture*, 15:4 (1982), pp. 16–30

Murray, Venetia, *High Society: A Social History of the Regency Period 1788–1830* (London: Penguin, 1998)

Paulin, Tom, *The Dog-Star of Liberty: William Hazlitt's Radical Style* (London: Faber & Faber, 1998)

Radford, Peter, *The Celebrated Captain Barclay: Sport Money and Fame in Regency Britain* (London: Headline, 2001)

Reid, John C, *Bucks and Bruisers: Pierce Egan and Regency England* (London: Routledge & Kegan Paul, 1971)

Rendell, Jane, *The Pursuit of Pleasure: Gender, Space and Architecture in Regency London* (New Jersey: Rutgers University Press, 2002)

Schlicke, Paul, 'The Pilgrimage of Pierce Egan', *Journal of Popular Culture*, 21:1 (1987), pp. 1–9

——, *Dickens and Popular Entertainment* (London: Allen & Unwin, 1985)

Thomas, Donald, *Cochrane: Britannia's Sea Wolf* (London: Cassell, 2001)

Worrall, David, 'Artisan Melodrama and the Plebeian Public Sphere: The Political Culture of Drury Lane and its Environs, 1797–1830', *Studies in Romanticism*, 39, 2 (2000), pp. 213–27

Online Resources and Articles

British History Online <http://www.britishistory.ac.uk/report.asp?compid=43376>

Hubbard, Alan, *The Independent* (14 January 2007), <http://news.independent.co.uk/world/americas/article2152439.ece> [accessed September 2007]

Oxford Dictionary of National Biography <http://www.oxforddnb.com>

Waddell, Sid, <http://www.sidwaddell.compsyswebdesign.com/q.htm> [accessed September 2007]

Westmacott, Charles Molloy, ('Bernard Blackmantle'), *The English Spy*, 2 vols. (London: Sherwood, Jones & Co., 1825–6), <http://www.gutenberg.org/etext/20001> [accessed April 2013]

Index

Aaron, Barney 23
Ackroyd, Peter 74, 76, 77, 78
Allardice, Robert Barclay 15, 20, 72, 87, 89, 213
Americans (US) 12, 14, 31, 53, 106, 113, 150, 153, 180, 203, 217–18, 222

Badcock, John *see* Bee, Jon
Barclay, Captain *see* Allardice, Robert Barclay
Barrymore, Earl of 88
Beardsworth, John 177
Beaumont, Barber 170, 176
Bee, Jon 17, 29, 36, 127, 178, 204
    Boxiana IV 17, 29, 55, 61, 65, 72, 80, 84, 86, 94–6, 99, 102, 106, 112, 114, 119, 127, 132, 142, 145, 150, 151, 156, 159, 160, 165, 169, 172, 175, 202, 204, 208
    Sportsman's Slang 17, 25, 35, 38–43, 63, 89, 144, 146, 154, 166, 174
    The Annals of Sporting and Fancy Gazette 17, 22, 60, 68, 80, 85, 105, 124, 154, 155, 171, 173, 174
Belasco, Abe 86, 111, 112, 131
Belcher, Jem 1, 2, 5, 50
Belcher, Tom 19, 52, 76, 81, 107, 156, 157, 194
Bell's Life 27, 134, 209, 210, 212
'Blackmantle, Bernard' (Charles Molloy Westmacott) 194, 195
Blackwood's Edinburgh Magazine 8, 25–6, 28, 124, 163, 186, 187, 194

Blücher, Marshall 134
Boxiana see Egan, Pierce and Bee, Jon
Boxing Reviewed 2, 3, 22, 56, 108, 136, 141, 172, 201, 207, 233
Bristol 11, 48, 80, 101, 107, 159, 160, 201
Broughton, John 9, 133
    Broughton's rules 9–10
Burney, Frances 206
Burns, Bob 80, 131, 146
Byron, Lord 6, 9, 32, 47, 49, 57, 92, 93, 103, 134, 148, 162–3, 173, 175, 188, 217
    Don Juan 149
    on foreigners 136, 138, 169

Calzaghe, Joe 225–6
Cannon, Tom 64, 90, 132
Carini, Tito Alberto di ('Venetian Gondolier') 20, 49, 112, 133, 136
Carpentier, Georges 223–4
Carter, Jack 57, 59, 121, 122
Castlereagh, Lord 90
Castle Tavern 60, 72, 136, 177, 194, 235
Clay, Cassius Marcellus (Muhammad Ali) 217, 218
coachmen 13, 43, 62, 66
Cobbett, William 2, 6, 91
Cochrane, Thomas 31, 138, 148, 169
cock-fighting 4, 7, 27, 69, 85, 101, 115–17, 127, 161, 199
Cooper, Jack 61, 81, 155
Corinthians 8, 27, 28, 35, 44, 59, 61, 72, 86, 90, 113, 164, 165, 183, 205

Covent Garden 71, 73, 77, 86, 90, 167
Cribb, Tom 14, 19, 21, 23, 26, 50, 53, 57,
    58, 81, 83, 85, 89, 97, 108, 113, 133,
    136, 141, 145, 178, 181, 183, 188, 212
    portrait 107
    and his tavern 79, 92–3, 195
Curtis, Dick 67, 68, 83, 84, 104

Deacon, William Frederick, *Warreni-*
    ana 32, 181, 187–91, 195
Dickens, Charles 5, 28, 33, 40, 59, 62, 120,
    123, 126, 154–5, 193, 195–9, 203–4,
    227, 231, 233
Dogherty, Dan 156–7
Donnelly, Dan 88, 104, 114, 156
Dowling, Vincent 5, 27, 29, 87, 124, 130,
    145, 153, 159, 170, 175, 194, 209,
    214, 220
    see also Fistiana
Drury Lane 77, 121, 171, 172
duelling 4, 22, 78, 173–4, 220

Edinburgh 89, 124, 155, 177
Egan, Pierce
    early life and career 15–17
    Book of Sports 17, 19, 48, 62, 64, 68,
        72, 74, 83, 85, 93, 104, 108, 114,
        116, 124, 127, 128, 136, 137, 140,
        143, 145, 146, 149, 153, 155, 170,
        171, 172, 173, 174, 177, 186, 195,
        201, 210, 211, 227, 229, 235
    Boxiana I 2, 8, 10, 12, 15, 16, 19, 20, 21,
        22, 23, 24, 27, 28, 48–54, 61, 72,
        75, 82, 83, 85, 86, 88, 89, 92, 97,
        104, 107, 108, 110, 111–15, 122, 127,
        128, 129, 133, 134, 136, 140, 141,
        143, 144, 147, 159, 160, 163, 167,
        173, 201, 222
    Boxiana II 15, 18, 19, 42, 54, 57, 60,
        76, 84, 91, 99, 111, 113, 120, 128,
        129, 131, 139, 141, 143, 144, 146,
        147, 154, 155, 156, 160, 167, 209

Boxiana III 6, 15, 19, 24, 25, 55, 56,
    57–9, 65, 66, 76, 80, 82, 83, 84, 88,
    90, 92, 97, 103, 104–7, 109, 113,
    114, 118, 119, 120, 121, 130, 131, 132,
    135, 137, 142, 145, 146, 147, 150,
    152, 156, 162, 165, 175, 176, 177,
    180, 182, 186, 219
Egan's Grose 16, 35, 37, 41, 49, 59
Every Gentleman's Manual 102, 210,
    213
Life in London 28, 29, 32, 33, 37,
    43–7, 57, 73–5, 76, 77–8, 104, 116,
    119, 123, 129, 145, 164–7, 191, 193,
    195, 201, 206, 207, 228, 230
Life of an Actor 33, 73, 77
New Series Boxiana 15, 17, 64–8, 82,
    90, 100–2, 109, 128, 132, 153, 155,
    168
Pierce Egan's Life in London, and
    Sporting Guide 17, 25, 65, 67, 79,
    87, 108, 131, 135, 157, 171, 207, 229
Pierce Egan's Weekly Courier 17, 48,
    67, 68, 163, 177, 229
Pilgrims of the Thames 44, 192, 219
Sporting Anecdotes 16, 40, 153, 165
The Finish to [...] Life In and Out of
    London 167, 211
Emery, John 136
English Spy, The 194, 235
    see also Westmacott, Charles Molloy
Epsom 68, 81, 146, 211
Evans, Samuel
    ('Dutch Sam') 27, 52, 54, 209, 226
    ('Young Dutch Sam') 4, 115, 125

female readers / spectators 12, 82, 123–4,
    164, 205–6, 224
Fewtrell, Thomas *see Boxing Reviewed*
Fistiana 5, 87, 124, 125, 130, 145, 147, 153,
    159, 170, 175, 209, 214
Fives Court 9, 39, 124, 157
Flaxman, John 104

France (and the French) 31, 50, 89, 107, 132, 133, 136–9, 141, 144, 145, 147–8, 153–4, 161, 166, 169, 171, 174, 224
Fraser, George Macdonald 228

gambling 3, 4, 9, 14, 20, 27, 41, 42, 51, 53–4, 58, 62, 63, 72, 75, 86, 88–9, 115, 117, 119, 121, 129, 131, 152, 156, 168, 169, 170, 173, 174, 176–7, 184, 190, 199, 205, 208, 210, 213, 216
George IV (Prince Regent) 1, 37, 85, 181, 183–5
Godfrey, Captain, *Treatise upon the Useful Science of Defence* 20, 21
Grantham 14, 83
Greece (and Greeks) 13, 107, 138, 166, 169
Gregson, Bob 6, 51, 83, 104, 113–14, 139
Grose, Francis 16, 36
Guest, Thomas Douglas 107
Gully, John 6, 7, 51, 83, 90, 92, 105

Hall, Stuart 179, 221, 222
Halton, Pat 67, 114
Harmer, Harry 60, 81
Hawkins, Jem 132
Hazlitt, William 19, 26, 78, 97–103, 107, 119, 123, 141–4, 149, 150, 151, 154, 161, 200, 208, 212, 213, 217, 231, 233
Heenan, John C 203, 204, 215
Henderson, Michael 221
Hickman, Tom ('the Gas-man') 19, 26, 56, 82, 85, 97–102, 107, 119, 141–3, 149–52, 175, 208, 212
Hindley, Charles, *The True History of Tom and Jerry* 39, 195, 207, 220
Hobhouse, John Cam 57, 91
Holt, Harry ('the Duffer') 146
Hooper, Bill ('the Tinman') 88
horseracing 4, 7, 49, 54, 68, 69, 93, 176, 177, 201, 210, 221

Hudson, Josh 55, 72, 83, 90, 152
Humphries, Richard 5, 23, 75, 97
Hunt, Leigh 91, 162, 163, 185

Ireland (and the Irish) 8, 15, 18, 24, 60, 79, 88, 114, 115, 156, 157–8, 160

Jackson, John 'Gentleman' 6, 9, 87, 92, 105, 110, 111, 113, 134, 142, 145, 162, 172, 182, 195, 217
Johnson, Samuel 40, 48
Johnson, Tom 3, 22, 67

Kean, Edmund 76, 77, 84, 121
Keating, Frank 228
Keats, John 179, 191
Knight, Charles 125, 193

Lancashire (fighting methods) 31, 154, 155, 190
Langan, John 8, 60, 79, 108, 157–8, 206–7
Lawrence, Thomas 105
Lee, Bruce 219
Liggett, Phil 221–2
London 11, 15, 29, 32, 35–6, 38–9, 43–6, 48, 49, 53, 57, 62, 63, 66, 68–9, 73–8, 83, 88, 90, 91, 95, 101, 104, 105, 114, 115, 134, 144, 154, 156, 158–60, 164–7, 172, 194–5, 199, 201, 230

Mailer, Norman 218
Martin, Jack 83, 90, 94–7, 103, 132, 165, 172
Marshall, Benjamin 105
Mellish, Harry 93
Mendoza, Daniel 12, 23–4, 25, 58, 75, 97, 110–11, 141, 142, 155, 212
Miles, Henry Downes 80, 220
see also Pugilistica

Molineaux, Tom 14, 23, 26, 53, 83, 85, 89,
        97, 106, 108, 112–13, 121–2, 129,
        133, 136, 155, 157, 188, 212
Moncrieff, W T 39, 195
Moore, Thomas 6, 32, 38, 47, 49, 180,
        186, 187, 188, 191, 195, 206
        Epistle from Tom Crib to Big Ben 181,
            185
        Tom Crib's Memorial 32, 38, 123, 137,
            148, 159, 182–7
Moulsey Hurst 61, 83
'Mr. M' 24, 105, 107, 131, 137, 145, 162, 175
Murray, John 57, 173

Napoleon 1, 31, 131, 148, 149, 150–1, 181,
        213, 222
Neal, Ned 4, 226
Neate, Bill 26, 80, 97–101, 107, 119, 141,
        143, 208, 212
Nelson, Horatio 1, 134, 148, 149, 150, 152
Newbolt, John Henry 204
Newcastle upon Tyne 11
New Monthly Magazine 8, 19, 154
Newgate Prison 57, 78, 91
Nicholls, George 21, 143
'North, Christopher' (John Wilson) 25
Norwich 56, 82

Oliver, Tom 61, 82, 88, 104, 114, 119, 152,
        175
Orwell, George 161, 214
Osbaldeston, George 210
Owen, Tom 25, 58, 84–5, 118, 220

Painter, Ned 82, 139
Pearce, Hen ('the Game Chicken') 1, 2,
        92, 108, 201
Place, Francis 210
Pugilistic Club, the 9
Pugilistica 80, 104, 156, 220
        see also Miles, Henry Downes

Randall, Jack ('the Nonpareil') 17–19,
        56, 58–9, 81, 92, 94–7, 103, 111–12,
        119, 120–1, 130–1, 132, 143–4, 151,
        172, 180, 182, 186, 189, 199, 218–19
Real Life in London 42–3, 54, 94, 110,
        138, 166, 172–3, 195, 201
*Remarks on the Influence of Pugilism on
        Morals see* Vasey, William
Reynolds, John Hamilton 116–17, 188
Reynolds, Tom 128, 144, 146, 172
Richmond, Bill 12, 23, 55, 59, 113, 122
Rimmer, Heskin 154

Sala, George Augustus 178, 179, 180, 202,
        210, 211, 212
Sayers, Tom 203–4, 215
Scotland (and the Scots) 15, 24, 31, 89,
        124, 136, 150, 155, 177, 231
Scott, Walter 28, 31, 32, 136, 139–40, 188,
        231
        The Two Drovers 31, 86
Sharples, George 17, 105
Shaw, Bernard 33, 125, 159–60, 161, 166,
        193, 200, 207, 215, 216, 233
        Cashel Byron's Profession 33, 150–2,
            164, 171, 193–4, 199, 205, 207
Shaw, John (Life-Guardsman) 139, 145,
        157
Shelton, Tom 60, 61, 81, 131, 135
Slack, Jack 56
Sloman, Charles 109, 163
Smeeton, George 15
Smollett, Tobias George, *Humphrey
        Clinker* 38, 73
Southey, Robert 135, 188
Sporting Magazine 3, 26, 27, 39, 172, 178,
        219
Spring, Tom 8, 79, 80, 81, 94, 101, 108,
        146, 157–8, 206
Stevens, Bill ('the Nailer') 106, 222
Stevenson, Harry 62, 104

Surtees, Robert Smith
  Jorrocks' Jaunts and Jollities 192
  New Sporting Magazine 27, 178, 192
Suvorov, Aleksandr Vasilievich
  ('Suwarrow') 149

Tattersall's 201
Thurtell, John 42, 62, 118, 168
Times, The 3, 87, 176, 215
Turner, Ned 61, 91, 97, 119, 160, 180, 182

Vasey, William 10–11, 115, 129–30, 133–5,
    155, 168, 171, 173, 175, 176, 200, 201
Vauxhall Gardens 66, 147, 171
Victorian, attitudes and scene 10, 27, 33,
    38, 69, 178, 203–4, 209, 217, 219,
    228, 231

Waddell, Sid 222
Ward, James (Jem) 61, 66, 72, 152
Ward, Joe 49, 122, 137
Waterloo, battle 132, 134, 139
Weekly Dispatch 4, 16, 151
Wellington, Duke of 14, 128, 130, 131, 132,
    145, 152, 153
Westmacott, Charles Molloy ('Bernard
    Blackmantle') 194, 235
Wilson, John ('Christopher North') 25
Windham, William 127
Wooldridge, Ian 228